Kira wanted him.

If she was to be his woman and none was to have any doubt of her status, his possession would have to be a public one. Thierry arched one brow, hoping she understood the import of what he asked, when she nodded quick agreement without breaking his gaze.

So be it. She would be his for this one night and all others. This moment was between the two of them in truth.

Thierry gave the amethyst scarf the slightest tug, loving the way she tumbled trustingly into his arms. Had he spared the time to think, he might have thought her relieved, but other matters were there to attend. Her small hands were on his shoulders, her breath in his ear, her scent filling his nostrils fit to drown him, her softness filling his hands.

His woman...

Dear Reader,

Unicorn Bride was the first of Claire Delacroix's stories of the lost kings of France. *Pearl Beyond Price* is the second. It is the story of Thierry de Pereille, and the beautiful Persian captive who joins him on his journey to seek the truth of his own heritage.

This month we also have *The Heart's Wager*, the sequel to Gayle Wilson's first book, *The Heart's Desire*. The duke of Avon needs rescuing and his wife sends her brother, Devon, to follow Avon's trail, in this compelling Regency era story of a hero and heroine who must overcome great danger just to survive.

And be sure and keep a lookout for our other two titles wherever Harlequin Historicals are sold: *Land of Dreams*, a heartwarming Western from March Madness author Cheryl St.John, and *The Bride's Portion*, a captivating medieval tale from author Susan Paul. We hope you enjoy them all.

Sincerely,

Tracy Farrell
Senior Editor

Please address questions and book requests to:
Harlequin Reader Service
U.S.: 3010 Walden Ave., P.O. Box 1325, Buffalo, NY 14269
Canadian: P.O. Box 609, Fort Erie, Ont. L2A 5X3

CLAIRE DELACROIX

PEARL BEYOND PRICE

Harlequin Books

TORONTO • NEW YORK • LONDON
AMSTERDAM • PARIS • SYDNEY • HAMBURG
STOCKHOLM • ATHENS • TOKYO • MILAN
MADRID • WARSAW • BUDAPEST • AUCKLAND

ISBN 0-373-28864-6

PEARL BEYOND PRICE

This edition published by arrangement with Harlequin Enterprises B.V.

® and TM are trademarks of the publisher. Trademarks indicated with
® are registered in the United States Patent and Trademark Office, the
Canadian Trade Marks Office and in other countries.

Printed in U.S.A.

Books by Claire Delacroix

Harlequin Historicals

* *Romance of the Rose* #166
  Honeyed Lies #209
† *Unicorn Bride* #223
* *The Sorceress* #235
* *Roarke's Folly* #250
† *Pearl Beyond Price* #264

* The Rose Trilogy
† Unicorn Series

CLAIRE DELACROIX

An avid traveler and student of history, Claire Delacroix can be found at home when she has a deadline, amid the usual jumble of books, knitting needles and potted herbs.

For all my wonderful friends at RWA Ontario.
Thanks.

Prologue

Maragha—in modern Azerbaijan—February 1265

Chinkai's body was as cold as the dawn.

Thierry gritted his teeth at the volume of spilled blood, knowing that he would never grow used to the killing.

The wan fingers of light straining above the horizon did naught to warm the air, though their meager illumination showed Thierry the pallor of the old warrior's skin. Chinkai had been dead for some hours, mayhap since the previous eve. Too late, Thierry recalled that the grizzled warrior had left the khan's funeral celebrations and not returned.

That Chinkai's death was not a natural one was beyond doubt. No mistaking was there the viciousness of the slash across the throat that had ended his life, nor the copious quantity of dried blood staining his *kalat*. Indeed, it seemed the old warrior's eyes were still glazed with shock at the suddenness of his own demise.

Thierry swallowed carefully and forced himself to touch the older man's wizened flesh. 'Twas cold as stone.

Indeed, he had expected naught else, but still his bile rose. He lifted his gaze and scanned the silent camp, seeking some clue of what had transpired but knowing all the while he would find none. Just Chinkai, dead and alone on the grassy plain.

But one thing had Chinkai and Thierry in common and Thierry could not evict the thought from his mind. Thierry eyed the corpse as though willing it to confirm or deny his fears.

Both had aspired to be khan.

Had Chinkai died for his ambition?

The old khan was dead and opportunity was ripe for the selection of a new khan. But three candidates were there within the tribe. The third, Abaqa, was the son of the old khan. Though this assured him naught, Abaqa was known to be ambitious.

Now Chinkai drew breath no longer and Thierry could not help but wonder how ambitious Abaqa truly was.

Thierry jumped at the muffled sound of a footfall, only to meet the bright gaze of Abaqa. He stiffened warily despite himself and hoped naught of his thoughts showed in his expression.

Was he to join Chinkai this very morn?

"Too much drinking for our old comrade?" Abaqa inquired cheerfully. Thierry met the speculation in the other man's eyes and knew Abaqa saw more than his words revealed.

"Hardly that," Thierry replied tightly. "His throat has been slit."

"Ah." Abaqa jammed his thumbs into his belt as he paused beside the pair. Thierry was forced to look up from where he squatted to hold the other man's gaze. "Mayhap a squabble over a woman," Abaqa suggested with calm disinterest.

"I should think not," Thierry said dismissively. Abaqa's brows rose.

"Mayhap you *should* think so," he said silkily.

It seemed he had guessed aright. Thierry let his gaze drop to Chinkai and willed his heart to slow.

'Twas evident he was being threatened, though Thierry would know clearly how or why. Should Abaqa be behind

Chinkai's death, Thierry would hear the threat fall in full from the man's lips. He straightened slowly and braced his own hands on his hips, savoring his height advantage over Abaqa.

"Indeed?" he asked stonily.

"Indeed," Abaqa affirmed. His dark eyes narrowed as he assessed Thierry. "'Twould seem to be unhealthy to not share my opinion these days."

"Your sire is but dead three days and no guarantee have you of the khanate," Thierry observed with forced calm. Abaqa's brows arched high.

"Nay?" he asked with feigned surprise. "Tell me not that you, too, believe the best-qualified man will hold the position."

"Always has it been thus," Thierry argued, but Abaqa laughed cynically.

"Nay," he whispered with evident delight. "Always has it been the *survivor* who became khan and none other." His eyes widened slightly as he watched Thierry absorb the assertion, then he stepped back and glanced to the fallen man with open disgust. "Fool," Abaqa muttered deprecatingly, the single word telling Thierry to be on his guard.

Thierry had best take to sleeping with an eye open.

Unexpectedly those bright eyes swiveled to lock with Thierry's regard once more, though this time the hint of a mocking smile played on Abaqa's lips. "No one else need see this but you," he whispered. A chill tripped down Thierry's spine but he refused to look away.

"Chinkai's absence is not likely to go unnoticed," he commented. Abaqa's smile broadened.

"My sire will be buried in the full Mongol tradition," Abaqa reminded him. "Who will know if one human sacrifice is a little more cold than the others?"

He would feign a sacrifice to cover his crime? Thierry was shocked that even Abaqa could be so callous. But one glimpse of the determination in the set of the other man's chin told him that he was a fool to even doubt the other man's intent.

"You cannot do this thing," Thierry protested, knowing the futility of his objection even as he made it.

"Nay, I can and will have it done. I, however, will be occupied with becoming khan." Abaqa paused dramatically and eyed Thierry. "Which is why you will do this," he added quietly. "For your new khan. I trust you will make a good show."

"You cannot know that you will be khan," Thierry argued tightly. Abaqa leaned closer, his sharp scent invading Thierry's nostrils with a vengeance.

"I *will* be khan," Abaqa growled. "And you will kiss my boot, one way or the other. Just as Chinkai did. Do you understand our ways that much, outsider?" This last was delivered with an eloquent sneer.

Outsider. Despite all Thierry had done and all the years he had labored for the exaltation of the tribe. How many assaults had he led? How many successful forays had he planned? And all of it meant naught because of the taint of his mixed blood. Rage rose within Thierry that he should be so threatened at the very moment when all he had aspired to dangled within reach.

"Kubilai himself once told me that there could be no outsider with the legacy of Chinggis Khan's blood running in his veins," Thierry said. Abaqa laughed, and the brittle sound carried far in the chill morning air.

"That same lineage runs in my veins, as well you know," he argued. His lip curled before he continued. "But 'tis not thinned with western swill."

The two men's gazes locked and held for a charged moment. "Face the truth, Qaraq-Böke," Abaqa hissed. "The best man will be khan and that man will be me. You will kiss my boot or not live to tell the tale."

Clearly unless Thierry was willing to adopt Abaqa's tactics, the khanate would not be his. He dared not look to Chinkai, though the fallen warrior's image was crystal clear in his mind.

He was not willing to pay that price. He could not slaughter Abaqa to ensure his own ascendancy.

At the same instant that Thierry realized he was not prepared to commit murder, he saw in Abaqa's expression precisely the opposite. Abaqa would stop at naught to be khan. Thierry would be wise to mind his back, at least until Abaqa was certain of his ascendancy.

And until Thierry decided what path he would take from here.

"I will see to Chinkai," Thierry conceded gruffly. Abaqa grinned anew, displaying his array of yellowed teeth.

"Always did my sire consider you to be an intelligent man," he purred. "Mayhap he was right about something." He winked evilly, then turned and positively danced back to the camp. Thierry watched the older man go as he struggled to rein in his anger. Little option did he have, in truth. His own pride to the contrary, his only real choice was to do Abaqa's bidding.

At least for the time being.

He fought against the ground swell of disappointment that raged through him. So long he had labored for naught!

But Thierry had waited for his opportunity before and it seemed he would wait for it again. Time could only make his position stronger, and he was yet young. Even without his intervention, Abaqa could not live forever.

Thierry could afford to wait and work a little longer. He would continue. He would follow Abaqa's bidding. He would form another plan. And one day, the fate that he coveted would be his alone. It was his destiny.

But on this morning there was Chinkai. The camp was stirring to life and Thierry gritted his teeth as he bent to bear Chinkai away. Only too well did he understand that failure in any task Abaqa granted him would be seen as a sign of disloyalty to the new khan.

And no intention had Thierry of granting Abaqa such an easy victory.

Far across the plains of Asia, a man awakened in the night, haunted by ghostly visions of unicorns. Angry unicorns whose manes were snarled and whose feet tore impatiently at the ground, they set his heart to furious pounding.

He tossed and turned and tore himself from sleep. The sound of his ragged breathing filled the room. He stared wide-eyed at the ceiling and fancied he still saw their blazing eyes.

He shivered despite himself. A dream. 'Twas no more than a dream. Dagobert clutched the coverlet as he fought to slow his breathing in the calm of the house. His palms were damp. To his astonishment he realized that 'twas heavy red samite that filled his hands, not the cotton coverlet he knew should be there.

He needed not to look to know 'twas the banner of his house, the one he knew to be safely stored away. 'Twas the one graced by the image of a single prancing unicorn that was inexplicably unfurled over the bed.

But look he did.

'Twas that very one. His heart missed a beat and an unfamiliar panic uncoiled in his veins. What did it mean? Why had the dream come to him?

The wan moonlight played tricks with his sight, for the embroidered gems encircling the beast's brow appeared as pearls in its otherworldly glow. Well did Dagobert know that Alienor had chosen the blood red floss of rubies for her work. He blinked, his heart raced, but the vision remained stubbornly unchanged.

He exhaled shakily and looked to his slumbering wife, noting how the moonlight traced the filigree of silver in her dark tresses cast across the pillows. The vestiges of his disturbing dream made him seek out the echo of his lost son's features in her peaceful visage. When he found what he sought, he closed his eyes against the pain of recollection.

But one thing had he promised the boy and that one thing he had not done. How he hated a task unfulfilled. Was this dream a reminder of that failure?

Dagobert looked to his sleeping wife once more. For a moment he feared that she was as insubstantial as the capricious moonlight, the ghostly pearls, his lost son. He tentatively touched one fingertip to her cheek, half-afraid of what he might feel.

The warm satin of Alienor's skin reassured him, as always it had. He released the breath trapped in his lungs and let his fingertips slide over her cheek in a slow caress as determination filled him anew.

So far they had come, so much they had lost, yet this one greatest treasure remained his. Dagobert smiled in relief and closed his eyes, willing his mind to supply the tang of salt air that had teased his nostrils in his dream.

That alone had been welcome. 'Twas the smell of home. 'Twas the smell of the wind vaulting over the high walls of his ancestral home of Montsalvat. Too long had he been without the bite of that wind against his skin.

Suddenly Dagobert knew with unerring conviction that his son yet lived and that he would find him at Montsalvat. That was, without doubt, the message his dream bore. His eyes flew open, though this time he saw naught but the ceiling itself arched above the bed.

There could he tell the boy of his heritage, he concluded with rising excitement. There alone could he complete the task that had been set before him. There alone could he happily pass from this world, should his time deign to come. Resolution flooded through him and he gathered Alienor close to his side, anticipation flickering to life within him.

Time 'twas to go home. And should the ghosts of the past demand to be confronted, Dagobert would meet them at Montsalvat.

Back in Languedoc, far west of both Thierry and Dagobert, the rising sun gilded the azure of the Mediterranean and burnished the ramparts of a fortress perched high in the hills. In the stables of that fortress, name of Montsalvat, an old knight urged yet another goat kid into the world.

A good spring it was proving to be and milk in ample quantities would they have this year, he thought with pride.

He turned the new arrival, showing the young goatherd how to clean the mucus from the creature's nostrils before he noticed the deformity.

The beast had but one nub where a horn would grow.

Eustache's breath caught in his throat at the sign, for it could be naught else. He reached out and touched the creature's damp brow, ignoring the mother's protesting bleat.

'Twas time again. Twenty years had it been since a goat had been born thus at Montsalvat. Twenty years. He had almost begun to fear that he would not live to see the next attempt to regain the lost legacy.

But here was no mistaking the portent of this oddity. 'Twas rare that the beast who graced the standard of the Pereilles came to life, and when it did so, especially here at the family's home, all knew to be prepared.

Eustache let the thrill of anticipation ripple through him as he stroked the newborn's brow. Time again to stake the ancient claim that had long been denied. He would indeed see the day.

His mind raced with possibilities, his excitement rising that he might yet again lay eyes on his old comrade, Dagobert de Pereille. And the son! A mere babe he had been when they had left these walls behind, but that had been twenty years past. The babe must by now be a man.

Would this be his time? Would he gain the prize and vindicate his family?

Eustache straightened and stood suddenly, his mind filling with the responsibilities before him. Aid would be needed, arms and men and supplies. As temporary master of Montsalvat, the provision of all fell to Eustache.

All his knighted life had he served the Pereille clan and he would not fail in this task. A list began to form in his mind even as he left the stables, but Eustache smiled as he stepped out into the first blush of the dawn. They would be relying upon him to be prepared. And Eustache knew well what had to be done.

Optimism buoyed his step as he crossed the bailey. Mayhap this time the battle would be won. Mayhap this time all would be settled. He dared to hope for a moment, before his usual practicality settled in.

If naught else, 'twould be good to see what kind of son Alienor and Dagobert had wrought.

'Twas a day of beginnings and endings, a day on which all three men stepped onto the bright path of their destiny, though none of them knew where that path might lead. An old dream was there to pursue, a yet older score to settle, and none could foresee whether the demand for vengeance or the desire of ambition burned with the brighter flame.

Or mayhap a conquest of a gentler kind would win the day.

Chapter One

*Tiflis—between the Black Sea and the Caspian Sea—
October 1265*

Thierry knew the pearls were counterfeit.

He rolled the pearls leisurely across his palm under his would-be ally's watchful eye. He wished he could either dismiss or justify his conviction. The gems looked real enough, but a glimmer in the other man's eye had triggered Thierry's suspicions.

And once active, his suspicion was not readily dismissed.

'Twas true that there were a goodly number of the gems in the velvet sack he had been offered as tribute, all of it summoned in but half a day. He eyed the ivory spheres speculatively, hoping the other man merely thought he was assessing the value of the offering.

In truth, he supposed he was.

No salve to his pride was it to be treated as Abaqa's runner, even after all these months, and he bit down on the increasingly familiar taste of annoyance. Still was he required to fetch tribute, to know all the while that each offering was considered a reflection of his own loyalty. Thierry gritted his teeth and let the gems play in his palm.

The pearls caught the light and indeed they gleamed with the luster of true pearls. This observation only served to give Thierry a grudging admiration of the counterfeiter's skill.

The other man made a nervous little laugh that drew the gaze of both Thierry and his old companion Nogai.

"Surely such an expensive gift is adequate," he said tentatively, the scholar's soft voice translating immediately after the man spoke. The four men virtually filled the small office, though the two townsmen managed to leave an eloquent space between themselves and the Mongols. The unexpected comment prompted Thierry to give the man a slow and thorough perusal.

He struggled to keep his lip from curling at the softness of the man the town revered as their leader. The flesh was loose around his middle, the pallor of his hands made him look almost feminine. Still worse, there was a light of fear in his darting eyes. This was a man? A leader? One entrusted to negotiate the town's safety? 'Twas almost too much to be believed.

Never did the kind of man these merchants and townsfolk chose as leaders cease to surprise Thierry. No blade could this man swing, no knowledge had he of summoning and dispatching troops, no ability had he to defend his town.

Which explained the presence of Abaqa's army camped just outside the town walls.

Thierry's eyes narrowed thoughtfully. He watched the man's flustered response to that move with interest before once more looking down to the gems cradled in his palm. Undoubtedly this was a shrewd man of business who could more than adequately govern his people under normal circumstances.

A man who likely thought he could outwit simple barbarians.

"Soon enough we shall see if the gift is adequate" was all he said, savoring the guttural sounds of the Mongol tongue. An admirable language it was for issuing threats, and that alone made him glad to have learned it.

The scholar Thierry had pressed into service translated his words and the townsman blanched. Nogai chuckled and the other man recoiled slightly, though he tried to hide the gesture. His glance darted once more to the little velvet sack in trepidation. Thierry spared the man an intent look as he tucked the sack into his tunic, watching until he swallowed nervously.

Counterfeit beyond doubt.

Thierry toyed briefly with the idea of taking retribution now for the insult, his gaze steady on the other man while he reflected. But better 'twas to leave such a task to Abaqa, for he would relish it more than Thierry.

Revealing naught of his conclusion, Thierry held the man's gaze for a long moment. Fear grew in those eyes as the other man's imagination evidently conjured recollections of Mongol retaliation.

A reputation was not necessarily a liability in these matters.

Satisfied when the man's eyes flicked to Nogai as though he expected the pair of them to fall immediately upon him, Thierry turned silently on his heel. He strode back out into the sunlight, the scholar and Nogai in his wake. He sensed rather than saw Nogai leer with deliberation at the town leader before he followed.

Thierry considered the twisting street, carefully gazing in first one direction and then the other. The agitated man he had left behind was forgotten as he planned his next step. His own survival in Abaqa's camp had to be ensured, first and foremost.

"We should return to camp," Nogai suggested. Thierry only shot a sharp glance in his direction.

"Not yet."

Nogai frowned and folded his arms across his chest. "Why ever not? Surely you have not forgotten that we ride to battle tomorrow? This is but another whimsical test of Abaqa's, and already have we expended too much time upon it."

He waited with obvious anticipation, but Thierry merely shook his head again.

"We are not yet done" was all he said. He ignored the anticipation in the eyes of his *anda*.

A pearl merchant was what Thierry needed.

A tribute of false pearls would not be good for the town leader's health, nor indeed that of the town, should Abaqa discover the forgery. However, Thierry knew that it could also bode poorly for his own longevity and this interested him above all.

If he could expose a forgery before it created undue embarrassment, his usefulness would be assured.

For now. Thierry lifted his nose to the wind and determined that the souk was to the right. He gave no explanation to either of his companions before he strode determinedly in that direction, leaving them to scurry in his wake.

Kira frowned irritably at the bowl of pearls her father had left her to sort before his departure to Constantinople.

Naturally he had not granted her the task of sorting the pearls without a smug smile.

So my daughter fancies herself worthy of becoming a pearl merchant. Kira could hear his mocking tones as clearly as if he stood beside her, and she grimaced yet again at the memory.

She would not cry. She had not cried when he beat her and she would not do so now. Had she not the opportunity she had wanted?

Then prove yourself. Tell me where they are from. Still she could see him as he taunted her from the door. His condescending smile had told her that he had no doubt she would fail.

But she would not fail. Kira set her lips stubbornly. Here indeed was her chance to finally prove herself worthy of her father's love. As worthy as a son could she be to aid in his business, and succeeding in this test could only prove that fact.

She would succeed. Kira did not fool herself, for there was much she needed to learn. No advantage had her sire granted her in teaching her only his native Persian, insisting that that language alone be spoken in their home. She well knew that as a merchant, he conversed readily in half a dozen tongues. But even Persian, as universal as it was, was often not enough within Tiflis itself.

Despite that handicap, Kira would prove herself. She was determined to do so. And this was the first necessary step.

Sadly, the truth was that her father had included some pearls of ambiguous origins, no doubt deliberately. Indeed, 'twould not have been much of a test otherwise. She had already sorted out the obvious forgeries, but well enough she knew what her punishment would be should she make a single mistake.

Hundreds of gems there were. Kira squared her shoulders and took another handful of pearls. She slipped a half dozen of them into her mouth.

Salt. She spat the first one into the brimming bowl of pearls she had already determined to be from the Red Sea. Good sense did it make that there were more of them mixed into the batch, as they would fetch less at market. She nodded approvingly at her judgment.

Salt and salt again. Two more joined the bowl, then two less salty, but still saline.

The last pearl she rolled tentatively around with her tongue, wanting to be sure before she decided. Well could a pearl merchant's reputation be shattered by the selling of lesser pearls as better ones and she schooled herself to be cautious.

Definitely sweet, she concluded with conviction. Definitely from Oman. The pearl joined a mere handful reposing in the second dish of sorted pearls.

Mayhap she was getting better at this, she thought with a rush of pride. She had been quicker with that mouthful. Feeling more optimistic, she scooped up another half dozen pearls and popped them into her mouth.

A guttural declaration drew her startled gaze toward the sunlight flooding from the market. A man's tall frame blocked the light. Kira squinted at the man silhouetted in the alcove leading to her father's shop, unable to make out his features in the shadows yet curiously aware of the weight of his gaze upon her.

Evidently her silent reaction was not the expected one. Kira's heart tripped in trepidation. He repeated whatever he had said the first time, with a heavy emphasis more than adequately tinged with impatience.

No idea had Kira what he said and she knew not what to respond. She stood reluctantly, painfully aware of her short stature and wondering how on earth she would explain that she could not do business until her father returned.

"Where is your father?" another voice demanded breathlessly in familiar Persian. Kira looked past the massive man to find a well-known but markedly nervous face.

"Johannes," she said with mingled relief and pleasure to see the scholar.

The forgotten pearls beneath her tongue stumbled unexpectedly from her lips when she spoke. Kira gasped as they danced to the ground and scattered. They glimmered in the shadowed shop and rolled away to hide in the corners.

Half-wit, Kira cursed herself, bending hastily to retrieve the gems as her color rose.

In the same moment the tall man muttered something vehement that could have been a curse and took a hasty step backward.

Another male voice protested and Kira confirmed with a quick glance that there was a third man behind the tall one. He was considerably more agitated than his companion. He gesticulated to the fallen pearls, his hasty words similarly incomprehensible though he said much, much more.

Kira hastily gathered the errant gems before they were lost. She dropped them into her pocket and straightened, only to find all three men regarding her with utmost solemnity. The hairs pricked on the back of her neck. Kira looked instinctively to the tall man. His expression was tinged with a healthy measure of suspicion.

Suspicion of *her?* Why?

The tall man's retreat had taken him out of the shield of the shadows and Kira spared him a questioning glance, undeterred by his stern countenance. He was heavily tanned or else darker of skin than she, his expression hard and uncompromising. His shoulders were broad, his forearms heavily muscled, his strong legs planted against the dirt floor like veritable tree trunks.

Kira fancied he would be about as easy to move as a firmly rooted tree and had little doubt he earned his way as a mercenary of one kind or another. He was garbed in a rough manner unfamiliar to her, his blue tunic, although as dirty as his dark blue trousers and heavy boots, unexpectedly trimmed with lavish gold embroidery.

Fear flickered within her but she refused to indulge it. Who were these men and what did they want? She met the steely glint of suspicion in his eyes, something about his very stillness making her wish he had stayed in the shadows. He apparently had a similar effect on the normally garrulous Johannes, who spared a quick glance to the tall man in much the same manner as one would regard an unfamiliar and potentially vicious dog.

Kira looked to the third man, his Asiatic features making her heart still. He sported a pointed goatee and thin mustache, unlike his companion, who was clean shaven. Both men wore their hair tied back tightly and bound into a braid, but the very sight of the shorter man's distinctively narrow eyes fed Kira's fear.

It could not be, she told herself wildly, even as she watched Johannes eye the two foreigners. Kira shivered at the possibility she could not even voice within her own mind and willed herself not to take a step backward. Never had she shown her sire her fear. She would show none to these strangers. Kira swallowed carefully and deliberately squared her shoulders.

"My father has gone to Constantinople, so the stall is not open for business," she explained formally to the scholar. The expression of raw fear that transformed the older man's features startled her and she flicked a glance to the impassive warrior.

"Nay, nay, nay," Johannes fussed, literally wringing his slim hands before himself. "This is not good, not good at all."

The tall man barked something short but incoherent that was clearly a demand. Kira's trepidation rose as Johannes responded quickly in kind, the third man's dark eyes bright in the shadows as he watched.

"What is this about?" she demanded, her uncertainty making her speak more sharply than was her custom.

The tall man's eyes narrowed speculatively and he spoke tersely to Johannes. The way his gaze wandered over Kira sent reluctant color rising over her cheeks.

She was *not* that sort of woman.

Kira lifted her chin indignantly and boldly held his gaze. She knew that her heavy, draped and hooded djellaba thrown over her high-necked *kurta* was demure beyond even the current mode, and that her full *chalwar* trousers hid all but her ankles from view. No need had she to tempt the glances of men in town, for that, too, bore the price of her father's lash.

Was that amusement briefly flickering in the warrior's eyes? Kira dismissed her whimsical thought out of hand, knowing intuitively that a sense of humor would not be an attribute of this rough warrior. Indeed, she had not found it an attribute of men in general, unless they mocked at another's expense.

"He wants to know when your father will return," Johannes translated. Kira shrugged in response.

"Just last week 'twas that he left," she confessed, incapable of tearing her gaze away from those scrutinizing eyes even though she felt that they bored into her very soul. "No less than a month could his journey require."

The warrior nodded curtly, apparently having understood the gist of her response from her gesture, and barked an order to Johannes. The scholar raised imploring eyes to Kira.

"Some pearls he needs valued immediately for the Mongol khan," he whispered. Kira felt her eyes widen in surprise despite her determination to keep her thoughts hidden.

Mongols. 'Twas true, then. Her gaze flicked reluctantly back to the third man with his characteristically Eastern features as though to verify her original suspicions.

When the Asiatic man grinned wickedly, Kira inhaled sharply. Her gaze danced back to the tall man seemingly of its own accord. He was watching her with that unnervingly silent scrutiny. Kira took a slow breath as she came to terms with Johannes' revelation.

No need had she to look into either pair of cold eyes again to know that these men would slaughter anyone who did not do their bidding. 'Twas all part of their daily business, she had little doubt.

No wonder Johannes was terrified.

But she would not give them the satisfaction of seeing her fear.

Kira drew herself up straighter and endeavored to look confident of her own abilities. No heart had she for abandoning Johannes to this forbidding man's disapproval.

"A rough value can I give him of the gems," she offered, the strength of her voice surprising her. Johannes translated her words and Kira took a deep breath, willing her heartbeat to slow. Truly she hoped that she could fulfill this task.

And her father thought that *he* had left her a test of her abilities. Kira licked her lips nervously as the warrior slowly slid a small pouch from his tunic. Could she do this? In truth there was little choice now. The warrior said something directly to her and Kira was forced to meet his compelling gaze once more though she did not understand his words.

"He says that the way pearls drop from your lips when you speak is a sign you can be trusted," Johannes supplied.

Kira swallowed with difficulty, knowing that she dare not reveal the truth of what he had obviously misinterpreted. She reached for the bulging velvet pouch, startled at the jolt that tripped over her skin when the warrior's rough fingertips brushed hers.

His skin was warm.

Suddenly Kira was aware of him in a much more intimate sense than she would have preferred. The unexpected contact and the faint waft of his musky scent awakened something within Kira that would have been better left slumbering.

She snatched the bag and backed hastily away, hating the knowing expression that lit his eyes at her move. Curse him for presuming to guess her thoughts. For no flattering thoughts had she of a barbarian warrior, regardless of his own interpretation of her response. Kira lifted her chin defiantly and glared at the tall man.

"Time will this take," she managed to say, forcing herself to continue even when that jaw hardened with displeasure. "Mayhap you could return later."

Impossible 'twould be to work under this merciless scrutiny. Irrational 'twas and she knew it, but Kira wanted this man out of her father's shop. Now. She felt agitated as she never had before and told herself 'twas the man's very stillness that unnerved her. And the way he watched every move so impassively. 'Twas unnatural.

Her heart sank when Johannes' voice faded, his translation not even complete before the warrior shook his head with certainty. He bit out something that Kira had no trouble recognizing as a recrimination or a threat or both and she felt her cheeks heat again. Too much 'twas to have him question her honesty.

"No intention have I of cheating him and you had best make that clear," she told Johannes tersely. She felt the heat of an indignant flush staining her cheeks but did not care. "An honest house is this. 'Twas only my suspicion that 'twould be easier for me to concentrate on the task without supervision that prompted my suggestion."

A flurry of Mongol followed her words and again the warrior shook his head, deliberately settling himself onto an inverted oil vessel that her father had abandoned in his packing. He braced his elbows on his knees, looking even more immobile than he had before, and growled one last comment.

"He says you will have to get used to him," Johannes supplied in a small voice. Though his words came as no surprise to Kira, her heart took an unsteady lurch as she met the warrior's resolute gaze.

Fine. She dropped the sack of pearls deliberately on her worktable. The sooner the pearls were assessed, the sooner he would be gone. And a good riddance 'twould be.

She was annoyed, of that there was little doubt. Thierry found the unexpectedness of her response curiously amusing. Fear he was used to, but disgruntled cooperation was a response that was entirely novel.

Evidently the woman was a witch.

Those full lips had tightened, and the teeth that had flashed when she smiled earlier were gritted together in a clear bid for self-control. The soft gold of her complexion was now tinged with a more ruddy hue. She cleared her work space brusquely of other gems, the expression in those wide dark eyes mutinous at a minimum.

For all of that, though, she did his bidding. Thierry supposed another less perceptive than he might have been fooled, but he saw every minute sign of her displeasure. That such a small and feminine creature would even consider defying him was as fascinating as it was unprecedented. Thierry could not help but watch her tiny hands as she worked.

Though she refused to glance in his direction, Thierry knew she was completely aware of his regard. He leaned back against the wall, fingering the hilt of his blade speculatively. What manner of woman spewed pearls from her mouth when she spoke?

A puzzle that was, but no less of one than her response to him. Why was she not terrified? Certainly the thin scholar had made it clear that he was Mongol. Fear had flashed through her eyes, telling Thierry that she was well familiar with their reputation. But she had not recoiled in the manner of most soft urban women who had seen naught of life.

What kind of woman would have the audacity to act thus? A Mongol woman, surely, but this woman's delicate features hinted naught at Eastern blood.

A witch she must truly be. Indeed, 'twas well Thierry had guessed her game, for he would need to guard himself against her sorcery. No other explanation could there be. Convinced of his own logic, Thierry watched the woman with grim determination.

Incredibly, his suggestion that she might cheat him if left alone seemed to have struck a nerve. That aroused Thierry's curiosity. Surely these town people did not expect foreigners to trust them?

Or mayhap she simply disliked that he had guessed her game so early.

"Mayhap you should have the pearls assessed back at camp," Nogai suggested.

Thierry stiffened, hearing the leer in his old companion's voice. He did not have to look to know full well the path his *anda*'s thoughts had taken. Though the woman's garb was cut full, 'twas clear enough that she would be small and shapely. He stifled an uncharacteristic surge of annoyance at his old companion's appetites.

"They will be assessed here," he said flatly, hating Nogai's knowing chuckle. Thierry felt the other man lean closer, fully anticipating that his next words would be for his ears alone.

"Tempted, are you not?" Nogai whispered mischievously. Thierry did not acknowledge the taunt, staring resolutely forward. He was *not* tempted. Women did not tempt him. "Well should you be, for she is a tasty morsel, indeed." When his words still garnered no response, Nogai dropped his voice yet further. Thierry struggled not to bristle.

"Mayhap should you not be interested, I should sample her myself."

"Nay!" Thierry bit out the denial more harshly than he intended.

The woman glanced up like a frightened doe, her startled expression making him consider apologizing.

Apologizing? Khanbaliq loomed in Thierry's mind and he straightened his shoulders deliberately. 'Twas only the soft folk of Khanbaliq and other courts who apologized to women. Urban folk. He tried unsuccessfully to summon a sneer. A Mongol would not apologize. Thierry held the woman's startled gaze for a charged moment, then her color rose and she turned abruptly away.

A Mongol he was these days and he had best recall that fact. This woman he owed naught. Thierry felt his eyes narrow as he recalled the way the pearls had spewed from her lips. And the tingle she had launched over his skin when their hands had accidentally brushed.

"A witch is she," he pronounced, as much to remind himself as anything else. To his completely unwarranted relief, Nogai's manner cooled immediately.

"Touch her not," Thierry added testily.

"Nay," Nogai concurred. He even took a wary step backward, unconsciously granting the woman more space. "No telling is there what price she would extract for that."

The scholar drew himself up taller as though he personally took insult for the charge. One cold glance from Thierry silenced any protest he might have made.

The woman's gaze flicked between the three of them uncomprehendingly. Clearly she sensed that they discussed her. All three men remained stubbornly silent, even the scholar refusing to clarify the charges for her. The woman's lips thinned in annoyance and Thierry almost smiled.

Smiled? First apologizing, then smiling. Surely his wits were addled this day. Thierry scowled. 'Twas the witch and her sorcery that did this to him. She spun with a defiant flick of her chin and carried a broad vessel back into the shadows.

Where was she going? Thierry panicked and jumped to his feet.

For his obvious suspicions he earned a scathing glance from the lady in question that effectively checked his pursuit. Thierry almost smiled at her indignation, but the ripe curve of her buttocks outlined when she bent to scoop water from an urn halted that rare impulse before it had truly begun.

Nogai made an admiring sound under his breath that Thierry alone seemed to note. She was yet more shapely than he had guessed and Thierry's mouth went unexpectedly dry. How long *had* he been chaste? He could not cease fingering the hilt of his blade, though he told himself the gesture was merely a habit.

She propped the brimming clay bowl on her hip as she returned. The further evidence of the slender curves hidden beneath the full cotton garment fed Thierry's awareness of both her and his own increasingly agitated state. Abruptly and uncharacteristically he wished he had been able to completely adopt his tribesmen's penchant for simply taking whatever they wanted.

The value of the pearls was all he was here for, he reminded himself sternly. Once he had that information, he would return to the khan's camp. With Nogai alone. Abaqa would have his tribute from Tiflis, such as it was, and they would ride to battle on the morrow.

He watched the woman settle the brimming bowl on her worktable. Her hands were long fingered and graceful for all their delicate size, though Thierry knew not why he noted such a thing.

'Twould be ridiculous to undermine any of his aspirations for what could amount to no more than base desire. Abaqa might not thrive as long as his sire, and Thierry might yet have the opportunity to vie for his ambition. No woman was worth jeopardizing all of that.

The woman moved quickly, her sudden gesture as she cast the pearls into the vessel catching Thierry's eye. He leaped forward in alarm, too late to intervene, as the contents of the velvet pouch spilled into the water.

A trick 'twas! And too absorbed had he been in his own troubles to anticipate her move!

Nogai swore. He lunged forward in the same moment as Thierry. The two of them towered over the woman as she glanced up in alarm. Thierry peered into the depth of the water, his anger flaring when he realized he could not see the pearls.

They were gone! He had failed!

The vessel had some sort of false bottom, Thierry concluded in dismay. He cursed his own stupidity in letting his baser instincts cloud his normal caution.

He would not grant Abaqa such an easy victory.

The woman's eyes widened when Thierry hauled his blade purposefully out of his belt. He silently applauded how well she played her role for she looked confused, then perfectly incredulous to find the unsheathed blade right beneath her nose. She met his gaze, her beautiful dark eyes startled. Thierry hated himself for his inexplicable urge to reassure her.

Was she not bent on deceiving him? Did such intent not grant him the right to take her life? Why then did he have this inexplicable urge to stroke the furrows from her brow?

"Tell him that this is the best way to find forgeries."

She spoke hastily to Johannes, the translation making Thierry frown. He watched with amazement as she gestured to bobbing orbs on the surface of the water. She murmured something else, and the scholar's quick translation sparked Thierry's interest.

"You have been tricked."

He dared to wonder in that moment if his own assessment of the gems had been correct. The woman quickly plucked the "pearls" that floated off the surface of the water as Thierry watched. Before he could intervene, she offered them to him with a dismissive gesture that told Thierry more than eloquently their authenticity. They *were* counterfeit. He grudgingly acknowledged her skill as he looked at the "gems," lowering his blade but not yet ready to put it away.

"Counterfeit," Nogai breathed. Thierry felt his friend's regard upon him. "You suspected as much before we even came here, then?" he demanded admiringly. Thierry merely nodded, watching the woman carefully to see what she would do next. "City dwellers," Nogai sneered as he shook his head. "Surely they cannot think we are such fools as to let such an insult pass?"

"The matter is best left to Abaqa," Thierry said calmly, a newfound admiration in his gaze as he watched the witch.

Mayhap he had misjudged her. She flicked a self-conscious glance to him and flushed in a most fetching way. Thierry's gaze dropped to her lips. She licked them and something raged to life within him.

Thierry frowned and tore his gaze away. He filed the false gems carefully in one of his pockets that Abaqa might be shown the fullness of the insult. He peered into the depths of the bowl with curiosity, all too aware of her sweet scent. The water had cleared and Thierry counted ten pearls nestled together in the bottom.

'Twas obviously a magic trick of hers to be able to so easily sort the wheat from the chaff. Though he knew not the means of her sorcery, Thierry respected the result. She pushed up a sleeve to reveal a slim and honey-hued forearm and scooped the remaining pearls from the base of the bowl. Was her skin the same shade everywhere? The question was more intriguing than it ought to have been. Thierry abruptly held out his hand to claim the meager spoils, uncomfortable with the direction of his thoughts.

To his complete astonishment the woman plopped the gems into her mouth.

Nay! She meant to swallow the only part of the tribute that was valuable!

Rage filled Thierry, rage with himself for being so fool-ish as to trust a stranger. He dove across the narrow table separating them. The vessel of water toppled precariously. The woman cried out and stepped back in surprise, but Thierry was quicker.

His hands locked around the slim length of her throat with practiced ease. The water splashed over their feet. The scholar shouted in dismay, Nogai swore yet again, but Thierry had no time for qualms.

He could not let her swallow them.

That one thought filled his mind even as he noted the softness of her skin beneath his hands. The woman's eyes opened even wider as his grip tightened purposefully. He noted with some satisfaction that fear had finally claimed her.

He flexed his fingers so they would not slide over her silky skin of their own accord. She had tricked him!

The witch choked unevenly and spat a half dozen pearls to the floor, tears filling her dark eyes as still she coughed. Out of the corner of his eye Thierry noted that Nogai re-trieved the gems.

There had been ten pearls in the water, Thierry was cer-tain of it.

Four there were still unaccounted for and well he in-tended to wait them out.

He gave the woman a little shake and she made a gur-gling sound deep in her throat. Furious that she had so de-ceived him and was showing a perverse inclination to expire at this most inopportune time, Thierry released her throat and slapped her back hard.

Another pearl leaped to the floor.

Three more! He smacked her shoulder blades once more when she still choked, ignoring the older man's fervent and useless prayers. A second gem made the jump, rolling across the dirt. Finally a third gleamed as it fell from her lips. The woman drew a shuddering breath and cleared her throat slowly, wiping her tears as Thierry glared at her im-patiently.

One more there was.

When she spoke, he would have the last pearl, he resolved grimly. His eyes narrowed at the look of outright hostility she shot at him. Traitorous witch! He gripped her shoulders that she might not bolt and waited patiently.

"You stupid fool!"

She spat an insult he had no interest in understanding. Thierry watched her full lips with growing disbelief when no gem dropped from them. He frowned at her tirade even as the older man translated, the indisputably angry words flowing over him unattended. There could be little doubting her meaning, those brown eyes flashing with fury as she wagged an admonishing finger beneath his nose.

"Look what you have done with your meddling!" she charged angrily. *She* was angry? Thierry inhaled slowly when the scholar's words made clear her accusation that he was at fault.

Mayhap she was annoyed that he had foiled her plan, he speculated thoughtfully. Otherwise she might have had nine more pearls. His lips set grimly.

No right had she to the khan's tribute. To think he had thought her insulted by his earlier charge that she meant to cheat him. She had simply been annoyed that he had so accurately anticipated her intent. A fool he had been to trust her at all. Thierry regarded her coldly, then held out his palm between them in a silent but eloquent gesture.

The woman shook her head firmly and pointed to her stomach once more.

"Ways there are to retrieve something swallowed," Nogai asserted calmly as he unsheathed his blade. The woman took a hasty step backward, evidently needing no translation of the other man's intent.

"Aye," Thierry agreed and headed purposefully for her.

The gem would be his. She darted to the back of the shop in a futile effort to evade him. When he cornered her, her breath was coming in quick gasps, her eyes and the hasty flutter of the pulse in her throat revealing that she was finally truly afraid. She said something that was obviously an entreaty, but Thierry had no intention of following Nogai's suggestion.

He would not question why. He pressed down on her shoulders until she dropped to her knees, unable to help noticing how tiny she was as he closed one hand around her jaw. The other slipped into the thick silk of the hair at her nape.

Soft, he marveled, hesitating for an instant. Years had it been since he had felt anything so soft as this woman's hair. She spared him a terrified glance that recalled him fully to his senses. Thierry pushed his finger into her mouth and down her throat.

She clutched at his hand, her grip surprisingly strong as she coughed and gagged. Thierry knelt over her as she dropped to all fours, sensing that the pearl would shortly be his.

Her offering, though, was completely devoid of gems.

A witch she was, indeed. He glanced to her speculatively, finding her looking thoroughly human with those tears of exertion streaming over her cheeks. Despite her state, she managed to glare at him indignantly. Thierry once more stifled that unfamiliar urge to smile.

Instead he frowned and held out his hand once more.

"Gone 'tis," she insisted, the scholar's rapid translation filling Thierry's ears. He refused to look away and she pointed emphatically to her stomach. "None have you to thank for that but yourself," she chided, her chin tilting up defiantly.

Something about her indignant response niggled at Thierry, even as her lack of fear intrigued him. He looked quickly to the scholar, wondering if he had misunderstood her intent.

"What does she mean?" he demanded impatiently, still not relinquishing his grip on her shoulders.

His fingers curled around her and without thinking, he drew her closer. The spice of her skin was intoxicating and he forced himself to look away as he gathered his jumbled thoughts. Thierry felt rather than saw her look to the scholar in turn. Her breathing quickened when he simply responded without translating.

"The flavor of a pearl reveals its origin and hence its value," the older man supplied quietly. Thierry glanced back to the woman in time to see her flick a glance filled with trepidation up to him. She demanded something of the scholar, presumably an explanation, and he noted that her voice had risen.

"She should have told me her intent," he growled, staring at her so hard that she seemed compelled to look to him anew. When she did, he savored his threat, relishing the sound of the Mongol tripping off his tongue as she shivered beneath the weight of his hands. "Now she will have to pay the price."

Chapter Two

The warrior released his grip on her so abruptly that Kira nearly fell back on the floor; Johannes' translation of his last words no reassurance at all. What did he mean? Her mouth went dry as he retrieved the pearls from his companion and jammed them back into the velvet sack. He shoved it into his tunic as he turned slowly and regarded her.

She would not cower.

Her heart began to gallop, however, her mind filling with a thousand possibilities. Would they kill her now to retrieve the gem? Kira had barely the chance to note a newly decisive gleam in his eye and panic before the warrior had closed the space between them and tossed her over his shoulder.

She struggled instinctively against him, earning herself a stinging slap on the buttocks and a tightened grip on the back of her knees. In truth, the blow hurt little but her pride. The other Mongol laughed, his lecherous grin right before her, and Kira cringed in anticipation of her fate. The time of reckoning had come and there was naught she could do to turn the tide. The warrior turned abruptly, the echo of his low voice rumbling against her thighs in a most disconcerting way.

'Twas intimate beyond compare to be pressed against him thus. Kira desperately tried to put some distance between the warrior's warm flesh and her own. His heat rose through his garments to taunt her breasts, her thighs, even her palms pressed against his shoulders. 'Twas futile she knew to struggle, but Kira could do naught else.

"He says to tell you he means to have the pearl," Johannes offered as he appeared abruptly before her eyes. His own dark eyes filled with sympathy before he continued. "One way or the other."

Kira's mind recoiled in shock at the promise in those words, but the warrior was ducking back out into the sunlight. His long strides took them across the market square and away from the only home she had known in record time.

"Johannes!" Kira cried out. She noted suddenly that the busy market had fallen silent as all simply watched her being carted away. "Johannes! You must help me!" Although Johannes had trotted into the market behind them, the warrior's determined pace was quickly leaving him behind.

Much to Kira's chagrin, Johannes seemed to be making no efforts to close the gaping distance. Would she be abandoned by her neighbors to the Mongols' whim? What would her father have to say of this? Worse yet, she was leaving the shop untended in his absence. Kira cursed her own sorry hide for failing in yet another of her sire's tasks. Never would she prove herself worthy of his love this way.

"Johannes!" The other warrior strode behind her captor with equally long steps. When Kira made the mistake of meeting his eyes, he very deliberately licked his lips. She recoiled, but he laughed harshly. Only too readily could she imagine what this one had in store for her. Truly she had fallen into the hands of the devil's own spawn.

Mayhap it would have been a mercy if they had her killed quickly.

"None can help you but yourself, child," Johannes called from far behind them. Kira heard the thread of fear in his voice. She looked desperately to the old neighbors in the market, dismayed to find them clearing out of the

Mongols' path, as well. They stood silently aside with terrified expressions.

But when had they ever helped her? Indeed, she was a fool to be surprised. Kira gritted her teeth and lifted her chin. How many times must they have heard her cry out during the night? How many times had they heard the bite of her father's lash finding its mark and done naught for her? How often had she greeted her fate alone before?

How often, indeed.

No one to help her but herself. Truly, naught had changed.

Kira's breath abandoned her lungs in one sharp move when the Mongol unexpectedly tossed her across the back of a horse. At least he touched her no more, though her skin still tingled from the imprint of his hands.

The beast wore a high red saddle, caparisons rich with embroidery hanging over its sides. Though the trappings were dirty and showing signs of wear, the horse's chestnut coat was glossy as though it were well tended. It pranced impatiently beneath her weight, yet more evidence that it suffered naught beneath this man's hand.

Mayhap another tended his beast, she told herself stubbornly. It could not be that a Mongol showed concern for any other than himself. Kira slanted a glance at her captor and confirmed her own silent judgment. Certainly no kindness ever passed from the hand of this stern man. Had he not slapped her own buttocks? Truly, men were all the same.

The horse took another nervous step and the ground moved dizzyingly beneath Kira's gaze. She inhaled sharply at the promise of her first horseback ride and fought against the bile rising in her throat. Too unsteady a perch was this for her taste, and the journey had yet to begin.

She found the weight of an uncompromising hand in the small of her back and the warrior's knees nudging her shoulder and thigh before she could collect her thoughts.

Warmth flooded through her garments and across her skin from that outstretched palm, and Kira panicked.

He muttered something impatiently when Kira struggled to right herself. She glared up at him through the tangle of her hair.

"I will not ride like a sack of grain," she informed him frostily, taking refuge from the barrage of unfamiliar feelings in anger once again.

He seemed somehow to understand, for one hand gripped her hair and hauled her upright painfully to sit before him in the saddle. Kira voiced no complaint, merely gritted her teeth. She would show no weakness. She felt the other Mongol watching them, painfully aware of his poorly concealed amusement. She stubbornly ignored him as she fought against her rising fear. What did they intend to do with her? Her imagination was only too ready to supply the obvious alternative. Her warrior made a demand, an imperious point of his finger making it clear that he intended her to ride astride.

Like a common whore. Never. Kira shook her head immediately at the inappropriateness of that, watching his lips thin to a grim line. 'Twas bad enough to guess her fate without having to agree to the deed. Without preamble the warrior pushed her head resolutely back down toward his knee.

Well, if that was her choice, she would ride astride, Kira resolved. Anything would be better than the indignity of riding like a sack of grain. Not to mention that she would likely become ill in such a posture. She impatiently pushed aside his hand and sat up once more, gripping the horse's mane as she struggled against her full djellaba to lift her leg over the creature's back.

The Mongol muttered what was surely an oath. Kira flushed as his hands closed firmly around her waist as he lifted her high. Only too aware was Kira that his hands fully encompassed her waist and she felt claimed by him in some inexplicably new and disorienting way.

Nonsense. Kira's cheeks flamed yet ruddier beneath the other Mongol's interested eye. Full *chalwar* trousers she wore and naught was there for him to see. And well they both knew that she was no whore.

Even if he might mean to change that fact. Kira felt her hands begin to tremble as though they were not a part of her.

Kira leaned forward but evidently 'twas not the warrior's intent that they be separated, for one muscled arm locked around her waist. He imprisoned her easily against his chest, her arms pinned to her side beneath his relentless grip.

She struggled indignantly, the recent wounds on her back stinging with friction from her efforts as she roundly cursed his familiarity with her. The unmistakable feel of something hardening against her buttocks brought her to a flustered halt.

Kira panicked silently, for no doubt had she what that something was. A virgin she might be, but she was not a fool. A woman need not be a whore to know what was what in this world.

Would he possess her here and now if she vexed him? No good could come of this, to be sure. At this very real indication of what might be in store for her, fear threatened to overwhelm Kira. How often had her father threatened her with the beating of her life if a man laid a hand upon her? 'Twould be her fault alone, she had been made to understand, and the lash a necessary punishment. A fine match did her father intend to make for her one day, a marriage that would financially assure the leisure of his days.

Only an ungrateful wretch of a daughter would steal the promise of that away from her sire.

Surely her maidenhead could not be the price he would compel her to pay her for swallowing the pearl?

Kira's heart chilled and she felt herself begin to tremble as the possibilities became more clear. No doubt had she that a Mongol would take what he wanted, regardless of her entreaties. She felt the blood drain from her face at the realization that no explanation would suffice for her father.

His future would be destroyed and 'twould be all her doing.

The warrior's fingers fanned to close more resolutely around her elbow, eliminating any option Kira might have had to move farther away. She stiffened at the restriction and he grunted, though it seemed that she could no longer feel his arousal.

No time had Kira to reflect upon the matter, for his stirrups jingled and he dug his heels into the horse's side in that same moment. The creature seemed to have been waiting only for such a sign to flee the town at a recklessly wild pace.

She shrank instinctively back against the warrior's strength as the horse ran, certain she would be bounced loose and shattered like a doll on the ground. She clutched at the sinewy forearm wrapped around her, knowing her nails were digging into his flesh but unable to check her fear.

Her loose hair flailed around them, its binding long gone and her hood fallen away. The man behind her cursed again as Kira clung to him. He dropped the reins and she thought her heart might stop in terror. The beast ran unchecked! They would be thrown to the ground and their bones broken in a hundred places! Had this warrior not a scrap of mercy in his soul?

His freed hand swept savagely around Kira's head, his rough thumb brushing her nape and sending an unexpected shiver down her spine as he gathered her hair and twisted its length. 'Twas long enough that he could grip the ends in the hand clasped over her elbow. No reassurance did she take from the ease with which he accomplished his objective and nonchalantly picked up the reins again. Kira tugged against this new restraint, feeling hopelessly tethered even as she bounced precariously on her unsteady perch.

She would be jostled until everything within her was shaken loose. That was to be her fate. Powerless would she be to even stand when this wild ride was completed. Indeed, she could fairly feel the bruises rising on her buttocks already.

Her father would have much to say to her about such inappropriate behavior.

The Mongol said something to her, but she shook her head uncomprehendingly until his free hand curved firmly about her knee. No time was this for further familiarities. Kira recoiled from his touch. He repeated his command more slowly and did not release her knee, pressing the joint firmly into the horse's side and holding it there.

He gripped the horse with his knees, she realized suddenly, glancing down to find his knees clamped against the beast's ribs. Kira tentatively followed suit, imagining that his muttered response as he released her knee was approving.

'Twas better! Kira fancied she had a steadier perch. Her panicked breathing slowed with the realization that she was not likely to topple to her death.

Not until she returned home to her father, at least. Her heart sank.

If indeed she lived long enough to do that. Kira sighed and stubbornly blinked back her tears.

She would not think upon her fate. She would not even speculate on this barbarian's plans for her. Kira lifted her chin and surveyed the grassland sweeping beneath the horse's feet.

As her heartbeat slowed, she forced herself to concede that riding a horse was not so terrifying at all. Indeed, she felt warm and secure, though certainly such feelings were completely unwarranted. 'Twas only the fact that she could no longer see the warrior's cold expression that allowed her to relax, sitting as she was, virtually in his lap.

Kira became suddenly aware of the strength of his thighs behind hers. That recently awakened tingle struck again with new vigor. Though his grip around her waist was uncompromising and she knew there was no escape, the warrior did not hurt her. Could he truly be as brutal as she feared? Kira looked down to his fingers wrapped so proprietarily around her elbow, hating herself for liking their tanned strength.

Who knew what those hands had done? The man was a Mongol. A barbarian.

Mayhap she was losing her mind. Certainly the jumble of emotions churning within her this day could not be sorted into any order. Mayhap the warrior was saving her hide for some other fate. Kira chilled at the thought and refused to reflect on it further.

In the distance a dark smudge grew more distinct. Kira gradually picked out the forms of horses grazing all around an apparent settlement. Gradually it became clear that the smudge across the landscape was composed of thousands of round homes. Kira had little doubt what sort of settlement they approached.

'Twas the Mongol camp. A cold trickle of dread meandered into her stomach at the sight. What gruesome fate awaited her here?

Thierry rode directly to his own yurt, liking its welcome familiarity. The round felt tent gave him a sense as close to homecoming as he found these days.

But he would not indulge himself in another recollection of Khanbaliq. Truly he could not recall when those images had last haunted him as they did this day. But no time had he for such poignant and pointless reminiscing.

The woman had clenched up before him as the camp came into sight. Once again he stifled the urge to reassure her. Had she not tried to trick him once already? Indeed, there was no way of telling what sort of treachery was filtering through her mind even now.

A witch she was. He should know better than to trust such a lovely face.

Undoubtedly she was used to turning her beauty to her advantage. 'Twould not work this time, Thierry reminded

himself determinedly. He halted the horse with a barely
audible sound and nudged his knee beneath hers. She apparently understood his intent, letting him lift her knee over
the horse's back with his.

At least she was not a fool, he concluded with an unwarranted rush of pride. He savored the pleasant feel of her
cradled in his lap before he slid to the ground. Was the rest
of her as soft as her hair? She gained her footing less
gracefully than he had expected. That as much as anything
was an indication of her unfamiliarity with horses.

That could well be changed. Thierry was amused when
the witch immediately tried to pull away from him. Where
did she think she might find safer haven than with him in
this camp? Nogai would offer her company, 'twas true, but
somehow he doubted that kind of companionship would
please her.

Thierry kept a firm grip on the end of her hair that had
her shortly spinning to a stop, her eyes flashing angrily
when they met his. Nogai laughed at her predicament and
she spared him a hostile glance before she confronted
Thierry once more.

She spat something, but the translator had been left in
Tiflis. Mayhap not the best conceived plan, but then,
Thierry needed no more from her than the pearl. Her anger was fascinating though, and Thierry watched her, unable to help being intrigued.

"Mayhap you will find out firsthand the cost of coupling with a witch," Nogai taunted. The woman flicked him
a venomous look, though she could not have understood
the comment. Thierry chose to ignore the gibe.

She demanded something breathlessly, her tug on her
hair communicating her request. Thierry almost smiled at
her foolishness as he shook his head slowly. Her lips set
mutinously and she crossed her arms under her breasts.
Bewitching she was indeed, with those dark eyes shooting
sparks. Thierry resolved in that moment to show both her
and Nogai that he was unaffected by her charm.

He coiled her long hair once more around his hand, compelling her to come closer to him as he watched her silently. Her eyes widened in trepidation when he very deliberately repeated the gesture. She swallowed but took the requisite step closer. He wound her hair around his hand over and over again until his fingers were almost touching her throat. Thierry allowed himself a moment to flex his fingers in the thick mass, marveling at that softness, noting her discomfiture as she stared up at him helplessly.

Her skin was so golden a hue, he mused, recalling only too well the delicacy of her throat beneath his hands, the ripe press of her buttocks against his groin. He should not have teased her with his arousal, he knew, but she was so tempting, he had done so before he thought.

And now, he concluded as he looked into those wide brown eyes, she was certain that he intended to ravish her. He saw fear in those dark depths now where none had lurked in the shop. Her fear struck a nerve within him, as had her fearful response on the horse, dissolving his lust before it could truly take possession of him.

Dismissing his recurring urge to reassure her, Thierry nudged her impatiently forward. He felt his brows pull together in a frown of displeasure, even as he reminded himself that 'twould be much easier if she remained afraid of him.

Women were a liability, an indulgence that made a man soft. And softness made a man vulnerable to his enemies.

Like Abaqa. Thierry's blood ran cold as he noted again the woman's delicacy.

This woman in particular was not to be trusted. Thierry had only to keep the witch close until the pearl reappeared. A day, mayhap two, depending on what she ate. Mayhap he would even return her to Tiflis unscathed if she granted him the gem quickly enough.

Making him soft already she was, he concluded angrily to himself. No Mongol would have considered setting her free. Did the blood of the great Khan not course through his veins? He opened the flap to his yurt with a savage sweep and shoved the woman inside, leaving a chuckling Nogai outside.

A day might well be all he could afford of her company.

Kira had not expected the interior of the brown tent to be so luxuriously appointed. She gaped openly at the thick, patterned rugs covering the ground. Embroidered cushions were scattered in one corner, a small unlit stove in the other with various cooking implements and small vessels. A brass lamp hung from the central pole that supported the roof, though it, too, was unlit and her captor showed no inclination to light it. He left the flap open behind them, his grip unrelenting in her hair as he bent and hauled cushions into a pile around the pole.

One tug on her hair had Kira on her knees and she protested, earning a hostile glare. The warrior broke into a spate of Mongol longer than anything he had said to date, angrily gesturing to their surroundings with a broad sweep of his free hand.

"No idea have I what you mean," she countered irritably. "If you think that I will hold my tongue simply because you bid me do so, then you are indeed sorely mistaken—"

Kira got no further before the warrior scooped up a thick scarf and shoved it uncompromisingly into her mouth. She struggled against him as he tried to tie the gag. Kira managed to bite him hard enough that he cursed and released her hair to better finish the job. 'Twas all the encouragement Kira needed to make a run for the open flap. She got no more than two steps before the warrior grimly swept her off her feet.

He was coldly angry, that much was readily apparent when he cast her onto her back on the cushions. Kira squirmed but he dropped one knee onto her belly, lowering just enough weight onto her to keep her captive but not crush her. His eyes flashed as he lashed her wrists to the pole with crisp efficiency. Another scarf served to bind her ankles. The ends of the one filling her mouth were knotted behind her head so that she had no hope of breaking free.

She was trapped!

The warrior glared down at her for a long moment, and Kira feared her heart would stop in terror when he bent toward her. Kira's mouth went dry as her mind flooded with the certainty that he would surely rape her.

He merely tugged on the scarf knotted around her ankles so that her knees were forced between her elbows and tied it to the post, as well. He cast a blanket over her in evident disgust. Then he braced his hands on either side of her shoulders and barked out several terse, incomprehensible commands.

She had to break free somehow. Kira wriggled defiantly against her bonds, her movements setting the pole wobbling unsteadily. They both glanced up as the tent swayed. Kira stilled, then he glared down at her once more. A short lecture was undoubtedly what he was delivering, his hand signs making it more than evident to Kira that her fighting could haul down the tent.

Precisely, she thought victoriously. The warrior must have guessed the direction of her thoughts, for he shook his head with that maddening slowness. He moved out of her line of sight, then returned with a thick scrap of wool felt that looked much like the fiber of the tent itself. The warrior stood over her, mimicking the sway of the tent before dropping to his knees and pressing the piece of felt over Kira's nose.

The wool itched for an instant, then she realized she could not breathe. Her eyes widened in horror at his meaning. He would sit by and let her suffocate? Surely not! she thought wildly. His untroubled expression shocked her, answering her doubts more eloquently than words.

They were barbarians, one and all, these Mongols.

The warrior stood slowly and cast the piece of cloth aside, satisfaction gleaming in his eyes that she had understood his meaning. He lifted the lantern from the pole where it dangled over her head and set it beside the stove.

Kira frowned at him, unable to believe even a Mongol could be so callous.

Barbarian.

The final piece of the puzzle dropped into place when the warrior strode purposefully out of the tent, dropping the flap in his wake.

The tent fell into darkness in the same moment that Kira realized that he was leaving her alone. The muffled sound of his horse's footfalls made her feel more abandoned than she had in all her life.

Indeed, she knew not even whether he would return. And that possibility troubled Kira more than she knew it should.

"The others will well enjoy this news," Nogai commented wryly.

Thierry gritted his teeth as he dismounted, wishing there was some way he could keep the tale of his deed from spreading through the camp. But Nogai was not known for holding his tongue, especially once he had some *qumis* under his belt. The fermented mare's milk was intoxicating beyond anything else Thierry had ever sampled and enough to loosen the most reluctant tongue.

That Nogai's tongue was willing made the liquor's effect all the worse.

"The tribute will be well received," he restrained himself to commenting, knowing full well that this was not the news Nogai meant. His companion laughed and clapped him on the shoulder.

"But naught compared to the news that the Qaraq-Böke has taken a woman," he teased in a low voice. Thierry spared Nogai a scathing glance.

"I take no woman," he insisted. Nogai laughed again and Thierry was dismayed to feel the back of his neck heating.

"Good news that is, for should you not claim her, there will surely be others willing to take on the burden of the task," Nogai remarked lightly. Thierry stopped dead on the path, waiting until Nogai did likewise and turned to meet his eyes. The horses nickered in the darkness behind them. The revelry from the yurt ahead beckoned them onward.

"The woman will surrender naught but the pearl," he growled. Nogai lifted his brows eloquently, evidently not convinced.

"And then?"

"She will return to Tiflis," Thierry insisted, disliking the slow grin that spread over Nogai's features.

"Surely you jest," he charged. "No time had you to ride to Tiflis on this day and even less time have you to return there. Do you forget already that we engage the Golden Horde tomorrow?" Nogai rubbed his goatee with an affected gesture of recollection. "'Tis a battle of some import, as I recall. Mayhap I err, but 'twould seem that might distract your interest from one, admittedly small, woman." Nogai paused, darting a sidelong glance in Thierry's direction before he turned to swagger confidently to Abaqa's tent.

How Thierry loathed it when Nogai insisted on seeing matters as they were not.

"Unless, of course, your interest in the woman is more than passing." Nogai cast the taunt insouciantly over his shoulder as he walked away. Thierry stalked in pursuit, his expression turning grim. No time had he for this nonsense and already was he regretting this excursion into Tiflis.

"My interest is solely in regaining the pearl," he reiterated doggedly.

"Aye, one pearl is well worth this trouble when already you have nine," Nogai remarked with the innocent air of a child. Thierry did not trouble himself to respond to that comment. He was not in the least surprised that Nogai could not leave the matter alone. "Mayhap if you are not interested in her charms, you might indulge an old friend's fancy?" Nogai suggested impishly. Thierry's gut went cold.

"Naught but the pearl," he repeated stonily. He hated the way Nogai shook his head and clucked his tongue.

"And the good people of Tiflis will believe that?" he scoffed. "The woman will be outcast on her return, re-

gardless of what tale she tells. And well enough we both
know how outcast women earn their keep throughout the
world." Nogai's voice dropped confidentially and as he
leaned closer, Thierry struggled to bolster his resolve
against the appeal of the inevitable suggestion.

"Should she be fated to be condemned, should you not
at least avail yourself of the pleasure of her companionship?" he whispered temptingly.

Thierry did not even dare to imagine such a thing. Already was he far too aware of the woman's allure. And the
reminder that her reputation had already been destroyed by
his capturing her was less than welcome.

He thought of the way her eyes flashed in anger and
something clenched within him.

Naught had this to do with retrieving the pearl that was
rightfully part of the khan's tribute, he reminded himself
savagely. The woman would have to come to terms with her
own fate when she returned to town. Had she not swallowed the gem, he would not have been compelled to bring
her along.

His had been a perfectly logical choice under the circumstances and certain was Thierry that the khan would
feel the same way. He shot a hostile glance in Nogai's direction by way of answer and stalked ahead to the well-lit
tent, leaving his companion to trail behind.

"And who will be sifting through her leavings, I wonder?" Nogai taunted unrepentantly, though Thierry resolutely ignored him. "Well would I like to see you on your
hands and knees at that task," he jested. His laughter did
little to ease Thierry's own doubts about the situation he
had wrought.

"Mayhap you should find somewhere else to sleep to-
night," Thierry found himself saying. 'Twas unreasonable
how he hated the thought of his companions looking upon
the softness of the witch as she slept.

Nogai laughed. "Then none will know if you keep your
word," he taunted. Thierry ignored him though the accusation made his ears burn.

The pair of *keshik* guards at the opening of Abaqa's yurt stood aside when they recognized Thierry and Nogai. Thierry hesitated on the threshold, disliking that the sound of revelry was so high this early in the evening. In no shape would these men be for battle on the morrow, he thought with disgust, knowing that Nogai had oft proved that very same prediction wrong.

Mayhap if he had more Mongol blood within him, he might have similarly been able to fight well after a night of drinking.

Odd 'twas that of late all seemed to remind him of the deficiency flowing through his veins.

The khan made a beckoning gesture to Thierry that struck him as slightly mocking. He stonily refused to take offense. Abaqa had made his position clear and Thierry knew well the alternative to doing the khan's will. No matter if this subservient role increasingly chafed at him.

No matter if he was a better warrior than his khan. No matter at all.

"Come tell me of the results of your labors," Abaqa invited, no evidence in his tone of how much he had imbibed.

"Tribute from Tiflis, as you requested," Thierry offered matter-of-factly, pulling the small pouch of genuine pearls from his tunic. The khan riffled through the meager offering skeptically.

"'Tis not much," he commented, as though the insufficiency pleased him in some way. A victorious sense flooded through Thierry at the knowledge that he had not failed as anticipated. He dug the remainder of the pearls from his pocket with satisfaction.

"This part of the tribute are frauds," he added. The other man's eyes lit with a predictable gleam.

"Frauds? They dare offer frauds as tribute? Mayhap we should visit Tiflis," Abaqa suggested. A rousing cheer filled the tent. "Berke and his Golden Horde first," he shouted over the enthusiastic response of his men and turned a smug smile on Thierry. "An old score have I to settle there," he added in an undertone. "Those around me know that I do not soon forget a slight."

Thierry met Abaqa's gaze as toasts were raised by the assembled commanders at the idea of two battles in short order. He saw the animosity reflected there as their gazes locked, but refused to look away as another round of raucous music broke out. The shaman pounded his horse-headed staff on the ground and the men stamped their feet in time, until their laughter broke the rhythm.

Abaqa smiled and the tension was broken. He glanced over his military elite indulgently as he quaffed his own draught. Thierry followed his gaze and was caught short by the knowing expression etched on the features of the shaman. That man was avidly watching his discussion with Abaqa from the other side of the yurt.

The shaman's gaze brightened as he noted Thierry's regard. Thierry stifled his inevitable sense of dislike when the man threaded his way across the yurt to stand just behind the khan. He nodded to the religious man. The shaman smiled archly and responded in kind.

Had the man divined something of this battle already? Did he know anything of the woman captive in Thierry's own yurt? A sense of vulnerability assailed Thierry and he suddenly wished the woman was not there, whether she was his own or not. Better 'twould be for both of them if she was safely back in Tiflis.

The hair on the back of Thierry's neck prickled, even as he knew the very idea was nonsense. Naught could anyone see of the future. The shaman knew naught.

Abaqa rolled the pearls across his palm, much as Thierry had done earlier, and shot the younger man a sharp glance. "Clever you were indeed to suspect the value of the gems," he asserted quietly. His eyes narrowed slightly as he held Thierry's regard.

His tone was not approving. Thierry's pulse leaped in dismay. Something was wrong.

"Mayhap *too* clever," Abaqa added deliberately.

His unexpected words hung in the smoke-filled air as the other three men waited for him to continue. The pearls rolled across the khan's callused palm and gleamed in the flickering lantern light. The four men barely seemed to breathe, the flickering lamplight illuminating the curious stillness of their tanned features as the revelry continued unabated around them.

Had Thierry been too audacious? Had Abaqa's tolerance for his presence in the camp expired?

Would he share the same fate as Chinkai?

Abaqa poured the pearls into his empty chalice and considered them in the bottom thoughtfully for a long moment. He looked up suddenly, his bright gaze revealing that he enjoyed the air of anticipation surrounding him. He tapped the chalice methodically with one finger and held it up to Thierry's view.

"I once heard tell of another commander having a chalice made of the skull of an opponent who rode unsuccessfully against him," he mused. He held Thierry's gaze for a long moment. Were his words meant to be a personal threat? Thierry's pulse accelerated. Abaqa leaned forward with a confidential air that fully captured the attention of all three men.

"I would have Berke's skull bear my *qumis*," Abaqa concluded slowly.

He had named the khan of the Golden Horde, their opponents on the morrow. Thierry exhaled in silent relief.

Abaqa smiled a dangerous smile, making Thierry suspect that every nuance of his response had been detected. He struggled not to fidget with the knowledge that Abaqa was enjoying toying with him.

"'Tis time we saw what legacy you bear in your veins," Abaqa suggested with seeming indifference. His lids dropped as he watched his own fingertip slide around the rim of his chalice. Thierry wished he could see the expression in the older man's eyes. "You should have no qualms leading the right wing on the morrow," the khan added flatly and his lip curled condescendingly before he continued. "We shall see soon enough whether you are truly as stealthy as the black wind itself."

Thierry's heart skipped a beat at the risk and the opportunity, though he carefully schooled his features as he nodded.

Was this the opportunity he had been waiting for? Was this the chance that would prove his ability as a leader? A single *tümen* of ten thousand men riding under his command on the morrow. Should Thierry manage to prove his loyalty and survive this test, it could be the first step to establishing his own foundation of support within the tribe.

"May the Golden One's blood bring you luck," Abaqa concluded, his tone revealing that he expected exactly the opposite to occur.

And should Thierry fail? The expression in the other man's eyes told him that any failure on the field would be interpreted as disloyalty to the new khan. Abaqa held Thierry's gaze that he might see the fullness of the threat before snapping his fingers impatiently for more *qumis*.

"I thank you for your salute," Thierry said politely. He did not need to look to know that Nogai had detected the same skepticism in Abaqa's eyes.

Thierry's gaze sought the shaman's regard seemingly of its own accord. The shaman quirked a knowing brow and smiled a secretive smile. Thierry's resolve to ride successfully from the field redoubled in that one long moment.

He would show them all of what he was made on the morrow.

Chapter Three

Thierry was surprised to find the shaman behind them when he and Nogai finally abandoned the khan's yurt and gained the relative silence of the night. The man moved more silently than Thierry could fathom and he felt a twinge of annoyance at his presence. The shaman smiled anew as though he had detected the path of Thierry's thoughts.

"An assumption you make that you will succeed on the field tomorrow," he purred silkily. Thierry shot a glance to Nogai. His companion said naught, but 'twas easy to detect his nervousness at the unexpected comment.

"Not unreasonable would such an expectation seem to be," Thierry observed, hating that he was beginning to question the matter himself. No power had this man in truth, he reminded himself. Political aspirations of his own had the shaman and the truth was clear to all who dared to see. Indeed, how could he manage to divine the future before it occurred? Illogical 'twas.

The shaman's eyes glittered in the shadows and the moonlight gleamed on the polished wood of his staff. Beneath such light, the horse's head seemed to take on a life of its own and Thierry fancied that the hoof at the base of the staff stamped impatiently in the dirt of its own accord.

Suddenly the sounds of celebrating in the khan's yurt seemed much, much farther away. They were alone under the moonlight, just the three of them. The sounds of merrymaking were more muted than Thierry knew them to be in truth. Was this some sorcery of the shaman's? He looked into the ancient eyes of the shaman and felt as though they had been magically shifted to some other world.

Indeed, the world he knew seemed too far away in this moment.

Nonsense 'twas. But the shaman's smile widened despite Thierry's conviction.

"Naught have I to fear from you and your ambitious dreams," the shaman intoned as he leaned closer to Thierry. Nogai took a tentative step back, but Thierry refused to follow suit. He would not let this man intimidate him, no matter how close his words struck.

"Shown to me 'twas," the shaman hissed when Thierry said naught. He rattled the bag of sacred sheep bones he carried for making his predictions and his eyes narrowed as he leaned yet closer.

Thierry did not dare recoil or break the man's regard.

"The gods showed me their hand in your fate and 'twas not a pretty sight, Qaraq-Böke. Aspirations have you, 'tis evident to all, but all your ambitions will amount to naught. Tiflis was but the beginning." The shaman arched his brows high and sneered. Thierry knew a moment of dread but he stifled his fear, hoping it did not show in his eyes.

"*Naught*," the shaman repeated. He smiled with relish as he cast a scornful glance over Thierry. "A failure will you make of your life and, worse, 'twill be by your own hand that you fail."

That last proved the fallacy of the tale. Success did Thierry want and well enough did he know himself to understand that he would never forsake his own ambitions.

"Naught do you know of this," Thierry argued skeptically. The shaman's eyes widened at his disrespectful tone.

"Do I not?" he mused, his arching brow eloquently conveying his skepticism. "Mayhap you know better than I. Mayhap you can divine the future better than I. Mayhap you have garnered the support of more powerful spirits than I in your short life." His lip curled as he paused to glance over Thierry.

"Mayhap," the shaman sneered. "But I think not." He spun on his heel and his white cloak swirled out behind him, the colorful strips that hung from it dancing in his wake. "Mayhap we shall see on the morrow who knows best." He cast the words over his shoulder with a carefree air and they hung ominously in the night.

Thierry refused to respond. Nogai shivered openly when the shaman turned away, but Thierry resolutely held his ground as he watched the man go.

Threatened he had been before and he would not take this taunt any more seriously than the others. 'Twas but a game to disarm him and undermine his confidence.

Victory would be theirs on the morrow and Thierry knew the fact well. And when ultimately his own success was rewarded, as Thierry had no doubt it would be, the shaman's error would be clear for all to see.

Thierry let his horse run with the others for the night so that it might graze. For a long moment he let the harness swing from his hand, his gaze tracing the beast's path. What had he wrought of his life this day? Naught but trouble, as far as he could see.

And yet more trouble, of an entirely different nature, awaited him at his own hearth. He turned with a frown and stalked back to his yurt in poor humor. 'Twas humiliating enough for Nogai to joke about who would sift the woman's leavings, but 'twas doubly unnerving to find himself resenting the other men's delight in discovering that the woman was not his whore.

Never mind his rising anticipation at the knowledge that she awaited him just steps ahead. He should not have returned to Abaqa's yurt. Even if Nogai had insisted on a fortifying shot of *qumis* in the wake of the shaman's warning.

Thierry would ignore the woman. No use had he, after all, for women or the vulnerability they created. Thierry wondered if he had imagined the glint in the khan's eye when he had confessed to taking her. Foul luck it had been indeed that a flushed Nogai had spilled the entire story. Thierry had been asked for naught but affirmation, which he could not deny.

Witch. Already had she turned his life on end. Was she at the root of this new uncertainty stalking him? Had Abaqa changed his mind about Thierry in truth, or did he simply continue to toy with Thierry? And if Abaqa *had* changed his mind, had the witch somehow contrived the change? Did she take retribution for her captivity?

The thought was more than unsettling. Witchcraft or not, her very presence had undermined the security of his position within the tribe, just as he had feared. Women meant vulnerability in a culture where all pursued their own interests alone. 'Twas as simple as that.

Mayhap 'twas time enough he gave up this vagabond life. After all, the Mongol strain was but a quarter of what coursed through his veins.

The unexpected thought caught Thierry completely off guard. He actually considered the possibility for the barest instant before discarding it with disgust.

What nonsense was this? No other life had he. Khanbaliq tempted him, but he resolutely pushed that recollection aside, as well. Naught was there for him in Khanbaliq, even if he chose to ride across the width of Asia to return to that town.

This was his life. *This* was the path he had chosen. And the labor of his years was destined to bear fruit, sooner or later. Thierry could feel it. Mayhap it had been too soon when the old khan died, but he was young enough to wait out Abaqa's reign. And continue to consolidate his support while he waited. Leading a *tümen* on the morrow was but the first step. No interest had Thierry in casting all aside now for what amounted to no more than whimsy.

More nervous must he be about this battle than he had thought.

Thierry shoved open the tent flap in poor humor. The wan moonlight was enough to show that the woman was not only awake but watching him warily. What did she expect of him? he thought irritably. He trudged into the yurt and squatted down to light the brass lamp. Had she not tried to deceive him? Was she responsible for his woes? When the flame flickered to his satisfaction, Thierry swiveled without standing and silently returned her regard.

Was that relief he had briefly glimpsed in those dark eyes?

It helped his resolve not a bit that the golden lamplight seemed to heighten her soft femininity. The position her bonds had forced her to take showed the ripe curve of her hips to advantage from where he crouched. Her skirts had pulled up almost to her knees, leaving her feet and calves temptingly bare. Thierry fancied he could discern a hint of more private treasures in the shadows of her skirt. Her hair was cast loose over the cushions, dark and thick. He well recalled the smoothness of it between his fingers, and he shoved to his feet with a determined grunt.

Not for him was this.

He bent and untied her ankles with swift gestures, ensuring that he did not touch her flesh. Was it truly as soft as it appeared? His curiosity tempted him but he would not indulge himself.

She immediately straightened her legs, stretching with a wince. Thierry refused to acknowledge a nudge of guilt at the marks on her skin. She would not play on his sympathy so readily, he told himself, knowing without doubt that looser bonds would only ensure that she escaped.

Her movement revealed that she did wear *chalwar*, and he cursed his mind for the tempting images it had contrived. Naught could he have seen of anything. Clearly the woman's very presence was addling his wits.

Witch.

He untied her hands and she rubbed her wrists but once before she rolled and sat up. The motion brought her in such close proximity that Thierry could smell the sweet-

ness of her skin. The teasing scent fairly undid all of his resolve to leave her alone. Her hands leaped to the knot in the
scarf that gagged her when he did not immediately untie the
knot.

She hesitated, her eyes lifting reluctantly to his. Well
could a man drown in the fathomless appeal of those dark
orbs. And those lashes. Had ever he seen such lavishly thick
eyelashes? Like some forbidden princess she was and he
wondered if she deliberately flaunted her appeal.

Thierry nodded once and shoved to his feet, having no
interest in getting closer to her that he might loosen the knot
himself. She sighed with relief when that scarf, too, was
discarded. Thierry could not help but covertly watch the
rise and fall of her full breasts at the gesture.

How well would she fit beneath his hand? Too easily he
recalled the delicacy of her shoulders under his grip. Everything tightened within him and Thierry realized how
long he had been alone.

Because he had no space in his life for the vulnerability
women brought.

Somehow the reminder carried less conviction as he regarded the woman in the soft light. She watched him warily, as though she knew not what he might do, and Thierry
collected his thoughts hastily. He leaned over to grasp her
slender wrist and haul her to her feet.

She was so much tinier than he. For an instant Thierry
appreciated anew the difference in their relative sizes. He
liked the delicacy of her features, the fact that the top of her
head did not even reach his shoulder, the fragility of the
wrist within his grip.

She tipped her head back to meet his gaze questioningly.
Her lips were full and soft. Thierry wondered how she
tasted before the flicker of trepidation in her eyes hauled his
thoughts back to matters at hand.

'Twas best he ensured that she feared him. Her fear alone
could eliminate his desire, and business there was to attend
to. The sooner she surrendered the pearl, the sooner Thierry
could see temptation out of the way.

* * *

The latrine pits were behind the camp and open to the four winds. The emptiness of the plains surrounding them gave Thierry no qualms at letting the woman have some measure of privacy. He turned his back on her and scanned the distant hills with disinterest, forcing himself to breathe evenly. Even if she ran from here, he would catch her before she got far.

And 'twas far easier for her to search her own leavings.

When he heard her footsteps approaching, he glanced down at her, resolutely holding her gaze as he extended his hand once more between them. She shook her head firmly and he nodded.

A good draught of *qumis* was what she needed to set things on their way, he concluded. And the liquor would make her sleep soundly this night, as well, which was no small advantage, either. If he rode to battle on the morrow, Thierry certainly had need of his own rest. Little desire had he to spend his night awake and worrying about his fetching captive's escape.

Qumis it would be.

Kira shot her captor a glance of scathing suspicion when he offered her a battered tin cup. When she hesitated, he lifted his dark brows once, then drained half the cup's contents in one swallow. He offered the remainder to her once more.

Clearly she was supposed to drink it. Kira accepted the cup, sniffed tentatively and winced at its content's foul odor. Swill! She glanced to the warrior dubiously. He nodded once, firmly, and let his fingertips stray suggestively to the hilt of his knife.

Drink or die. 'Twas not much of a choice, but there was a possibility that this vile substance would not kill her.

A very small possibility.

But how would she ever force it down? Kira flicked a glance to the warrior, realizing in the same moment that there was no chance he might look away. She would have to drink it. She eyed the evil brew, took a deep breath and drained the cup in one swallow.

The liquor burned a path to her belly. Kira coughed at its unexpected heat and felt tears come to her eyes. The warrior swore under his breath. She took a shaky breath when she recovered herself and glared at him reproachfully through her tears.

He might have warned her that it was a concoction to be sipped.

The warrior said naught, merely refilled her cup. Kira almost rolled her eyes. Surely he did not expect her to drink more?

Although, to her surprise, the fire in her belly had diminished to a rather comforting glow. He hesitated before he handed her the refilled cup, lifting it toward his lips and making a series of sipping gestures.

Did he think her completely witless? That much she had deduced already. Kira knew her lips twisted scornfully before she could stop the expression. She nodded hastily and took the cup, dropping her gaze so she would not have to see his response.

Their fingers brushed inadvertently in the exchange, making Kira inordinately aware once more of the quiet intimacy of their surroundings. The drink unfolded a heat in her veins, making her uncomfortably aware of her companion's allure.

But this warrior had no use for her. Had he wanted her favor, he would already have taken it, when she was bound and unable to fight him.

Unless this liquor was part of a greater scheme. There was an unsettling thought. Kira's gaze slipped of its own accord to his full *chalwar* trousers. Her eyes widened at what she found and her gaze flicked immediately to his.

The warrior arched a brow, seemingly tempting her with the possibility.

Kira caught her breath. She was trapped in truth. No one would help her here, even if she screamed. Kira was suddenly, and mayhap tardily, well aware of the precariousness of her position. She inched backward, hoping he might not guess her intent.

His gaze hardened, making her heart skip a beat, then he pointed one finger at her. This was the moment Kira had dreaded, she was certain of it. She swallowed and nodded once in acknowledgement, powerless to look away from him. He quickly flicked his finger at the cushions on the side of the yurt farthest from the flap. Kira frowned uncomprehendingly and he growled in annoyance, repeating the gestures with the addition of closing his eyes and dropping his cheek to rest on one hand.

He said something to her in Mongol. He pointed to himself and gestured in the direction of the door, then said something else.

Was he telling her that they were sleeping separately? Impossible. Truly she was finding only the meaning she sought in his utterance. It could not be.

Kira carefully put down the cup and repeated his gestures rapidly. "I will sleep here and you will sleep there?" she asked doubtfully. It could not be so. The warrior watched her avidly. He nodded once when she finished and looked up at him inquiringly.

This was beyond belief. Surely she had misunderstood. Mayhap he meant *after* . . .

Kira had to ask the embarrassing question. There was no other way to be certain.

"Do you mean to couple with me?" she asked, feeling the heat of a flush stain her cheeks. The warrior's expression remained impassive and Kira knew he had not understood. She scowled. How . . . ? But of course.

Not having the audacity to look directly to him, Kira made a fist and inserted her other index finger into the space. She pumped the finger up and down in the space, certain there could be no doubting her meaning.

The warrior immediately shook his head quickly in denial.

He said something that Kira did not understand and she did not dare to be relieved too soon. With a grunt of frustration, he held out his hand between them. Kira stared at his outstretched palm for just a moment before she understood.

The pearl! He wanted only the pearl!

"No more do you desire of me than the pearl?" she demanded breathlessly, barely able to believe her luck.

The warrior said something and tapped his outspread hand with one fingertip.

Only the pearl. Praise be that her allure was so meager. Kira tucked up her feet and sipped at the contents of her cup with satisfaction, barely noticing how the warrior glowered at her change of mood.

He turned away and when his face was averted, Kira watched him with interest. It could be naught but this glow that had been sparked within her, but she noted for the first time his rugged appeal. If naught else, her warrior was well-wrought. Kira smiled to herself at the whimsy of the thought, her interest captured when he produced some flat bread and what looked to be cheese.

Indeed she was hungry. The warrior crouched down and made easy progress through the food. It seemed he had forgotten Kira's presence. She cleared her throat pointedly, raising her brows when she caught his eye.

The warrior shook his head firmly.

So she was to be starved! Fine! It seemed she had counted her blessings too soon. Kira drew herself up proudly at his refusal and defiantly took a great draught of the liquor as she held his regard. If naught else, she would drink!

The woman made it through another cup before she fell asleep. Thierry grudgingly admired her stamina as he sat motionless and watched the gentle rhythm of her breathing. She had slid down on the cushions and lay on her back with the confidence in sleep shown only by children and drunkards.

He cautiously moved forward but she did not stir, her breathing unaltered by his approach. Thierry knew she slept in truth. He crouched beside her, fascinated by the way her rosy lips had parted, the dark crescents of her long lashes splayed against her cheeks. He cast a glance over the length of her and wondered if townsfolk truly slept in their clothing.

He most assuredly did not. It took but an instant for the idea to trickle into Thierry's mind before he leaned over and carefully unfastened her djellaba. She stirred slightly and mumbled something in her sleep beneath his fingers.

Thierry froze, fearing he had awakened her.

But the woman fell silent once more and slumbered on. Thierry returned to his task, anticipation rising in his chest.

It was only the *qumis* that did this to him, he told himself resolutely. 'Twas the liquor alone that fed his fascination with her. He caught his breath despite his assertion when he peeled her *kurta* away, its removal revealing the drape of her trousers. Thierry's fingers trembled slightly as he divested her of the *chalwar*.

She was perfectly golden from head to toe, her skin as unblemished as the finest silk. Little doubt had he that she would be as soft, but now that opportunity beckoned, Thierry could not bring himself to touch her.

Her breasts were full, the nipples rosily dark, her waist temptingly small, her hips gently flaring. Her skin was so smooth that he almost could not believe it was real, even though the whisper of her breathing filled the tent. Thierry took an unsteady breath and reached out one hand tentatively to caress her flesh, just to be sure.

Vulnerability.

The word shot through his mind and brought his hand to a halt. The heat from her skin rose to tease his palm held less than a handspan above her. He swallowed with difficulty and pulled his hand back, knowing she was not his to touch.

But he could not tear his gaze away and he retreated just a short distance. He sat on the cushions, his bread forgotten as he watched her sleep. Thierry found himself memorizing every curve, noting every mole, every dimple, fascinated by the differences between the two of them.

Impossible 'twas that even a woman could be so small and perfectly formed.

She murmured once more much later and he feared anew that she would discover him, her incomprehensible words making those full lips stir in the most intriguing ways. Then she turned toward him. Thierry's heart fairly stopped, so certain was he that those dark eyes would fly open and instantly be filled with accusation.

But he could not move, watching transfixed as she rolled gracefully onto her stomach. Her hair spilled leisurely over her shoulder in a dark cascade that covered her back from shoulders to waist and spread over the cushions. She pointed her toes and he followed the gesture hungrily. She sighed as she nuzzled the cushion, the sound drawing his gaze back in time to see her slim fingers stretch to span the embroidered cloth. She murmured and rubbed her cheek on the cushion, sending her hair sliding into a glossy puddle on the carpet.

Leaving an angry network of scars on her back bare to his view.

Thierry frowned and blinked, but the marks remained. Did these townspeople flog witches? What else could have been her crime?

He dared to creep forward to peer at her marred flesh. Fresh red welts there were, signs of a recent lashing, for they could be naught else. Thierry leaned closer, inhaling deeply of her sleepy scent as he noted the healed marks below the new ones. He looked to the woman's features in repose and his scowl deepened. Habitual this had been, unless he missed his guess, and the matter did not sit well with him.

Who could willfully abuse such a small and perfect creature?

And what business was it of his to be angered by that fact?

Thierry hastily retreated across the yurt, fairly tripping over the unlit stove in his haste to put space between them.

He crouched down, his gaze returning of its own accord to thoughtfully trace the network of scars.

What could she have done to merit such punishment? 'Twas a puzzle he was unlikely to solve. He sat, only half aware of the silence gradually descending over the camp as he watched her sleep and teased his mind with the search for an explanation.

'Twas only much later when his own exhaustion threatened to claim him that Thierry could turn away. He retrieved the scarves from the center of the yurt and stared down at her for a long moment. He heaved a sigh before he bent to tie her ankles once more.

'Twould be foolhardy to trust her, he knew, but still he did not like his task. And was the task any less effectively done if he wound the cloth between her ankles that they did not chafe? Or what did it matter if the bond was less tight than it could be? She was drunk and fully asleep and he would bar the only exit himself.

Thierry tied her wrists together in the same manner, stunned when the woman rolled to her back. She stretched her bound hands high over her head even before he had knotted the scarf. The sight of her stretching right beneath him, her back arched and nipples straining high fed his imagination only too well. The idea of her beneath him in truth fairly undid his resolve not to touch her, and his hands shook slightly as he hastily tied the knot.

He promised her. Panic flooded through Thierry and he retrieved the blanket he usually slept in, hastily tossing it over her that temptation might be at least hidden from view. No consolation was her murmur of pleasure. He glanced down to find her smiling slightly in her sleep as she snuggled into the covering.

Considerably more disgruntled than he felt he ought to be, Thierry turned abruptly away. He shed his own clothes impatiently and rolled himself in a blanket with unconcealed annoyance, convinced that it was particularly cold this night.

* * *

Kira awoke with the sense that something had gone foul in her mouth. Her stomach rolled and her eyes flew open with the certainty that she had need of the outdoor facilities.

The shadowed interior of the tent drifted into focus and Kira frowned in recollection, not having any explanation at all for the soft warmth that caressed her skin. She put one hand down that she might sit up on the cushions, discovering that her wrists were bound in that same instant. Her feet were similarly tied and she scowled irritably, swinging her shoulders so that she abruptly sat up.

The blanket covering her midriff fell away. Kira gasped to find herself nude. Her breasts were bared to both the chilly morning air and the inscrutable gaze of the man crouched on the opposite side of the tent.

He neither moved nor spoke, but Kira was past expecting anything different from this warrior. She was mortified when he did not look away, though, and clutched the blanket with both hands, hauling it over her breasts. Barbarian. Kira hoped he had not noted the way her nipples had beaded under his perusal, knowing all the while how unlikely 'twas that he would fail to observe anything at all.

He stood, his movements as economical as always. Kira started when she saw that he wore naught at all, her gaze stopping stubbornly at the thick pelt of hair on his chest. As he moved closer and she stared at his chest, she noted despite the poor light that a mark stretched across his skin from beneath the wiry dark hair. The mark extended toward his shoulder and Kira discerned that 'twas in the shape of a cross.

Could he be Christian? Well she knew that the sect used the cross as the symbol of their faith but never had she seen a believer mark his own flesh. When he paused before her, she could see the distinctive port-wine color of a birthmark and frowned in confusion. He had been born with such a distinctive mark upon his skin?

Reluctantly, Kira looked up to meet his eyes and more immediate questions filled her mind. What had happened the night before? So little did she remember after his promise—if indeed he had promised what Kira thought he had. She panicked slightly at that acknowledgment, scooting backward when he took another step toward her. He paused, his eyes narrowing slightly, and she dared not drop her gaze for fear of what she might see. Too close he was, for she felt that she could feel the heat from his skin.

Worse, she could smell him, and the scent did naught to bolster her resolve. He smelled warm and spicy, and that unfamiliar warmth, which she could no longer blame on the drink, coiled once again in the depths of her belly. Kira clutched the blanket as she felt her color rise and knew she could no longer hold his regard.

"Well I thought that you did not intend to take advantage," she charged breathlessly, holding the blanket before her like a barrier as he regarded her silently. "Where are my clothes? Why am I naked? What happened?"

He grimaced and used the same sign language he had used the night before, speaking as he did so in that incomprehensible tongue. He pointed to her, bending to scoop up the cup he had offered her the night before and making a sipping motion. Kira nodded quickly.

That part she recalled well enough, she thought irritably, wishing he would hasten to the heart of the matter. He pointed to her once more, closed his eyes and dropped his cheek to one palm.

Kira nodded impatiently once more. "Aye, that I well enough understand, but I would know what *you* did last night," she insisted. When he did not immediately respond, she pointed imperiously to him and lifted her brows in silent query.

The warrior nodded, speaking quickly as he indicated himself and pointed to a discarded blanket by the tent flap. So he had done as he had said. Kira expelled a sigh of relief, the gesture bringing her bare nipples in contact with the soft wool once more.

"But what about my clothes?" she demanded with new-found dismay. He looked blank and she glanced pointedly down behind the blanket at her nakedness. He frowned and swept a hand before himself in a gesture that compelled Kira to note his nudity, dropping his cheek to his palm once more.

So, he slept naked. Kira shook her head resolutely when he gestured to her and lifted his brows. "Nay, I do not sleep naked," she affirmed, spotting her *kurta* with relief. She stretched to reach it with some difficulty and when she managed to grasp it, shook it in his direction. "I sleep with this."

He shrugged, as if disinterested, turning away to haul on his *chalwar* and his boots.

Kira stifled a very feminine surge of irritation that he had so little interest in her nudity. Not easy for her pride was it that he so readily admitted to finding her unattractive, and she struggled to her knees, letting the blanket drop away. Little point was there in shielding herself from him, for he undoubtedly had more interest in his horse.

Men, she thought with disgust, surprised to find his hand heavy on her shoulder when she tried to rise. How had he moved across the space so quietly and quickly? He frowned and shook his head, leaning over her to untie the scarf that bound her wrists.

That dark thicket of hair on his chest brushed against her shoulder and Kira took the opportunity to study him through her lashes at such close quarters. Though he was bigger than she, there was not an ounce of spare flesh on his body, all of it lean strength and muscle.

His eyes were gray, she noted with amazement, wondering at his heritage, for his eyes were not as narrow as the Mongols', either. She felt that increasingly familiar tingle of awareness when his fingers brushed her skin, knowing all the while that 'twas futile and foolish to feel anything at all for a bloodthirsty warrior like this.

But he had not abused her, she was forced to concede. Fixed on his task, he dropped to one knee to undo the binding at her ankles with surprisingly gentle fingers. Lucky for her 'twas that rape was not among his objectives, Kira concluded as she noted the disparity in their sizes once more. Little enough was there she might have done to defend herself against one so much larger and stronger.

Mayhap 'twas a blessing that he liked her not, she reflected, watching his strong fingers make short work of the tie at her ankles.

Her father might be pleased.

Surprisingly enough, Kira found that neither the warrior's apparent disinterest nor the promise of her sire's grudging satisfaction sat well with her. Clearly, her irrational thinking of the night before still plagued her.

Her stomach rumbled once more and the warrior spoke brusquely, indicating her garments with an imperious finger. Kira hastily donned her *kurta*, *chalwar* and djellaba, grateful that he seemed to understand her haste when he immediately opened the tent flap and hastened her to the latrine.

The most savage expulsion of her life left Kira weak-kneed with relief when 'twas over. She inhaled shakily, passing one hand over her sweat-beaded brow. Knowing she had no choice, she turned to look, gasping aloud at the sight of the creamy pearl reposing amidst the dirt.

Kira glanced to her warrior, but he was scanning the horizon, frowning thoughtfully at the dawn with his arms folded impatiently across his chest. Her heart pounding erratically, she flicked the pearl into the grass with her toe and rolled it around under her foot.

Convinced he was distracted, she finally picked up the pearl and slipped it surreptitiously into her pocket. She looked guiltily to him again, but he evidently had not noticed her furtive move and she willed her heart to slow.

For no intention had Kira of surrendering the gem as yet. At least, not until she knew his plans for her.

Kira knew only too much about broken promises. He might not have abused her so far, but Kira would be sure of his intent before surrendering her only asset. Well might the warrior be biding his time, only to strike a more telling blow once he had what he wanted from her.

Kira strolled toward him as nonchalantly as she could manage, rubbing her troubled stomach to ease its aching. He turned that sharp gaze upon her and frowned, extending his hand between them in silent demand. Kira jumped at the abruptness of the gesture, then shook her head. She hoped against hope that she looked as convincing as she had the day before. His scowl deepened as he glanced back to the space she had used, offering his hand once more insistently.

"Nay, I did not pass it yet," Kira lied. She shrugged as though she did not understand the matter.

The warrior's brow darkened thunderously before he abruptly strode back to the spot where she had crouched. The precision with which he went to the exact location sent Kira's heart plummeting. Much more had he observed than she had suspected and she feared suddenly that he might have seen her covert retrieval of the gem.

Had she left some mark in the dirt when she pushed it to the grass? She knew not and her heart pounded as she watched. He peered into the dirt, then strode back to her impatiently a moment later and grasped her elbow as he hastened her back to the tent.

Kira hesitated just inside the opening, not at all trusting his grim expression as he hauled on a short *kurta* with long sleeves that gleamed with the luster of silk. He left the *kurta* untucked and pulled a coat of mail over it, followed by a leather cuirass that laced over his chest. He looked as though he were dressing for battle, though Kira was an uneducated judge of such matters, and she could not help but wonder where he was going.

And what he was going to do with her.

Finally the gold-trimmed tunic he had worn the day before was pulled over the laced leather. He buckled on a scimitar, lashed a knife to the inside of his left forearm and scooped up an iron helmet lined with leather, jamming it on his head. His gaze fell on Kira as he fastened the strap under his chin and she fairly fidgeted beneath that steady regard.

He could not know that she had lied to him. Kira dropped her gaze that he might not see the truth in her eyes. Mayhap, with luck, he would merely think her uncommonly modest.

The warrior grunted to himself, undoubtedly making a comment on her response, and Kira dared to peek between her lashes as he retrieved his weapons. Had she not seen the evidence herself, she would not have imagined that he could look more forbidding than he had already. This sight, though, made her fold her hands cautiously together before herself.

For what battle did he gird himself? And what was going to happen to her?

She was only too well aware of the weight of his regard upon her, although she did not dare meet his gaze. Neither would she cower, and so the two stood silently for a long moment, Kira feeling each heartbeat pass with agonizingly slow speed.

The warrior remained silent, not a clue to be gleaned from his stony features when Kira glanced between her lashes yet again.

Mayhap he knew what she had done. Mayhap he had seen. Mayhap he was granting her one last opportunity to confess.

Mayhap she should have given him the pearl, she thought wildly.

No further time was she allowed to reflect upon the matter. A round shield, a bow and pair of quivers were the last items the warrior took. Then Kira found herself being hustled outside and through the rows of round tents, trepidation making her heart race.

Chapter Four

"Persian, are you?"

Kira started at the sound of that achingly familiar language and almost turned before she caught herself. She frowned and scrubbed the filthy garment she had been commanded to wash, wishing any would-be companions would leave her alone.

The warrior had left her to wash clothes under the direction of an ancient harridan, and wash clothes she would. At worst, the task occupied her hands, if not her mind.

Although there was absolutely no need to make idle conversation with any of the other women standing knee-deep in the stream. None whatsoever.

Why would any of these women talk to Kira? Grist for the gossip mill, no more than that. Surprisingly, her relief to understand anything anybody said had nearly overpowered her usual caution. Long ago Kira had learned that her business was naught but hers alone.

"Indeed, you well look Persian. Certain am I that I have not seen you in the camp before, so you must be newly arrived."

Unfortunately Kira's lack of response did not seem to be affecting the woman's friendliness. The woman dunked a garment alongside Kira and Kira noticed the dark gold hue of the woman's skin. Persian skin. Slender fingers had she, much like Kira's, though Kira could see that the nails had been broken, and graceful hands that moved as though they had once been pampered now bore hard calluses.

Kira's gaze dropped stubbornly to her own hands and the similarity was inescapable. Would her hands soon be so abused? And what of the rest of her? She plunged the dirty garment into the river up to her elbows so that her hands were lost in the murky water.

The woman sighed. "I had so hoped you would be Persian," she said softly. There was no missing the subtle recrimination in her tone, and the familiarity of the language rolled around Kira's heart, entreating her to respond. "'Tis tedious to have none to talk with in one's own tongue."

Curiosity got the better of Kira with that comment. Too close 'twas to her own thoughts that she could not at least look to this woman. Kira schooled her expression carefully before she glanced up.

Her companion could not have been more than a few years older than Kira, for there was a youthfulness to her complexion that could not be subdued. She was slim and a full head taller than Kira, her hands moving with the fluid grace of a woman of station. Her dark hair was long but coiled back behind her head, several threads of silver catching the sunlight.

She smiled and though the gesture was welcoming, it revealed the unexpected hardness that dwelled in her dark eyes. Bitter she was, for all her solicitude, and Kira wondered what she had endured in the Mongol camp.

Did Kira dare ask?

"I am Persian," Kira confessed in as noncommittal a tone as she could manage. The woman's smile broadened.

"And recently arrived?" she prompted.

"Aye," Kira admitted unencouragingly. No interest had she in sharing her entire sordid tale with this stranger. The woman waited expectantly, but Kira ignored her and returned studiously to her labor.

"Ha! Right on both counts I was, then." The woman picked up her own work with satisfaction, but Kira let the remark pass without comment.

The silence between them was an uneasy one and Kira fancied the other woman was waiting for a confession of sorts. Kira scrubbed the dirty cloth determinedly, well aware the watchful eye of the old one on the riverbank was missing naught of this exchange.

"Persian I was once, as well," the woman continued conversationally.

Kira gritted her teeth. Naught had she to confide in this woman.

More pressing matters had Kira to consider on this morning. Where had her warrior gone? Had he abandoned her for good or simply for the day? When would he return?

What would she do if he did *not* return? Not a backward glance had he cast in her direction when he had left her with the old one. Though it should not have surprised Kira, the matter bothered her more than she thought it should have. Nervous she was amidst these people, much more nervous than she had been before in his presence. Well enough she knew that the only change was the warrior's absence, but Kira stubbornly refused to think any further along those lines.

"The *kalat* of your man is that?" the persistent Persian woman inquired. Kira looked to her uncomprehendingly, not knowing the term. "His tunic," she whispered in explanation. Kira glanced down to find a blue garment similar to the one her warrior wore in her hands. Indeed, she had not taken the trouble to study the garment she worked on.

"Nay," she said flatly, surprised when the woman exhaled with a hiss. Her friendly manner disappeared so abruptly and completely that Kira could only watch the transformation in astonishment. What had Kira said to so dismay the woman?

"And you would wash the *kalat* of another so openly?" she demanded in obvious shock. Kira knew she looked blank, but she gestured with one hand to the old woman who had given her the work.

"She bade me wash it," she explained tersely. And little enough choice had Kira had in the matter. The Persian woman took a small step away from Kira's side as though fearing to associate with her.

"Then Black Wind is not your man?" she asked sharply.

Kira knew her lack of understanding showed and the other woman shook her head irritably. "The tall one who brought you here. He is called Black Wind," she said impatiently. Kira could not help but wonder at the import of his name. "Is he not your man?"

Kira shook her head. The woman glanced hastily from side to side before she leaned closer to whisper conspiratorially. "Have you not a man?" she demanded incredulously. Kira could but shake her head again. The woman looked surprised, then her eyes narrowed dangerously.

"Truly you cannot know the way of things here to speak to me without telling me your status," she informed Kira frostily.

"'Twas you who spoke to me," Kira observed with a grimace. Clearly the woman was mad. She plunged the garment into the brown water swirling around her knees to rinse it out, deliberately ignoring the anger emanating from the other woman.

"No matter who began the talk. 'Twas your place to tell me your lowly status," the woman maintained. Kira's interest was piqued by the reference. Lowly? "Claimed by one of the *keshik* am I," the woman continued in a lofty tone, "and of considerably higher rank than a common whore like yourself."

Whore? Kira dropped the garment into the water in her indignation. "No whore am I!" she asserted, and the woman laughed in disbelief.

"No secrets are there between we women," she said with a malicious smile. "All within the camp know there are but three kinds of women here." Kira knew her lack of comprehension showed and the woman continued scornfully. "Jest not with me. Openly claimed women like myself are there and whores who welcome any between their thighs."

Kira drew herself up taller. "Chaste am I," she stated proudly. "Clearly that makes me of the third type." To her surprise, the other woman laughed harshly once more.

"Aye, mayhap it does, though you may well regret your status soon enough."

"What mean you?" Kira demanded.

The woman smothered a smile and deliberately returned to her work. "War fodder are they," she supplied with evident enjoyment. "Like children and prisoners of war, women like yourself lead the army into battle."

"I do not understand."

"They are slaughtered first by the opposing army," Kira was informed with no small measure of relish. The woman smiled and turned deliberately back to her work. "Aye, more than one way is there to rid an army of extra and useless mouths," she commented, examining a tear in the garment as though they discussed nothing more alarming than the weather. "Mayhap if you had a whit of sense, you would part your precious thighs."

"Well you said yourself that there is no honor in that life," Kira snapped, disliking the woman's self-satisfied air.

"At least 'tis a *life*," she observed pointedly. "And should you not learn quickly the value of that, 'twill be of little import at all." The woman's eyes narrowed and she leaned closer to Kira to continue in a confidential tone that Kira did not trust. "Mayhap there are but two kinds of women in the Mongol camp," she murmured. "Those who choose to live, and those who die." Kira exhaled her breath slowly, feeling her stomach churn sickeningly as she looked in the direction her warrior had disappeared.

"Did they not ride to battle this day?" she asked, and was not relieved when her companion nodded amiably.

"Aye, that they did and a big battle 'twas to be indeed." The woman glanced up with bright eyes, a knowing smile playing over her lips as she regarded Kira assessingly. "And yet you are here, not before the troops," she observed coyly. "A pretty enough creature are you—mayhap Black Wind has hopes for you yet."

Nay, Kira thought wildly to herself. It could not be so. The warrior wanted only the pearl before he consigned her to her fate, for clear enough had he made his disinterest in her form.

Suddenly Kira was very grateful for her impulse to keep the gem and she stifled the urge to finger it where 'twas secreted within her pocket. Flatly refusing to reflect further upon her meager chances for the future, she carefully retrieved the garment from the muddy water and began to scrub once more.

The field was empty.

Birds wheeled overhead and called to each other, the dried grass of summer past waved in the wind and made a slight whispering noise as the wind slipped through it. The sky was a flawless cerulean blue and there was a faint hint of spring in the morning air.

The pastoral scene was markedly different than the one Thierry had expected. He stopped his horse in disbelief and eyed the view with skepticism. He squinted at the distant smudge of horizon but not a hint could he discern of the Golden Horde.

There was no enemy to engage.

"Where is Berke? Where are his troops?" Nogai demanded impatiently as he pulled up alongside Thierry. Thierry could only shake his head.

"I know not," Thierry admitted calmly. Nogai snorted and surveyed the empty field arrayed before them with open disgust.

"But our spies said they were here but two nights past," he protested. "With no less than two *tümen* of men. Promise of a great battle there was. Where could they have gone?"

That Nogai was disappointed, there was little doubt. Far to his left, Thierry spotted a movement, but did not bother to look closely. 'Twas the other flank, the left wing of Abaqa's own troops. Still unwilling to believe the evidence of his eyes, he scanned the horizon yet again.

Naught.

"Mayhap 'tis a trap," he suggested, unable to conceive how Berke could have concealed his men in the dead grass. No valley was there where Abaqa's troops could be drawn unsuspectingly and encircled. No hills, no river gully, no trees. Naught but flat, unrippled plain confronted him as far as the eye could see.

"One could only hope," Nogai commented in a disgruntled tone. "Never did I expect that we would have all but an opponent this morn." Thierry glanced to his old friend in surprise.

"Well it seems that you are disappointed," he said. Nogai grinned outright.

"I had thought to collect Abaqa's new chalice," he added wickedly. "Unsporting 'tis of Berke to deprive us of the game, especially when I have oft heard how skilled the Golden Horde is in battle. Well had I been looking forward to the chance to empty my quiver into the ranks of a worthy opponent." Thierry shook his head indulgently and frowned at the empty plain once again.

"'Tis most odd that they should be gone," he mused, almost to himself. "Well must it be a trap of sorts." He looked to Nogai to find his own speculative thoughts reflected there. "Could your bloodthirstiness be sated by pursuit alone?" he asked with a quirk of one brow. Nogai laughed.

"But one way is there to discover the truth," he said and gave Thierry a bold wink before he spurred his horse. "And mayhap there is still a chalice to be retrieved this day. If not, one might hope for some game, at least."

"Then we ride in pursuit." Thierry raised one hand to his troops and beckoned them onward with a shout as he spurred his horse. A glance to his left confirmed that the commander of that *tümen* had made much the same conclusion as Thierry, for those troops were also thundering onto the plain.

Thierry's lips thinned with determination. Even should Berke be laying a trap, he would be hard-pressed to deal with the full press of Abaqa's forces. Though if Berke truly traveled with two *tümen*, the match might be closer than Thierry would have liked.

Though the stakes were high, as well. The two hordes battled for dominion over these very grasslands, extensive and fertile lands imperative to the grazing needs of both nomadic groups. Without these lands, the sheep and horse stocks would have to diminish and Abaqa's tribe would suffer less wealthy circumstances, if not outright hardship.

Abaqa's sire had held these plains long, but his demise had opened the question again for his rival, Berke, who wished to expand. 'Twas Abaqa's first test as khan and one that he could not afford to lose.

And should matters go awry, Thierry well knew that the field commanders would pay the price for that loss.

Little doubt had he that Berke's logic was much the same, and he puzzled anew over the Golden Horde's absence. They could not have simply ridden away from a battle of import like this. Indeed, if Berke bested Abaqa here, he might well be able to absorb all of Abaqa's dominion by continuing to sweep south. A new khan was at his most vulnerable in the first year of his dominion.

It made no sense. Thierry's scowl deepened and he decided that Berke must have set a trap. A particularly devious trap that Thierry had best discern before 'twas too late. Indeed, he saw in this moment the fullness of the risk he had taken in assuming the command of the right wing. Much was at stake. Too much, mayhap.

Mayhap Nogai would indeed see enough battle this day to satisfy even his taste.

Far behind the departing troops the shaman sat motionless on his white horse and watched the dust rise in the riders' wake. He lifted his nose to the wind and listened to the voices of the spirits whispering in his ears, trying to discern more than they chose to tell him this day.

Death there was in the air, for naught else could that pervasive scent that tickled his nostrils be. Well the shaman knew that 'twas no normal smell he caught in the wind, but a precognitive one that he alone of the tribe could discern.

But 'twas there nonetheless, even if only to him, and the shaman knew not its source or meaning. He frowned and asked the elusive spirits, but they confided naught new to him. Their whispers assured him only that Death had passed and done his work already.

At least the Dark One came not for him this time.

Which gave the shaman pause to think. His eyes narrowed as Qaraq-Böke's horse was lost in the distance, and he tapped his staff thoughtfully. The Dark One evidently had not come for that warrior, either.

Unfortunately. Far easier would life be without the threat of a nonbeliever becoming khan, even in the distant future. Despite the shaman's efforts to undermine him, Qaraq-Böke continued to prove himself an able warrior. Indeed, should all continue thus, the shaman might well lose credibility with Abaqa, who was a believer. Only too willing had Abaqa been to believe his rival a poor warrior at first, but a few well-won battles might easily sway his mind.

And the shaman would have to ensure that he was not on the losing edge of that transition. He clicked his tongue against his teeth with dissatisfaction, wishing the spirits would be more forthcoming on this day. Something had gone amiss, for Berke's troops were inexplicably gone. And should there be no battle, Qaraq-Böke could not be "accidentally" lost in the fray.

The shaman pursed his lips and hoped the men he had commissioned had more sense than he expected they did.

He recalled Abaqa's unruly drinking and frowned. Unless he missed his guess, made even without the sheep bones, Abaqa would not boast the longevity of his sire. Nay, something had to be done about Qaraq-Böke before 'twas too late. Annoying 'twas that the man revealed no vulnerability, no weak spot that might be turned against him and that the shaman might use for his own advantage.

Even the shaman's threats and premonitions of the previous night had apparently not affected the impassive warrior. And genuine they had been, as well. The shaman shook his head, disliking even further that Qaraq-Böke did not listen to the warnings of the spirits. One thing 'twas to be a nonbeliever who would take little guidance from a shaman once empowered, quite another 'twas to be a fool.

Aye, Qaraq-Böke could not be khan, under any circumstances. And since the shaman alone saw the threat, then he alone must correct the situation.

If only there was some weakness he could exploit. If only...

But of course. The shaman's gaze drifted down the river to where the women were washing clothes. But of course. Too quick had Qaraq-Böke been to deny his interest in the Persian woman he had captured. That he had even bothered to capture her was of note in itself, when the man had not been known to ever take a woman.

The shaman smiled to himself, pleased with his own cleverness. Perfect 'twas. For who, other than a shaman, could coax a reluctant pearl from the woman's gullet without causing her harm?

The old crone who guarded the women would not dare to defy him.

This Kira did not trust.

The white-cloaked man who had claimed her from the river hauled her through the deserted camp, dodging between rows of tents with unexpected agility. His carved staff pounded regularly into the dirt as he walked, his other hand latched around her wrist with a will that brooked no argument. His long nails bit into her skin and Kira cringed at their yellow color, but made not a sound.

Kira liked not that the old harridan had made no protest. She liked not that she had never seen this man. She liked not that he dressed differently than the others. And she liked even less that her warrior was not here to witness the transaction.

Had the warrior passed her to another? Kira knew not and her heart pounded unevenly as her mind filled with ugly possibilities. That this man was not a warrior was evident by his dress, his staff making Kira wonder if he was some sort of religious man. He selected a tent that was white, not dark like the others, and impatiently tugged Kira inside. Her mouth went dry.

'Twas shadowed inside despite the light-colored fleece and her eyes took a moment to adjust from the bright sunlight, though her companion hesitated naught. He lashed her wrists to the center pole with frightening efficiency, much as the warrior had done the night before, but this time the rope gnawed into Kira's skin. She did not dare protest, but eyed him warily, wondering what lay in store for her.

The man pushed back his hood and smiled. Kira did not trust the sight.

She could not fathom a guess as to his age, which did little to reassure her.

Though his darkly tanned skin was smooth as a child's, something lurked in his eyes that spoke of knowledge beyond what could be gleaned in one lifetime alone. His smile was toothless, the braid of his gray hair thick and luxuriantly long. His hands were as strong as a young warrior's, as she had already experienced, yet his nails were as yellowed and long as a hermit's. A drum hung at his side and his carved staff was fashioned into a horse's head instead of a crook at its top. A trio of white animal tails dangled from the staff where the horse's mane might have been.

His smile made everything within her go cold.

He said something in that vulgar guttural language they all used. Kira did not understand, but she boldly held his gaze in her determination not to show her fear. He spoke again, and though she could have been mistaken, Kira fancied that the language he used had changed. Still she did not comprehend the words, however.

"Well do I understand that you possess one of the khan's pearls," he said next, his Persian so impeccable that Kira was taken completely by surprise.

To her own disgust she answered before she thought to do otherwise.

"Aye," she admitted. The man's eyes gleamed and Kira cursed her own stupidity. Thanks to her own loose tongue, he knew not only that she had understood but that she still had the pearl. A plague on herself for not being more circumspect.

"Aye," he repeated, clearly pleased with her response. "Then well should you know that I have been charged with its retrieval."

"By whom?" Kira demanded as though she had every right to ask. If her warrior had abandoned her, then she would know the truth of it.

The man turned slightly aside. "It matters not," he said smoothly. "All that is relevant is that you will surrender the gem to me."

"Unwilling 'tis to make its reappearance," Kira lied audaciously. The older man slanted her a glance that did naught to assuage her fears.

"Ways have I to convert reluctance to willingness," he purred as he abruptly pulled back a dark curtain on the far side of the tent.

Kira gasped when all manner of brass containers and small vials were revealed, their contents almost indiscernible in the shadows of the tent. Above the array, a carving of a man with blue skin hung, his cheeks puffed as though he blew out a flame. Beneath him was a figure of a woman, plump beyond compare and nude in her fullness. The mouths of both figures were smudged, as though offerings had been pressed against their carved lips. Kira shivered and struggled against the rope that bound her.

This she definitely did not like.

The man evidently forgot her presence as he made his preparations. As to what he prepared, Kira would rather not have known, but as she twisted futilely against the rope she realized that she might have little option. He began to hum to himself as he selected several vials from the collection. He lit a fire in the brass stove on the floor and mixed a concoction beneath Kira's horrified gaze.

Surely he would not expect her to consume this? Somehow Kira imagined its effect would be stronger than the foul liquor she had already imbibed in this camp. Wordlessly, the man lit an array of candles before the two figures. When he lit a cone and she smelled the perfumed smoke of incense, Kira had no doubt that his arrangement of vials served as an altar of sorts.

Nay, she liked this not a bit. He began to chant, his arms rising beside him as though he would embrace the sky. The candle flames seemed to leap higher, the sun brightened the white walls and roof of the tent, the faces of the carved deities glowed. His voice rose, the words incomprehensible to Kira. His foot stamped and the very ground vibrated.

He lifted the bowl containing his preparation high, then smeared some of it across the mouth of each carved figure.

He pivoted with an abruptness that took Kira's breath away. His eyes were closed, but he walked straight toward her. Kira panicked. She writhed and twisted, desperately trying to loosen the rope, but it remained resolutely knotted around her wrists as though 'twere charmed. He dipped his fingers into the lumpy mixture when he stopped beside her, and the smell was fit to make Kira retch. She jerked her head away when 'twas evident he intended to feed her the mixture.

Undeterred and without opening his eyes, he cast aside the bowl with a flick of his wrist. He grasped the back of her neck with one mercilessly strong hand without dropping any of the mixture from the other. He squeezed her throat threateningly, his other hand held before her stubbornly locked lips. Kira made an unwilling sound of protest.

The man's eyes flew open abruptly. His gaze bored into hers and Kira could not look away. He blinked naught and his gaze seemed focused deep within her soul. She felt suddenly certain that he was not of this world, though she could not have said where the thought came from.

"Open your mouth."

Kira heard the command echo in her own mind, though she knew the man had uttered not a sound. The candles he had lit sputtered, and fragrant smoke wended its way toward the ceiling as the carved deities watched avidly. Kira shook her head mutely, already feeling the man's will wind its way into her thinking.

His eyes widened and he leaned closer. His fingertips, covered with the foul-smelling concoction, touched her lips. Kira shuddered from head to toe and, against the silent protest of every fiber of her being, slowly opened her mouth.

The last thing she felt was the mealy texture of the substance forced into her mouth. Kira felt it slip traitorously down her throat, as though it had a will of its own, just before her surroundings faded to naught.

The women were not at the river when Thierry and his men returned.

For an instant Thierry feared the woman had come to some harm and his heart skipped a beat before he chided his own foolishness.

"Woho!" Nogai taunted. "Mayhap she had a better offer this night than yours!" Thierry fired an annoyed glance at his companion but Nogai only winked.

"I expect she is with the old one," Thierry said flatly. Nogai laughed, which did naught to improve Thierry's temper.

"That an old woman makes a better offer says little of your persuasive skills, my friend," Nogai teased. Thierry felt his ears redden and his irritation grew.

"Well I told you that she would surrender naught but the pearl," he growled, wishing he knew the source of his annoyance. Naught did it mean that she was not where he had left her. And certainly there was no reason for that twinge of disappointment he had felt when he had spied the empty river.

No reason at all. And there could have been no anticipation lightening his heart in returning to camp this night, especially after the complete lack of a battle this day.

Exhausted Thierry was from a fruitless day's ride in pursuit of men who were not there. 'Twas no more than that that made him leap to conclusions. The sun was sinking low and 'twas not unreasonable that the women had ceased their labor for the day.

It meant naught that she was not here. And his twinge of disappointment had been for no more than the delay. Now before he could retire, he would have to fetch her from the old one.

"Abaqa will be awaiting our report," he reminded Nogai tersely, not missing the way his *anda*'s brows rose.

"Mayhap he has had some news this day that will explain things," Nogai agreed. Thierry almost thought the other matter closed until the two dismounted and matched steps.

"And of course, the more haste is made to report to Abaqa, the sooner you might retrieve your fetching baggage," Nogai whispered mischievously.

"Clearly you have forgotten that the woman is a witch," Thierry snapped.

"Me? Nay, I have not forgotten," Nogai retorted confidently. "But 'twas not I who was so anxious to return to camp this night."

Thierry slanted Nogai a hostile glance and earned a merry grin for his trouble.

"I shall ensure the khan is quick," Nogai assured him. Thierry stifled a healthy urge to kick his friend and strode to Abaqa's yurt in poor temper.

Clear 'twas that he would have no peace until the woman was gone. Indeed, he hoped she had passed the cursed pearl this very day, that he might send her home. The thought sent a curious pang through Thierry that prompted yet another unwelcome recollection of Khanbaliq. He gritted his teeth and told himself that Abaqa's distrust was wearing down his resolve.

The sooner the woman was gone, the better.

The *keshik* guards at the khan's yurt stood aside when Thierry approached, Nogai in his immediate wake. Inside, Abaqa glanced up and grinned.

"Little enough chance had you to prove yourself this day," he commented, clearly in a jovial mood. Mercifully the shaman was nowhere in sight.

"What happened?" Thierry demanded tersely.

"Still you have not heard?" Abaqa's brows rose. "Berke died yesterday."

Thierry's heart leaped in his astonishment. "Of what did he die?" he asked.

Abaqa snorted. "Avarice," he retorted sharply. "Mayhap ambition beyond his station." He traced the design on his chair with one fingertip before glancing up sharply. "'Tis poor judgment to covet something that is mine," he said consideringly. Thierry went cold but refused to let Abaqa see that his barb had struck home.

"What did he covet of yours?" he inquired instead, knowing the answer all the while but unable to think of another alternative quickly enough. Abaqa shook his head indulgently.

"My territories," he said. He glanced away and his lips thinned dangerously. "My armies, my gold, my wives. All that is mine did he covet, for why else would he have invaded this territory as soon as my sire died?"

"I suspected as much but did not know for certain," Thierry said hastily. Abaqa leisurely looked him over, then snorted again.

"Indeed, you should understand the fact of the matter," he said. His voice dropped to a threateningly low timbre as his gaze locked with Thierry's. "'Tis not healthy for a man to crave what is mine."

"Who succeeds Berke?" Thierry dared to ask.

Abaqa smiled. "Why am I not surprised that you, of all men, would ask that question?" he mused. He tapped his fingers on the arm of his chair and regarded Thierry for a long moment before shaking his head, as if to clear it. "I know not. No clear successor is there."

"Then that is why they left the field," Nogai guessed. Abaqa flicked a glance to Thierry's companion.

"I would expect as much," he said quietly. "Undoubtedly, they have returned north to burn their Khan in a fitting manner. For the time being, it would seem there is no threat to me." Abaqa's gaze meandered back to Thierry and he raised one brow thoughtfully. "At least, not from *outside* the tribe," he added.

With that, the khan snapped his fingers and summoned a drink for himself, effectively dismissing the two warriors from his company.

An enraged roar woke Kira abruptly from her slumber.

Her father had discovered her crime. She cringed in anticipation of the lash's bite, and when none came, dared to take a breath. Kira opened her eyes with difficulty to find herself huddled on the damp ground, her wrists still bound to the tent pole, and recollection came flooding back.

She blinked to clear her foggy vision and the roar erupted again. Kira cringed at the proximity of the sound and her gaze flew across the tent.

The man in white stood before her warrior, his manner calm as he gestured toward her. The warrior was markedly less calm. Kira could virtually feel the heat of the anger emanating from him. His eyes glittered and his jaw was set. His companion with the goatee lounged in the opening to the outside. Kira met his gaze and he winked broadly. Her gaze skittered uncertainly back to the warrior.

What had angered him? And what price would his fury bear? Only too similar was this to her father's frequent tempers and she could only fear for the worst. Would he beat her? Rape her? No help was her addled mind in this matter, for it seemed to Kira that she could barely put two thoughts in order. Curse the white one and his mixture.

Should she surrender the pearl or was it already too late to save her own hide? She struggled against her bonds, able to think of naught but escape. To her dismay, her body did not readily follow her bidding and her clumsy movements were futile.

Her warrior barked a short question and the man in white shrugged. The warrior looked fit to explode when he jabbed one finger at the other man, his tight words evidently a threat of some kind. The white-robed man drew himself up taller at the apparent insult, but the warrior had already turned away.

To Kira's chagrin, the warrior turned his attention on her. She scurried backward but could not move far because of her bindings. Incapable was she of hiding her fear in this state, with her body fighting every move and the warrior's anger clearly beyond anything her father had ever let her see.

He squatted purposefully beside Kira. She cringed and his scowl deepened with displeasure as he untied her wrists. Fearing his anger was directed at her, Kira instinctively shrank away, only to have him glance to her in surprise. He touched the chafe marks on her skin with one gentle fingertip. She shivered, not knowing what to expect, certainly not expecting to look up and find him watching her with what might have been concern.

Not here. Not from this man. He cared only that she live long enough to return his property. Kira's heart skittered unsteadily, then lurched when he folded one heavy hand around hers. Naught could this mean, she told herself wildly, even as that increasingly familiar tingle of awareness launched over her flesh. The warrior snarled something at the man in white. That man shrugged indifference and the warrior's lips thinned.

He grasped Kira's elbows when she might have pulled away again, confusion puckering his brow when she gasped in response. He stood slowly and virtually lifted her to her feet, arching one brow in silent query. Kira nodded hastily, wanting no more than to be free of his unsettling touch.

When he released his grip on her, no one was more surprised than Kira that her knees gave out beneath her. She gave a little cry as she crumpled toward the ground again and heard the white one's knowing chuckle.

The warrior swore and scooped her up before she collapsed. The tent danced around them and Kira closed her eyes weakly, despising the single tear that crept out from between her lashes.

Weakness. How she hated weakness. Especially in herself.

The warrior said something and the white one answered with apparent reluctance. Kira squeezed her eyes tightly as the warrior carried her outside, the motion of his step making her stomach roll uncertainly. She leaned closer to his warmth despite herself and found his heartbeat beneath her fingertips. Its echo was curiously reassuring and she dared to release the breath she had been holding and relax ever so slightly against him.

Just for a moment. Until she could be strong again.

She was safe, Kira thought, feeling the fog in her mind advancing to claim her once again. Nonsense, she corrected sharply, knowing the first thought was naught but whimsy.

Curiously, Kira's conviction in that fact did naught to halt her fingers from spreading across his chest. Well it seemed she would grip the beat of the warrior's heart within her very hand as all faded to naught.

Chapter Five

When Kira awakened in the familiarity of the warrior's tent, 'twas nearly dark. She rolled over and found him watching her silently. Kira's breath caught in her throat. Their gazes locked and he moved not a muscle, as though he was waiting for her to collect her thoughts.

Disconcerting it had been, to say the least, to find herself relieved to see the stern warrior in the white tent. Kira could make little sense of her response. Certainly the man had done little to endear himself to her, though she had to admit that he had not been as cruel as she had anticipated.

At least, not as yet. 'Twas a particularly heinous tactic he had in mind, she surmised, for evidently he meant to gain her trust before abusing her.

Although she was forced to concede that she could scarcely have imagined that her maidenhead would be intact after an entire night in the Mongol camp.

He rose abruptly to his feet and closed the distance between them. When he bent over her, Kira refused to show her trepidation. Her mind was clearer for the sleep and she boldly held his gaze.

Had she not known better, she might have thought that he smothered a smile at that.

He urged Kira to her feet and her guts writhed. She gasped and he seemed to understand, for he hastened her immediately outside and toward the latrine pits.

* * *

Well it seemed that matters had changed. Though Kira knew that she had never been so thoroughly voided in her life as she had been in this camp, the warrior demanded naught of her when she had finished at the pits. To her astonishment he led her purposefully in the opposite direction from that of his tent. His silence seemed particularly ominous and Kira could not help but speculate whether she had been grateful too soon.

Mayhap the time of her reckoning had come.

He led her away from the camp. Kira hoped they made but a roundabout return, but when they stepped outside a cluster of tents, her heart began to pound. His pace continued relentlessly into the open fields on the far side of the camp and Kira knew she would not stride away from this place. Naught but the grasses weaving in the wind was here and her heart almost ceased to beat when he stopped abruptly.

Was it here he intended to take her? Or did he mean to retrieve the gem with his knife? The grass rippled around them and the uncanny silence of the plain filled Kira's ears. Indeed, none would hear her scream in these remote pastures. Her heart took off at a gallop at the realization, for 'twas quickly followed by the certainty that there was naught she could do about it. He was larger than her, stronger, undoubtedly more cruel. She could fight, but the battle would not last long.

Well it seemed that she could not draw enough air into her lungs and Kira feared she might faint. She felt the utter stillness of her companion and dreaded his intent before he raised his fingers to his lips and let out a long, low whistle.

Then he stood perfectly still, waiting it seemed, his grip relentless on her arm. Kira scanned the horizon in confusion, fancying she heard a faint sound stirring above the silence. The warrior squeezed her arm once and lifted a heavy finger to point into the middle distance, never uttering a word. Kira suddenly saw the dark shapes approaching.

What was this? Beasts he needed for his diabolical plan? She could not even imagine what wickedness he planned to wreak upon her.

Four horses became discernible as they drew closer, their manes blowing loose, their hoofbeats becoming more and more distinct. Kira glanced up and fancied that the warrior's features softened as he watched the creatures run. She could not be sure and looked back to the beasts in confusion.

They ran directly toward them. Kira was certain they meant to run right over them. There was a death she would expect to be painful, though it made no sense that the man beside her held his ground. When the creatures bore directly upon them and Kira thought she could see their eyes, she bolted.

The warrior impassively tightened his grip on her arm before she could take a second step. Well it seemed he had anticipated her move, but as the horses drew yet nearer, Kira could not even summon surprise.

They whinnied and she covered her ears with her hands, knowing they were too close to turn. Kira cringed and turned toward the warrior, his grip on her arm allowing her precious little movement, indeed. Her heart pounded and she cowered against him, but the horses veered off unexpectedly.

Kira glanced up in astonishment. Her fear transformed magically to delight when the horses cantered around them in an ever-tightening circle to slow their pace. He had summoned them. And they had come. Kira looked to her warrior with newfound respect. Never had she known anyone who had a way with beasts. The creatures walked the last few paces between them, one nuzzling the warrior's other hand with its nose.

They had not been trampled to death. Kira watched in amazement as the warrior scratched the beast behind its ears with what might have been affection. When the one with cream markings on its brown coat nudged its nose against her knee, she dared to stretch out a hand and mimic the warrior's gesture.

To her surprise the wild creature tolerated her tentative caress. Its coat was thicker and softer than she might have anticipated and Kira reached to touch the furry curve of its ear. The horse abruptly snorted and proudly tossed its head, backing away to fix her with an assessing eye.

She feared it would run away and the warrior would be angry with her, but the horse stood his ground and regarded her cautiously. Kira remained as still as she could, sensing this was part of the warrior's strategy with the creatures. She barely dared to breathe as the beast eyed her warily.

A long moment later, the horse stepped toward her again. It ducked its muzzle under her hand demandingly this time and Kira could not help but smile.

It liked her. She rubbed its ears, daring to press her fingers a little more firmly into the fur, and the horse amazingly leaned into her caress.

The warrior released her elbow abruptly, moving with a speed that startled her. In the blink of an eye he had cast a harness over the head of the horse before her. The creature tossed its head indignantly and pranced for a few paces. Her warrior did not relinquish his grip on the reins and the horse soon settled.

Could it be that the horse had been harnessed before? Kira could not imagine that a wild creature would take so readily to the restraint otherwise. But no time had she to reflect upon the matter. Suddenly the warrior dropped the reins to the ground and stepped on them, simultaneously gripping her waist and lifting her. Kira panicked.

He would not put her on this horse alone!

She struggled against him and the horse nervously danced sideways. The warrior dropped her to her feet once more though he did not release his grip on her waist. He said something quickly to her, but Kira could not understand him. She shook her head desperately, unable to think beyond her terror of being on the horse.

His voice dropped when he spoke again and she fancied he spoke more slowly. Despite that, Kira looked stubbornly at the ground, unwilling to aid him in any way with whatever foul plans he had for her. The warrior muttered something and gripped her chin, relentlessly forcing her to meet his eyes. Once again she was startled by their silvery tone, that momentary surprise long enough for him to snare her attention.

"Tiflis," he said slowly, his accent making it difficult for Kira to immediately understand his meaning. "Tiflis," he repeated. She nodded quickly. Tiflis. What about Tiflis? He pointed to her and the horse, turning to gesture toward the horizon past the Mongol camp. "Tiflis," he said again, and Kira understood.

He was sending her home.

Her heart fluttered but she did not dare to hope until she knew the fullness of his plan. Too good to be true this was and a catch there must be. Kira pointed tentatively to the warrior, not daring to touch him with her fingertip.

"Tiflis?" she asked. Uncertain she was whether he meant to accompany her, but he shook his head firmly. He repeated his assertion and Kira nodded once more.

She was going home alone. Was it possible that she had misunderstood him? One glance to the resolute gleam in the warrior's eyes destroyed that illusion. Relief flooded through her and she dared not think too much about the matter. No understanding had she of his reasoning, but she would grasp the unexpected gift with both hands and flee directly home.

But she had to ride this horse to get there. She turned a wary eye on the horse, knowing full well that the creature was her only possible means of transport. Mayhap to go home, she could conquer this fear.

When the warrior lifted her once more, Kira did not struggle and the horse did not stir as her weight was settled on its back. The warrior flicked an imperious finger at Kira's knee and she obediently lifted it over the horse's back, her color rising with the awareness that the warrior was seeing far more of her *chalwar* than was truly appropriate.

But well enough had he shown that he was not tempted by her, she reminded herself fiercely, accepting the reins from him as her nervousness rose.

Could she really ride this creature all the way home?

The warrior stayed her with one hand and she watched as he unlashed the sheath on the inside of his left forearm. A dagger obviously reposed within it and Kira's fear rose once again. What did he intend to do? Was this all a ruse to raise her hopes before he killed her? Did he mean to retrieve the pearl once and for all in this secluded spot where none might help her?

Kira recoiled when he reached for her arm. He frowned impatiently, the fact that he seemed puzzled by her response dissipating some of Kira's doubts. He tucked her hand firmly under his arm and pressed it against his side, leaving the soft flesh of her forearm turned up. Kira shivered, but he simply laid the sheath over her arm and lashed it there with his characteristic efficiency of movement.

When he released her arm and handed her the reins, Kira understood that he was giving her a means of protecting herself. When last had anyone given her anything? When last had anyone done anything for her at all? Kira looked to him in amazement, but he merely propped his hands on his hips and jerked his head in the direction she was to ride.

"Tiflis," he repeated yet again, sparing a pointed glance to the sinking sun.

Kira touched the hilt of the knife tentatively, struggling to accept what he was doing for her. A gift he had granted her that could save her life.

Impulsively she reached into her pocket and retrieved the pearl she had passed. She thrust her hand out between them and held the gem out to him at arm's length. 'Twas only fair, after all, that she give him the pearl.

He frowned as he held out his hand, then understanding dawned in his eyes as he realized what she offered. His gaze rose slowly to lock with hers and Kira fought the tremor that danced over her flesh when he deliberately took the gem from her fingers.

"Thank you," Kira said simply. She willed him to understand what she meant, touching the knife once more and laying a hand on the horse's neck.

The warrior's eyes gleamed and he rolled the lustrous pearl between his rough thumb and forefinger as he silently held her gaze. Something changed in his expression, though Kira could not have named that tentative softening in his eyes. Precious little chance had she to do so, for he half turned away and scowled when she did not urge the horse onward.

"Tiflis," he insisted flatly.

When Kira did not yet move, uncertain what kept her from doing so, the warrior raised a hand and gave the creature's rump a resounding smack. Kira yelped in surprise and desperately tried to grip the beast's round belly with her knees as it ran at breakneck speed toward home.

When she had gained her balance, she risked one glance over her shoulder to find the warrior far behind her, his hands propped on his hips as he watched her flight. The grasses waved about him but he stood completely motionless, silhouetted against the distant hills, the other three horses grazing nonchalantly about him.

Thierry found the yurt unnaturally quiet when he returned. He prowled around its interior restlessly, unaccountably annoyed that naught had appeared to change, when in fact so much had.

The shaman had moved openly against Thierry for the first time. No idle threat had he made this time, for in taking the woman, the shaman had challenged Thierry's prior claim. No doubt had Thierry that all within the camp already knew the tale. This could not bode well for Thierry's future.

Vulnerability he had feared, and vulnerability she had brought. Never had he been challenged like this; never had another dared. Although the woman was gone, Thierry wondered what fruit this incident would bear. Would his authority be questioned? His command over the *tümen* revoked? He knew not and liked not the uncertainty.

'Twas clear already that Abaqa was losing patience with him, though whether the two incidents were linked, Thierry could not say. Abaqa's threats were openly made this day and 'twas clear Thierry had gained naught of credit on the field. Berke's retreat had stolen his sole opportunity to redeem himself.

Would Abaqa cast him out? Or would he suffer the same fate as Chinkai?

Thierry scuffed at the carpets and scowled across the shadows of his yurt, startled to find his vision of the sleeping woman sprawled across his cushions as clear as if she were really there.

He turned away from the haunting image, dismayed to find his anger rising. She was gone. Headed home to her family where he should have left her. Thierry's gut clenched at the thought but he forced himself to face reality. Destined she was to spend her life sorting pearls. Mayhap she would wed one of those soft urban men. Bear him robust sons and delicate daughters.

Thierry strode out into the growing darkness, biting down on the bile that rose in his throat. She had not been his to touch. Though he tried to forget its presence, the pearl he had shoved into his pocket seemed to burn a mark in his thigh. Only too well did he understand that it was the pearl he had demanded. Thierry resolutely ignored the press of the gem as he decided to seek out some *qumis*.

He would not reflect upon the irony of the fact that she was gone just when he had naught left to lose.

No solution was it and well he knew it, but he would dismiss the woman from his thoughts this night one way or the other. And well might the *qumis* dispel some of the anger still simmering within him.

Thierry's blood heated at the realization that the woman could easily have been hurt. A fool he had been to take her from Tiflis for the sake of a pearl. Yet Thierry knew, in the same circumstance, he would make the same choice again. His fingers clenched in recollection of the incredible softness of her hair.

Mercifully, the shaman had sought the pearl first.

And the witch had tricked him. Thierry bit down his urge to smile once again and scuffed his toe in the dirt appreciatively. How she had managed to conceal the pearl from the shaman, he did not know. Mayhap her sorcery was stronger than his.

It mattered not the means. Yet again, Thierry could but appreciate the result. His gaze wandered over the tents as though he might see the distant town of Tiflis despite the obstacles and the darkness.

Stubborn witch, he corrected himself, and shook his head.

She was safer in Tiflis. Thierry forced himself to face the truth of that and sighed.

How he wished he could dismiss this niggling sense that all was not right. He had done his best for the woman. He had kept his word and she had surrendered the pearl. Their business was completed and he would do best to forget the entire matter.

Her own fate had the woman to meet. She had surrendered the gem and he had kept his promise. Now their ways must part. Despite his determined reminder, the thought did not ring as true as Thierry thought that it should.

And 'twas less easy than it should have been to turn his footsteps toward the khan's yurt and the promise of *qumis*.

'Twas dark when Kira first spotted the protective white walls of Tiflis. The sight of those walls suddenly made her consider the wisdom of her return.

How could she simply go home? How could she tell her father that she had abandoned his shop? How could she not tell him, when all the neighbors were certain to delight in sharing the tale?

What if some of the gems had been stolen in her absence? What if everything had been stolen? How would she ever explain? How would she ever repay the loss? Kira licked her lips nervously. An ungrateful wretch of a daughter she was, in truth.

But it had not been her fault.

The assertion rang boldly in Kira's mind and she was shocked by the audacity of her own thoughts. For the first time, Kira was not willing to immediately cede to the argument she knew her father would make. How could she make her father understand that she had been powerless against the warrior's will? Indeed, he had carried her bodily from the town, despite her protest.

It had not been her fault.

A dangerous thought that was and Kira instinctively shrank away from it. Better she knew than that. And even if it was true that the blame lay elsewhere, Kira knew well that her explanation would fall on deaf ears. She blinked back stubborn tears and forced herself to face the truth.

No excuse could there be for what she had done, especially if her father's shop had sustained damage. Kira eyed the approaching walls of Tiflis and could not imagine that the jeweler's premises could have remained untended all this time without consequence. She inhaled sharply, knowing she would taste the lash yet again on her father's return.

Still, the stubborn thought that this whipping would be undeserved could not be wiped from her mind.

Impudent. Good-for-naught. Lazy ingrate. Kira called herself a string of her father's favorite insults to no effect. No choice had she made in this, and though she had been left responsible for the shop, naught else could she have done. The warrior had carried her away, despite her protests, and her neighbors had helped naught.

A dutiful daughter would have contrived somehow to stay and protect the shop, she reminded herself fiercely to no avail. Well enough she knew the argument, but hearing it echo in her mind only angered Kira. She squirmed in anticipation of the new wounds she would sport for her own unreliability and tentatively glanced back where she knew the Mongol camp to be.

Without warning she recalled the weight of a man's fingertip on the reddened chafe mark on her wrist. A gentle and warm fingertip. Kira shivered in the chill of the evening air.

Would any in Tiflis believe that she had survived a night in the Mongol camp unscathed? Still more unlikely, would they believe that she had retained her maidenhead?

Well could she hear her father's accusations ring out. A faithful daughter would never have permitted herself to be in such circumstances. A worthy daughter would not cast her chastity into doubt. A loyal daughter would not selfishly jeopardize her sire's hopes for a secure future.

The charges rang false in Kira's ears, for well she knew that she could not have effected any difference in her situation. But nay. Unfair she was being to her sire. Wise he was and always right. Kira had the scars to testify to that. Her chin set stubbornly and she pulled the horse to a halt.

She need not go home.

The mutinous thought excited and terrified Kira simultaneously. Did she dare? Did she want to dare? Or would she meekly return to the shop and await her father's return, that he might beat her for something she had been powerless to change?

'Twas more than an unearned beating at stake, though. Well enough Kira knew that no honorable man would have her after this. Not with such a taint on her name as having spent a night within the Mongol camp. Suspicions would fester in whatever remained of Tiflis despite her claims of innocence, and her sire's dream of buying his leisure with Kira's hand would fade to naught.

Kira needed not long to see where that path led. Her life would become less than it had been, for there would no longer be any promise of reward. Kira frowned in confusion as once again she compared how the warrior had treated her with her father's treatment.

No sense did it make that a barbarian who cared naught would show her greater kindness than her own sire. Well did Kira know that her father loved her, but her frown deepened as she struggled to make sense of it all.

Mayhap love was an overrated commodity.

The thought made Kira feel guilty as soon as it formed. How could she think thus of her own sire? How could she even conceive of such a thing when he had cared for her and raised her all these years? Truly her father's cry of "ingrate" was a proper one.

Kira hung her head in shame. Mayhap her father was best left without an ungrateful daughter such as herself. Mayhap her absence alone would make him happy. Kira bit her lip and considered her plight as the horse nibbled disinterestedly on the grass.

She could not shame her sire by coming home after this.

But if she did not return to Tiflis, where could she go? Kira glanced reluctantly again over her shoulder to the horizon.

War fodder, whores and claimed women. Was there a role that she was worthy of in that? Mayhap 'twas the sole choice that would do honor to her sire.

Kira could not imagine that she deserved any better for so failing her father and she inexpertly urged the horse to turn around before she had time to question her choice.

The moon was setting when Kira fancied she caught the scent of roasting meat on the wind. She shook her head, knowing that her mind was teasing her achingly empty stomach. Surely the Mongols had already retired, as she would dearly love to do.

She rested her cheek against the horse's sleek coat as it closed the last increment of distance to the camp, liking the way the creature's warmth penetrated her skin when she closed her eyes. The creature's pace had slowed, but Kira cared naught, for well she knew it must be tired, as well. She closed her eyes and let the scent of the horse's fur fill her nostrils.

Indeed, riding was not such an ordeal as she had once believed. And had Kira not had the gift of a horse, how might she have returned so rapidly to the camp?

Who would have guessed that something she so feared could have become her ally?

The horse nickered and Kira reluctantly sat up as the camp came into sight. Fires there were burning despite the fullness of the night, their golden light flickering between the tents, much to Kira's surprise. Laughter rose to her ears, that tempting scent of roasted meat making her belly growl anew.

The Mongols were awake.

Her warrior might still be here. Only now, Kira realized that she had been concerned that the Mongols might have left. Were they not nomads, in truth? Incredible 'twas that such knowledge could send relief flooding through her, and Kira wondered what had happened to her once clear thinking.

But in truth, the warrior was the only soul who had ever shown her any consideration. Kira looked to the blade lashed to her arm in confusion and not for the first time marveled at his deed.

Mayhap he had simply not had time to take his hand to her.

But nay. Unfair that was, for had she not slept in his tent unescorted? Kira frowned, still unable to understand the man, yet wishing she could check her anticipation at the possibility of seeing him once more. Though he might not be as enchanted to see her. Kira frowned.

What sort of reflection on her life was it that a Mongol warrior had shown her the greatest kindness she had known?

A traitorous thought that was, and Kira would not indulge it further. Had her father not fed her all these years? Kept a roof over her head? Clothed her after a fashion? Surely she was the most ungrateful child ever born to man, as he had been so fond of reminding her, if she could not value such luxuries that many others did not know.

What was she going to do now that she had found the Mongols? How would she find her warrior? The tents looked much the same and continued endlessly one after the other. And well she knew that she could not ask after him, for she spoke no Mongol.

Kira hesitated on the fringe of the camp, filled with uncertainty. Mayhap she should have left some message for her father. Guilt consumed her and she sat and inventoried her shortcomings by rote. Ungrateful, lazy, stupid, slow, scrawny, weak, female . . .

The laughter of women startled Kira abruptly out of her thoughts. Her glance darted from side to side as she sought some place to hide, but the cursed horse whinnied just as the women came out of the shelter of the clustered tents. Their voices stilled and Kira froze, any explanation dying on her lips. Her mouth went dry, her heart ceased to beat while the women eyed her silently.

Finally one of the women stepped forward and held a flickering lantern high. Kira could not speak, even when she recognized the nosy Persian woman from the stream. The woman smiled and Kira's heart went cold.

"You came looking for Black Wind," the woman commented with a measure of amusement. Kira shook her head in immediate denial, her heart recovering to run at an erratic pace.

"Nay, I . . . I . . ." Kira stammered, then swallowed resolutely and held up her head proudly. No gracious explanation was there for her behavior and little point could she see in not being direct after she had come so far.

"I cannot go home," she stated flatly. The woman's eyes sobered as she held Kira's regard, then she shook her head disparagingly and smiled a fleeting sad smile.

"Nay, none of us can," she said quietly, a thread of understanding in her tone. Much to Kira's surprise, the woman stretched out one hand welcomingly. "Come with us," she invited. Kira could not believe her ears.

What did this woman expect in exchange for her aid? Kira regarded the woman's hand with suspicion, knowing full well that no one offered assistance to another without another objective in mind.

"What do you want from me?" she demanded coldly, disliking this false pretense of friendship. The woman's expression became surprised.

"Naught," she said quietly, but Kira shook her head.

"Too much have I seen of the world to believe that," she retorted. The woman's gaze flicked assessingly over Kira once more and she nodded deliberately before she took a decisive step closer.

"I have been abandoned and turned out of home," she confided in a harsh whisper, her eyes gleaming in the shadows. "So well I know that 'tis easier to face this with others than alone."

Kira said naught, certain her face showed that she was unconvinced.

"Are you not hungry?" the woman asked. Kira was forced to acknowledge at least to herself that she was. "What will you eat on your own? A huntress are you, then?" The woman smiled and half turned back to the camp. "Lift your nose and smell the meat we eat this night. And tired are you after your ride? Blankets aplenty are there here to sleep under and felt tents to take shelter within."

"And what price must I pay to so indulge myself?" Kira demanded suspiciously.

The woman's voice dropped another increment. "You must trust me," she said slowly. "As I must trust you."

"A high price, indeed," Kira scoffed, though her skepticism was fading quickly.

"Aye, we both have much to lose," the woman agreed.

The silence stretched between them as they regarded each other solemnly, then the woman extended her hand once more.

"What choice do you imagine you have?" she whispered. Kira was forced to face the truth. As war fodder, she had none too long to live, anyway.

"None," she admitted heavily, hesitating for a moment before she slipped her hand into the other woman's warm grip.

The woman's fingers tightened over hers and Kira was surprised to find herself reassured by the gesture. She slipped from the horse's back and held fast to the creature's reins. Her nerves settled a little more when the beast she had grown to rely upon showed no reservations in following the Persian woman into the cluster of tents.

When Kira awoke, sunlight was shining brightly through the partially opened flap of the tent and she could smell it heating the wool felt overhead. She frowned, thinking herself in her warrior's tent once more, and wondered whether the ride to Tiflis and back had been a vivid dream.

She rolled over, fully expecting to find him watching her with that inscrutable expression on his face, but instead she met the sharp gaze of the Persian woman. Events of the previous night came back to her in a flash and she dropped her chin to the cushion, unable to deny her disappointment.

"Good morning," the woman said. Kira halfheartedly returned the greeting. How many more mornings would she see now that she had committed herself to becoming war fodder? How many days until the Mongols rode to battle once more? Kira sighed and rolled over.

"More enthusiasm will you need to show should you wish to snare a man," the woman commented dryly. "Mayhap a smile would be in order once in a while." Kira spared the woman a dark look.

"I do not expect to be claimed," she informed her tersely, not liking having false possibilities dangled before her.

"Too pretty are you to become a whore," the woman observed matter-of-factly. She dug out some flat bread and offered it to Kira, smearing some white cheese across the top of it. Kira accepted the offering gratefully, surprised to find it quite flavorful. The woman's eyes narrowed speculatively. "Unless you are not as chaste as you would maintain."

Kira grimaced at that. "Never have I known a man," she clarified flatly, secretly amazed to find herself discussing such personal matters with a relative stranger. But something there was about this life-style, something more earthbound than town living that made such conversation seem natural. And what matter if the woman thought her common? Kira would not live long enough to be troubled by such a judgment.

The woman leaned forward purposefully. "Surely you cannot believe yourself destined to walk in front of the armies," she charged. Kira glanced up from her meal in surprise.

"Aye."

The woman shook her head in unconcealed disgust and shoved to her feet. "Fool!" she snapped, leaning over to clutch a handful of Kira's hair and let it run through her fingers. "Have you never seen yourself in a glass? Truly you could aspire to being claimed, should you only trouble yourself to make the effort."

"Do not jest with me," Kira insisted through the tightness of her throat. "Well enough do I know my shortcomings."

"Believe what you like," the woman declared with a wave of her hand. She propped her hands on her hips as she regarded Kira. "But well enough did I see the look in Black Wind's eye when he brought you to the stream. That man was not aware of whatever shortcomings you imagine yourself to have."

Kira's heart leaped but she refused to indulge herself in any such hopeful whimsy.

"He is in the camp, you know," the woman confided and Kira looked to her in shock. "Aye, they all are. All of the *ba'atur* remain." At Kira's evident confusion, she grimaced and explained. "The blooded ones, the 'nobility' one might call them for lack of a better name. Drinking and celebrating Berke's army's retreat they were in the khan's

tent all last night. Likely all of this day and night, as well."
She folded her arms across her chest and held Kira's gaze.
"Well enough do I know that 'tis simple to tempt my man
when he stumbles home after one of these binges. Would
you not tempt Black Wind?"

Kira drew herself up proudly. "I would not become a
whore."

"'Twas not what I suggested," the woman countered irritably. "A claimed woman is as close to a wife as one may
be here. A ceremony have they, but 'tis neither Zoroas-
trian nor Moslem, so I feel not wed in my match."

"But they claim to be wed?"

"Aye, in their own terms," the woman agreed with a
world-weary shrug.

"Your man is faithful to you alone?"

The woman laughed. "Aye, to me and his four other
women should the mood to claim another not take him."

Kira shuddered. "I could not do this thing."

The woman leaned over her and there was no denying the
intelligence that sparkled in her eyes. "You would be
alive," she reminded Kira in a low voice. "And you would
be protected should you be claimed by a blooded one like
Black Wind."

Kira nibbled her lip, barely daring to be tempted by the
possibility. "Why is he called that?" she demanded
abruptly. The woman shrugged.

"His name he would not give when he rode in, so one
was given to him. Few questions are asked of any who
would join, especially one who fights as well as he. Claimed
to have the great one's blood in his veins, though none believed him until he began to show the signs."

"The signs?"

"Luck," the woman supplied flatly. "'Tis clear the gods
and the elements smile upon him, for little he takes on fails.
He is a blessed one, despite the stigma of his mark." She
leaned closer and her voice dropped to a confidential whisper. "'Tis said he bears the mark of some dark god on his
chest and that it cannot be removed. Those who ride into

battle with him say it glows so that it can be seen through his *kalat* and that the enemies fall back in fear from the sight.''

Kira did not dare to let her skepticism show, but merely held the woman's gaze with what she hoped might pass for amazement. Superstitious nonsense. 'Twas a birthmark alone her warrior sported, liken to many others Kira had seen except for its distinctive shape.

"But his name?" she prompted.

The woman shrugged. "Rode in from the north, he did, and so stealthily did he pass that none heard him afore he stood before the khan's own tent. Directions they call by colors here, and 'north' to you and me is 'black' to them. 'Tis said he passes as silently and appears as unexpectedly as the north wind itself, hence the name Black Wind."

And was about as warm. Kira regarded her bread with disinterest, unable to reconcile herself to the woman's suggestion despite the quiver of excitement fluttering within her stomach.

"I do not believe he can be tempted," she protested, then glanced up when the woman laughed again.

"*All* men can well be tempted," she assured Kira confidently. "Come and I will show you. A little *qumis* and a few hours of dancing and you will be ready to show the man your charms."

"But—" Kira protested halfheartedly, her words silenced with a cutting glance from the other woman.

"Would you rather live than die?" the woman demanded flatly. Kira found herself nodding.

"Aye," she admitted, knowing it to be the truth.

"Then surely coupling with a man cannot be too high a price to pay," the woman observed. Seeing Kira's doubt, she gave her a maternal pat on the shoulder. "I would not see you die, child, especially when one such as Black Wind desires you."

"He does not," Kira argued, but the woman only smiled.

"Naught do you know of men if you believe that," she chided, and Kira dared to hope. The woman extended her hand again. This time Kira let herself be pulled to her feet, her own tentative smile matching the woman's confident one. "Well do I think dancing will suit you," the woman mused. "What is your name, child?"

"Kira."

"Kira," she repeated carefully as her gaze ran over her. "Named for the sun, are you. Does the sun not choose life every day?" The woman leaned closer and her voice dropped to a whisper. "Would you not choose life, little Kira?"

"Aye," Kira said after a moment's pause, her voice growing firmer with her burgeoning conviction. Optimism burned brightly within her now that she gave it rein and she dared to hope that her warrior could indeed be tempted to claim her for his own. "Aye," she said again. "I will choose life. Teach me what I need to know."

Chapter Six

Thierry could not believe his eyes when he saw her in the khan's own tent two nights after he had sent her home.

Surely 'twas a trick of the light, or the copious amount of *qumis* he had imbibed, for his woman appeared to be among the dancers. Serfs and whores they were, by and large, women who ensured their own survival by the granting of their ample favors.

No place had his witch with them. Surely his eyes erred.

"Time enough 'tis that you showed interest in the fair sex," Nogai jested beside him.

Thierry acknowledged that he was probably not as circumspect about his intrigue as usually he was. Indeed, it mattered little now. Invincibility was of import only for those who had power, those with something worth stealing. A battle that had not been meant quite simply that Thierry had had no opportunity to prove himself. And unproven, he had no power within the tribe.

The smoke was thick from incense in the khan's tent and the cloying sweetness stung Thierry's eyes as he dared to peer once more at the dancers. His eye fell immediately on the same tiny figure and he shook his head stubbornly. In Tiflis she was, but his fogged mind refused to relinquish its certainty. 'Twas a trick of the flickering lamplight alone.

Indeed, she heavily favored his witch, but her movements were more languid. A drum was struck, bells shaken and the women took to a cleared space on the floor, their hips undulating in time to the music. A confusing swirl of scarves temporarily obscured his vision as the women ran in a tight circle amidst the sound of applause. When they stopped, he glimpsed a trim ankle before the flowing cloth drifted down to hide it from view once more. Thierry looked up to find his woman not two arm's lengths before him.

There was no disputing his impression now. 'Twas her, though her gaze was less sharp than he recalled.

His heart skipped a beat. He saw that the slowness of her movement was probably *qumis*-induced and stifled an indulgent smile. Her large eyes appeared yet wider and darker with the sweep of dark kohl accenting them. Her lips seemed ruddier and fuller and he had no doubt they had been painted, as well. She met his eyes and smiled timidly before she rolled one shoulder in an amateurish parody of the more experienced dancers.

Thierry licked his lips and glanced away, unable to account for the sudden dampness of his palms. How had she come to be here? No explanation could he find for her presence, especially dancing as she was, though Thierry cared little for that fact. In truth, he was pleased to see her again, though he would not have admitted as much to another living soul. Could he have missed her? Impossible, but he definitely felt better than he had just moments before.

He could not help but turn his gaze upon her once more.

'Twas endearing how she tried to dance like the other women, her innocence as obvious as the nose on her face. Thierry felt an unexpected glow of affection swell within him as he settled back to sip his *qumis*. Yet again in this woman's presence, he was tempted to smile.

"Witch." Nogai reminded Thierry of the danger she posed with the terse word, but Thierry silenced him with a glance.

No interest had he in any superstitious nonsense, though little indeed did it please him to know that Nogai had discerned the direction of his thoughts so readily. Naught did he need to spoil the sweetness of this moment. Even if she should be gone by the morrow, Thierry would savor this chance to see her again.

And he had naught to lose by making his interest clear. The very thought sent a heated spark of anticipation running through him. Thierry told himself 'twas naught but the *qumis,* though indeed he knew better.

The men hollered and hooted at the dancers in typical fashion, several of the women blowing kisses and making beckoning gestures as they danced. The witch looked only to him and only briefly before her gaze dropped to the floor. Thierry saw that she nibbled her bottom lip occasionally, her nervousness more than readily apparent, her color unnaturally high.

The gracefulness of her every gesture recalled the sight of her gloriously nude all too readily to Thierry's mind. He licked his lips, feeling the spark kindled within grow to a flame. The yurt was suddenly much warmer than it had been, to Thierry, at least, but still he could not look away from the unexpected sight of her dancing.

'Twas when she glanced at the other dancers and mimicked their gesture, tossing aside the large emerald scarf wrapped around her fully, that Thierry realized this could not be some harmless indulgence. Though she threw the silk aside with less practiced aplomb than her companions, her grace was made evident by the gesture.

As was much of the rest of her, he acknowledged with some discomfort. Thierry straightened slowly at the sight of her bare midriff, knowing full well that there was a mole to the left of her navel and liking it not that everyone else in the khan's tent knew it, as well.

The thought of touching that mole tempted him, but he ignored it.

A crisscrossed red scarf bound her breasts, another in brilliant blue girded her hips. An array of other scarves in bright hues hung from or around the blue one, the moving gaps between them affording tempting glimpses of her shapely legs. The men's hooting troubled Thierry now as it had not before and he wondered how many were gazing upon the soft flesh of his woman. The very thought made him cringe, illogical though that was. No claim had he here.

This time when she rolled her hips, it garnered more of a response from him than a cringe, though Thierry dared show naught of his feelings. Nogai whistled loudly but Thierry remained stock-still. The woman looked to him and smiled tentatively once more when she met his eyes. He refused to show any sign of her effect upon him. She must have discerned something in his expression, though, for she raised her hands over her head as the tempo of the music increased. She rocked her hips in time, the very provocativeness of the gesture shocking Thierry, though his companions seemed to have another response.

The woman smiled slowly and Thierry knew she had guessed that he was not unaffected. But what was her objective? Surely she could not mean to tempt him? Not after her relieved response the other night to his stated intention to leave her be?

The very possibility was provocative, but Thierry refused to let himself indulge in such whimsy. She could not be tempting him. She took a step closer to him, seemingly oblivious to the other men in the tent. She spun on one toe and unraveled another scarf from her hips. As yellow as the sun it was. Thierry wondered how he could ever have thought her dancing amateurish when she deliberately cast it to him.

Mayhap he had misinterpreted. The invitation was blatantly unmistakable. He snatched the scarf from the air, schooling his features to remain impassive. Deliberately he sipped his *qumis* and held her gaze. Well it seemed that she intended to tease him this night, but he would know her desire with resounding certainty before he did anything in response.

Her ankles and calves could be seen more clearly since the yellow scarf had been removed. Thierry admired the view, even as the lewd calls of his companions fairly made his ears burn. Fortunate 'twas that she could not understand the Mongol tongue. He followed one leg upward, devouring the sight of her golden curves until finally he met her eyes once more.

Still she regarded him as though he were the only man in the tent. The realization fed the heat already burning within him. When her slender hands fell to another knot on her hip, Thierry's heart leaped. No desire had he for more of her to be displayed to common view lest another be tempted to make her his own.

'Twas time. He tapped his index finger on the floor of the tent directly before him. Something flickered in the woman's eyes. Her color blossomed anew but she took the steps needed to bring her directly before him.

And resumed her dancing.

Thierry immediately regretted his impulse. He was inundated by her sweet scent and clenched one hand around his cup in a bid for self-control. Too tempting 'twas to have her swaying so seductively directly before him. Should he care to look straight ahead from his seat on the floor, he could fairly stare right into the most fragrant part of her. Thierry resolutely avoided the option.

Instead he made the mistake of looking up to her face.

Vulnerability he saw in those dark eyes. And fear. What had brought her to this camp? He wondered what she had found in Tiflis. Had the marks on her back anything to do with her return? She spun on her toe again and he caught a glimpse of her back, relieved to see that she sported no fresh wounds. What then? Had she come back for his protection? Deliberately was she tempting him and Thierry could only assume that she wanted him to claim her.

His woman. Bewitched he must be, for the idea held no small measure of appeal.

But two days past, he would have declined, regardless of the spell she cast over him. Even this day, he would decline the offer from any other without regret. But in truth, this witch provoked him even when she sought no such end. This night he knew not how he might resist her allure. Naught had he to lose indeed by the softness of a woman, for he was powerless in a society that held only power in esteem.

He could do as she asked.

Thierry's heart leaped at the very possibility but he forced himself to consider the realities. She was a virgin, unless he knew absolutely naught of the world. Was this truly the price she was prepared to pay? No merchant would have her for certain after this.

Mayhap Nogai had been right and none would have her now.

If only he could be certain 'twas what she wanted. Thierry tapped the floor closer to his knee and she instantly took the requisite step. The smell of her engulfed him and he blinked disconcertedly, his gaze dropping abruptly from the swaying silk to her feet.

Her delightfully small and well-formed feet.

A red mark there was, mayhap a callus, that had not been there before. Thierry reached to touch the spot on her instep without thinking, startled at the contrast between his rough hands and her smooth skin. She laughed unexpectedly at his touch, her foot wriggling away as she shivered. Thierry glanced up at the unexpected sound in time to see her eyes glimmer with mischief. An amethyst scarf was unknotted from her hips, those tiny feet playfully dancing a hand's span away.

Thierry looked up in confusion, surprised to find a flurry of soft purple enfolding his senses. He pulled the silk from obscuring his vision and held fast to the end. She danced at the other end of the scarf, undulating with the increased tempo of the drum. Thierry saw naught but her golden loveliness.

She could be his.

When her eyes met his again, he held her gaze and deliberately put his cup aside. She licked her lips nervously but neither broke his regard nor ceased her dancing. With an abrupt flick of his wrist, the amethyst cloth danced out of her grip and fluttered through the air to Thierry.

She looked confused, but little time did he give her to reflect upon the matter. No sooner had he the scarf within his grip than he snapped it again, sending a furl of silk to encircle her hips. He snatched the loose end out of the air and, much to the approval of his companions, pulled her resolutely closer.

She smiled openly at him and danced within the circle of silk, stretching her arms high in that pose that so enflamed him. Thierry gripped the scarf in one hand and reached out to touch the softness of her ankle once more. Instantly she planted her feet on the floor, the music becoming a frenzied beating at that same point. She shimmied her hips in a timeless move, the vibration fueling Thierry's desire.

Unable to help himself, he let his fingertip trail leisurely up her leg. To his surprise, she shivered but did not move away. Thierry looked up to meet her eyes, seeing his own desire reflected there. Deliberately did she tempt him, he was certain of it, the light in her eyes making him believe she wanted their mating as much as he did.

As smooth as satin was her skin. Thierry swallowed as that fingertip dared ever higher. Not only did she not move away but she slipped one foot farther away from the other. Thierry's heart pounded at the promise of that, and he allowed his finger to relentlessly continue.

The drumbeat slowed to a repetitive pounding, a pulse that was taken up by dancers and crowd alike. The golden light of the lamps flickered restlessly. The tent resonated, the women pumped their hips, the men stamped their feet and Thierry looked into the acquiescent eyes of his woman.

When he encountered the dampness at the juncture of her thighs, all else was forgotten.

She wanted him. Her eyes widened at his bold touch, but she neither ceased dancing nor looked away. Indeed, it seemed to Thierry that there were none but the two of them within the smoke-filled tent.

But there were more than the two of them. And if she was to be Thierry's woman, she would be his alone. Not a private society was this one and well enough he knew that only a deed witnessed by many was believed to be the truth. The evidence of one's own eyes alone could not be disputed.

If she was to be his woman and none were to have any doubt of her status, his possession would have to be a public one. Only that would leave no doubt. Thierry arched one brow, hoping she understood the import of what he asked when she nodded quick agreement without breaking his gaze.

So be it. She would be his for this night and all others. His path resolved, he willfully forgot the others in the yurt once more.

This moment was between the two of them, in truth.

Thierry gave the amethyst scarf the slightest tug, loving the way she tumbled trustingly into his arms. Had he spared the time to think, he might have thought her relieved, but other matters were there to attend. Her small hands were on his shoulders, her breath in his ear, her scent filling his nostrils fit to drown him, her softness filling his hands.

His woman.

She was on her back beside him in a flash, her gleaming hair spread over the bright carpets layered on the tent floor. Thierry was atop her in a heartbeat, his *chalwar* torn open. Incense and her scent mingled in his nostrils, the *qumis* burned hot in his veins, the pulse in his ears echoed the beating drums. He hauled the scarves out of his path and buried himself within her in one move, deaf to the cries of the men around him.

Her gasp he heard alone. He whispered some reassurance in the Frankish tongue he had not dared to let pass his lips in years before her sweetness overwhelmed him. Too tight was she for him to last, but mayhap 'twas better for this to be concluded quickly. He thrust within her and felt the bite of her nails in his shoulders. He managed to thrust only once more before he arched back and spilled his seed.

Witch.

His witch. Thierry collapsed atop her, knowing he had never been so completely claimed. It seemed her softness invited him closer and he was sorely tempted to fall asleep

thus. No one would lay an abusing hand upon her again, he
thought fiercely, daring to whisper once more within the
soft curve of her ear. She was his and his alone.

She was silent beneath him, her breath coming in anxious spurts, and Thierry reluctantly acknowledged the press
of men around them. No place was this for such a sweet
union. The deed had been done and now he would have his
temptress to himself.

Her eyes were closed when Thierry dared to look and he
knew a moment's doubt, but he resolutely shoved to his elbows. Business was there at hand. The deed was done, but
he must ensure that none doubted the evidence of their
eyes. Ample time would there be in privacy for the slow
loving he longed to savor with her. The night was yet young
and his anticipation at the promise of that thought rose
much more quickly than he could have expected.

Flooded with a protectiveness he dared not explore, he
pulled his cloak to cover her as he withdrew, leaving himself exposed to draw the men's attention from her. His. A
murmur went through the tent as Thierry stood slowly over
his woman, his feet braced on either side of her draped and
prone form. Slowly he met the gaze of every man in the
yurt, daring each to acknowledge the evidence of her broken maidenhead smeared upon his flesh.

No doubt would there be on the morrow that he had
done this thing. No question would there be to whom this
woman belonged. She had curled up at his feet beneath the
cloak, yet again reminding him of a small cat, though her
hands concealed her face from view.

One of the other men reached for the cloak with a mumbled joke, but Thierry drew his blade in a flash. The point
at the man's throat halted his gesture before he could un-
veil the woman. He swallowed carefully and straightened
beneath Thierry's gaze, though none moved to aid him.
The tent fell yet more silent as the others awaited the out-
come of the challenge.

"None shall look upon what is mine," Thierry growled.

The stillness in the tent was so complete that he had not a doubt all had heard his claim. Once again he met the gaze of each in turn, waiting until the challenge faded from each pair of dark eyes before moving on. Satisfied, he deliberately sheathed his blade, adjusted his *chalwar* and crouched down to pick up his woman.

She recoiled from his touch, the accusation in her wide eyes when she pulled her hands away fairly sickening him.

But no time was this for dissent. Thierry hoped she saw the warning in his eyes before she buried her face again in the folds of the cloak. He reached for her anew, hoping none had witnessed her response other than him. He only dared to exhale when she did not fight him and he stood with her cradled in his arms.

Lighter even than he had expected was she and he marveled once more at her delicacy, letting his hand spread to span the slenderness of her waist. He felt the tension coiled within her and understood suddenly the shock their coupling must have been. No easy task had it been for her to allow his touch this soon, he was certain. Deciding on this path had taken courage and Thierry's admiration surged for his woman. Soon enough would he show her that the reality of coupling had not to be such a hasty deed.

Impossible 'twas to check his pride that she was his in truth, that he had been the first and that there would be no others as long as he drew breath. Thierry resolutely held her closer, determined to sweeten her recollection of their first mating before the night was through.

Ways there were of pleasing a woman and though he had long been chaste, he was well enough acquainted with such techniques. Indeed, the very thought of touching her in more private circumstances lent purpose to his step as he left the khan's yurt.

'Twas only when he gained the outside air that Thierry discerned her quiet sobbing. His lips thinned at the muted sound, his elaborate rationalizations forgotten as he roundly cursed the barbarian he had become.

* * *

She would not cry.

Kira willed her tears to stop, certain the warrior would think her a complete fool for such behavior. Though little enough did she care what he thought after what he had done to her.

Like animals had they coupled. Before an audience of yet baser animals. What kind of people dared to watch such intimacy? Certainly Kira had expected that their mating would be an inevitable result of her dancing, should she be successful, but never had she imagined 'twould take place in public.

Indeed, she could scarce believe it now.

And why had this made her cry when her father's frequent beatings had never drawn a tear? Although there had been a twinge of pain and certainly some discomfort, what had happened this night could not compare to the painful bite of the lash she knew so well.

'Twas the shock alone that fed her tears, Kira told herself stubbornly, even as they refused to halt. Naught could her response have to do with this man. It could not, for she knew naught of him. And no credence would she give to the ache between her thighs. Little enough excuse was that for tears.

The night air was cold but Kira flatly refused to huddle any closer to the uncompromising man who carried her. What had she done? No gratitude had she anymore for the *qumis* that had fed her resolve and loosed her inhibitions, for its heat had completely abandoned her. Kira shivered, hating the filmy veils that clung silkily to her flesh.

Cold and alone she was with the man who had claimed her. Kira dared not look up to his face and stayed huddled within his cloak as she struggled to come to terms with what had happened.

Had this not been what she wanted?

Her traitorous body was too aware of the lean strength of his chest as the warrior carried her away from the scene of the spectacle they had made. She heard his solid footfalls in the beaten-down grass and felt the determination in the arms that held her against him.

No doubt his expression was as stonily impassive as ever. She despised him suddenly for granting her what she had asked of him, wishing too late that the loss of her maidenhead might have been a sweet mating. His fault it was that she had been forced to make such a choice, for had he not stolen her from Tiflis and the life she knew? Had he not taken her to the Mongol camp from which she could never return home?

Truly, it seemed she had plenty for which to blame this man, and her silent tears rolled unchecked over her cheeks.

But 'twas she who had chosen him of all the men assembled there, and indeed Kira could make little sense of her choice. Surely she could not have any regard for a man with whom she had never spoken? Surely she could not feel anything but disgust for a man who had done what he had just done?

Kira's feelings on the matter were more confused than she would have liked them to have been. Too comforting was his warmth for her taste, too easy would it be to subside against him and let him gather her yet closer.

Or worse, to let him touch her with such familiarity again. The scent of his skin reminded her that her own desire had not been quenched in her shock and she fidgeted as she struggled to dispel such inappropriate thoughts. She should loathe him. This warrior deserved no more than that.

He ducked into the enveloping shadow of the tent they had already shared and Kira's pulse quickened. Did he mean to mate again? And yet more troubling, why did the thought prompt anticipation to mingle with her fear?

She gasped when he crouched without striking a flint, cradling her yet closer in his lap. Too aware was Kira of the darkness pressing around them and the distant sound of merrymaking. Indeed, the shadows made her yet more aware of the warrior's proximity, his scent filling her lungs and heightening the intimacy of this setting. Mayhap 'twas better to be in public after all, she thought wildly, trying desperately to scurry away from him.

His arms tightened around her, checking her retreat as he kept her resolutely in his lap, and he muttered something under his breath as he sat down. Kira froze, startled that his tone did not sound angry, and listened attentively for some abrupt change in his manner.

When none came, she dared to glance up through her tears even as her heart thudded in her ears, cringing at the shadow of his hand rising above her. His hand paused for a moment and she knew he had noted her fear before he gently pushed the hood back from her damp face.

He had left the tent flap open and Kira could discern his features in the half-light. His eyes were gleaming in the shadows and she fancied she saw concern in his expression, though she hastily dropped her gaze and refused to indulge her whimsy.

If only she could stop the flow of these cursed tears.

To Kira's surprise, a rough thumb slid slowly across her cheek, collecting her tears in a single gesture. She watched transfixed as the warrior raised his hand and carefully licked the salty drops from his own flesh. Kira dared to meet his gaze, her mouth going dry at the intensity of his expression.

Slowly, as though he feared to startle her, he repeated the gesture and wiped the tears from her other cheek. Never did he even blink, let alone break her regard, and Kira's chest clenched as his tongue languidly collected his new harvest of tears from his thumb. Something awakened within her again but she refused to indulge it, forcing herself to recall the kind of man she confronted.

A Mongol. A barbarian. A ruthless warrior. Kira swallowed carefully, not daring to believe the thought that immediately crossed her mind when he reached for the new tears on her cheek.

He simply could not be apologizing. What could a man such as this know about such social niceties? His very tenderness fed her tears and they flowed with new vigor despite her efforts, leaving Kira powerless within the maelstrom of her conflicting emotions. How could this man confuse her so? And why did he do so?

He leaned slowly toward her and Kira's breath caught in her lungs, his move reminding her suddenly that she was cradled in his lap. His other hand was curled surely around her waist, his fingers gripping her pelvis with a gentle firmness. The strength of his thighs was bunched beneath her and when his free hand curled under her chin, Kira was stunned to hear a faint sigh escape her own lips.

When the tip of his tongue touched her cheek ever so gently and lifted away another tear, Kira shivered. He pulled her closer within the circle of his embrace as though he thought her cold and her fingers spread of their own accord to fan out on his shoulders. His careful removal of her tears was eroding any thought that he was to blame for her horrendous fate and she could not fight her instincts on this matter.

He *was* apologizing.

Kira's heart melted at the realization, his touch igniting her desire once more. Indeed, she was only too aware beneath his gentle assault that the unfamiliar tension within her when she had danced for him had not been released. She was agitated deep inside and though she knew not what to do about it, she imagined her warrior did.

When his lips closed firmly over hers, Kira could think of naught but gaining that release. He nudged open her lips with his tongue and the world spun giddily at the warm spice of his kiss. Kira closed her eyes as she submitted and clasped her warrior's neck, liking the feel of his corded strength beneath her hands.

She trembled when his fingers gripped the hair at the nape of her neck, her back arching high when his other hand explored the fullness of her breast. He teased her nipple with work-roughened fingers and Kira nearly cried out at the pleasure that coursed through her from that point.

Emboldened by his sure touch, she dared to run her hands over the breadth of his shoulders. Without breaking his languorous kiss, he guided her hands to the front of his *kalat*, his own hands roving to curve around her buttocks. Kira's heart leaped to her throat and her fingers trembled, but she unfastened the ties nonetheless.

She hesitated for a moment, then slipped her hands beneath both the fur-lined tunic and the silk shirt beneath. His skin was as warm and smooth as heavy satin left in the sun, the wiry hair on his chest tickling her fingers. Kira recalled only too well the sight of his nudity the other morning, and her pulse accelerated.

She found his nipple and gave it an impudent pinch, liking the way he jumped in surprise. Before Kira could savor the unexpected moment, he shifted her weight in his lap and she was startled by the press of his hardness against her buttocks. The warmth of his hand landed flat on her bare stomach and Kira froze, suddenly certain that she knew what he was about.

This was no apology, she thought wildly. He meant only to earn her complaisance that he might take her again this night. What a fool she had been! This man had no regard for her feelings! And she had virtually begged him to make her his whore.

Kira squirmed in panic, but the way the warrior's strong fingers slipped purposefully beneath the scarf wound about her hips brought her struggles to an abrupt halt. The warm span of his fingers speared through the tangle of hair at her crotch, the very possessiveness of the gesture making her suddenly afraid.

Mayhap her feelings about another coupling this night truly would carry no weight.

Kira met the warrior's gaze tentatively, feeling completely captured beneath his grip. He was watching her, though she should have anticipated that, just as she should have expected his stony expression. He did not move and she had the sense he was waiting for her reaction.

Much as she was waiting to see what he would do next.

The two regarded each other silently for a long moment, Kira only too aware of the sound of her agitated breathing filling the tent.

Then the warrior's finger slipped decisively lower. Kira caught her breath, knowing his destination without a doubt yet powerless to stop him. A jolt tripped through her when he touched that spot again, the one he had teased briefly in the other tent.

Kira panicked. She would not couple with him again this night. She was sore, she was confused, she was tired and rather less than herself thanks to the effect of the *qumis*.

And he was teasing her, breaking down her resistance with single-minded resolve just so they could mate again. No regard did he truly have for her, for had she not seen his lack of response to her nudity the other morning? Indeed, he had only partaken of what was offered. No remorse did he feel for his deed, and at her telling response to the gentle pressure of his fingertip, Kira thrashed in an almost certainly futile attempt to gain her freedom.

To her astonishment the warrior let her go.

Chapter Seven

Kira gained her footing in a flurry of tangled silk, and felt an utter fool when the warrior did not move at all in pursuit. She gulped unsteadily to regulate her breathing, finding herself snared once more by his assessing regard.

Again they watched each other warily.

Kira began to wonder if he had turned to stone in truth, then his eyes narrowed suddenly and he abruptly stood. She darted out of his range and he spared her a glance that could have been indulgent had it come from any other man.

With smooth gestures he lit a lamp and hung it from the central pole. He carried a flame from the lamp to a small stove reposing in one corner, his intensity in focusing on his task leaving Kira feeling as though she had overreacted. Indeed, it seemed unlikely that this supremely unconcerned man even knew she was with him, let alone that he expected her to couple with him. Kira shifted her weight uncertainly from one foot to the other, not knowing what she should do next.

Should she run?

But where else would she find haven on this night and in this camp? Had she not wanted him to claim her? Evidently he had done so and it seemed that her place was here.

Even if her companion was markedly disinterested in that particular fact.

He filled a large pot with water and set it on the small stove. Kira nibbled her lip, wondering what was his intent.

To her surprise he began to peel off his clothes and methodically fold them before laying them neatly aside.

He meant to couple again! Kira panicked anew. She
scurried to the farthest side of the tent. Full well did she
know that she would be able to do little to fend him off, but
Kira kept her distance. No reason was there to make his
conquest an easy one.

The warrior continued disrobing, clearly undeterred by
her actions. Not a glance did he spare in her direction, even
when he stood splendidly nude, and Kira acknowledged a
niggle of doubt as to his objective. Could she have misread
him? The pot of water steamed and he squatted before the
short stove to pour the water into a bowl. He rummaged in
his saddlebags, producing a length of cloth, from which he
tore a shorter piece, and a brown block that fit easily into
his hand.

Only now did he turn to Kira, and she was disconcerted
at how readily he looked directly to her. Indeed, the man
fairly had eyes in the back of his head. He offered the trio
to her, but she hastily shook her head. Kira scurried backward, not trusting him enough to close the distance between them. The warrior shrugged and plunged the block
into the water.

Only when it began to lather on his skin did Kira realize
that it was soap. Considerably coarser and darker soap than
she knew, certainly, but still she licked her lips carefully at
the very promise of a bath. Filthy she felt after these past
few days. How long had it been since she had indulged in
the luxury of bathing twice daily? Indeed, that ritual of her
life in Tiflis seemed but a distant memory.

Of course, she would have to disrobe to wash properly
and that was out of the question.

Kira stubbornly turned her back on the sight of her warrior's nudity and folded her arms across her chest. She
could well enough go without a bath this night.

Although, she conceded as she spared a glance down to
the filmy array of garish scarves beneath his heavy cloak,

the man could not see much more of her than he already
had. And had she not been nude in his presence before?

She flicked a glance over her shoulder to find him scrub-
bing his body with evident relish. He ran the wet cloth over
his skin with a flourish, closing his eyes as the warm water
ran over his skin.

Curse him. Had she any idea that the man had a sense of
humor, she might have thought him deliberately teasing
her. But not this man. He glanced up and their gazes locked
for a long moment, Kira fancying she spied a glimmer of
something in those silver depths before he abruptly returned to his task.

She turned and stared resolutely at the cavorting shadows thrown on the tent wall. Had she not been in the river
but two days past? How dirty indeed could she be? Her
belly itched at the thought. The warrior made some low
sound of satisfaction in his throat and splashed in the water with obvious pleasure.

Well it seemed to Kira that her very skin crawled at that
unwelcome reminder. The river water had been filthy and
brown. And that *had* been two days past. She noted the
dark line beneath her nails as the splash of his bathing
taunted her anew.

Enough.

The man had seen and indeed sampled all she had.
Foolish pride would not keep her from being clean. Kira
dropped his cloak from her shoulders and bent to untie the
knotted scarves with shaking fingers before she could
change her mind.

Her nipples beaded as she turned to confront him in her
nudity and she could not have met his eyes to save her life.
She tossed her hair over her shoulder as though untroubled and resolutely crossed the tent to demand the soap
with one outstretched hand.

The warrior did not surrender the soap.

Kira gritted her teeth before she looked up to meet his
eyes, only to find him shaking his head with that madden-

ing slowness. He said something that was evidently an explanation and she was certain he was denying her a bath.

Of all the wicked ways to tempt her! Anger shot through
Kira. She heartily wished that she could tell him in no uncertain terms what she thought of such churlish behavior.

Indeed, it might be worth telling him, whether he could
understand her words or not.

Kira propped her hands on her hips and opened her
mouth to do just that, only to find the warrior's heavy finger firm against her lips.

It was wet, and a trickle of warm water ran over her chin
from his hand, but Kira could not move to stop it. Her eyes
widened in surprise.

Kira reluctantly met his gaze as she fell silent, unable to
deny the twinkle she found there. The very sight disconcerted her with its unexpectedness so that she lost the thread
of her argument. Instead she found herself nodding dumbly
when he held up one cautionary finger and cocked a brow.

His wet skin glistened as he tossed his water out the tent
flap and she could not help but notice the play of the mus-
cles across his back. Kira set her lips stubbornly, mentally
granting him but an instant more of tolerance before she
made her thoughts most clear.

To her surprise he filled the bowl with the remainder of
the hot water and offered her the bowl. Indeed, it seemed
he had divided the water in half as if he fully expected her
to bathe despite her original refusal.

It irked Kira that he found her so predictable, the reappearance of that twinkle in his silver eyes doing little to
improve her temper. A new length of cloth did he tear, offering it and the block of soap with all the gallantry of a
foreign courtier.

Curse him.

Kira snatched the soap and cloth in ill humor, momentarily grateful that he did not seem determined to aid her in
this task at least.

Although, the way he casually turned aside and ignored
her nudity left something to be desired, as well. He laid out

a pair of blankets nonchalantly near his folded garments, evidently completely oblivious of her nakedness or even her presence. At least he could glance in her direction once in a while, Kira thought irritably as she scrubbed her skin. The man could make a pretense of being attracted to her, if truly he had claimed her.

Unless he thought her merely a whore. Kira's eyes widened at the possibility and her fingers fumbled so that she nearly dropped the soap. Could she have sacrificed her virginity for naught but a night?

'Twas unthinkable, but not so easy to dismiss as Kira might have liked. She looked to the warrior to find him squatting atop the blanket, apparently at ease with his own nudity and watching her carefully. Kira had the uncanny sense that he had sensed her distress over that last thought, though truly there was no way he could know what was in her mind. He cocked one dark brow, as though inviting her to explain. Kira wished she could.

Somehow she sensed that he might reassure her, irrational though that thought was. What *had* she done? Tears blurred her vision once more but Kira refused to let them fall, stubbornly reminding herself that she was yet alive. Had that not been the point of surrendering her virginity? To ensure her very survival?

But had that truly been achieved? Kira wished she had some assurance as to the security of her role, whether she be whore or claimed woman.

She frowned and scrubbed the remainder of the soap from her skin, surprised to find the warrior looming in her peripheral vision. His brows tightened together as though he, too, was frustrated by their lack of common language, then he began pointing around the tent. Each time he pointed, he said something terse, a word or mayhap a phrase, but Kira knew not what was going on.

When he pointed to his tunic and stated *"kalat,"* she suddenly understood.

He was naming objects in Mongolian. Kira nodded quickly, glancing around for some way to indicate that she understood him. Her gaze fell on a tin cup and she pointed inside it.

"*Qumis,*" she said hopefully. The warrior nodded once with evident satisfaction. He held her gaze and pointed to the middle of his chest.

"Thierry," he said firmly. Kira felt her eyes narrow, for the word did not sound Mongolian to even her untrained ears. He repeated it, though, and she realized he was telling her his name.

Thierry. Kira almost said his name herself, having an inexplicable urge to feel the word roll over her tongue, but checked her response just in time.

She would *not* say his name. She would not forgive him so readily. Not until she understood whether she was his woman for good or his whore for this night alone.

And neither would she couple with him again, should she have any choice in the matter.

The warrior watched her expectantly, but Kira stubbornly said naught as she lifted her chin high. She certainly would not tell him her name, for that would be worse than saying his. That silver gaze bored into hers, as though willing her to understand, but Kira resolutely made no acknowledgment of his demand.

Finally he gestured to her and cocked one brow questioningly, but Kira shook her head adamantly. She would not tell him. His lips thinned and he turned away, indicating with one hand the blankets he had unfolded and beckoning to Kira. She shook her head again, pointing determinedly to the other side of the tent.

She would not sleep with him.

There was no doubt that she had displeased him with that. The warrior folded his arms across his chest and shook his head just as determinedly. Kira straightened her shoulders, knowing that she had no intention of acquiescing to share a bed with him this night. Had he not let her sleep in privacy before?

A male voice raised in song outside the tent drew Kira's attention away from their contest of wills. Two women giggled before the man outside began to laugh raucously, as well. No doubt there were some indulging themselves this night. They were close, though, and she wondered fleetingly, as their voices drew yet nearer, if they intended to come right into the tent.

Kira looked back to the warrior in trepidation. He counted off three fingers and gestured outside with those fingers, then pointed to the side of the tent where Kira had intended to sleep. She shook her head quickly, certain he was just trying to frighten her, but he nodded confidently and repeated the gesture. They could not be coming here. Had she and the warrior not been alone here before?

The voices grew yet louder. The warrior watched her silently and Kira wondered if that night had been an exception. Certainly the tent was much too large for one man alone. Kira licked her lips nervously as the laughter grew nearer.

Well it seemed that their privacy was to be short-lived.

Still Kira hesitated as the voices outside grew in volume, jumping when the warrior unexpectedly scooped up his silk *kurta* with uncharacteristic impatience and strode across the space between them. He planted himself between Kira and the tent flap, shooting her a murderous look when she might have stepped away. He shook out the folded shirt with a snap of his wrist.

An instant later her vision was clouded by the undyed silk as he hauled it over her head. The lustrous fabric slid over her face, releasing the warm scent of his skin. Kira closed her eyes for a moment, opening them to find the singing man and two women staggering into the tent. Only just in time had the warrior covered her nudity and she was astonished to find gratitude flooding through her.

Surely she was confused this night to feel gratitude for the warrior who had taken her so publicly. Truly the *qumis* had addled her mind.

The newly arrived man whistled appreciatively and made a drunken grab in Kira's direction. The warrior moved quickly to kick out the other man's ankle, sending him sprawling on his face, much to his women's giggling delight. The fallen man laughed and shook a finger at the warrior as he rolled to his back and made some jest, though indeed the warrior did not seem to see the humor in the situation.

Kira barely had time to note that the man was the same who had been the warrior's companion earlier before she was scooped off her feet. Her breath caught and she was unexpectedly deposited in the middle of the unfolded blanket.

The warrior had dropped down beside her before she could voice her complaint, one arm clamped around her waist while the other swept the blanket over them in a savage gesture. She glanced up to find a dangerous gleam in his eye and a stern set to his mouth that effectively checked any impulse to make any protest clear.

Indeed, he seemed quite agitated that his companion had reached for her, his relentless grip on Kira naught if not possessive. His very response seemed to make his ownership clear, and Kira could not help but wonder at the cause.

Could she have been claimed after all? If so, for how long and on what terms? She glanced up at the warrior's stern countenance and he seemed to sense her doubt, for he caught her eye even as his fingers spread to span her waist. He tucked her slightly closer to his side and, knowing she had little choice in the matter, Kira settled against his hard warmth to sleep.

She supposed the morning would show more clearly her role. Kira bit down on her frustration, knowing there was naught she could do to make the matter clear sooner.

But tired she was and he was wonderfully warm. Mayhap 'twould not be so bad to sleep here. Indeed, what had she to fear from this man now? The warrior spoke to his friend, his voice rumbling beneath her ear in a most pleasant manner, and Kira dared to settle more thoroughly against him.

Thierry, she thought dreamily, saying his name in her mind despite her resolve not to do so as sleep crept up on her.

She was afraid of him.

Why else would she refuse to tell him her name? Thierry knew she had understood his request, for there was no lack of intelligence in those dark eyes. She had simply denied him, and though her refusal had stung at the time, he could well understand her uncertainty.

The shaman says a curse comes to a man who takes a witch. Indeed, I could not help but ask him the way of it. You should know that he was most interested in the matter.

Nogai's taunting words burned in Thierry's mind yet again and he gritted his teeth. Ironic 'twas that she seemed afraid of him, for the shaman had evidently made it more than clear that he would be the one to pay the price for this night's mating.

The curse? Aye, that will interest you, I should imagine, for 'tis an ugly fate. 'Tis said 'twill shrivel and fall off once it has been buried in a witch. 'Tis thus the shaman says and well you know he has seen much in his day.

A lie. A whimsy. It simply could not be that this sweet creature could extract such a toll from his body. Despite his doubts, Thierry could not help sparing a glance beneath the blanket to check.

Indeed, it seemed this witch made him larger, not smaller. He swallowed a smug smile at the thought.

And what did Nogai know of such matters? Superstitious he was, even beyond the inclination of the others within the tribe. Apt he was to believe every tale from abroad and see signs in the most mundane occurrences.

The shaman predicted your lack of success at Tiflis, did he not?

Nogai's closing taunt echoed relentlessly within Thierry's mind. Had the shaman truly said as much? Thierry did not know, Nogai's manner indicating that the prediction had been well-known. Had he had a downfall? Certainly Thierry had lost an opportunity to prove himself, but his conviction that his time of ascendancy was upon him had diminished naught. He was not quite ready to concede that he had failed.

Although Abaqa's manner lately had been less than encouraging. Thierry shifted restlessly, unable to dismiss the veracity of that last thought, his own wishes to the contrary.

Mayhap the shaman was right about taking witches.

Thierry looked down as the woman sighed, hearing evidence in the change of her breathing that she was truly asleep now. He shook his head mutely, unable or unwilling to condemn her so readily as a witch. Intrigued him in a most unnatural way she did, but that alone did not provide the proof he desired. Indeed, the pearls had fallen from her lips but once and once alone.

He recalled the scholar's assertion that the taste of a pearl revealed its source, and wondered. Could she have been assessing pearls when they came upon her? A most practical solution to the puzzle was that and Thierry tried to assess it independently of its allure.

She could be naught but a woman stolen from her home. A fetching and frightened woman who had deliberately tempted him this night to ensure her own survival.

Or mayhap a witch.

But claimed she was. By him. And together they must find their path from this night onward. Somehow he had to earn this tiny creature's trust without the ability to simply talk to her.

Thierry lay on his back and stared at the roof of the yurt, ignoring the giggling that accompanied Nogai's sport as he puzzled over what to do. His thumb stroked the softness of her shoulder blade absently, the soft puff of her breath against his skin and the tentative press of her fingertips on his chest filling him with an unusual contentment.

How much did she understand of what had happened this night? Thierry knew not and suspected that only time

would reveal the truth to her. No way had he of telling her
that he intended to keep her by his side without fetching the
annoying scholar from Tiflis. Soon they would be on the
move again and it would be unreasonable—not to mention
unpleasant—to be permanently blessed with that man's
company. Nay, this was an obstacle he and his witch had to
conquer alone.

He could only make his intent clear by keeping her at his
side, and that would take time.

In the interim, he would set himself to the task of earning her trust.

No intention had Thierry of partaking of her charms
without her explicit consent again. Not only did the very
recollection of his deed make him cringe inwardly, even
knowing the necessity of it, but 'twas clear that she intended to extract a toll from him for it, as well. Beside the
risk of the shaman's threats coming true, there was the un-
questionable fact of her newfound distrust of him. The
price was clearly too high all around.

He would have her come to him when next they mated.

Thierry frowned thoughtfully, knowing well that this
night must have been less than a pleasant experience for
her. Would she even *want* to come to him after such a mating? Doubt grew within him as he stared down at her, as
peaceful in sleep as a child.

Impulsively, he bent and brushed his lips across her
smooth brow, liking the way her silky hair caressed his
nose. The very softness of her triggered his arousal once
more and Thierry wondered in that moment how he would
keep himself from her, mayhap indefinitely.

Wither and fall off. Truly the shaman knew naught of
what he spoke and Thierry was tempted to show him the
evidence of that himself. This witch would keep him en-
gorged when even she ignored him, let alone when she
turned her will upon him.

But what if she never came to him again?

As Thierry stared down at her, an idea formed in his
mind, tempting him with the possibility so that it could not

be denied. Mayhap if he showed her the pleasure that could be hers from this pastime, she would eventually come to him of her own volition.

Mayhap 'twas worth a try.

Kira was having the most wonderful dream.

Her mind was repainting the memory of the loss of her maidenhead and well she knew it, but she granted her imagination free reign, knowing that a dream could hurt naught. She was floating in a warm sea of silk, drifting languidly while a school of little fishes nibbled at her thighs. Kira sighed and stretched amidst the soft swirl of silk, smiling to herself when the teasing fishes ventured higher.

They were nudging at the apex of her thighs where that sensitive spot was concealed. Kira spared not a thought before she parted her legs to grant them access. They dived gleefully through her nest of curls and she imagined the sight of them disappearing into the secretive darkness before their nibbles stole her breath away.

She twisted away from temptation but the persistent fishes followed her diligently, their feather-light teasing sending a tide of warmth coursing through her. The sea of silk grew warmer, or else her skin became more sensitive, for it seemed every fiber of her being had come alive.

Kira dared to part her thighs yet farther, gasping aloud when yet more fishes attacked her breasts with their seductive touch. She felt her nipples bead beneath the warm assault and arched high, stretching her hands above her to encounter a broad pair of shoulders that were decidedly not fishy.

Kira's eyes flew open. Her heart fairly stopped at the silhouette of her warrior bent over her, his mouth gently tugging her nipple to an impertinent point. She watched in amazement as he lifted his head an increment and pursed his lips. The warm breath that fanned over her skin launched an army of goose pimples across her flesh. Kira shivered and he spared her a fathomless silver glance.

Their gazes locked for a long moment in the night shadows, the sounds of the others sleeping filling Kira's ears as she silently regarded him. Then the warrior's fingers moved expertly within the warm shelter of her dampness and all thought fled her mind. He leaned toward her purposefully and Kira closed her eyes as his lips found hers, knowing she was too aroused to deny his touch now.

Her senses were filled with the smell and the taste of him, his warmth, his strength. He coaxed and cajoled her flesh and, as surely as if she had willed it herself, Kira felt the fires kindled beneath her skin once again. Her legs shifted restlessly beneath the blanket as he ran an intoxicating row of kisses under her chin. She thought her heart would burst when he nuzzled her earlobe, his breath tickling the tender flesh there before he boldly licked behind it. Kira shuddered but her response gained her no respite from his fiery touch.

Those fingers between her thighs caressed and kneaded incessantly, demanding yet more of her even when she knew not what to do. She felt a moan rise to her lips but her warrior was quick to swallow the faint sound, his firm lips locking over hers once more. The move brought his bare chest into aching proximity with hers and Kira arched high at the persuasive brush of those wiry hairs against her aching nipples.

Suddenly a frenzy was loosed beneath her skin and she writhed against it. Her fingernails dug into his shoulders when his fingers continued to demand. It was too close, too much, too overwhelming and nameless, this tension that would not be denied.

With an abruptness that took her breath away, everything clenched within Kira. She made a cry into the warrior's kiss as the convulsions swept through her. For an instant her heart stopped, her lungs clenched and her womb contracted with a strength that astounded her. She saw a blinding light behind her eyelids and felt a frisson of heat fit to fry her skin.

Then there was naught.

Naught but the darkness, the sound of her breathing and the gleaming silver of her warrior's eyes. A seductive warmth flooded leisurely through her and she snuggled deeper into the embrace of the blanket. Kira barely had time to spare him a smile before she slipped back into that silky sea of dreams once more.

The summons from the khan came before the dawn.

Thierry was awake and heard the messenger's pace on the grass before the man even reached the yurt. Instinctively he knew that he was the one being summoned. 'Twas the time of reckoning, unless he missed his guess.

'Twas a relief in a way to know that Abaqa would finally make his move, and Thierry found himself unnervingly calm. The *keshik* guard ducked his head into the yurt without preamble, his uniform revealing his regiment as the khan's private guard. He nodded once when he met Thierry's gaze, then ducked back outside.

Thierry extricated himself slowly from the delightful tangle of silk and softness that was his woman. He did not want to wake her so early and moved carefully, bending to tuck the blanket carefully back around her. She nestled down into the wool, rubbing her cheek against the spot where he had rested. His heart leaped, but Thierry refused to permit himself any romantic whimsy.

She had sought him out for his protection. He had granted her request in exchange for the pleasures she could grant him. 'Twas best to keep matters simple between them. He would keep his end of the bargain and that was all there was of import here.

Well it seemed that the light of morning had restored his reason.

He could not halt his quick visual check before donning his *chalwar*, grunting with skeptical satisfaction that all was as it should be. As though it could be any other way. Shrivel and fall away. Naught did the shaman know, that much was clear. Was he not a warrior trained to believe solely the evidence of his own eyes? Rationale alone would govern his thoughts. Thierry could not completely quell an unexpected surge of scorn that these Mongols should be so gullible.

But was he not part Mongol? And what precisely was the other part that of late had made him think himself separate from them? Thierry dressed hastily, as though running from his traitorous thoughts.

As he made to join the messenger outside, he found himself unable to subdue the urge to look back on his woman one last time. She would be safe here with Nogai and well he knew it. Not wanting to look like a complete fool, Thierry made a pretense of adjusting his scabbard as he surreptitiously slanted a glance in her direction.

She slept, as before, with all the innocence of a child.

He wished suddenly that she would not awaken before he returned.

Nonsense. Foolish whimsy. The khan was summoning him this morn and well he should know that this interview would require his full attention. Changes were afoot. Thierry snapped the buckle on his belt and strode out into the waning darkness. The men exchanged another terse nod and the messenger set a quick pace for the khan's yurt.

Chapter Eight

Abaqa was eating dates, or more accurately, was having dates fed to him by one of his wives. He smiled a predatory smile at Thierry's appearance and Thierry noted that 'twas his western wife draped by his side. From Constantinople had this one come, to forge an alliance, although Thierry had seen precious little evidence of such a truce.

Though truly, with the current state of affairs in the Byzantine Empire, it seemed there was little enough to be gained from a link with the Byzantine royals. Undoubtedly the woman was better out of her homeland. The men exchanged greetings politely, the guard stepped back and Thierry waited patiently. The khan chewed thoughtfully for a long moment.

"Had Berke not died in so timely a fashion, you might have had expectations," he said finally, emphasizing the last word in a most pronounced way.

Aye, Thierry conceded to himself, he had had expectations when he had ridden from the camp. The retreat of the Golden Horde had stolen away the promise of the fulfillment of his ambitions, but still he could hope 'twas but a temporary setback.

Even if the shaman's actions and Abaqa's words told him clearly otherwise.

"Mayhap," he agreed carefully. "'Tis of little import now."

"Mayhap not," the khan said enigmatically. He waved away his wife with an impatient gesture, fixing his gaze on Thierry. He smiled slowly, evidently realizing that he had captured the younger man's attention, and carefully folded his hands together before he spoke.

"As the commander I know you to be, you must realize that this battle was our last chance to expand to the north." Thierry nodded, unable to divine the path of this discussion. Such matters were well-known, even within the ranks.

"Constrained on every side are we now, even with the Golden Horde's retreat. No interest have I in their lands north of the plains that are clearly ours once more, for the land is useless for grazing. Clear enough 'tis, as well, that the lands north of Tiflis have already been raided so extensively that there is little enough remaining to take from them. The size and value of the tribute you collected from Tiflis can only be taken as a sign that 'tis time to find greener pastures." Abaqa spoke quietly, studying his fingernails with more interest than seemed appropriate. "The time has come that we must explore our final option."

Thierry's mind readily supplied dozens of equally drastic possibilities. He intuitively disliked that the khan was telling him about this, not at all comfortable that his destiny was apparently entwined with this option.

Not a good sign for his own fate could this be, for he was not usually among Abaqa's confidants.

"We must make an alliance with the Franks," Abaqa concluded, raising his dark eyes to meet Thierry's. Thierry knew his surprise showed, for he had not the chance to check it.

"The Franks?" he asked when it seemed he was expected to say something.

"Aye," Abaqa grunted, and frowned. "Palestine do they hold and many a time over the years have they contacted us about combining our forces against the Mamluk dogs. Now they have lost Jerusalem, a matter of much import to them, though 'tis truly a hopeless town to hold. A question of religion is it undoubtedly. Well do we know that their emis-

saries are oft filled with this unreasonable desire to see us
baptized." He plucked another date from the bowl his wife
had abandoned and plopped it into his mouth.

"In truth, 'tis why my sire refused to trouble himself with
them. Who indeed can imagine a man of such faith at
war?" He made a vague gesture, and truly, Thierry could
not imagine the Buddhist monks he was familiar with
wielding a sword. Not even the shaman in the camp picked
up a blade, though that man was filled with enough threats
and dire warnings to suffice.

"My wife, though, knows of these Franks," the khan
confided, leaning forward to prop one elbow on his knee.
"Ravaged Constantinople they did once in their religious
lust and left most of the city for dead." He met Thierry's
gaze and Thierry noted the spark in the man's eyes.

"Such information leaves me pondering this Frankish
alliance," Abaqa continued, nibbling the clinging bits of
date from his fingers with affected nonchalance. "I would
know what kind of men they are." His voice dropped
slightly and Thierry stiffened. "I would have a military man
provide me an assessment." That dark gaze swiveled back
to pin Thierry to the spot. "I would have *you* find out."

"What do you mean?" Thierry asked pointedly. 'Twas
evident what Abaqa meant but he wanted to hear the matter stated clearly.

"I would have you ride to this Paris of theirs as an emissary. My greetings will you carry and mayhap my encouragement of a treaty, depending on the evidence before
your own eyes."

Thierry swallowed carefully, knowing full well the impertinence of the question he would ask but having no
choice. He had to know.

"Why me?"

The khan smiled a predatory smile that told Thierry that
he was not expected to succeed. "Well it seems to me that I
recall hearing a tale that you speak the Frankish tongue,"
Abaqa commented idly. Though this was true, Thierry
suspected 'twas not the fullness of the tale. The shaman's

silhouette separated from the shadows behind the khan. The man's eyes gleamed and Thierry knew a moment of dread to have his suspicions so readily confirmed.

Was he being sent on a futile mission in the hope he might not return?

Truly it seemed that his fate was not to be markedly different from that of Chinkai. But at least Thierry had a chance of surviving. And survive he would, despite the conviction of these two men.

"Aye, I have spoken the Frankish tongue," he agreed carefully. "Though it has been many years."

"The road is long," Abaqa said offhandedly. "Much time will you have to practice." His eyes brightened and he leaned forward once more. "There *is* another reason," he confided in a low voice. Thierry's heart began to pound.

"Aye?"

"Aye. Show me your mark."

Thierry frowned in confusion, then reluctantly unfastened his *kalat*. Only too well did he know the suspicion the Mongols had of his birthmark, though he gave it little heed. Had his father not sported one much like it? And what had it to do with this mission? He bared the port-wine stain to view, surprised to hear a woman's gasp.

"'Tis the mark of the Christ," the khan's Byzantine wife declared breathlessly. The shaman's eyes glittered triumphantly and the khan's smile widened.

Thierry watched in stunned amazement as she darted forward to gingerly trace the outline of the mark with a quivering fingertip, though she did not touch his flesh. Her hand paused and hovered before him as her gaze flicked audaciously to his, then danced away, her head bowing as she dropped to her knees before him.

Thierry glanced up in surprise to meet the knowing smile of the khan. He felt the woman's lips brush across his boot.

"They will believe you," Abaqa growled with satisfaction, his gaze sweeping scornfully over his wife.

Thierry's head reeled but he took a step back from the kneeling woman and cleared his throat deliberately. "When shall I leave?" he asked hoarsely.

"This very day," the khan asserted curtly, snapping his fingers impatiently at his wife. "No need is there for you to ride all the way back to Tabriz with us. The way is shorter from here."

His wife stood hastily and scurried back to his side, her eyes downcast once she noted her spouse's dissatisfied frown. Gravely had she erred in dropping to her knees before any other but the khan himself. Thierry hoped he would not have to pay for her insolence.

"The message will be ready shortly." The khan tented his fingers together and smiled yet again as he met Thierry's gaze. "Mayhap that rebel Nogai would be well advised to accompany you," Abaqa added in a dangerously low tone. Thierry's heart clenched that his fall from grace should implicate his friend as well, but there was little he could do about the matter now.

"After all," Abaqa commented under his breath as he selected another plump date, his easy manner apparently restored, "I have no space in my camp for ambitious men." The men's gazes met and held once more. The glint in the khan's eye told Thierry that 'twas not Nogai's ambition that troubled him.

Indeed, he was being cast out of the camp, Nogai condemned to accompany him because of their long and openly acknowledged friendship. Thierry flicked a glance around the yurt and met the satisfied gleam in the shaman's eye once more.

The other man tapped his staff on the ground with satisfaction, the tails attached to the horse's head carved at its top dancing in the fitful light. No doubt had Thierry that his influence was responsible for this discussion. As their gazes held, the other man smiled slowly, his gaze dropping pointedly to Thierry's crotch.

"I would assume," Abaqa commented with feigned disinterest, "that I would have no reason to concern myself about witches in the camp on the morrow."

"Witches?" Thierry asked mildly, refusing to be goaded. He held the shaman's gaze until the man's smile faded before looking back to the khan.

"Aye, *witches*."

"Naught do I know of witches," Thierry commented, watching the khan's brows rise.

"You coupled with one before us all last night!" the shaman charged abruptly as he strode forward. All within the yurt looked up with interest, but Thierry maintained his calm.

"Claimed a woman, I did, in the usual manner," he declared softly.

The shaman's eyes gleamed and he shook his head. "Nay, she is a witch, for Nogai told me so and well do you know it, as well." The shaman leaned forward confidently and Abaqa watched him avidly. "'Twas her sorcery alone that gave her the strength to refuse my elixir," he whispered ominously.

Thierry saw the truth flicker in the old one's eyes and knew that his woman's refusal to surrender the pearl to the shaman had not been taken well. Yet again, he wondered how she had contrived to hide it, though it mattered naught now. His disagreement with the shaman had precipitated Abaqa's move and naught could change the matter.

All the same, he could not suppress a flicker of pride that she had bested the shaman.

Thierry shrugged with mock complacency. "Witches, shaman, holy men. Are you not all the same in truth?"

"Nay!" the shaman claimed wildly. "Evil are witches, for they twist the hearts and minds of men and destroy their form." Again that glance dropped and Thierry noted the khan's interest in the same part of his anatomy.

"Well it seems that you have erred in this prediction," Thierry stated quietly. "Indeed, the reverse seems true."

"He lies," the shaman whispered to the khan.

"Mayhap you would like to see for yourself," Thierry suggested silkily. Both men's eyes widened and the shaman's voice dropped to a hiss.

"Best he leaves the camp with his witch immediately, for no good can come of his presence. Have you not seen how the gods have turned against him? His golden luck is gone and with it, any need for us to shelter his kind."

"I shall be gone as soon as the message is prepared," Thierry interjected flatly. No interest had he in hearing any more of the man's nonsense.

Threatened the shaman was undoubtedly by the promise of another within the camp who might lay claim to his influential role. Women and men both could be shaman within the Mongol tribes, and Thierry was sorely tempted to make some brash claim of his woman's influence. The khan looked as though he would ask a question but Thierry spoke quickly first, knowing all the while the impertinence of the deed.

"My woman and *anda* will accompany me," he concluded, backing away before both men's relief.

Good 'twould be to put this life behind him, for thoroughly tired was he of the suspicions and superstitions that traveled with it. A relief 'twould be indeed not to be looking over his shoulder at every turn in anticipation of a betrayal. The matter was settled with Abaqa finally, and though Thierry hated to admit his ambitions thwarted, in a sense he was relieved. No more would he bow and scrape under the implied threat of his own demise.

A simple man he was again. A warrior, a mercenary, a blade for hire once the khan's message was delivered. No future had the Mongols in these parts, penned in as they were, and Thierry lifted his nose to the wind.

His mind filled with possibilities of adventure and fortune to be gained in other foreign lands just over the horizon. Had he not always had the certainty that he was destined for greatness? Mayhap his destiny was with others than the Mongols. So close he had come here to gaining ascendancy, only to have victory stolen away by foolish errors. It seemed the fates did not see success for him here. But still he had learned much these years and such experience would come readily to his hand when he had need of it again.

The land of the Franks beckoned. It could not be coincidence that sent him to the land where he had been born, the land that he had never known. A new spring was there in Thierry's step when he gained the outside and he thought he saw promise even in the rain. Always had he lived in the East and he wondered for the first time what had compelled his parents to leave their homeland so soon after his birth.

But no option had he of asking that question, with angry words and the width of Asia between himself and his father. And no need had he of an answer, in truth, for he was heading to his native land this very day.

Did Dame Fortune await him there?

Kira awoke to the drone of rain on the tent. She snuggled deeper into the warmth of the blanket, not knowing whether to be disappointed or relieved to find her warrior gone.

Had she dreamed that magical interval in the night or had he truly touched her? An exploring finger revealed the slick dampness between her thighs and she smelled her own scent heavy beneath the blankets. Kira's color rose and her certainty grew that the warrior would certainly think her no better than a whore for her shockingly loose behavior.

Indeed, she could scarce believe she had acted thus herself.

A woman groaned and a masculine voice raised in sleepy complaint. Kira closed her eyes again to feign sleep and rolled over to covertly seek out the source of the sound. The warrior's companion sat up with a scowl and scratched his bare skin, sparing a terse comment to one of the women who slept beside him. She argued briefly but he cocked his head uncompromisingly toward the tent flap. Kira slid farther under the protection of the blanket as the woman roused her companion with irritable resignation. The two of them, their kohl eyeliner smeared and hair bedraggled, made their way out of the tent.

Was this the way of whores in the camp? Kira hunkered down under the blanket and wondered what her warrior would expect when he returned. Would he similarly send her on her way? And where exactly did these women go?

The sound of breathing filled the tent again in the women's wake, the warrior's companion sprawling on his back and snoring with his mouth open as though he had not even awakened a moment past. Kira dared to peek around. She decided immediately that she liked the look of this one even less when he slept. Rougher he appeared than her warrior, more poorly groomed, dirtier and evidently of lower rank.

Well it seemed that she might have done worse the previous night. Kira shivered. But what had she gained? Would her warrior return to similarly oust her?

It seemed forever had come and gone in the time she lay there and fretted over her status, though indeed the tent had only become incrementally lighter when the warrior made his appearance once more. Kira's heart jumped at the decisive opening of the tent flap, no doubt in her mind who would stand framed against the morning's grayness should she dare to look.

But she could not. She squeezed her eyes shut and pretended to sleep as her heart pounded in her ears. Mayhap then, he would not have the heart to awaken her and cast her out, though well enough did Kira know that she was hoping thus in vain.

The tent was silent except for the other man's snores, the very air charged with expectancy. Well did Kira know that she was being watched again, but she resolutely kept her eyes closed.

If only she could slow her breathing or unclench her fingers beneath the blanket.

The warrior took a barely audible step and Kira heard whatever he carried drop to the ground. She tensed when she felt him stretch his length out alongside her, bracing herself for the worst.

Naught happened. Kira fancied she could feel his breath fan her skin, his breathing annoyingly more regular and slower of pace than her own. She panicked, knowing that she would do well to fool him at such close range, and desperately hoped that he merely intended to fall asleep once more like his brethren.

A sharp tap on the end of her nose made her jump. Kira's eyes flew open to confront the knowing expression in the disconcerting gray gaze so close to her own. Was that amusement that almost tugged at the corner of his lips? Indeed, it could not be and she stared back at him fearfully, uncertain what he intended to do now that he had discovered her ruse.

To her surprise he merely coaxed her to sit up before him. Kira shivered and clutched the blanket to her chest, not entirely convinced that his intentions were good ones. The way he moved to sit directly behind her fed her trepidation and she felt herself stiffen at his proximity.

Then his fingers were in her hair. Kira almost leaped skyward in alarm until she realized that he was finger-combing its length. She twisted slightly to look at him, only to earn a quick condemnation and a gentle finger beneath her chin urging her to face forward once more.

No desire had he that she witness whatever vile deed he had in mind, Kira thought bitterly. She jabbed her chin into the air stubbornly, certain she would see that he had not an easy way of whatever he intended to do.

There was no mistaking the rhythmic tug of having her hair braided, though Kira fought the evidence for a more rational explanation. He was grooming her? How could this be? It defied reason that he would do such a thing. She twisted around, not knowing what to do in the face of this unexpected development, and her gaze fell upon the burden he had dropped.

Clothing. Similar to his in style it looked, but smaller of cut.

Was she to have these clothes? And was this a sign of possession? Kira glanced over her shoulder uncertainly. The warrior had finished her braid and was tying the end with a short length of rawhide. He met her gaze, one end of the rawhide in his teeth, and raised his brows expressively.

Kira fought the urge to smile at his unexpectedly playful expression and quickly turned away from him. Her heart pounded erratically and she told herself not to be a fool. The man had no interest in her. Likely he knew she had no garments and would see her garbed before tossing her out.

The assertion did not ring as true as Kira thought it should have, for surely a man who cared naught for her would not worry whether she was soaked in this rain. But then, surely a man who cared naught for her would not have pleasured her in the night as he had.

Mayhap she merely knew too little about men who cared naught. Well did her father care for her, this she knew without doubt, and that alone should have told her that affection was a demanding burden. Mayhap a lack of regard was a less painful obligation.

Kira frowned, knowing herself to be more thoroughly confused than ever she had been. She closed her eyes and let the scent of the warrior's skin fill her nostrils, acknowledging that his very presence calmed her fears. Mayhap that was enough.

Mayhap that would have to be enough.

The warrior urged her to her feet with a hand beneath her elbow. He indicated with an imperious finger the deep blue *kurta*, *kalat* and *chalwar* he had brought, and Kira reached for the loose shirt. A solid finger on her shoulder brought her up short and she cursed herself for making the mistake of meeting his eyes. Too aware of him was she in the humid warmth of the tent with the beat of the rain filling her ears and the memory of his intoxicating touch heating her cheeks.

He pointed to the silk *kurta* she wore and said something, his gesture indicating that she should remove it. Kira's face flamed but he remained resolute.

'Twas his shirt, after all, she supposed. Kira dropped her gaze miserably, uncertain she could cavalierly disrobe before him this morning. His flat palm intruded on her peripheral vision, that signal of demand that he knew she understood. Kira nodded quickly. He would have his *kurta* but she would grant him no view of what was beneath. 'Twas irrational and well she knew it but still she could not do it.

She squared her shoulders to brace herself before meeting his gaze once more. With a swirl of one finger, she tried to show him that she wanted him to turn around. His features remained impassive and he showed no signs of moving. Kira sighed, gritting her teeth as she resolutely gripped his arm and tried to turn him. Well enough she knew that he had no interest in her form, but still her modesty compelled her to maintain some dignity.

At least she would not be forced to confront the disinterest in his eyes. She gave his elbow a resolute shove and, to her surprise, he complied.

No need had there been to be so readily complaisant, she thought irritably. At least the man could pretend to having some interest. Unreasonable she was being, and Kira was fully aware of her erratic mood, though this uncertainty over her fate did her temper few favors.

She desperately wished there was some way to know her status once and for all.

Kira spared a glance to the other occupant of the tent to ensure that he was sleeping, then hastily peeled off his silk *kurta*. Having no idea how much time the warrior would grant her to change, she quickly donned the garments he had brought. Kira frowned at the padding in the hips of the loose *chalwar* trousers, certain it would make her look hugely round. With a muttered sound of disgust she removed the pads and cast them aside, then hauled the fur-lined tunic over her head just as the warrior turned around.

He nodded with what might have been approval and pointed to a pair of boots Kira had not noticed before. She jammed her foot into one, lacing the open front up to the

knee similar to the way the warrior wore his. Kira picked up
the other boot, seeing out of the corner of her eye that he
had dropped to a crouch and was quickly rolling up the
blankets she had just abandoned.

He said something to his companion, who snorted in his
sleep but continued to snore more or less undisturbed. A
frown briefly darkened the warrior's brow as he put the
blankets aside, then he stepped over to shake the other man.

His companion sat up with alarm, his gaze focusing reluctantly on the tent around him. He blinked and frowned,
the pair exchanging a quick volley of comments as Kira
watched. The other man looked perplexed and made a demand, which the warrior answered with a single terse word.

He straightened abruptly, leaving his companion with a
moderately dazed expression. The warrior collected a pair
of leather saddlebags and matter-of-factly packed the
blankets away. He removed a pair of heavy cloaks, casting
the shorter one about Kira's shoulders before he donned the
other. His companion seemed to take that as a sign of some
kind, for he stood so quickly that Kira had no chance to
avoid a glimpse of his nudity.

She stared stubbornly at her freshly booted toe, not
knowing what was happening and uncertain she even
wanted to know. Then the warrior loomed in her peripheral vision and she glanced up to find him tossing one of the
saddlebags over his shoulder. He handed her the other one
and gestured her toward the tent flap, his companion hauling on his boots as he hastened to follow them out into the
rain.

The surrounding tents looked dejected in the gray morning light, their heavy felt sagging with the weight of the
rain. Misty 'twas and damp, and Kira shivered within the
warm embrace of her new clothes. She glanced back to find
her warrior hefting onto his shoulders a saddle that he had
left just inside the tent.

Her pulse leaped when his companion followed suit. She
needed little imagination to see that they were leaving the
camp. Her warrior's gaze met hers and Kira's heart gave an

unsteady lurch, the sensation leaving her unsure whether to be pleased or not that he had not so far cast her aside.

Would he take her with him, wherever he was going? Or would she be consigned to the ranks of the whores servicing the camp? Kira licked her lips carefully, trudging in the direction he indicated with trepidation weighing heavily on her heart.

The realization that the price for taking a witch was evidently quite low pleased Thierry more than he would have preferred. Touching her had reassured him yet again that the shaman had evidently misunderstood the inclination of her powers, if indeed she was a witch at all.

Simple 'twould have been to be able to blame this small woman for the khan's decision of this morn, but Thierry knew 'twas not the case. Only too aware was he that his becoming an outcast had been in the wind afore he knew she was in the camp.

Thierry's optimism about visiting his native land dismissed any such worries out of hand. A new future had he in the land of the Franks and Thierry was assailed by a sense that his would be a noble destiny there. In fact, he was feeling remarkably hale this morn, despite the khan's choice. His woman walked before him, her hips swaying temptingly, and he acknowledged himself to be feeling healthy, indeed.

But a few hours since they had coupled and already he was anxiously wondering how long 'twould take her to come to him. Truly he had denied himself too long.

The shaman was a fool.

He watched his woman's shapely buttocks and recalled the flutter of her heart beneath his hand. Something clenched within him at the memory and he vowed silently that she would come to him again. Had he not pleased her in the night?

Unless she had no recollection of his touch. Thierry searched his mind for some minute sign she had made this morn of her newfound awareness of him. Not a gesture, not a glance, not a flush could he recall that might signify that she, too, had needs. Indeed, she seemed yet more supremely unaware of him than before.

Could it be that witches truly had no need of men? Could this be the price of taking one? To be enchanted and have no hope of possessing her again? The very possibility of that being true made Thierry itch to make her taste her need once more.

But nay. He had vowed to himself that he would wait for her. Khanbaliq invaded his thinking yet again and for the first time, he felt a wave of ingratitude toward his sire.

Curse the man for teaching him to hold the sanctity of a vow above all else.

Chapter Nine

"Congratulations," the Persian woman purred into Kira's ear.

Kira turned away from the latrines, astonished to find anyone else awake in the silent camp. The Persian woman smiled knowingly. "Well did I tell you that you were too pretty for war fodder. And no doubt was there left that Black Wind chose you as his woman."

Kira felt her brows rise skeptically. "Indeed, the deed could scarcely be missed," she commented sourly as she adjusted her *chalwar*. The other woman gripped her arm, and Kira glanced up in surprise.

"Know you not what he did?"

"Aye." Kira winced in wry recollection. "I know well enough what he did."

The woman smothered a smile. "Nay, Kira, not that. You do understand that 'tis their way to stake a claim publicly?" she added in a lower tone. Kira felt her eyes widen.

"I do not understand," she said carefully, not daring to believe what the woman seemed intent on telling her. Surely 'twas not a custom to possess a woman before all the others?

The Persian woman nodded slowly as she saw comprehension dawn in Kira's eyes. "'Tis evident he wanted to leave no doubt that you are his," she hissed. "Possessiveness in a man is good sign, indeed."

Kira's heart leaped and she flicked a quick glance to the warrior standing at the far side of the latrine. He was facing toward the open fields behind as though completely unconcerned with her actions, but well enough she knew by now that he was fully aware of what she did and precisely where she stood.

In a way, such an awareness was strangely comforting. Had it been someone who threatened her this morn, instead of merely the chat of this woman, Kira knew that little could go amiss before her warrior was at hand.

She rather liked that. The other woman chuckled and patted Kira companionably on the shoulder, jarring her out of her thoughts.

"Aye, little Kira. Well do you know what I mean. Make no mistake, for Black Wind has claimed you for his woman."

Black Wind. Was that what "Thierry" meant? Kira turned to the other woman and looked right into her eyes. "How do the Mongols say 'Black Wind'?" she asked.

The woman looked surprised, then smiled confidentially. "Qaraq-Böke," she said, much to Kira's confusion. Naught at all did that sound like "Thierry." So harsh was the word in contrast to the name that the warrior had given her that Kira's heart began to pound.

Surely he could not have told her the name he would confide in no other here?

"No other way is there to say it?" she demanded breathlessly. The woman shook her head quickly, confusion lighting her eyes.

"Nay, Kira. 'Tis Qaraq-Böke he is called. Would you not say it to me first?" she asked helpfully. "Well you should know that but a slight inflection changes the meaning of a word in their tongue. I would not have you insult him when all seems to be progressing so well."

Kira smiled and glanced to her warrior as the surety of her conclusion flooded through her. "I will not insult him," she murmured with growing confidence. She gave the other woman an impulsive hug before she spun away, filled with an uncharacteristic optimism.

"I fear we are leaving and would wish you good luck," she said gaily. The other woman looked mildly surprised, but Kira waved and danced away. "Thank you!" she called before turning to her warrior triumphantly and granting him the same sunny smile.

For Kira had no doubt that her warrior had confided in her his real name. And that was more a sign that he had claimed her for his own than anything the Persian woman might have told her.

He turned to watch her approach, his sight landing unerringly on her as though he knew exactly where she was the entire time. Kira's pulse echoed in her ears and she stifled her jubilant smile as she fairly skipped across the grass to him.

He had told *her* his name after but a few days. And these people had known him years without learning his true name. Indeed, that could only be a good portent of things to come.

Something had changed in her assessment of him, though Thierry could not guess what 'twas. He puzzled over it as he saddled his horse in the misty rain, well aware of her complacency as she stood beside him. Calmer she seemed and he risked a covert glance in her direction to find her expression uncharacteristically patient.

Surely a woman would fuss over the foul weather? But nay, she merely stood and watched him work as though she would learn the task. Aye, he thought sourly, a woman afraid of horses well needed to know how to saddle a beast.

What game did she play with him now? Did she mean to steal a horse and escape him in the night? The idea that she might never come to him had unnerved Thierry more than he was certain it should have. Well he knew his current mood was the result. He spared her a glance and she met his gaze pertly.

Thierry spun back to his task, his fingers fumbling with the horse's trap. Indeed, the woman would make him skittish with her incessant changes of mood. Well it seemed that he could not foresee what she might do. 'Twas a new sensation and not one that Thierry was finding enjoyable.

Predictable had her response been when he had awakened her in the night, though he could not have expected her passion. And truly, had he troubled to reflect upon the matter, he might have anticipated the way she had recoiled after their mating.

But how or why had she ended up in Abaqa's camp again? Sent her directly to Tiflis he had and he wondered what had changed her path. There was a puzzle. And what had originally given her the audacity to openly defy him, a Mongol, in her father's shop?

Witch, he concluded readily, sparing her another covert glance. Naught did it help matters that the garb he had obtained for her accented her petite figure. Even without the padding in her *chalwar*, her hips were delightfully rounded and her waist small enough that he longed to fold his hands around her.

She smiled at him and Thierry's heart fairly stopped.

He felt the scowl darken his brow as he abruptly turned back to the horse's harness. Glad he was that she had not done *that* sooner, for the sight was fetching, indeed. Too readily did he recall her laughter when he had tickled her foot in the khan's yurt. That delicate foot with its high arch and tiny red callus. Thierry swallowed carefully and fastened the last strap on the harness.

Suddenly Thierry was markedly less certain of his ability to keep his vow.

He gestured to another of his horses and then to her, making a mock riding movement. Her eyes widened and she looked from the saddled horse to the unbridled one in momentary confusion. She pointed to him with one slim finger, her blank expression all the question Thierry needed.

He pointed to himself and laid one hand on the saddle. The horse stepped sideways, anxious to be on the run. His woman pointed to herself tentatively and Thierry pointed to his horse, then the other and shrugged.

"Tiflis?" she asked. Thierry shook his head firmly, surprised that she did not seem disappointed by the news. Had she not family in Tiflis?

"Paris," he informed her, but her expression changed not. Mayhap she had not heard tell of the Frankish city.

"Constantinople," he said flatly, hoping she knew the name of that city.

Her expression revealed that she was familiar with the town, the way she hastily laid one hand on his saddle beside his, showing at least an awareness of the distance. Aye, well he could imagine that she did not want to ride all that way alone with her uncertainty of horses, but he had had to offer the choice. For the sake of his vow, if naught else.

Thierry glanced down and was struck again by the difference in size between their hands lying so close together on the red leather saddle. He deliberately tore his glance away from her small hand and met her eyes.

"Constantinople?" she asked, pointing to him, then herself.

Any fear she had shown of him seemed to have dissipated rapidly, Thierry thought irritably, not in the least pleased that any sexual interest in him had seemed to depart along with it. Had he not ensured she was pleased? How long would she force him to endure the haunting scent of her skin?

How long could he endure her proximity without the barbarian within him bursting forth once more?

When Thierry forced himself to nod in response to her question, she pointed inquiringly to Nogai, then to all the horses, and he nodded once more. She chewed her lip for an instant, firing his desire to taste her anew. Evidently unaware of her impact on him, she patted the embroidered saddle once more and indicated herself.

"Constantinople," she said with a decisive nod.

So be it. Thierry nodded and swung up into his saddle.
He gave in to his impulse and gripped her around the waist
when he leaned down, savoring the fact that his hands virtually encompassed her as he lifted her into the high saddle behind him.

The cursed witch smiled at him again before he managed to turn away.

Had the other women told her something? Thierry knew
he called more hastily to Nogai than was his custom, the
proximity of his woman troubling him as they rode out of
the sleeping camp.

The ride did naught to improve his mood.

Their lack of a common tongue irked Thierry more than
it ever had and he found frustration chafing at him as they
rode west. Too tempting indeed was it to have her ride behind him, every step of the horse sending her breasts pressing against his back. Well it seemed to Thierry that he could
feel the imprint of her nipples, though 'twas impossible
through all the layers of clothes between them.

He refused to ride at a slower pace in deference to her
unfamiliarity in the saddle or the weather. A mission had
he from the khan and no woman would hinder his path.
The assertion sounded like an excuse even to Thierry's ears,
but he rode on determinedly, even as the rain soaked them
to the skin. This was his life, a mercenary's life, he thought
stubbornly. Well enough had she chosen to be with him—
now she would see the fullness of the path she had taken.

They stopped but once to let the horses drink from a
river. To Thierry's astonishment the woman complained
naught. She merely offered a slightly more tired version of
her smile when he climbed into the saddle again. Impossible that she was not uncomfortable. Indeed, his own wet
garments were chafing.

But nay. She simply brushed her wet hair out of her eyes
and slipped her arms cautiously around Thierry's neck
when he lifted her high. It helped his frustration not one
iota that she was apparently perfectly content with both her

choice and his denial of his own needs. The wave of possessiveness that shot through him had him placing her before him in the saddle before he dare to think. Nogai smothered a smile, but Thierry flatly refused to indulge his friend's humor.

They stopped finally when the moon was high overhead. The rain had slowed to a fitful drizzle and the woman stirred sleepily when Thierry dismounted. The gently rolling land extended as far as the eye could see in every direction and he frowned at the thought that they would have to stop in such an open place. At least the horses could readily graze.

Her eyes opened blearily and she met his gaze with less than her usual clarity of vision. Thierry folded his hands together and dropped his cheek to rest on one as he had once before. She smiled yet again, a softly seductive and sleepy smile that sent a startling pang directly through him. She slipped from the saddle like a woman in a dream, folding her arms about herself and shivering slightly as she glanced around.

"Mayhap we should kindle a fire," Thierry suggested.

Nogai laughed. "Oh, aye, well do I recall that always do we kindle one," he jested. Thierry felt his neck heat at the reminder that they seldom kindled a fire except on nights of dire cold. Which this one was not. Already was he more than fully aware himself that 'twas the woman's presence that had prompted his suggestion. Still, he did not appreciate Nogai reminding him of that fact.

Civilized 'twould be to warm themselves on such a damp night. Indeed, 'twas only sensible to ensure none of them sickened on the long path to Paris, lest the khan's message go undelivered.

"'Tis a cold enough night to merit one," he snapped, only too aware of her gaze upon him.

"Certainly," Nogai agreed with mocking deference. "I would not have you catch a chill at your sport this night." The shorter man turned to dig his tinderbox from his saddlebag, shooting a bright glance over his shoulder. "That is, unless the shaman spoke aright and you have naught with which to make your sport."

Thierry bit back a sharp retort, gritting his teeth as he resolutely unfastened his horse's saddle. Such a comment deserved no response. Nogai chuckled to himself and Thierry felt his ears burn, so certain was he that the woman looked between the two of them in confusion.

He lifted the saddle to the ground, dropping the saddlebags alongside. With a quick gesture he unfolded a blanket from one pack and cast it over the saddle, beckoning to the woman without meeting her eyes and patting its seat. She immediately did his bidding, a fact that pleased him more than he thought it should have. He folded the blanket around her with a brusque gesture, not waiting to see whether she smiled or not.

"Oho, surely the place of a woman has changed now that you have taken one," Nogai taunted. "Should she not be tending to our needs, instead of the other way around?" Thierry remained stubbornly silent while he removed the rest of the horse's harness, setting the beast free to run with its companions.

"She is tired," Thierry argued, knowing that Nogai would not leave the matter alone.

"And we are not?" the other man demanded archly. Despite his protest, he dropped to his knees and began to rummage in his tinderbox. "Should you spoil her now, no chance will you have of having her do your bidding later," Nogai advised. "Soon enough will you weary of her charms and wish she was doing all, as other women do." Thierry's lips thinned as he passed his friend a pair of fagots from his pack.

"'Tis not the way of my kin to leave the women do all," he muttered. Nogai looked to him in astonishment.

"Your kin?" he demanded with interest. "Naught have I ever heard you say of your kin afore."

"And now you have," Thierry retorted curtly.

What had prompted him to speak of personal matters with Nogai? Never had he even mentioned his family; indeed, none of the Mongols even knew his true name. The woman he had told already. Thierry slanted a wary glance in her direction, not in the least reassured by that realization. Why had he confided in her? He frowned and gestured pointedly to the unlit tinder.

"Are we to have a blaze this night or not?"

Nogai's brows rose, but he said naught else as he struck the flint. An awkward silence settled between the pair of them, a silence curiously unfamiliar for all the times they had sat together wordlessly on the plain.

Hot tea did they make to accompany the yogurt and flat bread they carried, though the meal was consumed wordlessly. The rain made the fire fizzle fitfully, and though Thierry knew his friend was curious, he could not speak of Khanbaliq and what he had left behind.

This woman was reminding him of matters best forgotten. Mayhap that was the root of her sorcery.

"Mayhap the fire was not such a good idea," he conceded finally when it fizzled to smoke yet again. Nogai's grin flashed opposite him before he sobered.

"The wood will do us for another night," he agreed quietly. Thierry smiled in turn, reassured that his reticence had not offended his friend. Nogai winked unexpectedly and jerked his head toward the woman. "Should you wish your sport this night, you had best be quick about it. She looks on the verge of sleep."

Thierry glanced to his woman in time to see her stifle a yawn, and barely checked an affectionate smile from spreading across his features. No sport would he have this night, nor indeed any other, he reminded himself firmly, without her express consent.

But no need was there for Nogai to know that. Thierry agreed and kicked out the fire, spreading his second blanket on the damp ground before coaxing the woman to lie down. She curled up immediately within the wool, looking very feline before she spared him an inquiring glance.

Thierry knew not how to tell her 'twas up to her whether he joined her or not, so he simply stood and held her gaze.

Finally she shivered with exaggerated tremors and reached out one hand to pat the expanse of blanket behind her. Thierry needed no second invitation, his anticipation firing as he dropped behind her. He thanked his lucky stars that he had not had to endure the waiting much longer, astonished when she did not unfurl her blanket to welcome him against her warmth.

To his surprise, his woman cuddled up against him and made a sound of satisfaction much like a contented purr before she closed her eyes. Thierry regarded her in amazement, knowing she could not be feigning the way her breathing slowed in sleep.

Nogai's smothered chuckle did little to ease his annoyance. Thierry hauled his cloak and the end of the blanket over himself in dissatisfaction, telling himself that 'twas his imagination alone that she smiled against his shoulder in her sleep.

The woman grew increasingly more comfortable in Thierry's presence as they drew ever nearer to Constantinople, though indeed she did not show any signs of planning to invite him between her thighs once more. Indeed, she cuddled against him on the third night as though his presence was no more threatening than that of an indulged family pet.

Tempted he was to not sleep with her at all, but he could not deny her his warmth. The nights were growing colder and she was small. When he felt her shiver, something nameless within him prompted him to ensure she did not fall ill.

A far cry indeed were these feelings from those he expected from the independent barbarian he knew he had become. Was it possible she was awakening all that was not Mongol within him? The return of such tender feelings did not sit well with Thierry, especially when the woman granted him naught with which to assuage his own needs.

For truly the shaman knew naught of what he spoke, the proof of that fact keeping Thierry from sleep. Except that mayhap this desire without release kept him snared within her web, be it a trap of sorcery or simply her soft femininity.

His vow irked him, but he would not break it now. Only the certainty that the woman rode with him because of her fear of the horses kept him from touching her again in the night. Clear 'twas that she had not the nerve to ride alone, should she be given a choice.

Mayhap for the sake of his vow he should give her a choice, Thierry concluded savagely. As though she sensed the direction of his thoughts, she wriggled closer and sighed with contentment. Thierry gritted his teeth at the invitingly ripe curve of her buttock pressed against his thigh.

Like some cursed lapdog did she treat him, not a Mongol warrior.

For a tempting moment he half considered doing something dramatic to show her the error of her ways, but the soft sound of her breathing brought him up short. Asleep she was already and he had not the heart to awaken her. Thierry folded his arms behind his head and stared into the fathomless indigo of the night sky.

Lapdog. He fairly snorted at the thought. Had she not been shocked when they had coupled before the others? Mayhap he should shock her again. Nogai was not much of an audience, but he would do. She was small enough that she would not be able to keep him from his goal, were he truly set upon it, he reasoned savagely.

She rolled over and the feather-light fall of her delicate fingers on his tunic brought all such thought to an abrupt halt.

Thierry stared at her relaxed fingers, unable to quell his satisfaction that she was showing signs of trusting him. And there was the matter of his vow. Not to mention his own desire to love her tenderly and gently when next they mated.

Even if it killed him, he must grant her the opportunity to come to him.

And well it might kill him if she persisted in smiling at him with such maddening sweetness, but going no further.

The muted sounds of the night reached his ears and Nogai began to snore with characteristic relish as they lay once again on the open plains. The woman burrowed into the warmth of Thierry's shoulder and he stared unseeingly up at the stars, wishing she might come to him soon.

Very soon.

The warrior was sleeping when Kira awoke. She remained nestled against him as she watched the sky tinge pink to greet their fourth morning of travel. Her buttocks ached from their ceaseless riding and she felt filthy beyond compare, but at least she was warm. And mercifully the rain had stopped. Kira was relieved that her clothes were finally drying and vowed she would never take such simple comforts for granted again.

How long until they reached Constantinople? Indeed, she had little idea how far the great city was, even from Tiflis, let alone what kind of pace they made. And why were they going there? What would happen when they arrived? No clue had Kira and she stifled anew her impatience. She wished she could remember what her warrior had said first, before he had said "Constantinople." Had it been the name of another town? Was Constantinople simply en route or was it in the vicinity of this other place? Had that been the name of a place at all?

Annoying 'twas beyond compare that Kira did not know and yet more so that she could not ask. She would simply have to wait and see.

The warrior's arm flexed, shifting the weight cast across her waist, and Kira watched him sleep. No less threatening did he look in peaceful repose, the line of his mouth as uncompromising as ever it was. She squinted and tried to imagine his lips curved in a smile, without success. At least he had claimed her for his woman and she had the certainty that she would not be cast before the advancing army as war fodder.

Though still it irked her that he obviously had no desire for her form. Why then had he claimed her? Impossible 'twas that he might have felt some responsibility for tearing her from her home, for he was a mercenary. That much was clear to even Kira's inexperienced eye. No feelings had this man, though truly she had expected that he might be more lustful.

It must be that her inadequacies did not tempt him.

What would happen if another crossed their path who did tempt him? Indeed, what fate did he plan for her, if not as his woman? Surely even a Mongol man took his pleasure with his woman more frequently than this? Kira knew not and wished that she knew more of men and their ways.

Or even that she was capable of asking him for the truth.

Could the Persian woman have been mistaken? Could he be taking her to Constantinople to meet some other, even less attractive fate? Kira considered the uncompromising lines of her warrior's sleeping visage and could not imagine that 'twas so. For all his stern manner, he had shown her a manner of kindness she had not known before and she would not condemn him out of hand.

Nor would she reflect upon her fate should one who did tempt him cross their path. Naught could she do if he chose to cast her aside, and she could not worry about troubles before they came. This was her life. For now, she would take life, such as it was, and be grateful for each day.

Indeed, she had little choice.

Kira rolled out of the warrior's grasp and listened, fancying she heard the sound of running water. How enticing 'twould be to have a bath and scrub this mire from her skin! And should she be quick about it, the men need never know.

She slipped carefully from the warm clutch of the blanket, holding her breath as she watched the warrior. He did not awaken, or else he feigned sleep so well that she could not discern the difference. He did not appear to notice her departure from his side, a fact that did little to bolster Kira's pride. The other one snored undisturbed.

Soundlessly, Kira unfastened the warrior's saddlebag, surprised to find its contents meticulously well organized. She found the soap and the length of cloth, sparing a covert glance over her shoulder before she hastily pursued the sound of running water.

Thierry knew something was amiss as soon as he awakened.

She was gone. At the realization that the woman was not beside him, his eyes flew open to scan the camp. Nogai snored comfortably but not a sign of her was there. His heart missed a beat.

Had another stolen her away? Or had she run from him?

Thierry was on his feet in a flash, the sight of his opened saddlebag bringing a frown to his brow. He squatted and checked the contents, surprised to find his soap missing.

Then he heard the running water. His mind put the pieces together and he breathed a shaky sigh of relief.

Bathing she was again. He shook his head tolerantly at the fancies of urban women and shoved to his feet. His gaze scanned the horizon as he listened and he picked out the change of vegetation at the edge of a rise. The river was there. Too readily did he recall the bronzed perfection of her skin, the realization that it had been long since he had gazed upon his woman following quickly in the memory's wake.

She would be bathing nude, he was certain of it. Thierry licked his lips and stared resolutely at the ground. No business had he watching her. Had he not made a vow? Had he not pledged to leave her be? How would he deny himself with her loveliness arrayed before him again?

Water splashed and he turned immediately at the sound. She might have slipped. Indeed, another could have come upon her at her leisure. Unable to check his steps, Thierry followed the sound of the water. After all, he told himself self-righteously, 'twas unsafe for her to bathe unescorted. Who knew what manner of bandits and vagabonds frequented these hills?

Though at the sight of his woman thigh-deep in the river and gloriously nude, all thought of anyone else was dismissed from Thierry's mind.

She was more beautiful than he recalled, her skin that even golden tone, every facet of her figure delicately wrought. His desire fired with an intensity that astounded him as she bathed, completely unaware of his presence. Thierry could not move from where he stood, everything within him captured by the sight of her.

She turned and he fairly heard her gasp when she saw him.

They both froze in place, eyeing each other warily. She vainly tried to cover her bare breasts with the small bar of soap and her tiny hands. Thierry could think of naught but covering them with his own hands, the thought thickening him in a denial of the shaman's dire prediction.

An instant later he was striding down the bank purposefully, abandoning his clothes as he splashed into the water. He noted with amazement that she held her ground, but even that observation did not slow his pace. The river swirled about her hips, its water icily green, its chill sending her nipples into pert peaks. Thierry knew he had never desired a woman more, but he finally stopped a pace away from her with uncertainty.

He did not want to frighten her again. And he had vowed to let her come to him.

Thierry looked into the dark glory of her eyes, the sight of her hesitancy renewing the hold of his vow over his desire. He held out his hand for the soap with matter-of-fact ease and she immediately surrendered it, as though glad to abandon its burden. Their fingers brushed accidentally in the transaction, sending a jolt through him. He glanced to her eyes again, surprised to find a scarlet flush burning her cheeks.

Thierry cocked one eyebrow inquiringly and his woman became truly agitated. Her color rose impossibly higher and she gestured hastily to his arousal, her gaze dancing nervously to meet his before she averted her face with a jerk.

Surely this could not be. Could his temptress doubt her
own charms? Thierry lifted her chin with one finger that
she would be compelled to meet his gaze. The way she
swallowed awkwardly beneath his touch fed the tenderness
flooding within him.

So, she did not understand the reason for his state. He
glanced down to himself, then looked to her, willing her to
understand that 'twas the sight of her that enflamed him.
She hastily shook her head and looked away nervously once
more.

Nay, sweet witch, Thierry thought affectionately. The
fault was indeed hers and he impulsively decided to make
the matter most clear. Well should she understand the
power she held over him. He tipped her chin once more and
held her gaze for a long moment, letting his fingertip slide
slowly down to her collarbone and trace its shape. Thierry
let his gaze follow his fingertip, knowing all his hunger for
her must be blazing in his eyes.

She shivered beneath his perusal, but did not move away.

His fingertip lovingly slipped over the full curve of her
breast, outlining the dark circle of one areola with what he
hoped was evident admiration. The nipple tightened, the
woman gasped and Thierry marveled anew at the softness
of her skin. Well could he lose himself in her softness and
warmth, the feel of her beneath one finger loosening his
resolution to keep his pledge.

His finger slid tantalizingly lower, tracing a lazy pattern
back and forth over the silhouette of each rib. Thierry leisurely encircled her navel with that feather-light touch,
pausing to tap that enchanting mole but once. His gaze fell
to the dark tangle of curls and he knew his stamina could
not bear the test.

Should he touch her there, he would be lost.

Thierry flattened his hand instead and caressed the silky
curve of her hips with his palm. He nearly closed his eyes
in pleasure as his fingertips rolled over the smooth indent
of her waist. He exhaled unsteadily, never having antici-

pated that such a slow and simple gesture could ignite him so fully, and dared to meet her eyes once more.

Disbelief shone in those dark depths and Thierry could not understand the sight. Could she truly doubt that she aroused him beyond compare? But one other way was there to make the matter most clear.

His fingers slid over her and abruptly speared into the hair held tight by her braid, his thumb tipping up her chin as he possessively kissed her. Thierry poured all of his passion into his kiss, willing her to understand her effect on him. Magnificent she was; indeed, he had never seen another who fired his desire so. He wished he knew the words to tell her so, hoped that his urgency would be communicated by his kiss.

Thierry's heart pounded when his woman tentatively placed her hands on his shoulders and leaned against him to taste him more fully. The casual brush of her nipples against his chest was enough to drive him to distraction, but he willed himself to keep a slow pace. He pulled her yet closer, cradling her head in his palms as he deepened his kiss. To his complete astonishment her tongue mimicked the gesture of his and nudged against his teeth.

The tentative flicking of her tongue made Thierry doubt he could control himself. He felt himself press against the softness of her stomach and heard himself groan aloud.

'Twas too much that she should kiss him thus when he had made such a vow. No more could he stand without the assurance that she would come to him fully. Indeed, he only fed his own madness by touching her thus. The embrace had to stop.

Determined to keep his word, Thierry tore his lips from hers and turned to stalk out of the water, blind to everything before him. Only the weight of her gaze upon him did he sense until he crested the small rise alongside the bank and scooped up his clothes.

He was back in the camp, agitatedly listening to Nogai's contented snores, before he realized he still held the soap.

Chapter Ten

Kira's fingertips rose to her lips in wonder as the warrior disappeared from sight.

'Twas not possible. She quivered inside with that same tension he had roused in her before. But the evidence he had given her was undeniable.

The man desired her. Her. Kira of Tiflis with her scarred back and ridiculously childlike body. With her breasts her father had called too small to nurse a babe. Had her sire not oft told her that she looked much like a poorly fed orphan? How often had she been reminded that he would be hard-pressed indeed to find her a spouse? Ingratitude it had been surely that had made her grow up in such an unattractive fashion to challenge her father's objectives.

But this man seemed to desire her. 'Twas too much to be believed. Kira straightened her posture with an unfamiliar measure of pride.

Mayhap she was simply the only female hereabouts. That thought eliminated her pleasure. Well enough had Kira heard that men needed a woman regularly to satisfy their desires. 'Twas evident that she alone was female of the three of them and that no other women had crossed their path these past days. She nibbled her lip thoughtfully, unable to suppress the argument that came immediately to mind.

No denial could she make of the heat burning in the warrior's eyes when he looked at her. Nor could she deny that he had claimed her in the camp, over all the other more amply endowed and more graceful women. Kira the warrior had chosen alone. Kira of Tiflis, over all the other women there. And clearly, he wanted her to know that that had not been an impulse regretted. The warrior still desired her. Kira allowed herself a brief flicker of pride and stifled a triumphant smile.

She was his woman, Black Wind's woman to the exclusion of all others.

Thierry's woman. Her pulse filled her ears at the heady reminder of his confidence.

Mayhap he had claimed her that she might have protection alone, she reasoned, still unable to accept what her heart told her was the truth. Mayhap he had thought himself responsible for her plight and aimed only to right the wrong.

Mayhap. But that argument's power was naught in the face of the incendiary kiss he had just granted her. Kira touched her lips wonderingly once more and permitted another thrill to trip along her veins. Indeed, she well enough understood what he was trying to tell her when he pressed against her.

Her warrior wanted to bed her again. Should she have had any doubt of that fact, the red flush rising on the back of his neck as he stalked away would remove all doubt.

But why had he left? Was it not the Mongol way to simply take what one wanted? Kira shook her head and rinsed her skin, reasoning that had the warrior wanted her, he might have taken her many times by now. She must have misunderstood him.

But he had simply pleasured her that last time he had touched her. She halted and considered that. No sense did it make that he could desire her and not take her again. Kira frowned and strode to the bank in his wake, absently picked up her clothes and began to dress.

Suddenly Kira recalled his manner with the wild horses on the plain and froze mid-gesture. She saw him again, standing silently and waiting for the skittish horses to approach him.

'Twas immediately clear to her. The warrior was waiting for Kira to make a sign that she wanted him. The conclusion was inescapable and Kira smiled in delight. No move would he make without her encouragement.

No barbarian way was that and her heart warmed at his consideration. Could he have understood her dismay after that first mating? Could he have shown her pleasure that she might understand 'twas not all pain?

Could he truly be waiting for her to indicate that she wanted him?

The very thought was both dizzying and intoxicating. Kira knew not what she would do. *Did* she want him? She scarcely knew, though when he touched her as he just had, she could think of naught but having more. She recalled the weight of his hands upon her skin and the fullness of him within her and shivered in anticipation.

Could she be so bold as to choose to mate with him again?

But how would she tell him what she wanted, if indeed another mating was what she wanted? Could she be audacious enough to show him without the fortifying strength of the *qumis?*

Clearly, touching his lips with her tongue was not enough, for she had done that moments past and he had left. Kira bit her lip, certain she had been bold beyond belief in making that gesture, but it had not sufficed. She knew not whether she could summon the nerve to do more; indeed, she was not certain she wanted more, but her heart was pounding when she climbed the rise and made her way back to camp.

Surely if he did desire her, mating with him again would better ensure that he not cast her aside. Kira frowned as she considered the wisdom of that and wondered if she was making all of this out of whole cloth. Could she have read more into his behavior than was warranted?

She crested the rise to find him watching a pot on the fire with a decidedly disgruntled air, and could not dismiss the thought that she had read him aright. A lightness buoyed Kira's heart and she acknowledged a sense of relief that he would leave her alone while she considered her options.

Consider them she would, for time aplenty had she to think while they rode. And should she decide that a coupling was what she truly desired, some way would Kira find to tell her warrior.

To tell Thierry, she corrected herself, and found herself smiling once again as she stepped toward the makeshift camp.

The setting sun turned the domes and spires of Constantinople to burnished gold, making the city look yet more exotic than even its reputation. Beyond the walls of the city the Bosphoros shone like indigo silk, reflecting the golden light of the setting sun. Lights gleamed from the windows of homes within the town, the bright pinpoints echoing the stars just becoming clear overhead.

Thierry sighed with satisfaction that they had made it this far before nightfall. They would reach the city gates with adequate time to enter the city before they were locked for the night. A hot bath, a hot meal, a firm straw pallet before the fire were all he wanted this night.

And the softness of his woman curled before him. She sat silently now, but he felt her awe and wondered if she found the size of the city as overwhelming as he did. Well would she appreciate the small luxuries to be found within the city walls and he found himself spurring his horse onward that they might find an inn yet sooner.

"Did I not know better, I would think you rode to the very gates of the city," Nogai commented. Thierry shot his companion a telling glance.

"What would be wrong with that?" he asked.

Nogai snorted. "Well you know that these town folk will not tolerate our camping right outside the gates," he scoffed. He lifted his nose to the wind and gestured off to their right. "A fine rise is there to shelter our camp from the wind this night."

"I make no camp this night," Thierry said calmly. Nogai's startled expression made Thierry writhe inside. Was it so unthinkable that he should desire some comfort this night?

"Surely you cannot mean to enter the city?" Nogai demanded skeptically.

Thierry could but nod. "Aye."

"And stay there?" Nogai dropped his voice to an incredulous whisper. Thierry nodded again. Nogai swore in eloquent disbelief and Thierry felt his lips thin in irritation.

No crime was it to not want to sleep on the cold ground again.

"'Tis the woman making you soft," Nogai accused unexpectedly. Thierry swiveled and glared at his friend.

"Well you know that she cannot tell me her desires," he retorted.

Nogai sniffed. "From Tiflis is she," he said with a sneer. "No soothsayer does it take to guess that she would prefer to stay at some foul inn in town."

"I intend to take no foul accommodations," Thierry argued, but Nogai simply laughed deprecatingly.

"*All* inns are foul, by their very nature," he scoffed. "Filled with vermin of all orders and ripe with the mingled scent of many men. Disgusting 'tis to sleep in such close proximity with others, without the bite of the wind in your nostrils and the sound of the waving grasses in your ears."

"Warmer 'tis there," Thierry interjected, having little interest in Nogai's ode to nomadic life. Often enough had he heard this particular piece of poetry to be warned of its charms.

"Warmer?" Nogai demanded archly. "Mayhap, but at what price? Filled with scent is the air, such that a man might fall dizzy in confusion. Meat and smoke and skin and incense and dozens of unnamed smells wrought from the decadence of living such entangled lives."

"No worse than a full yurt does an inn smell," Thierry argued.

Nogai raised one brow. "But amidst strangers," he hissed. "'Tis unthinkable to mingle thus with those who share no blood."

Thierry returned his friend's skeptical expression. "No kin are you and I," he felt obliged to point out, but Nogai simply smiled.

"To be *anda* is no small link," he argued. "Sword brothers we are sworn to be, and well you know that 'tis as strong a link betwixt us as blood."

"Then no trouble should you have sharing a room in an inn with me," Thierry countered reasonably.

Nogai recoiled in horror. "You cannot mean to sleep within the walls of the town?" he demanded again. Thierry nodded and Nogai's lips thinned as the argument grew more serious for him. "Why would you do this thing?" he asked scornfully. "Never have I known you to turn your back on the plain when there was a choice."

That assertion rang annoyingly true in Thierry's ears but he drew himself up taller. "A warm bath would I have this night and a hot meal in my belly."

Nogai's eyes narrowed. "Hot tea have we had almost every night," he observed in a low voice. "And the ground is soft enough to service a man's needs."

This last pricked Thierry's pride and his response sounded colder than he had intended. "What mean you by that?" he asked coldly.

Nogai snorted. "Methinks the woman makes another woman of you," he charged. The air was silent between the two of them for a long moment, then Thierry spurred his horse onward.

"Sleep on the plains like a dog if you will." He cast the comment over his shoulder. "I would sleep soundly this night."

Nogai muttered something deprecating under his breath before he spoke clearly enough for Thierry to hear. "And

how would you sleep soundly amidst whores and thieves?''
he challenged.

"Better than I would on the ground with the bite of winter in the air," Thierry retorted hotly. Nogai's horse galloped up beside him and Thierry glanced to that side to find
his friend's features distorted in scorn.

"Next will you be wanting a bath more than once a
year," he taunted. Thierry felt his eyes blaze in anger.

"Mayhap you should consider the same," he snapped.
Nogai drew himself up with affront.

"Thinking more like that of townsfolk than tribesman is
that," he declared savagely.

"And no less valid for all of that," Thierry retorted
coldly. Nogai's lip curled in a sneer.

"Well it seems that you are other than the man I have
ridden with all these years," Nogai accused. "Man and
Mongol both was he, but you show signs of becoming soft.
No doubt 'tis the result of cosseting a woman better left to
clear the paths for the army."

Something clenched within Thierry's gut at that and his
tone was harsher than any he had used with Nogai before.
"Mayhap 'tis but the greater part of my heritage asserting
itself," he concluded fiercely. "And well it seems time for
it to take precedence. Have I not become a barbarian in
putting it aside all these years?"

"You have become a Mongol," Nogai stated flatly.
Thierry shot him a cold glance.

"Aye. 'Tis exactly that of which I speak," he said quietly. "Sleep in the grass if you will. I would seek the warmth
of shelter from the elements this night."

"Expect me not to seek you out within the town," Nogai
called after him stubbornly, but Thierry did not grace him
with a reply. With the length of time that had passed since
Nogai had last bathed, Thierry was certain he could find his
anda by smell alone no matter how far afield he made his
camp.

Kira knew not what to think when the warrior's companion veered his horse away from them and galloped into

the low hills outside the city walls. His terse whistle had the other horses running in pursuit of him, leaving Kira and her warrior with naught but the horse they rode. Where was he going? Never did he look back, and though Kira understood the two men had exchanged angry words, she could not help but wonder what had come to pass.

And of what import was it that they had reached Constantinople? Why had they come here? What did the warrior intend to do now that they had?

More importantly, what did he intend to do with her? Too late, Kira regretted not granting him access between her thighs again, for it seemed she had not guarded her value to him well by making that choice. No reassurance did a covert glance to his set features grant her and she could not help but fret about her fate. Too easy would it be for him to abandon her here. She fidgeted restlessly before him as they passed under the shadow of the city gates.

It seemed the warrior knew his destination well and that fact did naught to reassure Kira. Did he mean to be rid of her immediately? Did he make for the slave market that she might at least bring him some ready coin? One so small as she would not fetch much of a price, Kira warranted sourly, the very thought perversely pleasing her. Should he so heartlessly cast her aside, 'twould suit her well that he saw little gain from the transaction.

But instead, he rode his horse into the courtyard of what looked to be a domicile. Darkness had fallen and the light of lanterns gleamed through the arched windows, casting shadows into the whitewashed yard.

A young boy came and gripped the horse's reins, offering greetings in a rapid sequence of languages until the warrior responded. Kira fancied she heard Persian trip from the boy's tongue, but before she could be sure, he had moved on.

The exchange was made in the warrior's tongue until the boy abruptly shouted a summons into the building. A portly man filled the doorway a moment later, his manner businesslike as he evidently negotiated with the warrior.

No imagination did Kira need to guess what was being negotiated. 'Twas insulting to be treated thus, though she supposed she had been a fool to expect more. And the loss of her innocence had undoubtedly only dropped her value.

If indeed the warrior had seen fit to confide that fact.

No trouble had Kira summoning an image of the retaliation that would be sure to bring from this portly man, or mayhap his customer, on the morrow. Her back had barely healed, but she had little doubt 'twould soon be bleeding once again. And all to fatten the purse of a barbarian.

A barbarian she had been fool enough to almost trust. Kira gritted her teeth defiantly and pulled forward, leaving some distance between herself and the warrior. What had her lack of resistance netted her? Naught but speedy delivery to the house where she would undoubtedly be doomed to slave the rest of her days, in one manner or another.

Curse this Mongol.

A bargain of some kind was struck hastily, leaving Kira surprised that the heavy man had not seen fit to examine her before his purchase. Mayhap he desired her only for domestic tasks. Indeed, though that was a relief, Kira knew she should have expected naught else. Had her father not made her lack of charm evident? And 'twas clear now that this warrior had but toyed with her when he had implied otherwise.

Mayhap she deserved to slave in this man's kitchens for her foolish hopes. But no doubt had Kira that she had just been sold, no less that there was naught she could do about it. Her face flamed as she dismounted before the warrior.

She would not look to the barbarian who had committed this indignity. She would not grant him the satisfaction of seeing her disappointment. Why had she been so foolhardy as to not fight a man like this?

To Kira's astonishment the warrior dismounted and cupped her elbow in his hand. He guided her into the house, the portly man stepping back from the doorway and granting them a paternal smile. Kira's certainty faltered briefly before her conviction redoubled.

He was but seeing her to her quarters. No doubt he expected she would grant him some sweet leave-taking, but Kira had a surprise for this Mongol. He might well have sold her, there might well be naught she could do about that, but she would not fall prey to his rough charm yet again.

They climbed the wooden stairs to the second floor and Kira's confidence uneasily slipped yet another notch. No servant or slave slept upstairs, at least not in Tiflis. She shot a wary glance to her companion, only to find him thoughtfully watching his step. The older man bustled up the stairs behind them, his incomprehensible chatter flowing over Kira as the warrior did not respond. His grip remained warm on her elbow and she wondered if she might have misinterpreted.

But nay. Why else could they be here? He meant to leave her and ride back to his friend. There could be no other reason.

The warrior ducked into a room on the right with a frown tugging at his brows, his gaze assessing as he glanced over the room's contents. The other man trotted around them and struck a flint to light a lamp. The flame cavorted wildly for a moment, sending golden light dancing around the room.

'Twas a fine room and Kira could not help but notice that fact. Larger 'twas than any she had ever known. A wide window there was overlooking a quiet courtyard and surprisingly sweet night air wafted through the opening. Though the pillows stacked in one corner were showing their age and worn in spots, Kira thought them the most lavish she had ever seen. The floor was tiled and swept clean, naught else but a table and that lamp in the room.

Surely these fine quarters could not be for her.

The warrior nodded and the two men exchanged a few terse sentences. This was it, Kira thought. This is where he means to leave me. Her heart plummeted and she could not honestly tell herself 'twas because of the state of the home to which she had been sold. Indeed, the portly man looked quite kindly.

'Twas the thought of the warrior leaving her alone that troubled Kira, and the realization of that fact troubled her yet more. She had grown used to him, against all odds, and well she knew she would miss the weight of that silent perusal upon her.

Indeed, were she being truly honest with herself, she knew she would miss more than that.

Kira covertly glanced through her lashes to the warrior, just in time to see him dig in his tunic and hand the other man several coins. Her eyes flew open in shock, yet the older man smiled as though naught was amiss. He tucked the coins into his own pocket, waved cheerfully and trotted to the door to disappear.

Kira was dumbfounded. What had transpired? She could not have been sold, for the warrior had paid. Could this be an inn? Had he purchased accommodation that he might abandon her here? Kira spun to confront him, only to find his assessing gaze upon her once more. 'Twas as though he waited for her response and for the first time, his thoughtful manner thoroughly irked her.

"What do you do here?" she demanded angrily, knowing full well that he had no understanding of what she said but needing to voice her frustration. "Why have you brought me here? Who is that man? What manner of establishment is this? And what is going to happen?"

The warrior regarded her for a long moment, then closed his eyes and rested his cheek on his palm in a gesture she recognized well enough.

Sleep.

"But *who* is sleeping here?" she asked tersely, pointing to him and to herself rapidly. She threw up her hands in confusion and a frown flickered across his brow. He indicated Kira, the pillows in the corner and repeated the gesture. Kira frowned in turn.

"And what about you?" she asked. "Do you truly intend to leave me here alone?" He returned her questioning glance blankly and Kira sighed heavily. She pointed to him, mimicked his sleep signal and waved broadly to the world at large.

The warrior pointed resolutely at the same pile of cushions and Kira's breath caught in her chest at the heat in his eyes.

He meant to share her bed here.

"And the other one?" she asked breathlessly. "Where is he to sleep this night? Watching will he be like the others were before?" The warrior propped his hands on his hips and Kira knew he had not understood her question. She made a riding motion, then pulled back the corners of her eyes with her index fingers in a mimicry of the other warrior's features.

She thought for an instant that her warrior almost smiled but the impression was gone before it began.

"Nogai," he said flatly and she assumed 'twas the other one's name.

"Nogai," Kira repeated, adding the sleep gesture and shrugging. The warrior pointed out the window. Kira fancied he indicated the hills beyond the city walls. He added a terse explanation but she knew not what it said. Indeed, it mattered little, for well enough did she understand the situation.

Well enough, indeed, for it seemed she could not keep the heat from her cheeks. She could not bear to ask him the question that filled her mind, and looked down to the tile floor in confusion. Did he mean that they should couple here this night? Had she but imagined that he had granted the choice to her?

The warrior rummaged in his pocket, his movement drawing Kira's reluctant eye. To her surprise he produced a pearl. He rolled the gem between his thumb and forefinger as he caught her gaze. They stared at each other for a long charged moment, and when he finally beckoned, Kira could not have refused him to save her life.

The room was warmer than she had noted on entering it, the sounds carrying from the rest of the house muted to her

ears as though they were a world away. Indeed, it seemed
once again that there was naught but the two of them in the
whole of the civilized world. The warrior's eyes gleamed as
Kira slowly closed the distance between them, leaving her
feeling as helpless as a fish on a lure drawn ever closer.

She paused directly before him and he held the pearl up
between them without breaking their regard. He rubbed the
thumb and forefinger of his other hand together and Kira
immediately understood his question.

He desired a value for the pearl. She glanced to the gem
for the first time and was startled by its familiarity. Surely
this was the gem she had swallowed.

Kira glanced back to the warrior only to find an unmistakable twinkle in his gray eyes. He made an exaggerated
swallowing gesture, then pointed to her. Evidently intent on
ensuring she did not doubt that 'twas the same pearl, he
flattened his palm between them as he had repeatedly asked
for the gem and dropped the pearl into his own palm with
a dramatic flourish.

'Twas the same pearl.

Kira reached for the gem to value it, grimacing when she
realized where it had been and how she had to assess it first.
She tapped her own lips and winced anew as she indicated
the pearl. Kira could have sworn the warrior's lips twisted
with mirth, but before she could be sure, he had bent over
his saddlebags.

A tin cup was pressed into her hand as he pulled the cork
from a wineskin with his teeth. Kira recognized the smell of
the *qumis* as soon as it was opened and shrank back, certain she need never taste that substance again. Despite her
reservations, the warrior poured a little into the cup and
dropped the pearl into the alcohol. He lifted the cup from
Kira's hand, swished the gem around, then tipped the cup
toward her.

The pearl glistened from its repose and Kira knew 'twas
as clean as it was like to be. She plucked it out of the liquid
and slipped it onto her tongue. She closed her eyes and let

the flavor of the *qumis* slide away as she concentrated on the cleaned gem.

'Twas sweet, was all she had time to think before the warrior's roughened hand closed around her neck. Kira's eyes flew open and her gaze leaped to his, only to find that twinkle dancing merrily in his eyes. He tightened his grip ever so slightly in mock menace and cocked a warning brow.

'Twas a joke.

Indeed, it had to be, though never had the man made a joke before. Kira caught his eye once more, the telltale crinkling at the corners of his eyes confirming her thoughts. She giggled unexpectedly at this insight into his personality and he wiggled his brows with vigor. Kira was completely unable to check her laughter when his eyes widened dramatically and his grip tightened with mock threat. She laughed aloud and the pearl danced from her lips.

The warrior made some charge over his shoulder as he ducked in pursuit of the gem. Kira shook one finger at him admonishingly, unable to completely quell her smile.

"'Twas your own fault for teasing me so,'' she accused him laughingly. The corners of his mouth tweaked and he shot her a telling glance as he straightened. Then he sobered with feigned tolerance, sending a mock scowl of disapproval in her direction as he dropped the gem into the *qumis* and swirled it around once more. He shook his head, as though severely plagued by the whimsies of women. Kira swatted him before she thought twice.

But a glimmer of the purposefulness in those silver eyes had she before he dropped the tin cup and reached for her. Kira squealed and ran, making it no more than halfway across the room before she was abruptly scooped off her feet. She laughed again as the warrior easily spun her around into his arms, her laughter fading only when she was looking up into his gleaming eyes.

Kira fell abruptly silent. The warrior's tentative smile fled. His fingers fanned out as he held her closer, his gaze running over her features as though he would memorize

every detail. Kira caught her breath at the admiration she
saw there, knowing that it could not be feigned, but unable to doubt the evidence of her eyes. The warrior leaned
toward her, then hesitated, his silver gaze rising questioningly to hers.

Unable to check her impulse, Kira reached up to twine
her arms around his neck. 'Twas all the encouragement he
needed and she was folded against his strength before she
knew what she was about. His lips were gentle upon hers,
firm yet cautious, as though he feared she would rebuff his
advance. Kira opened her mouth and leaned against him.
She could not have denied his tender assault for any price.

Impossible 'twas that he found her desirable, but time
and again he had shown her exactly that. And no doubt had
Kira that she desired him. She recalled the weight of him
within her and fairly writhed at the memory. Would he
come to her again? Did he truly wait only for her invitation or did he intend to join her this very night? Kira was
shocked to realize that she could imagine naught but being
with him again.

The warrior lifted his head and gazed down at her
warmly for a long moment before setting her gently on her
feet. He took her hand and tugged her to the table, pluck-
ing the pearl from the cup and handing it to her once more.

Business first, Kira thought savagely. Indeed, she could
not help but wonder if she was reading too much into his
actions when he acted with such single-mindedness. But
still, she obediently fingered the pearl, peering at its surface and leaning closer to the lamp to assess its color.

'Twas a fine gem, of that she had little doubt. But how
would she tell him its value? Only Persian currency did she
know well. Kira's brow puckered. She was not certain even
what coin they used here in Constantinople, let alone what
currency her warrior might be familiar with trading.

As though sensing her conundrum, the warrior pulled a
mélange of coins from his pocket and spilled them upon the
table. A small assortment 'twas, though they were mostly
unfamiliar to Kira. A pair of gold coins there were that she

knew to be bezants, though she knew not their relative value. A trio of silver coins with strange symbols upon them had square holes cut in the center. There were also several thin and bright silver pennies with notched edges that she had seen afore, but knew not the value. Kira's heart sank in defeat just before she spotted the silver dinar.

Good Persian currency, as her father would have said. Kira plucked the coin triumphantly from the jumble and laid it beside the pearl. She held up three fingers and tapped the coin, pointing to the pearl.

Three dinars. 'Twas a good gem. The warrior cocked a skeptical brow and Kira nodded vigorously. How could she tell him how good 'twas?

"'Tis from Oman," she said, waving the pearl beneath his nose and not knowing how much he comprehended. "The best pearls come from Oman. *Oman,*" she repeated deliberately. "And 'tis large—" she made a spreading motion with her hands "—and smooth. Not a blemish is there upon it." Kira turned the pearl under the light so that he might note the perfection of its luster. "And its color is almost white, which is most valuable."

Kira glanced around the room for something with which to indicate color. She shrugged and pointed to the oil in the bottom of the lamp, shaking her head disparagingly at its yellow tone, then pointed to the whitewashed wall and nodded with approval. She held the gem against the wall comparatively and nodded yet more. When she looked back, the warrior nodded in turn and Kira felt a thrill of victory surge through her veins. Had he truly understood her?

He crossed the room to her with long strides and her heart began to pound at his intent. But he merely lifted the pearl from her fingertips and turned to leave the room.

Did he mean to abandon her here? After their embrace, the thought was even more abhorrent than it had been before. She could not let him walk away from her! Kira panicked at the very idea and flew after him to clutch his sleeve. The warrior turned to look down at her with surprise.

"Surely you cannot mean to leave me here," she argued. Kira heard her words fall in a breathless rush but was powerless to halt their flow. "No one do I know in this city and indeed not a coin have I with which to feed myself or—"

The warmth of the warrior's finger fell against Kira's lips and she fell immediately silent. Her gaze rose tentatively to his, the warmth she found in his regard unnerving her, yet setting her heart to racing once again.

He held his fingers and thumb together, lifting his hand to his mouth as though he ate something, and met Kira's gaze questioningly. She exhaled shakily and granted him a smile.

Aye, she was hungry and she nodded quick agreement. The warrior nodded, pointing to himself, then outside the room. He pointed to Kira in turn, very firmly indicating the room.

She was to wait? But what if he didn't come back? Some of her fear must have shown in her eyes for the warrior resolutely gripped her chin. He pointed to himself, then made a walking motion with his fingers, walking those fingers back into the room. He indicated Kira, then himself, then made the eating gesture again before meeting her gaze inquiringly.

He was going to fetch some food. And what would follow? Kira licked her lips nervously and flicked a finger at the pile of cushions. She pointed to him, then herself, then to the cushions. He nodded, dropping his cheek to his palm.

'Twas not what she was asking. Kira swallowed before she slipped her finger into her fist, pumping it as she had once before. Despite the heat burning in her cheeks at her audacity, she managed to look up to the warrior's eyes.

He shrugged. Kira blinked but once before the weight of his finger landed unerringly on her chest. He tapped her there solemnly, the somber warmth in his eyes fit to drown in before he turned and walked to the door.

It took Kira a long moment to understand, but when she did, she could scarce believe it.

The warrior was granting her the choice.

Kira's heart began to pound and she nearly gasped aloud at his generosity. She had not misread him. Indeed, it seemed she had judged him too harshly. Her stomach skipped unsteadily at the realization that he was a more honorable man than she had yet known or dared to believe.

Kira could not let him simply walk away! She flew in pursuit of the warrior, finding him half-shrouded by the shadows cast across the stairs by the time she breathlessly gained the doorway.

Chapter Eleven

"Thierry!" she cried without thinking. The warrior halted abruptly and she imagined 'twas surprise that flickered across his features as he turned silently to face her. Kira tapped herself on the chest, unable to contain the happiness bubbling up within her.

"Kira," she informed him. "My name is Kira." He inclined his head slightly so that she could not see his expression in the shadows, then his eyes shone as he looked back to her.

"Kira," he repeated softly, a slight question in his tone, the way he rolled the *r* making her name sound strangely exotic. Kira nodded mutely and he shook his head as though amazed. "Kira," he mused, almost to himself. Kira could not help but wonder what he was thinking.

Then he glanced up abruptly, his bright gaze pinning her to the spot. "Kira," he repeated, and quirked one brow as he held up his right hand. "Thierry," he added with deliberation. He twined his index and second finger together, then gave them a resolute shake. "Kira. Thierry," he said resolutely.

Wonder of wonders, as Kira held his gaze in her surprise, for the first time she saw her warrior openly smile.

She gasped at the way the expression softened his features, then ran toward him, unspeakably encouraged by his response to learning her name. He scooped her up triumphantly, his grin widening as Kira laughed with delight and clasped her arms around his neck. Then his lips were on hers, his hands urging her closer, and she gave herself fully to his embrace for the first time. She was his woman. Not a doubt was there lingering in her mind and Kira intended this night to see that Thierry had none, either.

He groaned when she let her tongue meander into his mouth. Something primitive and feminine thrilled within Kira that she could garner such a response from him. Without breaking their embrace, he swung her up into his arms so that he clasped her knees against his chest and strode purposefully back into their room.

Indeed, Kira reasoned, she was not that hungry. Thierry kicked the door shut behind them and Kira closed her eyes when his lips traced a burning path down her throat. She ached with the need to feel him within her. The cushions pressed against her back before she knew they had crossed the room, and Kira savored Thierry's weight atop her. Her man. He unfastened the front of her *kalat* and Kira was surprised to find his fingers shaking.

Nervous he was! Her heart swelled with tenderness at the sign. Surely he could not doubt her response? Kira lifted his hands and pressed a kiss into each palm, stretching up to kiss either corner of his mouth before touching her lips to his. Thierry shivered and Kira could not believe the evidence of her own senses.

This magnificent man desired her but still he granted her a choice. An unbearable sweetness flooded Kira and she could think of naught but laying his own fears to rest.

Kira knelt before Thierry and purposefully set to unfastening his garments. Thierry made to assist, but she pushed his hands away, waving a resolute finger under his nose. The corner of his mouth quirked but he did her bidding, kneeling silently before her as she worked. 'Twas a heady power to have one so much larger than she at her command and the knowledge made Kira bold. She was well aware of the warmth of his gaze resting upon her and let her own admiration show when she had bared his chest to her view.

She leaned forward and carefully licked one of his nipples. Thierry caught his breath but no intent had Kira to grant him any quarter. She laved the nipple and ran her teeth across it until it tightened defiantly, then turned her attention on its mate.

When they both met with her satisfaction, Thierry's breathing was ragged and his eyes glittered. But still he kept his hands at his sides, and Kira savored the unfamiliar sense of power flooding through her.

For whatever reason, he was granting her control of their loving. And Kira aimed to see that Thierry did not regret it. This night would he know fully how much she desired him.

This night she would seduce him anew, knowing fully what she did.

Kira climbed to her feet beneath his gaze and slowly began to peel off her garments. Thierry appeared transfixed. The admiration she saw in his eyes made her audacious and Kira cast her garments aside with abandon, leaning temptingly close to him as she bared her shoulders. Thierry swallowed carefully when her *kalat* and *kurta* were discarded, his gaze fixed on her bare breasts. Impulsively, Kira teased them to peaks that matched his own beneath his sharp regard. He clenched his hands and deliberately unclenched them but did not make a move toward her.

Kira smiled and shed the rest of her garments, feeling more desirable than ever she had imagined she would. She unfastened the tie in her hair and shook out her plait, letting her hair cascade over her shoulders. Thierry's nostrils flared as Kira pulled his *kurta* and *kalat* over his head, but still he did naught. And when Kira pushed him in the chest with one finger, he obediently rolled back to sit against the wall.

She knelt before him and unfastened his boots, feeling incredibly forward when she tugged his *chalwar* from his hips. The sight of Thierry's arousal did naught to reassure her that she was not being too bold and her gaze flew uncertainly to his. Thierry smiled and cocked one brow eloquently, signifying that he intended to wait for her lead.

Kira felt her breathing quicken when she reached for his braid. He leaned away from the wall and Kira knelt by his hip, tantalized by his proximity. His hair was thick and silky. Well aware was she that his hand rested directly beside her knee, that her breast fairly brushed his arm. She could smell his skin and the scent taunted her with the promise of what was to come. Her fingers fumbled momentarily but she recovered herself enough to unplait his hair and spread it over his shoulders.

'Twas lighter than she had expected, more chestnut than black in shade, its texture more wavy than straight. Kira brushed its thickness back from his temple and leaned forward to press her lips there.

She could not stop once she had touched him, for the taste of his skin was as intoxicating to her as the most potent *qumis*. She traced little kisses all around his ear and along the line of his jaw. His scent and the heat rising from his skin drove her to distraction and she dared to rest her fingertips on his shoulders. From there they seemed to move of their own volition to trace mirrored paths across his shoulders and chest. Kira caught her breath at the feel of him.

"Thierry," she whispered shakily behind his ear. He shuddered from head to toe at the flurry of her breath there and suddenly his restraint finally broke.

"Kira," he growled as he twisted, but Kira was aware of naught but his hands upon her.

He rolled her summarily to her back and she could not cease touching the smooth warmth of his skin. Kira arched against his weight and tangled her fingers in his hair. She loved his strength, his heat, the unexpected gentleness of his touch. Thierry's mouth closed around her breast demandingly and she cried out at the sweetness of his suckling. She writhed against him and he ducked to assault the other breast, his hands cupping her ribs as he teased her nipples to peaks that rivaled the state of his own. The tension rose within her again and she wanted naught else than to touch and taste him everywhere.

His tongue was in her navel, his hands bracketing her pelvis, then Kira gasped aloud as he moved yet lower. His palms slid over her thighs in an endless caress as his tongue dove between her legs, and Kira found herself shamelessly arching to meet his touch. Only too well did she recall the pleasure he had granted her from that tender point. Indeed, the memory had haunted her and this night she knew she would taste it fully again.

Though she squirmed against him, Thierry granted her no respite from his devilish tongue. Kira's heart leaped in anticipation when she felt again that quickening beneath her skin. Her nails bit into his shoulders and she strained against him in pursuit of that elusive pleasure.

Certain she was that her cry would be heard all the way to Tiflis when it came, but powerless was she against the hot wave that coursed through her veins. She stretched high as she cried out, her hips bucking in an ageless dance that she could not contain. Kira reached fully the crescendo she had but tasted before and fell shivering from the heights to land securely in Thierry's arms.

Had she not been so exhausted, she might have been mortified at her wanton behavior. But then she saw Thierry's slow smile of satisfaction as he loomed possessively over her and she breathed in shaky relief. Kira reached up to touch the side of his face, loving how different 'twas in texture from her own and marveling that this man was hers. She ran her fingers lightly across his shoulders and nuzzled against his chest as he leaned over her.

His feather-light kisses dotted her eyelids, her brow, her earlobe, the underside of her jaw, and Kira fairly purred with pleasure at the attention he was lavishing upon her. Indeed, she nearly felt fit enough to scale those heights again and she opened her eyes to find his gaze sparkling bright in the half-light.

Unable to deny him the pleasure he had granted her, Kira reached up to touch her lips to his. Thierry's hand enfolded the back of her neck, the other cupping her breast. When his thumb dragged leisurely across her taut nipple,

Kira knew she had to sample him fully this night. She squirmed beneath him and when he lifted his weight, she purposefully locked her legs around his waist.

Thierry caught his breath, but Kira held his gaze in silent challenge. She smiled slowly and let her fingertip trail provocatively across his lips. He opened his mouth and she continued her caress across his teeth. Thierry bit gently on her inquisitive finger and Kira lifted her hips demandingly against him. His eyes widened at her impulsive mood and she had but an instant to smile before he slipped within her.

Thierry moved slowly, as though he feared to frighten her. Kira willed herself not to be afraid of this natural union. Gentle he was, the concern in his eyes now showing her that she had not been mistaken to trust him. When he rested fully within her, he paused and Kira moved slightly to accustom herself to him. Thierry blanched as he closed his eyes and Kira could not believe the extent of his weakness for her.

She rolled her hips experimentally in a parody of the dance she had learned and watched him grit his teeth. Kira nearly laughed aloud at the possibility that she might be able to please him as he had pleasured her. She arched back and deliberately stretched her arms above her head, dancing as well as she could stretched on her back beneath him.

Thierry's eyes flew open, his eyes blazing with desire. Kira merely granted him a cocky smile and continued her "dance." He reared up onto his knees abruptly and carried her with him, both of his hands clasping around her waist to hold her upright before him. Kira dropped her toes to the ground and stretched high to dance, loving the strength of his grip and the flame smoldering in his eyes.

Thierry tipped back his head and roared as he began to lift her up and down. The very movement made Kira almost forget to dance, for he rubbed himself against her so that that secret spot was reawakened. She met his gaze and saw the awareness of what magic he wrought gleaming there.

Knowing 'twas his intent, she could not deny him. Kira stretched high, struggling to dance even as the heat gathered within her. She writhed within his embrace as they danced together in a timeless tempo, their pace increasing to a frenzy. Then Thierry arched high and stiffened, his gesture driving him against her so that Kira cried out in his wake and collapsed bonelessly against his chest.

Impossible 'twas to believe that she had feared this union. The promise of coupling thus over and over again fairly made her weak, and Kira closed her eyes against the rise of exhaustion. The man would see she never slept. Kira smiled secretly to herself, deciding that she might ensure he never slept.

But the languor stealing through her in the wake of their loving could not be denied. Mayhap later she would see he never slept, she reasoned as her eyelids drooped closed. Barely did Kira feel Thierry's lips brush across her brow before she slipped into the netherland of sleep within the safe haven of his embrace.

Kira was still sleeping soundly when Thierry slipped reluctantly away from her side. Dawn had come and he had not moved as was his wont, but he could linger no more. The road to Paris was long enough without staying abed all the day. He smiled to himself as Kira rolled over and burrowed into the warm spot he had just abandoned. Indeed, he felt more lighthearted than he had in years.

All because a woman had confided in him her name.

Although 'twas true Kira had granted him more than that. Thierry almost whistled with satisfaction as he hastily dressed, only the fear that he would awaken her keeping him silent. No sound may have crossed his lips, but Thierry was more than aware that his expression was not nearly as stern as usual.

Mayhap 'twas not so bad to see the civilized man revived within him. Mayhap there was another future for him than the one he had hoped for within the Mongol tribe and lost in the blink of a capricious eye. Mayhap something of import awaited him in his homeland.

On this morning it seemed all was possible. Thierry almost considered the tangled mess he had left behind in Khanbaliq, but checked his thoughts just in time. He spared a last glance to the sleeping beauty dozing peacefully on the other side of the room and shook his head.

Even Kira could not heal that wound. Enough should it be that she appeared capable of healing all the rest.

He hesitated on the threshold for a long moment, watching her sleep. Knowing he had no choice but to fetch supplies did little to bolster his resolve to leave. Thierry stood silently for a long moment. Never would Kira know he was gone, for he had noted already that she was a sound sleeper. And should he move quickly, they could be on their way before the sun reached its zenith.

Nogai was undoubtedly waiting impatiently at the gates already. That thought spurred Thierry on and he closed the door to the room carefully behind himself as he departed.

The souk in Constantinople was as colorful and busy as any Thierry had yet seen. Indeed, if he had not such a finely honed sense of direction, he might easily have found himself lost amidst the confusion. All manner of goods were there for sale, fineries collected from all corners of the world, their attributes recited to the thronging crowd by numerous self-assured merchants.

Thierry pushed his way through the crowd and acquired the goods he had need of, ignoring the rest. Dried meat, flat bread, some cheese and dried fruit. Another pair of blankets did he buy, for the air would be growing colder as they traveled farther north. No need had Kira of catching a chill.

His business completed, Thierry swiveled at the savory scent of freshly roasted lamb, thinking to fetch Kira a treat, only to have his attention snared by an inconspicuous shrouded shop.

Round gems gleamed in the shadows and a black-robed man sat nodding behind the display. His beard fell long and white over his chest, his thick eyebrows the same shade, his black turban making his face look more lined than mayhap it was. He glanced up and met Thierry's gaze and those dark eyes flashed knowingly. The man beckoned with a bony finger and Thierry could not help but comply.

The man was a pearl merchant, the richness of the gems arrayed on the dark cloth enough to take even Thierry's breath away. And fine gems had he seen in his days. But never any like these.

Despite himself, he was fascinated by their colors and shapes. Pink pearls there were and even one of palest green, ivory ones and those of outright yellow, and finally those of gleaming white. Not all were round and he marveled at their shapes, some twisted and convoluted beyond belief. 'Twas a sight Kira would appreciate, and half a mind had he to fetch her. Even tiny pearly Buddhas were there and he raised a skeptical glance to the keeper.

"All genuine they are," he declared flatly, touching the Buddhas with a gnarled fingertip. "From Cathay are these. Men there have learned the art of the oyster well. Little bronze statues do they plant in the creatures and the creatures know naught but to create pearls of them, just as they do with grains of sand."

"'Tis amazing," Thierry commented.

The elderly man nodded sagely. "Buddhist, are you? A fine talisman is one of these for a fighting man."

"Nay," Thierry said flatly.

Not yet willing to leave, he let his gaze rove over the display once more and found his attention captured by an oddity of a pearl. On a fine gold chain 'twas, as though meant to be worn around a woman's neck, though the gem was misshapen. Despite its deformity, the pearl had a certain grace, however, and Thierry was intrigued at the way it caught the light.

"Ah," the old merchant breathed. "Fancy the *aljofar*, do you? Have you a woman, then?"

"Aye," Thierry admitted warily.

"Aye, and good luck an *aljofar* is for a mate," the older man confided. "'Tis traditional, you know."

He hooked one finger beneath the chain and let the gem swing before Thierry. Thierry reached out to touch the stone and knew as soon as 'twas cradled within his palm that he had to have it. As a token of his regard for his Kira. Only fitting it seemed to pledge himself to her with a pearl when 'twas pearls that had brought them together.

Pleased with his logic, Thierry dug in his pocket for the pearl Kira had granted him. Yet more fitting 'twas that one gem should be bartered for the other. He offered it to the old merchant, who accepted it with an assessing frown. As Thierry watched, he rolled the gem between his fingers, bit it, peered at it, then met the younger man's gaze.

"Two dinars," he offered.

Thierry shook his head firmly. "Well I am told that it is worth three," he said. The merchant cocked a skeptical brow. "From Oman 'tis," Thierry added, repeating Kira's claim as though he knew exactly the import of it. The merchant's white brows rose and he plopped the gem into his mouth.

This time Thierry knew better than to react. He stood and waited, wishing he could fully dismiss his worry that the man could easily swallow the gem and trick him out of its value. Too much trust did this pearl business require, he concluded sourly, just as the merchant spit the pearl back into his hand.

"So 'tis," he conceded. "Three dinars, then."

"The *aljofar*," Thierry bargained. The merchant feigned surprise and frowned.

"A precious gift is an *aljofar*. Not a mere frippery to be cast aside when modes change," he argued with a scowl. "This pearl and two more dinars."

Thierry shook his head firmly. "Simply the gem," he bargained.

The old man granted him a wary glance. "For a woman do you want this?" he demanded.

Thierry nodded resolutely. "For *my* woman," he corrected firmly.

The merchant stifled a smile and rolled Thierry's gem across his palm. "Your first woman, then?" he asked in a more welcoming tone.

Thierry cocked an imperious brow. "My only woman," he affirmed flatly. The merchant shook his head and lifted the *aljofar* by its chain once more. He let it swing before him as though considering the wisdom of what he thought to do.

"The pearl and one dinar, then," he offered genially. "An offer 'tis that you will not match anywhere else, for this *aljofar* is worth far more."

Thierry knew from the old man's tone that he would go no lower, but he wanted the gem. He frowned and watched it swing innocently from its chain, as though it deliberately tempted him.

To think that he was considering paying coin for a trinket. When last had Thierry honestly purchased something other than essentials? To turn out hard-earned coin to cultivate a woman's smile was beyond belief.

But 'twas for Kira. And to be granted another sight of Kira's smile. Well Thierry wanted her to have it and already could he envision the gem against her golden skin. 'Twas inexplicable, but there 'twas.

Thierry dug in his pocket for the coin and fairly shoved it at the merchant. The old man bit the coin in turn, then offered the *aljofar* to Thierry with a small smile.

"Well enough do I remember being young," he mused with a twinkle in his eye. "Mind you always hold her in such regard. 'Twill ensure that your lives be long and happy together."

Thierry looked down at the gem in his hand with satisfaction and smiled himself as he met the older man's gaze once more. "I would thank you for both the gem and the advice," he said sincerely. "Well it seems that we have made a good beginning."

The merchant smiled and inclined his head. Thierry was unable to stifle his own smile as he headed back to the inn. He indulged his desire to whistle, certain that naught could go amiss with his world on this day.

Kira was just awakening when he returned. She granted him a sleepy smile before she snuggled beneath the blanket yet again, and his heart swelled.

Impossible 'twas that she could arouse him with such an innocent gesture, especially after their activity of the night before, but Thierry's mind readily enumerated possibilities. He laid his purchases aside instead of packing them immediately away, wanting to linger here but a little longer.

Feeling uncharacteristically playful, he scooped up a pair of blood oranges from his newly acquired stores and dropped beside her on the blanket. Kira opened one eye warily, but he leaned back leisurely to lie beside her. She yawned and stretched and nestled her cheek against him. Thierry felt her gaze upon him as he quickly peeled the orange skins away with his short knife.

Evident 'twas that Kira was hungry, as well, for her eyes gleamed and she soon sat up with interest. The move sent that shimmering curtain of her hair falling over her shoulders and bared the smoothness of her shoulder to his view.

Thierry was seized by a desire to know the taste of that specific spot. Though he well knew he would unable to cease his sampling there. Eternal temptation was clearly the price of taking this witch for his own. Thierry swallowed and carefully schooled the motion of his blade. Nogai would be waiting. They had no time for such whimsy.

Though if nights like this last were any portent of the future, he could scarce complain at the price.

When he offered Kira a segment of orange, a wicked glint lit her eye that should have warned him. Well enough should he know that that expression foretold mischief of the first order. Thierry but waited to see what she would do. His heart took an unruly skip when Kira simply parted her lips invitingly. Full well did she know how she tempted him, he was certain of it, but he played the innocent.

He carefully placed a segment in her mouth, feeling his desire rise anew when she closed her eyes with undisguised pleasure and her dark lashes fluttered over her cheeks. She closed her lips and he was certain this had been timed to trap his fingertip within their softness. Thierry slowly pulled his hand away.

Kira rolled to her back as she chewed at a fascinatingly languid pace and made a very feline sound of satisfaction in the deep of her throat. When she rolled back to her side, the blanket dropped yet lower, though she seemed not to notice.

She met Thierry's eyes and smiled seductively before she opened her mouth expectantly once again. Thierry separated another segment, astounded to find her coyly beckoning him with her tongue. He halted and she giggled, as though amazed at her own audacity, then curled closer to him. Thierry shook his head and fed her another piece.

Witch. A trickle of juice escaped from the corner of her lips and it seemed he could not tear his gaze away from its path. Thierry watched as the red drop trickled over her chin and disappeared over the soft curve of her jaw.

Little imagination did he need to picture its path beneath the blanket and the realization barely formed in his mind before he impulsively dove in pursuit of its sweetness. Kira giggled, her laughter halting uncertainly when he boldly licked the juice from beneath her chin. Their gazes locked for a heated moment, then Thierry deliberately bent to kiss her.

Kira responded as enthusiastically as she had the night before, though she tasted yet sweeter from the orange. Indeed, Thierry knew he could readily drown in her sweetness once again. His fingers wound into her hair, his appetite for her not nearly sated, and Kira pulled him yet closer.

'Twas only the intrusive thought of Nogai impatiently waiting that forced Thierry to finally lift his head. Kira was flushed in a most delightful manner, her eyes sparkling bright.

The road was long to Paris, Thierry reminded himself resolutely when she wiggled and her breasts were bared to his view. Her nipples tightened beneath his regard and he swallowed carefully.

Passage on a ship did they need and the tide would be going out, he forced himself to recall. Thierry cleared his throat studiously, torn between his desire and the need to resume their journey. Kira reached up to run a hand gently over his face as though she sensed his indecision, then plucked the second orange from the floor.

Did she understand or was she but toying with him? Though truly if Kira had set her mind upon mating anew, Thierry could scarce escape her. Nor indeed did he want to. Her eyes sparkled with mischief as though she had guessed his thoughts. She held the fruit aloft, shook her head firmly and Thierry knew she had something else on her mind. Fascinated, he could but watch.

"Thierry," she said, laying the flat of one hand on his chest. His heart thumped beneath her hand but her fingertips danced away as she similarly indicated herself. "Kira," she said pointedly.

When Thierry nodded understanding, Kira pointed to the orange and cocked a questioning brow.

She wanted to know the word for orange. It could only mean that she desired to learn to speak with him. Should he teach her Mongol or Frankish? Would she know the difference?

Thierry took the fruit from her and turned it thoughtfully in his hand while he considered the matter. 'Twas Mongol he spoke on a daily basis, Mongol he spoke with Nogai and Mongol she likely should learn. Thierry looked Kira in the eye and intoned the Mongol word for orange.

To his surprise Kira frowned. She explained something rapidly that he could not understand, then pointed resolutely to the orange once more. Thierry repeated the word. Kira shook her head. She tugged the corners of her eyes so that they were tilted and pulled thin as she had once before.

"Qaraq-Böke," she said with her eyes pulled back, then shook her head firmly again. Kira looked him directly in the eye and let her hands fall. "Thierry," she said once more. The challenging glint in her eyes willed him to understand.

Thierry almost jumped at his intuitive grasp of her meaning. Kira wanted to learn Frankish, not Mongol. But how could she possibly know that he had taught her his Frankish name? He stared back at her dumbly, unwilling to trust his intuition.

Kira made a sound of frustration back in her throat and frowned. "Qaraq-Böke," she said again, as though fearing she had mispronounced his name. Her voice faded uncertainly as she watched for his response.

Thierry's surprise that she knew the name the Mongols had assigned to him was so complete that he could not hide his response. Kira shook her head in denial when she noted his understanding. Not Qaraq-Böke, he understood, and wondered if she was denying him. His heart stilled in fear.

Then Kira said "Thierry" again and nodded emphatically.

'Twas not the man but the language she denied. Kira wanted to learn Frankish. Somehow she knew about his name, of that Thierry had little doubt. And she knew that Thierry was his Frankish name. He regarded his woman with newfound respect. She must have gleaned something of that in his expression, for she grinned outright. Kira demandingly pointed to the orange anew, as though he might have forgotten her intent.

"Orange," Thierry supplied.

"Orange," Kira repeated with solemnity. She said the word thrice more, then glanced to him for approval. Indeed, her expression was so hopeful that he could not deny her. Her accent was dreadful, her pronunciation marginal, but Thierry imagined that she might be understood.

At least by him she could be, and he rather suspected that might be the point. He nodded approvingly. Kira said the word several more times as though she sought to memorize it, then her gaze swiveled determinedly back to Thierry's.

No imagination did he need to know that she would want to know more words, and he decided to rein her in before she overstepped herself. Useful 'twould be for them to understand each other and he would not have her exhaust herself with her enthusiasm.

"But ten words a day," he told her. He propped himself on his elbows over her and held his hands open to her when she regarded him blankly. "Orange," he repeated and folded in his thumb.

Kira's evident confusion was replaced by understanding and she nodded emphatically. She tapped the blade strapped to the inside of his arm and he acknowledged a surge of pride. A useful word to know 'twould be.

"Knife," he said. Kira repeated the word carefully until he nodded approval.

But a glimpse had Thierry of that mischievous twinkle in her eye before she framed his face in her hands and pressed a light kiss to his lips. She lifted her brows in silent query and he shook his head bemusedly even as he accommodated her. Witch. Trust her to want to know the name for that.

"Kiss," he informed her.

"Kiss," Kira repeated with such concentration that Thierry could not help but tease her.

"Kiss?" he demanded, arching his brows high as though she had made a request. "Aye, Kira." He swooped down and kissed her, liking the glitter of satisfaction in her eyes when he propped himself above her once more.

"Kiss," Kira said breathlessly. She grinned and snapped her fingers demandingly when Thierry did not immediately comply.

Mayhap 'twas not the best word to have taught her so soon, Thierry reasoned as he bent over her once again. Yet he was unable to quell this lightness that seemed to buoy his heart when she responded to him with such ardor.

"Kiss," Kira whispered against his jaw. Thierry let her roll him to his back so that she was sprawled atop him. He glanced down at her naked buttocks and growled appreciatively. He playfully pinched her. Kira giggled and scrambled up his chest.

"Kiss," she insisted and bent to taste him yet again. Thierry cupped her buttocks in his hands and pulled her closer, more than pleased with this new balance between them. How many nights of Kira's intoxicating kisses would it take to reach Paris?

Thierry suddenly recalled the *aljofar* and decided in that same moment to save the gift for a special occasion. Mayhap Kira's first Frankish sentence.

Mayhap when she learned the name for that even more seductive pastime.

He groaned at his body's response to the reminder and tore his lips from hers, knowing full well that they would never leave the inn at this rate. Thierry reached across the floor and managed to grab Kira's trousers. He wagged them purposefully beneath her nose.

"*Chalwar,*" he said firmly. She pursed her lips in a mock pout.

"Kiss?" she negotiated coyly. Thierry shook his head resolutely and rose to his feet before his desire had him acquiescing to her request. High was the sun and 'twas time enough they sought passage on a ship bound westward.

"*Chalwar, kurta,* tunic, djellaba," he insisted as he tossed her each item of clothing in turn. He turned to face her once more and gestured toward the hills. "Nogai. Paris." He made a riding motion and Kira exhaled with exaggerated dissatisfaction.

"*Chalwar,* kiss, *kurta,* kiss," she suggested cagily, laughing aloud when a frown of exasperation crossed Thierry's brow.

Truly they would never leave Constantinople at this rate. Did the woman not know how much her simple kisses affected him? Thierry spared her a glance and, from the glint in her eye, rather suspected that she did.

Though surely if she was dressing, there could be no harm in a few fleeting kisses.

"Aye," he agreed before he thought too much about the matter. Kira glanced up questioningly from donning her *chalwar*.

"Aye?" she asked doubtfully. Thierry nodded emphatically, trying to indicate that *aye* meant assent. Naught had he to fear, though, for clearly she understood. No sooner had Kira fastened her *chalwar* than she launched herself into his arms.

"*Chalwar,* kiss," she reminded him archly.

He gazed down into her sparkling eyes, well aware of the full warmth of her bare breasts pressed against him and the weight of her tiny hands on his shoulders. Irresistible she was. Indeed, when the point was made so compellingly, Thierry could do naught but comply.

And but hope that he could stop with a kiss.

Kira was satisfied enough with her situation to be openly curious when Thierry rode with a definite objective in mind. They met a heartily disgruntled Nogai at the city gates, and she blithely ignored his muttering as Thierry proceeded through the bustle of the town to the market.

Thierry was teaching her his language. Truly it seemed he had claimed her fully after all, and her heart soared with delight.

Kira's nose was assaulted by the strong odor of fish and her eyes widened at the lavish catch displayed in the market stalls. A rare luxury had fish been in landlocked Tiflis and she was amazed by both the variety and sheer amount of fish offered for sale. Like the farmers who seldom ventured into Tiflis she was, for she could not cease her curious peering at such unfamiliar sights.

The cobbled road angled down and the smells grew stronger. The people looked rougher and more men were there in the crowd than women. Without thinking of the matter, she moved incrementally closer to Thierry and felt his grip tighten possessively around her waist. Kira smelled salt and wet hemp and heard the creaking of wood. She was puzzled for an instant by the unfamiliarity of it all, until she saw the bobbing masts of the ships.

Tales she had heard aplenty of these vessels that crossed the seas, but never had she seen one. Indeed, she had never seen the sea. The sparkling water that stretched as far as the eye could see behind the boats fairly took her breath away.

"Are we going to take a ship?" Kira asked as she twisted to look to Thierry. He seemed to be watching for her reaction, for his expression softened slightly when their eyes met. Kira indicated the ships questioningly and he nodded once.

But where were they going?

"Paris?" she asked, but Thierry merely shrugged. He held up one finger and dismounted, passing the reins to Nogai as he strode down the wharf. The pair silently watched him disappear into the crowd, then their eyes met in mutual wariness.

Nogai said something but Kira shrugged that she could not understand. He frowned anew and exhaled impatiently before pointing deliberately to the sun. Kira nodded and Nogai traced a path with his finger where the sun would go over the course of the afternoon. He spread his hand open and glanced to where Thierry had disappeared, then shrugged.

Thierry might be gone for a while, Kira guessed, and she nodded understanding. Nogai gestured to a shady corner of the busy quai and seemed to be indicating that they wait there. Kira nodded and he heaved a sigh of relief. Nogai dismounted and ushered the horses to the space he had indicated.

Kira slipped from the saddle, a little disconcerted that Thierry had so completely disappeared, and retrieved a blanket from Thierry's pack to sit upon. She spread out the blanket, wondering how long he might be, and was startled by Nogai's grunt of approval.

Kira spun to find the Mongol grinning. Before she could question his intent, he produced a curious bundle from his

own saddlebag. Kira thought it at first to be a brightly
painted box, but nay. Nogai peeled off a thin layer and Kira
saw 'twas a pile of such layers. He offered her that first
layer and Kira turned it over with fascination.

A painting 'twas on some thin matter like parchment,
softer to the fingertip yet stiffer and she fancied more du-
rable. On one side there was a black image she thought to
be an Eastern character of some kind, on the other was a
colored image of seven golden coins.

She looked questioningly to Nogai and he mutely handed
her another card. The black image was the same but the
other side carried a colored image of three golden cups.
Kira frowned in confusion, her gesture enough to prompt
Nogai to explain with enthusiasm.

His words flowed over Kira uncomprehended but she
watched his actions avidly. He dropped to his haunches and
quickly sorted the cards into four piles. That done, he
picked up one pile and sorted it quickly into order. Kira was
surprised to see that there was a card to represent gold coins
of every number from one to ten.

Fascinated despite herself, she squatted opposite Nogai
and spread out the pile of cards with gold cups on them.
Similarly, every number was represented there. Nogai
spread out the other two piles and Kira noted the same
pattern echoed in staffs and what looked to be tree
branches.

Unexpectedly, Nogai scooped up all of the cards and
mixed their order together. He split a number of them between himself and Kira with alarming speed, leaving the
remainder piled in between them. At his imperious gesture, Kira turned over her cards to find an assortment of
numbers and images.

A contest it must be. And a way to pass the time while
they awaited Thierry. Like chess 'twas, Kira concluded, but
the tools of the game were lighter and more portable,
making them more suited to the Mongols.

Kira met Nogai's gaze questioningly and he smiled in crooked triumph. His dark brows lifted high, his eyes twinkled and he held up one finger as he began to explain.

Nogai shouted with feigned relief when Thierry reappeared, and Kira could not restrain her laughter. Winning she had been, though she imagined the Mongol had been contriving that she did so. He said something accusatory to Thierry and grinned. Thierry snorted, but his gaze was warm when he offered Kira his hand to help her rise.

She felt her cheeks heat as the recollection of their night before flooded into her mind but Thierry was bending to fold the blanket with businesslike ease. He and Nogai discussed something briefly, the cards disappeared and they began to lead the horses toward the wharf.

They halted beside a bobbing ship and one of the horses balked at being led aboard. Kira could not blame the beast, for one look between the small vessel and the vast extent of the sea was enough to make her question the wisdom of their move.

"Genoa, Paris," Thierry murmured into her ear. Kira glanced up with surprise. He pointed to the ship. "Ship, Genoa. Horse, Paris," he explained.

Kira spared the ship a skeptical glance that she hoped might communicate her misgivings. Thierry folded her hand reassuringly within his and urged her to follow him aboard as he spoke. His explanation was long enough that she understood naught but her name, though his low tone worked its magic upon her.

Had she not already trusted him with unexpectedly good results? Truly, the man saw to her safety and comfort more than anyone she had ever known. And with the promise of more of his leisurely loving, Kira knew she would have been a fool to turn away.

She trusted Thierry. The revelation was not as much of a shock as she might have expected it to be. She was his woman and he treated her with greater deference than many men undoubtedly treated their wives. Surely she could not ask for more. She would remain by his side wherever he chose to ride.

Her decision made, Kira granted Thierry a sunny smile and followed him onto the ship that would take them across the sea to mysterious and distant Genoa.

Chapter Twelve

By the time the snows were thawing alongside the road to Paris, Kira had missed three bleedings. There was no escaping the fact that she was pregnant with Thierry's seed.

Sick she had been from the second week out on the six-week ship voyage to Genoa, sick enough to not care about anything other than sleep. Nogai had lost a gaming partner and Thierry had lost a lover in her illness. For her part, Kira had lost weight, despite Thierry's efforts to encourage her to eat. Grateful she had been for his warmth when she was possessed by chills in the night and he held her close.

Indeed, she knew not whether she would have had the will to survive without his quiet strength. An unexpectedly playful side of him had she discovered as they lay together in the berth and he taught her yet more Frankish. And his relief when they had reached land and she had managed to smile for the first time in a month had been marvelous to behold. Indeed, 'twas too easy to grow fond of the man. Nary a thought had she spared to her missed bleeding under the circumstances. Surely all would be restored to normalcy once she began to eat again.

But north they rode without cease and still Kira had not bled. That fact had made her start to calculate on her fingers and more than once had she glanced into her *chalwar* for some confirming sign. The second miss was soon enough after their arrival in Genoa that she granted herself the benefit of the doubt.

The miss of the third bleeding left no question. With child she was. With Thierry's child, beyond doubt. Kira fancied she could detect a rounding of her belly and 'twas that that first made her consider the repercussions of her pregnancy.

'Twas not surprising in itself, for Thierry and she had been amorous enough before her illness to well justify the conception of a babe. Indeed, 'twould have been surprising had they *not* conceived, and she wondered if Thierry had considered the matter at all.

Did he desire children? 'Twas difficult to guess, for his wandering life did not appear a suitable one for rearing a family, at least to Kira's mind. But Mongols must have children and she supposed he might think differently than she. Did Mongols raise families the way her neighbors in Tiflis had done? Or did men leave women to that domestic task and simply ride on? Kira knew not and liked that not at all.

Was it truly the same to be claimed as to be wedded? Too late, Kira doubted the Persian woman's word. Indeed, who knew what obligations a Mongol might consider to be his as a result of such a bond? 'Twas clear enough that Thierry's behavior owed much to Mongol traditions, whatever his own lineage. What would Nogai have done with a pregnant woman?

More importantly, what would Thierry do with her? Would he leave her? Kira could hardly bear the thought.

Kira knew not the answers to any of the questions that plagued her and little did the matter aid her sleeping. She was compromised as surely as she could possibly be, and yet no husband had she to claim responsibility for her pregnancy or her child.

Indeed, she might simply ask, yet Kira shirked every opportunity. Only to herself in the night would she admit that she feared Thierry's response. And naught could she deny Thierry, even with all her concerns, when he turned to her in the night. Only one thing did Kira know with absolute certainty, though the fact did little to console her in the aftermath of their sweet loving.

There was no doubt that her sire would be ashamed of what she had become.

Paris.

They were finally here and Thierry could not completely stifle his excitement. Home he had felt since they had first crossed into the lands of those sworn to the Frankish king. Though the sense had faded as they traveled farther north, he knew with increasing certainty that 'twas here, in the land of his birth, that he would find his destiny.

And only the matter of the khan's message kept him from immediately pursuing his fate. With that in mind, 'twas impossible to linger outside Paris. Thierry could do naught but head directly to the king's palace, determined to see this errand behind him. No doubt had he that the khan's message would be politely rebuffed. Indeed, he hoped for no less.

All of Europe beckoned to his ambitions and he was nigh impatient to begin. Well he knew that he had been born at a château known as Montsalvat, and he wondered how he might discreetly find its locale. 'Twas his time finally and Thierry was anxious for his destiny to begin.

Kira looked about with curiosity and Thierry noticed yet again that she was unnaturally quiet. Odd 'twas, the change in her, but he supposed she was yet unsettled by their sea voyage. Indeed, there was a pallor to the characteristic golden hue of her skin that could not be entirely due to the change of clime.

And something he could not quite place had changed in her manner, though he had puzzled over it often. Withdrawn she seemed, private, yet more affectionate than ever before should he touch her. Certainly he could make no complaint about her passion, for she had surpassed even his wildest expectations in their nightly couplings. Though it puzzled him that Kira would not touch him of her own accord, he assumed 'twas something in her upbringing that dictated her behavior.

Dame Fortune had indeed blessed him with a perfect mate.

He dismounted in the courtyard of the king, awed by the majesty of construction surrounding him. Nogai's gaze similarly roved over the high walls of fitted stone and the conical towers looming high above them. Pennants of azure and gold flitted against the winter sky high overhead. Thierry knew he was not alone in counting the sentries along the walls and he found assessment in Nogai's eyes when their gazes met.

"I like not how outnumbered we are," Nogai muttered.

"Diplomats are we, not warriors," he corrected his old *anda*, but Nogai's expression remained skeptical.

"So far," he conceded gruffly as he slipped to the ground.

A man cleared his throat delicately and Thierry spun to find an older man regarding them with evident disapproval. His tunic was as blue as the sky with golden flowers worked upon it, every scrap of his knightly attire perfectly in order. Yet despite the beautifully encrusted scabbard hanging by his side, Thierry knew this was not a man who had seen battle of late. The man scanned their travel-stained and clearly foreign attire with open disdain before he met Thierry's gaze.

"Have you mayhap some business in this courtyard?" he inquired icily, his tone indicating that he believed no such thing.

"Aye, a message have I for the king," Thierry explained, and one silver brow arched high.

"Indeed? From whom might this message be?"

"His most esteemed Second Il-Khan of Persia, Abaqa, son of Hülegü, son of Tolui, son of the Great Golden Khan himself, the immortal and most divine Chinggis Khan, sends greetings to the king of the Franks," Thierry supplied, well recalling the beginning of the missive he had been granted.

To his credit, the formerly impassive guard looked somewhat surprised. "Genghis Khan?" he asked and Thierry nodded. "Have you news of Prester John, then?" he demanded with enthusiasm. Thierry feared to show his ignorance as the man's expectation was evidently so great, but knew not what else to say.

"I know not this Prester John," he admitted warily. The man's lips thinned in irritation.

"A king of the East is he, as all know, who will aid us in defeating the Saracens," he retorted frostily.

"Saracens?" Thierry asked dubiously, knowing naught of this race.

"The godless infidels who have stolen Jerusalem from beneath our very noses," the man confided hastily.

Aha. A question of terms, 'twas, no more than that. Thierry sighed with relief. Indeed, they were back on familiar ground. Well aware of both Kira and Nogai's avid attendance, he felt them relax slightly at his evident relief.

"A proposal this is for an alliance against the invaders of Jerusalem," Thierry assured the man confidently. He removed a scroll of parchment from his *kalat* to illustrate his intention.

"Verily?" the man asked, a new light dawning in his eyes as he eyed the scroll. Well it seemed that his manner thawed slightly when Thierry nodded agreement. "Well can I imagine that the king will be interested in your message, then," he said, and there was no mistaking the haste with which he summoned boys to tend the horses.

"Your horses will be tended," he said crisply. "And I will alert the king's advisers to your presence. A common room is there inside and to your right, should you wish."

With that he turned and bustled efficiently away.

"What says he?" Nogai demanded impatiently.

"That we should wait inside," Thierry replied. Nogai pursed his lips in irritation.

"Truly urban folk are all the same," he muttered. "What feeds this dislike of wholesome air in the lungs? I suppose there is little chance of waiting outside?"

"'Twould be seen as rude, I am sure," Thierry observed tersely.

"Let us hope the matter can be managed hastily," Nogai said begrudgingly with a sigh of dissatisfaction. "This diplomacy is indeed a burdensome task." He spared a telling glance for the cerulean spring sky and trudged reluctantly through the portal in Thierry and Kira's wake.

The summons came none too soon to Thierry's mind.

The common room was noisy, smoky and filled with Frankish knights. Naught was his difficulty with any of this; indeed, it seemed wondrously familiar and had much in common with the atmosphere of a friendly yurt. However, they had been but moments in the room before one knight nudged his companion and gestured to Kira. Thierry had bristled but set his lips grimly, determined not to begin a battle. Outnumbered they were by far, as Nogai had already observed, and naught could he do but glare back at the offending knight.

Obvious 'twas that she was his, but well it seemed to Thierry that no one recognized that fact. He scowled darkly and glowered to no avail as yet more admirers turned an eye on his witch. Thierry was not in the least reassured when Nogai and Kira blithely spread out their infernal cards, clearly oblivious to both the attention they drew and Thierry's dislike of the same.

"The Mongols, you must be." A crisp voice drew Thierry from his dark thoughts and he glanced up to find another guard garbed in that same blue and gold. Tempted Thierry was indeed to greet the man with an enthusiasm far beyond expectation.

"The king will see you immediately," the man intoned. Thierry flicked a summoning gesture to his companions and the cards hastily disappeared. The guard turned and set a quick pace through the smoke, leaving them darting through the common room behind him and out into a high vaulted hall.

As they trudged silently in the guard's wake, Thierry wondered if the others were as awestruck by the evident size of the palace. The boisterous sounds of the common room faded behind them and naught could he hear but whispering footsteps mingling with their own solid trudging. Well it seemed that the labyrinthine corridors twisted off in every direction. Certainly the one they followed was wide enough for eight men to walk abreast and continued on endlessly.

Deeply nervous did it make Thierry to be so thoroughly surrounded by stone and the makings of man. He wondered fleetingly how Nogai could bear it, for that man had little tolerance even of small inns and taverns. Indeed, he had slept on the deck of the ship in fine weather and poor, rather than venture into the hold. Thierry did not dare look back to see the truth lest he give a sign of his own discomfort. The messenger moved with a light step and Thierry knew he had little option other than following this man deeper into the maze.

Kira seemed completely untroubled, a fact that left Thierry feeling that he had somehow fallen short. He knew he did not imagine her curious perusal of their surroundings and wished he could be so cavalier.

Being led into a trap they were. The certainty grew within him until it was unassailable. Though Thierry knew the thought to be a fallacy, still he could not dismiss it. Everything within him distrusted this place and this path.

They climbed two flights of stairs crafted from artfully fitted stone. The steps swept around in a spiral, the like of which Thierry had never seen before. He refused to let his impression of the craftsmanship show and stubbornly kept his features impassive. The messenger pivoted at the top of the stairs, and gestured grandly to a pair of extremely high doors.

"The throne room," he informed them without meeting their eyes.

At an imperious rap of his knuckles, the doors swung open soundlessly to reveal two doorkeepers garbed in that same blue and gold. The messenger fairly skipped across the threshold, evidently expecting them to follow. Nogai made a barely perceptible growl of dissatisfaction in the back of his throat. Thierry took a deep breath, knowing he could do naught but follow suit.

The Khan's message had to be delivered. He squared his shoulders, determined to fulfill his commission, and peered into the room.

The throne room was large beyond his expectations. The ceiling arched impossibly high above, apparently supported by an elaborate arrangement of arches that Thierry knew better than to trust with such a burden. Any fool could see that the ceiling was of carved and fitted stone and he cast it a wary eye. All of the room was beneath the stone, though, and no way was there to enter the room and still avoid the risk.

Liking it naught, Thierry stepped into the room, hoping his perfectly healthy caution of such nature-defying tricks was not misinterpreted by these Franks. An open floor space was there in the middle of the room, flanked by banks of benches that rose higher the farther they were from the center of the room. Courtiers were clustered in small groups here and there on the benches. At the far end of the room and facing Thierry was a dais. A number of men sat there, discussing matters amongst themselves. None of them seemed to be paying any attention to Thierry's entrance.

Neither did they seem concerned about the ceiling, much to his surprise.

Instinctively and out of long habit, Thierry quickly picked out the guards and the exits. Easy enough 'twas to find the guards, for they all wore the same colors, much as the khan's *keshik* guard did. Two guards there were standing slightly behind the king on the dais, another pair at each end of the dais. The two who had opened the doors he would reasonably expect to be armed, as would he expect any number of the courtiers to be similarly prepared to meet a threat.

Two doors were there on the far end of the room. The one below the dais did not appear to lead anywhere of good repute, for 'twas barred and of poorer manufacture. The one behind the king Thierry suspected led to his chambers, for 'twas finely ornamented and marked with those same golden blooms. He shook his head minutely, his sense of being lured into a trap redoubled by his observations.

But one exit. This he did not like, the rising banks of benches to the left and right reminding him only too well of a valley set for an ambush. A valley with but one escape. Thierry liked not that he was the one stepping willingly within the trap. Though he was but an envoy and surely had naught to fear, Thierry felt his pulse begin to race.

"The envoy from the Mongols," the messenger announced when they had crossed the threshold. The words launched an uneasy silence as dozens of murmured conversations halted as one.

The king looked up, pinning Thierry with a glance. His courtiers and advisers glanced up with curiosity. Thierry stiffened and gazed around the room, more than fully aware that he was being scrutinized.

When the whispering began, his pride set him in motion. Let them look, he thought ferociously. Of naught did he have to be ashamed. Thierry strode purposefully down the length of the room, summoning his most forbidding expression as he approached the dais. Only one man was he, but this king would know the might of the Mongol khan.

Thierry paused before the dais, absently admiring the way its design made it virtually impossible to assault the king from where he stood. The leap was too high. No wonder their weapons had not been removed before they were permitted entry. The realization fed his suspicions of the situation, but no time had he to indulge such whimsies.

A man on a diplomatic mission was he. The sooner this matter was completed, the sooner he and Kira could continue with their lives.

And the sooner he could seek out his ambitious dreams. His heart missed a beat in anticipation, but Thierry schooled his response. A task had he to fulfill first.

"Greetings to you do I bring from his most esteemed Second Il-Khan of Persia, Abaqa, son of Hülegü, son of Tolui, son of the Great Golden Khan himself, the immortal and most divine Chinggis Khan," he began. The king's brows lifted in surprise.

"Frankish do you speak," he observed quietly before a frown flitted across his brow. "And rather well. How came this to be?"

"Many skills have we of which you know naught," Thierry replied, striving to keep his manner and tone consistent with the missive he had been granted. No unnecessary information was he to grant these potential allies, he had been told, in case they became not allies, but foes. 'Twas the strength of the Mongols they should be given to understand and not one concession should he make.

"Indeed," the king commented mildly. Two of the courtiers whispered to each other and Thierry bristled when he saw that they gestured to Kira. The king smothered a smile and Thierry wondered how much of his response had been noted.

"Mayhap you would tell us your own identities afore reading your message," the king suggested.

"Qaraq-Böke am I called," Thierry informed the king proudly, not seeing any reason to discuss his own Frankish lineage. Was he not the messenger of the Mongol khan? "And the blooded warrior Nogai 'tis who accompanies me on this mission."

"And from whence do you issue?"

"We come bearing the message of Abaqa, Second Il-Khan of Persia."

"'Twas not my question."

"But 'twas my response."

The king held Thierry's gaze for a long moment, as though willing him to say more. Thierry remained reso-

lutely silent, knowing full well that he had not answered the
king's questions as he had wished.

This prying manner was offensive in itself and Thierry
did not feel that he alone should be the one to swallow his
pride. A frown darkened the king's brow for a brief moment when Thierry said naught else. The king made a
sound that might have been exasperation in the back of his
throat before he leaned forward slightly.

"Envoys we have had from the Mongols afore," he confided. "And yet naught has ever come from these liai-
sons."

"Well might one question on which side the fault lay,"
Thierry countered flatly.

"One well might," the king agreed readily. "Though
truly that is not my point. I would but ask you for some
indication that your khan sends this message in good
faith."

Thierry unfurled the scroll of parchment he carried,
knowing that the text would explain itself more fully than
he could.

"The truth lies here, as does the sign you seek," he said.

The king nodded. "Then I would have you read this
missive now," he ordered.

Thierry cleared his throat as he stretched the parchment
out before him. The moment was upon him and truly he
hoped all went well. "His most esteemed Second Il-Khan
of Persia, Abaqa, son of Hülegü, son of Tolui, son of the
Great Golden Khan himself, the immortal and most divine
Chinggis Khan, sends greetings to the king of the Franks."

A clatter of activity diverted Thierry's attention from his
reading at that moment. He twisted to find a large group of
armed knights entering the throne room. Thierry frowned
and met the concern in Nogai's gaze.

Who were these new arrivals and what was their intent?
Did these Frankish people regard diplomats differently
than the Mongols did? Was he a fool to assume that they
could come and leave here without being assaulted? Well
enough had Thierry already seen the difference in their

cultures, and the arrival of these knights fed his doubts. Suddenly Thierry was not so certain that their safety was assured and he swallowed carefully, even as he tallied a count of the new arrivals.

"What brings you here?" crisply demanded one of the courtiers.

The older knight who led the group assumed a cavalier air that Thierry knew was feigned. "Come to see the Easterners, have we," he responded lightly. He was tall, his voice resoundingly deep, his step surprisingly vigorous despite the snowy whiteness of his hair. He carried his helmet beneath his elbow, his sword hanging from his hip.

At their leader's words the others leered at the trio before the king and laughed amongst themselves. Almost might one think they were drunk, but Thierry was not ready to make such an easy conclusion. No reassurance was there in the fact that they were garbed similarly to their leader in mail and tunics with full weaponry.

Thierry acknowledged yet another increment of dread. To what battle did these knights travel? The king gestured to the new arrivals for silence and impatiently waved them toward the benches on either side.

"Provincials," he muttered disparagingly under his breath. His manner indicated that the explanation should have meaning to Thierry, though indeed he could divine naught from the single word. There was shame in dwelling outside the city? Well might he have thought 'twould be precisely the opposite, but no time had he to ponder the matter.

"Please continue," the king insisted when Thierry stood uneasily silent, and he reluctantly returned to his scroll.

"Heavily cursed have both our kingdoms been by that godless union of Mamluk dogs emanating from Egypt and the infidels from Syria, and in this slight we already stand of one accord. Well do we understand that the loss of the city of Jerusalem and the land known as Palestine is a thorn that sticks in the side of the Frankish people, just as the loss of the surrounding plains sorely vexes our tribes.

"We propose a holy union between our armies, that we should attack these territories from opposite sides in a common operation. If by the authority of heaven, we should conquer these people, you should have Jerusalem as our gift."

A murmur of discussion broke out on the dais and Thierry wondered if 'twas his imagination that made the response sound favorable. Mayhap the matter could be settled hastily and Nogai sent back to Tabriz with the response. Mayhap. Thierry cleared his throat pointedly and the courtiers fell silent as he continued.

"The divine hand is clear in this and well it seems this liaison has been ordained. A sign has been sent to us in the person sent before you, for Mongol he is, yet he speaks your Frankish tongue. Well this seems a portent that our alliance is a blessed one. As if this were not enough, there is yet another sign of heaven's intervention, for this same messenger bears the very mark of your Jerusalem emblazoned upon his flesh for all to see."

A tense hush fell after his words, the expectation more than Thierry thought the missive certainly demanded. But no time had he to puzzle over such cultural differences. The sooner this was delivered, the sooner he could seek his own fate.

As he had been instructed, he unfastened his *kalat* and bared his birthmark to the view of those on the dais.

To his astonishment, the king blanched.

The king then fell weakly back in his chair, the pallor of his complexion making him appear markedly older than he had just moments before. The courtier to his left swore, the one on his right crossed himself vigorously, a young boy appeared to lift a cup to the king's lips.

"He dares to venture openly amongst us," another courtier whispered inexplicably. He stared in open-mouthed disbelief at Thierry's bared flesh. Another closed his eyes reverently and raised his rosary to his lips as he mouthed a silent prayer. The last man on the dais clambered to his feet and shouted.

"Guards!"

The cry echoed eerily in the silence that had fallen in the throne room. Suddenly everyone who had frozen in place came to life and the room erupted in activity.

What had Thierry done? This response made no sense. But a glimpse did Thierry need of the guards on the dais drawing their swords to prompt him to draw his own.

"Fool!" bellowed someone far behind when it seemed that naught could make less sense.

Thierry spun on his heel to find the knights who had lately entered the hall leaping down to the floor. They were led by that same solidly set man, who had donned his helmet. Thierry had little doubt 'twas he who had bellowed, for purpose showed in every line of his figure as he closed the distance between them.

"What did you do?" Nogai demanded impatiently.

"No idea have I," Thierry confessed in bewilderment.

"Well it seems that we will have to defend ourselves before we might find out," Nogai observed dryly. The two men's gazes held but for an instant before they backed together out of long-standing habit. A wide-eyed Kira was trapped between the two of them.

"A fine choice of an emissary Abaqa made in you," Nogai muttered with dissatisfaction. He swung his blade and another grunted as his swipe found its mark. "Not long enough are we even here for a meal afore you strike offense. Well it seems the khan might have weakness in assessing diplomatic talents."

No time had Thierry to respond to the accusation, for two guards leaped at him. He swung and missed, then jabbed more successfully. Kira squealed and he pivoted deliberately to keep her sheltered behind him as he dispatched the second opponent.

He cast a dubious glance at the knights now reaching them. On whose side would they swing their blades? Indeed, their role would decide the fight, for should Thierry and Nogai stand alone, they were doomed. Nogai bel-

lowed as he impaled another attacker and Kira fairly
crawled up Thierry's back.

"Give me a knife," she demanded breathlessly. Thierry
but bared his forearm to her as he kept an eye on the
courtier stalking toward him, dagger in hand. Kira snatched
the blade. He knew not if she could wield it, but well
enough should she try.

Another shout and Thierry fired a glance down the room
to find the leader of the knights had dispatched one of the
guards from the door with a telling blow. Allies these
knights were, then. Thierry's pulse pounded at the revelation. Now they had at least a chance of escaping the clutch
of this infernal building.

"Guards! Guards! *Guards!*" One of the courtiers had
climbed onto his seat and shouted for aid. The king had
disappeared into his chambers behind, several of the
courtiers similarly gone. The remainder pulled concealed
daggers and swords from their garments and leaped into the
fray with a shout. The group of knights worked their way
down the floor with methodical ease, steel clanging on steel,
until their leader was alongside Thierry.

"Thierry de Pereille are you?" he demanded in a terse
undertone.

Thierry nearly missed a parry, so astonished was he by
the question.

"Aye," he agreed warily before he could think to do
otherwise.

"Fool," the man declared again, his green eyes snapping fire as he dealt a telling blow to another guard.
"Though I guessed as much when I heard Mongols came
calling. Well might I have thought your sire might have
raised you to have more sense than this." He grunted and
jabbed his sword into the gullet of an attacker. Thierry
struggled to make sense of the enigmatic comment even as
he fought.

How could this stranger know his name? And how did he
know Thierry's father?

"And who might you be?" Thierry dared to demand, earning himself a sharp glare from the older knight.

"Eustache de Sidon," the man spat. "Were it not for the pledge I took to your father, 'twould be your blood on the floor and deservedly so. Never have I witnessed such brash foolhardiness—"

A roar erupted from the end of the hall as a large contingent of the king's guards spilled into the throne room. The older man beside Thierry muttered something uncomplimentary under his breath that sounded markedly like something Nogai would say. He shot Thierry a scathing glance.

"Get out now," he dictated flatly. Thierry bristled at the order and met that frosty regard with no intent of complying.

"I will not flee like a woman," he snapped.

The other man snorted. "Nay, you will flee like a hunted man," he corrected. "As will all the rest of us now, I wager." He swore eloquently and visibly gritted his teeth, his voice dropping to a growl. "Indeed, I should have trusted the sign more. Had I but known, I would have brought them all." His gaze flitted over the walls of the throne room and he shook his head disparagingly.

"Such an opportunity wasted," he muttered, to Thierry's confusion, then spared the younger man a knowing look. "Well could we have regained the prize this very day," he asserted.

Before Thierry could demand an explanation, the older knight turned and bellowed once more. He raised his blade high as he faced the attackers.

"To the doors, I bid you!" he shouted to his men. They turned of one accord to meet the new arrivals, a collective roar erupting from their throats.

"Of what does he speak?" Kira demanded breathlessly. Thierry shrugged as they were swept forward with the crowd of knights.

"I know not," he confessed hastily. "But for whatever reason, they aid us." Kira tripped and he feared suddenly that she would be undertrodden in the rush. Too small was she to fend for herself in this press. He scooped her up protectively and tossed her over his shoulder, not missing the flash of an impertinent grin.

"Questions later," she advised in a whisper, and Thierry almost smiled. He but gave her knees a squeeze before one of the king's guards broke through the ranks. Thierry swung his blade with vigor and summarily dispatched his assailant.

The army of knights drove through the contingent of guards like a finely honed wedge. Thierry found himself, Kira and Nogai packed into the center of the group so tightly that he had not even the space to swing his own blade. Nogai's alarm was evident, for his nostrils flared agitatedly.

They gained the hall, then the staircase, the group of men pressing relentlessly on despite the cries of those who rose against them. The fan of air did Thierry feel and he exhaled shakily when they passed into the courtyard.

How would they find the horses? Their escape was doomed!

Barely had the fear formed than Thierry saw their distinctively shorter horses saddled before him. How had this happened? Thierry spared a glance to the older man, who grimaced and waved to his beasts.

"Hunted are we," he growled. "Have I not made the matter most clear? Hasten yourself, boy, or I shall truly begin to question whether you might be your father's son."

Nogai had already mounted and Kira was in Thierry's saddle an instant later.

"But seven short horses like this did I find, milord," a young boy informed Thierry solemnly as he made to mount himself.

"But seven have we," he confirmed tersely. He turned his back on the impertinent lad and swung up behind Kira.

"And fine creatures they be, milord." The boy bobbed a bow. "Fine thick coats have they and well it seems they must be well suited to travel—"

"Beauregard!" the older man bellowed impatiently from atop his own charger, and the boy winced. "Well I bade you be *mounted* when we arrived!" The boy's eyes widened in a manner that left no doubt as to his identity and he scurried toward a smaller pony.

"Aye, milord, but I had to confirm we had found all the foreign beasts," he explained hastily.

"I care naught for your excuses!" the man shouted, scooping up the boy with more care than his tone might have led one to expect. "I bade you find the Mongol's beasts—surely seven is plenty, even if 'tis not all." He dropped the boy into the saddle before him and gave the riderless pony a hearty swat across the rump.

"Hasten yourselves!" he bellowed once more.

Thierry dug his heels into his beast's side and whistled, sending the others running along with them. The troop of knights barely cleared the gates before shouts rang out from within the fortress behind. Thierry's heart nearly stopped when he saw the market carts and old farm horses cluttering the street, knowing with certainty that the king's troops would be upon them before they reached the city walls.

To his astonishment the townsfolk seemed well accustomed to this sort of interruption, for a bellow from Eustache sent them hurrying out of the path. The cry was taken up by the others. Nogai winked at Thierry before he lent his voice to the fray. The horses were given their lead and the cobblestones echoed with the thunder of their passing.

"Surely they will pursue us?" Thierry demanded. The older knight shot him an indulgent glance and ruffled the hair of the boy seated before him.

"Beauregard has a way with knots and harnesses that may keep them behind us," he commented with a wry smile. The boy grinned proudly at his master's praise. Thierry jammed his own helmet on his head, acknowledging he would believe that when he saw the evidence, and pulled Kira resolutely closer.

When they passed beneath the walls of the city without intervention, the knights hollered victoriously. Thierry re-

leased the breath he had not known he was holding and
deliberately loosed his grip on Kira's waist.

He noted with pleasure that they set a course to the south
where he had felt so attuned to the land. His relief must
have been tangible, for Kira grinned up at him as she
slipped his knife back into his scabbard. She curled closer
to him and pulled his cloak about her against the late-af-
ternoon air. Too comfortable she looked and Thierry was
prompted to jolt her just a little. When next the knights
bellowed, he raised his own voice so ferociously that she
covered her ears with mock fright.

"Kiss," she whispered. Thierry brushed his lips across
her brow, his gaze seeking out the leader in the throng of
knights.

"Later," he murmured into her hair and felt her pout.

But more important matters were there afoot now than
the exchange of kisses. Not only had Thierry to discover
what had happened in the king's throne room, but he
would know how this knight knew his name. And what did
this man know of his father? Well it seemed the man
avoided his gaze as they rode, but determined was Thierry
to learn the truth of the matter when they halted for the
night.

Chapter Thirteen

Kira liked not that Thierry had declined her a simple kiss of reassurance. And not enough was it that he had said "later," a word she had learned and liked little in itself, but his very manner was aloof. His lack of interest in her did not bode well, to Kira's way of thinking, for well she knew that she could not hope to conceal her pregnancy from him much longer.

Indeed, had he already noted it? Was that the reason for his disinterest?

She fretted as they rode and he said naught else to her. Darkness fell and Kira shivered in the chill, yet still the knights continued along the silent road. They rode without shouting or even speaking once the city was behind them, their passage through the quiet countryside almost soundless in itself. There was naught but the hoofbeats of the horses on the dirt, the occasional cough, the periodical jingle of the trap. The moon rose and Kira huddled closer to Thierry's warmth, not daring to hope when the lights of a building bobbed in the distance.

But stop there they did. A gate opened as they drew nearer and the knights rode directly within the building's embracing walls of one accord. Nary a word was said, the gate drawn up virtually on their heels and secured against the outside.

A great walled courtyard they stood within, a tall building to one side and the walls enfolding all within their protective embrace. Golden light and the scent of roasted meat spilled out of the building. The horses stamped in the courtyard, their breath making white plumes in the air as the young boys dismounted to tend them. The men spoke quietly to each other as yet more men and boys appeared from within to aid with the tasks at hand.

Thierry lifted Kira to the ground and she knew not what to expect. The white haired man who had shouted so much joined them, as did a heavyset man who had come out of the building. The three men conferred hastily, their words too low and quick for Kira to comprehend. Thierry listened and eventually nodded in agreement.

To what? The heavyset man snapped his fingers and a pair of women in those trailing skirts Kira had noted throughout this land hastened toward them. Thierry brushed his lips across Kira's brow once more and waved her toward the pair of women without any explanation. They smiled invitingly but she was not convinced of their sincerity. Accompany these strangers? Where and to what purpose?

"But, Thierry—" Kira protested, turning to find that Thierry had already walked away. She picked out his figure where he walked with the other two men, his head bent low as he listened. Kira suddenly felt more alone than she ever had before.

A hand landed awkwardly on her shoulder and Kira glanced up to find Nogai's expression surprisingly sympathetic.

He said something she knew to be a joke, even though she could not understand, and winked reassuringly. Kira smiled despite herself. He tapped the pocket where she knew he kept his cards and wiggled his brows questioningly. Indeed, Nogai must feel even more lost than she.

Encouraged, Kira nodded and gave Nogai's hand a squeeze before she turned to accompany the two women. Whatever their intent, there was naught she could do to fight it alone. Mayhap if Thierry trusted them, she should do so, as well.

Mayhap if Thierry had appeared to give the matter some consideration, Kira might have had more confidence in that conclusion.

The women's dastardly intent proved to be that of offering Kira a bath.

So delighted was she at the possibility that she could not be coy. Half afraid they were teasing her with the steaming tub, Kira clasped her hands together and looked longingly at the steaming water. One of the women laughed at her hopeful manner as she nodded.

"Aye, the tub is for you," she said.

"Well it seemed you might desire one after your ride," affirmed the other. Her eyes twinkled merrily for a moment, then she pinched the bridge of her nose theatrically.

"Aye, you know the truth of it." Kira laughed along with them, her pleasure at the prospect making it impossible to take affront. A bath. 'Twould be heaven itself to scrub this grime from her skin.

'Twas only when Kira was nude in the tub and the women disappeared with her clothes that she began to doubt the wisdom of her decision. Were they to leave her here with naught to wear? But nay, they returned before the water had cooled and urged Kira out of the tub. They offered her a long-sleeved white *kurta* that fell to the floor and Kira smiled in recognition of the familiar garment.

"*Kurta*," she said, but the women frowned.

"Nay, this is your chemise," one corrected. "My old one, actually, but 'twill fit you better." Kira repeated the word to herself and mentally chastised herself for speaking out so hastily.

"And your kirtle," said the other in a more kindly manner as she held out a bundle of cinnamon hue. Kira accepted the heavier garment and shook it out, surprised to find it of much the same cut as the one she had already donned. 'Twas the weight of the fabric alone that changed the garment's name? Curious 'twas, but she pulled it over her head as they indicated.

To Kira's shock they tugged on laces at the sides of the garment until it fit her figure snugly. She looked down at herself in amazement when they nodded approvingly, knowing she could never show herself in public in such a manner. Indeed, there was naught left to the imagination by such a scandalous garment.

The women tut-tutted, though, and coiled Kira's hair back with businesslike ease despite her discomfort with her garb. They draped a sheer wisp of cloth about her throat and more over her head and hair, tucking the ends into a stiffened circlet placed atop her head. Kira regarded them skeptically when they stood back to admire their work.

Surely no one appeared in mixed company like this?

The kindly woman's expression brightened as though she recalled something forgotten, and Kira almost applauded her memory. Surely there was a good bit of cloth missing. At the very least, she had need of *chalwar* and a djellaba to cover this indecently tight garment.

To Kira's astonishment the woman offered naught but a pair of leather shoes.

Kira shook her head firmly and lifted the hem of the kirtle and chemise to show her bare ankle. "Am I to have no *chalwar*?" she requested politely. The women frowned and Kira struggled to find a way to explain. "To cover my legs," she finally said. The two of them discussed the matter in excited whispers, turning of one accord to grant Kira indulgent smiles.

"We wear no such garment," they informed her.

This did not bode well, to Kira's thinking. Surely it could not be so? The women shook their heads and chattered too quickly to be comprehended, then finally lifted the hems of their own garments.

Their legs were similarly bare.

The sight made Kira yet more aware of the loose chemise brushing against her bare thighs and buttocks. No other conclusion could she make than the obvious one, and though she resented that these women had assumed her to have the same occupation as they, she could hardly blame their error. Indeed, without vows between them, was she truly any better than Thierry's whore?

They urged her to the door and Kira concluded that she was not to be granted a djellaba either. Well it seemed that simple modesty was not assumed to be one of her traits, and her color flared high as they descended the stairs to the common room.

Just as they reached the floor and Kira was painfully aware of the regard of the company of men upon them, another entered from the courtyard. The cold gust of air swirled around her bare ankles and made her shiver after the warmth of her bath. Kira felt a telltale prickling and knew without looking that her nipples had beaded. The sight was surely visible through the shockingly fitted cloth and she felt yet more self-conscious at the realization.

Crimson with mortification, she kept her gaze resolutely on the flagstone floor and followed the women as she was bidden.

"Kira."

Even the awe in Thierry's voice would not compel her to look up, for certain was Kira that he was as appalled by her transformed appearance as she. Had she any hope of being considered his only woman, that meager possibility had most assuredly been destroyed by her appearance in the garb of a whore.

"Kira." Thierry's finger was gentle beneath her chin. Though she was upset, Kira could not turn away from him. She reluctantly lifted her gaze to his, surprised to find no censure in his silver gaze. That her clothing did not trouble him was surely all the answer that she needed to confirm her status. Kira felt her tears rise and she shook her head weakly. To her astonishment, there was admiration in Thierry's gaze when it locked with hers once more.

"Nay, Kira," he murmured. "Be not so distressed. Your garments were worn and 'tis best you dress in the Frankish manner."

"But 'tis so different," she protested, knowing she referred to more than the garb itself.

Thierry shook his head. "Yet flattering to you all the same," he mused affectionately.

To be told that the garb of whores suited her was far from the confirmation Kira sought from him. A single tear escaped the trap of her lashes but Thierry gently wiped it aside with his thumb. A small smile played over his lips and he traced one finger lightly down her cheek as though he feared to touch her.

"You are beautiful, Kira," he whispered. Kira closed her heart to the aching tenderness in his voice.

"But the others—"

"Nay." Thierry interrupted her firmly, turning her chin with one warm fingertip so that she was compelled to look into his eyes again. "None is so lovely as Kira," he reiterated with a slight emphasis on her name.

'Twas enough to dissolve her reservations, at least for the moment.

There was no mistaking his pleasure with her appearance and the very fact of that made Kira's heart beat faster. Thierry found her fetching above the others. Whatever role she might play in his life, Kira could not deny that his appreciation pleased her. A flame there was in his eyes and she well knew that he desired her in this moment. It seemed not for the first time that there were no others than the two of them and her heart swelled with pride that this man should have chosen her.

A man made a raucous comment and she jumped at the proximity of his voice. Kira's color flared yet higher at the realization that they stood amidst a veritable army of men, and her gaze flicked nervously to Thierry's. His smile widened slightly, but he did not yet usher her to the board. Embarrassed anew by the lack of modesty of her garb, she raised her hands hesitantly to cover her breasts in the hope that he might understand.

"But, Thierry, 'tis so immodest. I fear to have any look upon me so revealed," she protested.

"Nay, Kira," Thierry murmured. Much to her surprise, Thierry took her hands within his and lifted them away from her. He pressed a kiss to the soft skin on the inside of first one wrist and then the other. A shiver raced over Kira's skin from the sensitive point and she felt her hand quiver within his grip.

"No shame should you have, beautiful Kira," he whispered against her flesh. Undeterred by her shiver, Thierry's lips nudged against her hand and he pressed a kiss into her palm. He straightened before her and folded her fingers over the spot he had kissed, as though her grip could hold his embrace captive there.

Kira smiled at the whimsy of his gesture and it seemed that the hall was cold no longer. Thierry placed her hand on his elbow and escorted her to the long table where Nogai and the leader of the other men already sat, seating her alongside him as though she were the shah's consort herself.

'Twas only much later, when the hall was filled with the sounds of snoring men and Thierry dozed contentedly beside her, that Kira dared to give herself a hard look. She felt the dampness between her thighs, the weight of Thierry's hand on her waist and the absence of any token or vow taken between them. No consolation was it that when Thierry touched her or granted her a tender look, she forgot all else but the magic wrought between them.

But that did not change the truth of it. Kira stared at the ceiling and forced herself to form the thought. She was Thierry's whore and all others knew it. 'Twas time enough she faced the fact herself.

Kira folded her arms about herself in the darkness, hating the kind of woman she had become. Unbeknownst to all who surrounded her, she let her tears creep silently over her cheeks and wondered what would be the fate of her child.

Thierry felt that he recognized the old château reposing on the hill before them ten days after they rode out of Paris. They had ridden hard, especially after that first night, and put the leagues rapidly behind them. The company of knights had also kept from the main roads and Thierry suspected their leader thought they might be pursued.

Old Eustache had confided naught else, much to Thierry's annoyance. "For home, with all haste," had been his anthem these days and when Thierry saw the dark gray edifice ahead, he suspected home was precisely where he was.

He urged his mount deliberately forward in the ranks until he was riding alongside the old knight. Eustache granted him a wary glance but said naught.

"Is this our destination?" Thierry asked.

The other man snorted. "Know you not?" he asked disdainfully.

"Nay, or I would not ask," Thierry responded tightly. He fancied the other man smothered a smile.

"Montsalvat 'tis called," Eustache supplied finally. Thierry felt Kira turn to look up at the forbidding facade of the fortress but did not look away from the older man. Montsalvat. The name he knew well from his sire's tongue, the name of the place where he had been born. Thierry's heart leaped in anticipation.

"And 'tis here you call home?" he asked.

Eustache shot him a sharp look. "Aye."

Realizing that the man was being unnaturally communicative, Thierry decided to ask more. "What happened in Paris?" he asked, watching the knight's expression close stubbornly.

"Naught have I to say of that, if indeed you do not know," he replied tersely.

"Will they not follow us here?" Thierry demanded.

The old knight snorted. "Have they a whit of sense, they will." His lips thinned grimly. "But we will be ready."

"'Tis more than clear you know something more of this matter," Thierry observed.

"And evident that you do not," the older man replied.

"And equally evident that 'tis a factor of import I do not know," Thierry snapped in growing annoyance. "Surely if you knew my sire, you would feel some compunction to confide in me this truth."

The older man's eyes blazed with unexpected anger. "Surely if I knew your sire as I did, I would respect his decision."

"What decision?" Thierry demanded.

"I will say naught of it," the older man retorted. "Mind the road!" he shouted suddenly over his shoulder to his knights. "Singly will we pass, if you please." With that, he urged his horse ahead of Thierry's mount and the conversation came to a frustrating halt. Naught was there wrong with the road that two could not ride abreast and Thierry knew Eustache was avoiding his questions.

But why? Suddenly Thierry realized that 'twas when he had revealed his mark that all had gone awry.

"What is the import of my birthmark?" he shouted at the back of the man ahead of him. Eustache stiffened, telling Thierry he had found the crux of the matter, but naught did the older man say.

Eustache touched his spurs to his mount as though he would outrun the question, but his opponent had no intent of being so easily avoided. Stubbornly Thierry kept his horse hot on the heels of the knight's destrier and they began the climb up the steep road to the fortress well ahead of the others.

"Tell me, Eustache," he called, but no sign did the knight make he had heard. "Well do I know that you know the truth of it. Confide it in me."

Eustache touched his spurs to his mount in response and raced up the twisting road to the gates.

"Would you have me pay the price of my life for your stubborn silence?" Thierry demanded impatiently, to no avail. Eustache reached the barbican gates and passed beneath the shadow of the tower with reckless speed.

"My father's mark is exactly the same," Thierry shouted as he rode into the bailey behind him. Boys came running from the stables as Eustache leaped from his destrier's back. The beast panted from its exertion but the older knight merely cast the reins impatiently aside.

"What means this cursed mark?" Thierry asked in frustration as he followed suit. Eustache glared at him.

"'Tis no *curse* to bear the mark of your line," he spat indignantly. Thierry sensed the thread of the tale.

"What line?"

"Ask your sire," Eustache ordered in disgust as he turned away.

"I cannot," Thierry retorted. The older knight spun on his heel and granted him a wary glance.

"Dead is he?" he growled. He propped his hands on his hips and Thierry imagined the matter meant more to him than he might be willing to reveal.

"I know not," Thierry admitted. Eustache's eyes narrowed.

"Then you had best find out," he concluded harshly, and turned away once more.

"Well do I know that you know this tale!" Thierry shouted as the other man stalked to the portal to the hall. "And well do I see that you hold my father in regard! Is it not a travesty of your respect for him to not confide this in me?"

That question struck the flint.

"Travesty?" Eustache whirled around furiously and stomped back across the bailey to confront Thierry. So angry was he that Thierry wondered what he had wrought with his accusation, just before he found a meaty finger poked into his chest.

"Travesty? Well would it be a *travesty* of respect to tell you this tale, boy, and had you a whit of sense about you, you would know it. Twenty-one years past, afore the Yule, were you born in *that* tower—" the finger jabbed to the château behind the indignant Eustache "—and not four months later a fire was lit in *this* very bailey that you might be granted the full legacy of your line." The finger swept to encompass the deadened grass in the bailey and returned to wag beneath Thierry's nose as Eustache's voice dropped. "Your sire chose to wait."

"What say you?"

"He granted you *naught* of your legacy at your birth or your naming," Eustache clarified, slowly enunciating each word. "Well had he paid the price for its burden and he wanted you to make the choice yourself of shouldering its weight."

"Well, I would choose it now," Thierry asserted firmly, folding his arms across his chest. "Tell me the tale."

"You know naught of what you speak," Eustache sneered. "All my knighted life I have served your family, and even now, in tending this keep, I hold to the word I granted your sire and his sire before him. Can you not see that confiding in you this tale would be the greatest travesty of all? Your sire chose to be the one to confide the tale in you himself, and well did I know of his intent." Eustache took a step away and resolutely held Thierry's regard.

"'Tis out of respect for your sire that I decline your request."

With that flat assertion, Eustache turned to walk more slowly to the hall. The other knights passed through the gates then, the jumbled activity of their arrival doing naught to clarify Thierry's thinking on the matter. Had his father declined him as heir? It sounded not that way, but he knew not what to think.

"What if he is dead?" He blurted out the question afore he thought. Eustache spun slowly and met his gaze assessingly.

"Then your legacy died with him," he said so softly that Thierry had to strain to hear the words.

Nay. It could not be. Destined he was for greatness and well he knew it. This was his chance! No one could steal that from him and Thierry would not permit another opportunity to be lost to him by some whim of the fates.

"Time do we waste!" he cried to the older man in undisguised frustration.

Eustache grimaced. "Time has been wasted afore," he said. "My word did I give to your father."

His father.

Khanbaliq. Thierry's mind wrenched back to those days and those angry words even as Eustache disappeared.

Surely Dagobert still drew breath. Surely 'twas not too late to seek him out and hear the fullness of the tale. Anger raged briefly within him that his sire had not already granted him the tale of his legacy, until a thought dismissed the accusation before it could fully form.

Likely 'twas Thierry had stolen the opportunity for his father's confidence by leaving so abruptly those long years past. He released a long, slow breath and turned to face out over the hills, blind to the stunning view as he remembered his departure from Khanbaliq. Thierry winced in recollection of the accusations he had hurled at his sire that fateful day and rubbed one hand across his brow. He halted midgesture as a thought abruptly occurred to him.

Was this what the shaman had meant when he had said that Thierry's success would be sacrificed by his own hand?

If Kira had thought Thierry distracted before, 'twas naught compared to his manner after his argument with the older knight on their arrival. He was upset beyond anything she had seen before and she wished she knew what to say.

Indeed, though she had understood much of old Eustache's words, his talk of tales and legacies was a complete enigma to her. Kira suspected that Thierry knew little more than she. Though somehow it all had to do with his curious mark.

He frowned, lost in his own thoughts, as they were shown to a large room in the tower. Kira waited but no others joined them and she felt a thrill of pleasure that they were to have some privacy. A civilized place this Montsalvat was undoubtedly. Time enough 'twas that they reached one.

A box made of drapes sat in one corner of the room and Kira regarded it with curiosity. When 'twas evident that Thierry was not in the mood to explain Frankish matters to her, she investigated on her own, leaving him scowling at the floor.

She pulled back the drapes, not knowing what to expect. To her surprise, 'twas merely a place for reposing, from all appearances. Cushions were scattered across the raised base of the box, those heavy drapes hanging all around. Kira felt the bottom of the box, pleased to find it quite soft beneath the blankets.

Privacy, in truth. She smiled with satisfaction as she tugged the drapes closed once more. A strange contrivance 'twas, indeed, though with the coldness the stone floors took in this country, it mayhap was quite sensible. And well was she ready to have Thierry to herself during the night.

"'Tis a bed, Kira," Thierry informed her, his voice unusually flat.

She spared him a glance to find him no more happy than he had been moments before. Well could Kira do something about that. And mayhap 'twas time to show him that she could grant him more than one might expect from a whore. She purposefully closed the distance between them and stretched to her toes to frame his concerned face in her hands.

"Nay, Kira," he said, shaking his head slightly as he frowned. Kira ignored him, reaching up to smooth the furrow from his brow with a gentle fingertip. She shook her head in mock disapproval and he smiled absently at her antics.

"Everything will be fine," she told him solemnly, wishing she was articulate enough in Frankish to tell him yet more. " 'Twill all work out in the end," she added confidently, telling him precisely the opposite of what she had been feeling these past days. But clear 'twas that he needed some reassurance, and mayhap if she played the role of wife and mate, he might see the appeal of the idea. Impulsively she stretched up and kissed him gently.

'Twas the first time she had initiated a kiss, although she had demanded many, and Kira rather liked the sensation. Thierry responded naught for an instant, telling her that she had surprised him, as well.

Kira deliberately nudged her tongue invitingly against his and gained the response she sought. Thierry inhaled sharply and lifted her against him as he deepened his kiss. Kira pulled him closer with satisfaction, rubbing his neck soothingly and liking the way the tension was easing from him.

Something there was that she could give Thierry. Something more than sexual release, for here she gave him comfort. And more, he accepted it from her. She dared to take encouragement from that meager offering. Mayhap he did hold her in higher regard than the Persian woman had implied that all Mongols held their women. Kira closed her eyes and dared to dream that one day she alone would be Thierry's woman.

Though she needed not his love, for love had already left its furrows in her back.

She smiled softly when he lifted his head and he traced her cheek with that roughened fingertip again. A habit 'twas becoming, and one Kira rather liked. She nestled her cheek against Thierry's palm contentedly.

"Kira, I must go down to the others for a time," he explained quietly. Kira nodded understanding. She could not restrain the urge to rub her fingertips speculatively over her lips as she watched Thierry go, unable to completely stifle her budding optimism.

Mayhap she could be Thierry's woman alone. Should the thought not have occurred to him as yet, she would endeavor at every opportunity to make it so. Indeed, Kira could not imagine that their thoughts were not as one when she met the warmth in his silver gaze. Dare she even wonder whether he already thought of her alone?

'Twas almost too much to be believed, but Kira dared to indulge her whimsy. She spun about the room happily, pausing to poke at a trinket box or a tapestry in gleeful disinterest. Here would they stay, she fantasized, here would they make their home, simply the two of them together. The two of them and their babe, and mayhap more babes after this one. 'Twas fitting that they stay here at

Montsalvat, where Thierry had been born, himself. And 'twas a place she suspected that she could find amenable, as well.

Kira closed her eyes and imagined telling Thierry of the child. Mayhap 'twould be all the impetus he needed to cast aside his wandering ways and settle here to live. Mayhap he would be delighted that they had wrought another so soon. Mayhap he would feel as wondrous of the new life forming within her as she did.

Mayhap. Kira's eyes flew open and her gaze landed on Thierry's saddlebags. Did she dare to make her desire known? She hesitated for but a heartbeat before deciding to unpack his belongings. Liked it here, Kira did. More, she would raise her child here within these sturdy gray walls. She would lift her babe high and show him the wonder of the view from this perch high above the land, let him fill his lungs with the scent of the sea.

What better way to show Thierry thus than to spread about his belongings as though they lived here in truth?

The rationale was inescapable and Kira set to her task with relish. The blankets she shook out and folded atop the bed. Thierry's brass pots and cooking implements she arranged neatly on the cold hearth. She ensured that they were clean, though she did not imagine he would cook anything here. Already the smell of roasted meat rose from the hall below to tempt her stomach and Kira found herself happily humming at her task.

His silk *kurta* that she had worn that long-ago night came next from the bag. She rubbed her nose in its softness and draped it over a stool with a smile of reminiscence. Always would she remember those first little fishes.

On the morrow she would wash their garments, Kira resolved, reaching into the bag yet again. A small bag she retrieved and assumed it contained coin. But nay, 'twas too light and its contents not bulky enough. With a frown Kira spilled the contents out into her palm and caught her breath at the sight.

'Twas an *aljofar*. She would have known the token anywhere.

A gift for a bride. The very fact that 'twas hidden away told Kira in a heartbeat that 'twas not meant for her.

Having the evidence for what she feared most cradled within her palm unnerved Kira more than she would have expected. Indeed, she felt that she had been dealt a telling and unexpected blow by this discovery. Would Thierry not have given the token to her already if he had meant her to have the gem?

Kira's hand shook at the truth of that and she hastily dumped both the pearl and its chain back into the small sack. Her vision veiled with tears and she shoved the bag back into his saddlebag. Bittersweet was the realization of how much she had longed to have Thierry as hers and hers alone.

Wanted Thierry as her husband and the father of her children, Kira did, and now that 'twas not to be, she dared to fully voice her desire. One man, one woman, as 'twas ordained to be. And she had thought mayhap...

But nay. Kira had imposed her own beliefs on her perception of the situation and seen only what she wished to see. No promise had Thierry made to her. No more did he seek from her than a man might expect from a whore. A fool she had been to tease herself with other possibilities. Had the Persian woman not made it clear that these Mongols took many wives and held not one above the others? Had she not been warned?

Could this sweet longing she felt to be with Thierry alone be love in a different guise? Well it seemed it shared the same serpent's bite as her father's love. Though in truth, the teeth dug deeper this time for all that they did not scar her flesh.

Had she fallen in love with Thierry? If so, it seemed she had gained precisely what she deserved for daring to have faith in tender emotions yet again. Kira dropped to sit on the stone ledge of the window, knowing the truth when she heard it. No sweetness was there in the realization that she loved Thierry as she stared down at the rumpled bag. Only too well could she still see that plumply expensive *aljofar* in her mind's eye and well Kira knew she would never forget it.

A token for another woman.

A token of Thierry's regard that she was not destined to wear.

And never would Kira wear one, even as a token of another man's regard, after bearing a child out of wedlock. No doubt would there be that she was no longer innocent. A life of shame stretched out before Kira and she found she liked the taste of it naught. She stared blindly at the small sack perched in the bag and suddenly realized the folly of what she had done in unpacking his goods.

Nay, she thought wildly. It must be precisely where she had found it. Observant Thierry was beyond belief and he must never know she had seen what he had hidden from her. Kira forced herself to recall the sack's original position and unsteadily put it back just so, then cast a nervous glance around the room.

Better 'twould be if Thierry had no idea she had opened the saddlebag. Her hands shook as she folded the blankets but she would not falter in this task. Kira inhaled shakily and choked back her tears as she carefully repacked his belongings. 'Twas obvious that Thierry had come to the land of the Franks to fetch his bride.

Indeed, it mattered naught whether her belly rounded or not, for he would soon cast her aside, one way or the other. Fretted she had for naught all these nights. Only a matter of time was it before Thierry cast her aside. And whither then? She knew not and could not bear to speculate about raising their child alone.

Despair welled up in Kira's heart as she completed her task and weak tears spilled over her cheeks unchecked. She dashed at them with her fingertips before she realized the futility of the gesture and sighed raggedly in acceptance of her fate. Would that she had never met Thierry. Would that she were back in Tiflis.

Kira sniffled, then hastily crawled within the comfort of the draped bed, wishing it truly could render her invisible to the world.

"Tell me not that you have troubles in this paradise," Nogai commented sardonically. Thierry glanced up from his wine as his friend dropped to sit beside him, and scowled into the red liquid anew.

"Well it seems that I must seek my sire," he muttered.

Nogai's brows rose. "First a family, now a sire. Suddenly your kin are being conjured from naught so quickly that I cannot keep a reckoning of them all." Thierry's glance slid sidelong but Nogai was innocently draining his own tankard. The Mongol tapped the empty pewter demandingly on the board and grinned when it was promptly filled.

"Fitting it seems that you would be in haste to leave the first decent place we have quartered," he commented.

"Montsalvat meets with your approval?" Thierry demanded tersely, indicating that his tankard also be filled. Drink aplenty was what he needed this night, for only with oblivion might he escape his memories.

"Aye," Nogai concluded with satisfaction. "Aim to sleep under the stars this night I do, as is fitting for a man. Have you seen the goats? Sturdy stock have they here and able herdsmen they must be. Even with the liability of this tower, 'tis an amenable place."

"Should you like it so well, you will undoubtedly be welcome to remain in my absence," Thierry responded sourly. He did not bother to acknowledge Nogai's glance of surprise.

"Truly you mean to leave?"

"I must seek my sire," Thierry growled.

"Ah." Nogai took a long draught of wine. "Have you any inkling where he might be?" he asked with apparent idleness.

"Khanbaliq," Thierry supplied tightly. Nogai choked in a most satisfactory manner.

"Khanbaliq?" he demanded in open astonishment. "Know you how far that is?"

"Aye." With greater precision than Nogai might guess did Thierry know the distance, for he had traveled it and he suspected Nogai had not. Without the endorsement of the khan, 'twould take a full year to reach Khanbaliq. And then what? Another year to return to the land of his birth? All to hear a tale he might have been told years past. All to hear a tale that might mean naught.

Or might mean everything. Thierry indulged himself with a venomous glance to the taciturn Eustache, who stubbornly ignored him.

Cursed man. Two years was Thierry to waste over this matter. Yet little choice had he. Thierry's sense that his destiny hung in the balance and that this tale could tip the scales could not be denied.

"'Aye,' says he, as though 'twere no farther than the town below this fortress," Nogai snorted into his tankard. He fixed Thierry abruptly with a bright eye. "What of Kira?"

"What *of* Kira?"

"Does she ride to Khanbaliq?"

Thierry's lips thinned. "Kira is my woman," he said tightly, as though that explained all. And to his mind, it did.

Nogai, however, snorted with undisguised skepticism. "And enchanted will she be with the sight of another ship in such short order, you can be sure," he commented dryly. Thierry refused to indulge him with a response and the two drank in silence for a long moment.

"Have you considered," Nogai began finally in a measured tone, "that such a trip might be difficult for one so small as she?"

He would *not* leave Kira behind. 'Twas unthinkable, and truly Nogai overstepped himself in even suggesting such a thing. Thierry bristled at the very thought and turned a chilling eye on his *anda*.

"What do you suggest?" Thierry demanded coldly. Nogai spread his hands carefully.

"Only that it might well be safer for Kira to remain here. Not so strong is she as Mongol women and well might she welcome the opportunity to wait behind such sturdy walls."

Everything within Thierry clenched at the very idea. Two years without Kira? Impossible. And naught would happen to her on the road—he would personally ensure her safety. Whereas here, who knew what fate might befall her?

"Kira is stronger than you know," he retorted frostily. Nogai raised his brows but said naught, philosophically taking a sip of his wine instead.

"When do you plan to commence?" he asked mildly some moments later. Thierry drained his tankard and banged it on the board yet again.

"On the morrow, with first light," he informed his *anda* tightly. "Well it seems that time is of the essence."

"Aye," Nogai responded with an easy grin. "Imperative 'tis that I should have some decent *qumis* in short order, instead of this thin swill that passes for drink in these parts." He drained his tankard, showing no trouble in swallowing the "swill," before he banged it on the board with a roar and a wink.

Chapter Fourteen

Not reassuring at all was the fact that Thierry did not return.

Kira curled alone under the coverlet within the secure embrace of the draped bed and watched darkness descend over the room. Thierry did not come. Raucous sounds rose from the hall below, their volume increasing as time passed with aching slowness and still Thierry did not come. The smell of the meat reached a peak and faded away to naught, yet no tread of a foot in the hall outside did Kira discern.

She huddled deeper within the blanket's warmth and wrapped her arms around her stomach, as though she would comfort her fledgling babe. Alone they were, and they had best become accustomed to that fact. Indeed, Kira might not even have the bed to hide within once Thierry discovered her state. An expensive indulgence it must be and she could not imagine that one would waste such richness on a pregnant concubine.

But what choice had she other than to stay? No coin had she with which to smooth her way back. And where would she go? Back to Tiflis? Indeed, she could not imagine that her sire would even welcome her there should she arrive with her belly swollen with child and no husband in tow.

The *aljofar* had value.

The traitorous thought held a certain appeal, though Kira's ethics rose in instant denial. She nibbled her lip in indecision. Did she dare?

Recollection of precisely who had compromised her had
her flying out across the room and rummaging in Thierry's saddlebags. Tears pricked Kira's eyes as the gem tumbled out into her palm, but she resolutely blinked them
away. Precisely how much value did the pearl carry? Was
it indeed worth betraying the man she had grown to trust,
however mistakenly?

Kira closed her eyes and placed the gem on her tongue.

Sweet. She stifled a curse and spat the pearl out with
disgust.

A plague on the man for buying such a good gem! She
cast the necklace away from her, not caring where it fell.
How could he manage such a feat? *Naught* did Thierry
know of pearls and yet he still acquired an exquisite *aljofar* for his bride. Unfair 'twas, and her indecision rose yet
higher at the evident value of the piece. Kira stalked irritably across the room and back to cast an accusatory eye
over the pearl. The gem winked innocently in the light cast
by the moon where its chain had snagged on the saddlebag.

'Twas worth good coin, that cursed pearl. Kira crossed
the room reluctantly to lift it from its perch and let it swivel
slowly from its chain before her. Good coin. Coin enough
mayhap to buy passage to Constantinople. The gem
gleamed invitingly as though it would tempt her to make the
choice, but Kira shook her head and heaved a sigh.

'Twould be wrong. She could not do it. Thierry had
parted with hard-earned coin to acquire a worthy gift for
his bride and no place had she to intervene. The *aljofar* was
not hers to take, one way or the other. Kira was but a whore
who had made the mistake of conceiving, and well would
she have to bear the burden of her error alone. She slipped
the pearl slowly back into the small sack and replaced the
entirety within the saddlebag.

Naught had she but the garments on her back and her
own resources. Precious little they seemed indeed to see a
way for herself and a babe, but somehow Kira knew she
would ride the storm.

And as long as she could, she would keep Thierry's protection.

Even if he could grant her naught else.

'Twas with the first light of the dawn that Thierry crept up the stairs. Not too drunk was he to have forgotten that Kira had not eaten, though admittedly he had recalled the fact rather late. His steps were rather more unsteady than he expected as he made a swerving path down the corridor, offering in hand. He scowled even as he wondered whether Nogai had spoken aright.

Had they been so long without *qumis* that they were less than they had been? Nogai had fallen asleep on the board from the red wine, and well enough did Thierry know 'twas not his wont.

Was Kira making them both soft?

The twinge of guilt Thierry felt when he nudged open the door and found the room within silent did naught to reassure him. Not even Kira's breathing could he discern and well he knew that his hearing was better than that.

Impossible that he was becoming an urban man. Impossible that he could not carry his *qumis*. Impossible that he could not discern the sound of a sleeping woman's breathing when she lay so close. Thierry stalked into the room in poor humor and fairly dropped the crockery of stew onto the table by the hearth so that it clattered noisily. Let Kira see the fullness of the man she had chosen. He burped fruitily, amplifying the sound with satisfaction.

Naught stirred.

'Twas disconcerting. Fear rose within him and he wondered suddenly if Kira inexplicably might have abandoned him. No reason had she, but still the room was too quiet. Thierry spun around in panic and surveyed his surroundings, finding his saddlebags precisely as he had dropped them.

Not a good sign was that. Indeed, it appeared that naught had stirred since his departure and the matter did not sit well. Thierry's eyes narrowed as he found no sign of

Kira, and his gaze landed on the bed. 'Twas the only place where Kira could be concealed and he strode across the room and ripped open the drapes.

Time 'twas they were on the road to seek his sire, and he told himself that 'twas that impatience alone that fueled his anxiety.

Kira slept curled in a tight ball. Little cat. Thierry released his breath slowly in relief and forced his fingers to loosen their grip on the drapes. He stood and gazed upon her, unaware of the smile that transformed his features as he leaned against the bedpost.

His Kira. Thierry's heart wrenched at the fragility of her. So tiny she was. Her breathing was soft enough that he fancied she barely breathed at all. No wonder he had not heard her, for she made virtually no sound. Only too well did he recall her illness on the ship, and the hand that would have urged her awake froze mid-gesture.

Was Nogai right? Would he threaten Kira's health by taking her on a journey that was sure to be arduous? Thierry reached out one tentative fingertip and gently smoothed the hair back from her temple. He admired the luscious sweep of her dark lashes upon her cheek and found his fingers trailing over her skin in a caress.

How could he bear to be without her for two years?

There was not just Kira's health to consider, though. Only too well did Thierry recall the gleam in men's eyes when they had looked upon her, and his hand clenched involuntarily. They could be set upon by bandits on the long road to Khanbaliq. Kira could be hurt. Worse, she could be raped or even killed.

How could Thierry live with himself should he be responsible for bringing her to such a fate? How could he bear to see her hurt?

What if something should befall him and she was left alone with Nogai? Would Nogai protect her? Thierry hoped so in the same moment he prayed Nogai would not see fit to claim his strong yet delicate little cat for his own.

Was that not the Mongol way? Thierry's gut twisted in indecision and he paced impatiently across the room. No sooner had he put distance between them than he was drawn back to gaze down at her as though she kept him on an invisible lead.

Witch, he thought affectionately, tempted by the luscious swell of her rosy lips. He sat carefully on the side of the bed and leaned over her, fancying that she sensed his presence when she immediately turned toward him.

What if some evil fate befell both Nogai and Thierry, leaving Kira truly alone?

Thierry's gut went cold and he shoved to his feet, the thought sobering him more than two nights' sleep. Had not old Eustache pledged his hand to Thierry's family? Would that old knight not see Kira protected? And safer she would be here, within the walls of the fortress Montsalvat, than anywhere on the open road he might take her. Eustache had said they were prepared to greet any pursuers from the crown, and the forces Thierry had already seen quartered here convinced him.

'Twas the only sensible path to take, despite his own misgivings. Thierry must think of Kira and her safety, not simply his own baser desires.

But how could he tell her that he did not abandon her here? Two years was long enough that any woman might have doubts. Would she believe any promise he made? Thierry propped his hands on his hips with dissatisfaction as he stared down at her once more.

Would she cry at the news? Thierry's innards writhed at the possibility. Never would he be able to leave without her, should she cry. But he could not endanger her. Thierry pressed a hand to his temples.

Would that he could be assured that she would be safe in his company, for his heart vehemently protested any other solution.

But nay. 'Twas illogical to jeopardize such a fragile creature so, purely for his own whimsy. Some of his possessions Thierry would leave that Kira might know he intended to return.

'Twas the way it should be. She would understand. Thierry's vision blurred as he stubbornly set about his packing and he forced himself to think of his return. Once he knew of his legacy, he would return and take Kira to his side once more. His woman she was and even the breadth of the Mongol empire could not change that simple fact. His fingers fumbled when he came upon the small pouch with the *aljofar*. He hesitated for a long moment, finally letting the chain and gem tumble into his palm.

Well should he have given Kira the token already. Thierry spared a glance to the bed, knowing that if she had awakened, he would have granted it to her now.

But nay. Kira slept on, oblivious to Thierry's anguish, and loath was he to awaken her for such an indulgence. And then he would be forced to explain all to her. Thierry jammed the *aljofar* into its pouch.

Witch. So completely had Kira ensnared him, yet she blithely slept while he wrestled with his feelings for her.

And what were his feelings for her? Strong indeed was this urge to see her safe, yet Thierry would not grant it a name lest he be compelled to look it fully in the eye. He thought of his parents, and for the first time considered that there might be a difference between claiming Kira as his woman and making her his wife.

But nay. Foolish whimsy that was. 'Twas all the same. The woman warmed his bed and knew the safety of his protection. What more could there be between man and woman? What more might one desire of a union?

Thierry thought unexpectedly of the way she had offered him comfort before he had gone down to the hall the night before and decisively snapped his saddlebag closed.

Mayhap 'twould be better that he was without her for a while. Mayhap this softness she had launched within him would disappear, should she not be constantly before him.

Mayhap that softness was not something to be distrusted. The taunting voice of temptation would not abandon him readily this morn, it seemed, and Thierry shoved restlessly away from the bed.

Enough. A task had he to perform and though 'twas one he would rather avoid, he would see the matter through. His father he would seek, his legacy he would know, his woman he would return for when all was completed.

And he would grant her the *aljofar* on his return. Thierry grimly shoved the pouch containing the gem deep within his *kalat*.

Despite his resolutions, he could not help but pause before he left and look down on her lingeringly once more. Would that he could commit her features to memory. Would that he could safely take her with him.

Would that he did not have to go.

Kira sensed the difference in the room as soon as she awakened. Something was amiss. She rolled over and peered out through the heavy drapes, squinting at the brightness of the sunlight that flooded the room.

Clear 'twas that Thierry had not returned to her, for she had not felt his warmth throughout the night, but there was something else gone awry. As soon as her eyes adjusted to the morning light, Kira saw that one of Thierry's saddlebags was gone.

It could not be. She flew from the bed, tripping over the cursedly long chemise these folk wore, and tore open the top of the remaining bag. His blanket, his cooking utensils, his tin cup, all were gone. Indeed, this bag was virtually empty and she wondered why he had left it behind. One blanket there was only.

Kira rummaged in the hidden shadows of the leather bag and encountered something hard. She drew it out into the light and bit her lip when she realized she held the knife Thierry had granted her once before. That time he had given her a means of protecting herself when he sent her home alone.

The message was clear enough to Kira's mind. Well it seemed he gave her the same means once again. Which could only mean that Thierry would be gone for a time. Kira sank to the floor beside his bag and turned the blade over and over in her hands.

Mayhap he was gone for good.

Mayhap 'twas his way of telling her to be gone when he returned.

And he had not even awakened her to tell her of his decision himself. Truly she had been a fool to expect anything else.

She would not cry.

How could he leave her without saying adieu? How could he abandon her here in this remote fortress with solely a short dagger to protect herself? How could he not have known that she bore his child?

Curse him! In a rare burst of temper, Kira swatted the saddlebag viciously and sent it rolling end over end across the stone floor. The blanket tumbled out and unfolded itself, another tin cup rattled as it danced across the flagstones. Kira scooped up the empty bag, shook it savagely and cast it against the far wall in disgust.

'Twas then that she realized what else Thierry had taken with him.

The *aljofar* was gone.

Thierry had gone to fetch his bride. The moment she had dreaded was upon her. Kira had been dismissed.

An overwhelming sadness threatened to engulf Kira but she stubbornly bit down on the tide. She would *not* cry. She would not be disappointed or hurt. Had she not known from the outset that he was Mongol? Had the Persian woman not warned her of their ways?

Had she not known better than to put her faith in him?

No matter that she had done precisely that. No matter that Thierry had not treated her in the manner she might have expected from a Mongol. No matter that he had been kind and considerate of her beyond anything or anyone she had ever known. Mayhap that just made the inevitable more bitter to swallow.

'Twas the cruelty she had originally expected from him, rendered all the more cruel by the kindness he had shown her first.

Curse him.

She was an abandoned whore who was with child. Kira jabbed her chin into the air determinedly. She owed her child more than wallowing in self-pity would earn him. Was his sire not a proud and tall man?

But she would not raise her child here in this place that brought a gleam to Thierry's eye. To this fortress she knew he would return. Mayhap he fetched his bride to bring her back here. At the very thought, Kira hauled the heavy kirtle over her head and began to hastily lace the sides.

Whatever the price, Kira and her child would not be here to greet him.

Thierry and Nogai were leaving the village perched on the side of the hill below Montsalvat when Thierry realized another party rode along the serpentine road toward them. He and Nogai exchanged a look and Nogai frowned.

"Think you that they follow from that king's court?" he demanded suspiciously. Thierry did not like that he had no ready answer, nor did he like that the party was too far away to be readily identified. His first thought was for Kira sleeping far above and he knew he could not simply ride away without knowing more.

"I would know their intent," he said, relieved when Nogai nodded agreement. They ducked into the shadows alongside the only tavern in the ramshackle village and waited impatiently for the others to approach.

As they sat, Thierry watched his horse's ear twitch complacently and reviewed what he had seen. The party was extensive, which did not bode well to his mind. But there seemed to be no haste to their progress, a fact both annoying and puzzling.

Surely invaders would approach quickly and attack before any guessed their intent? To that end, surely attackers would arrive in the night. But this road led to no other destination than the fortress. Well it seemed that Montsalvat would soon have guests, of one manner or another.

And Kira he had left alone within the fortress walls. Thierry stifled a foreboding sense that these riders came on a mission he would not like. Nogai settled himself back into the shadows with his usual calm and spared Thierry a telling glance.

Aye. Thierry gritted his teeth. They would simply have to wait, even though these riders seemed to be taking far too long to reach the town.

Well it seemed that he had lost his patience for waiting, among other things, these past few weeks.

"Töde!" called an imperious voice when Thierry thought he could surely remain quiet no longer. 'Twas a voice that Thierry remembered well and he stiffened instinctively at the sound, despite all the years that had passed since he had last heard it raised.

It simply could not be.

"Do pick up the pace, Töde. I would cross the threshold of Montsalvat yet again before I expire." The rumbling growl was so achingly familiar to Thierry that he closed his eyes for a long moment to regain his self-control. He felt Nogai's inquiring gaze upon him, but could not summon the words to explain through the midst of his surprise and confusion.

"Never is time wasted on caution, milord," a younger voice replied.

"Time aplenty have we already wasted on this trip and I would sit at a warm hearth with a cup of brew in short order."

"Our homeland 'tis, Töde, and safer than you might think," an equally familiar but feminine voice added persuasively.

It seemed that Thierry could not summon the air into his lungs.

Here. Now. Naught had he decided of what he would say, what he would do, what he would ask, having fully expected to have the width of a continent to summon his thoughts. But the moment was upon him already and naught was there he could do but face its demands as well as he was able.

Thierry straightened slowly and turned, the knowledge of what he would see not lessening the shock a whit. He took a deep breath and urged his horse out of the shadows into the road as the arriving party drew alongside.

The closest horse whinnied in surprise and took a double step. This drew the attention of the Mongol who rode alongside, his hand dropping to his blade with predictable speed.

Thierry moved naught as he met the steady gaze of his sire.

"You!" Dagobert inhaled sharply and hauled his destrier to an abrupt halt.

The others jostled to a halt and all fell silent. An expectant silence filled the crooked road, but Thierry could neither speak nor look away from the recollection in his sire's eyes. Dagobert squared his shoulders suddenly and his expression turned forbidding. In that moment Thierry knew he would have to be the first to speak and hoped he could do so. He cleared his throat, the clamor of his heart making it difficult to find fitting words.

"Hello, Father," he said simply.

The quiet words hung in the silence and it seemed the very earth held its breath. His sire's expression melted not a whit and Thierry feared that his greeting would garner no response at all.

A movement caught his eye and he noted his mother's presence for the first time. In the same instant he saw his father's restraining hand on Alienor's forearm and well understood the meaning.

This battle was betwixt the two of them alone.

Thierry noted the signs of his father's aging in the morning sunlight and endeavored to calculate how long it had been since they had exchanged heated words. Five years? Six? Thierry could not be sure, but well did he know that his sire's memory of that day had not faded, either.

He had been young indeed when he had ridden out of Khanbaliq in anger. And had sworn he would never return.

The hostility sat between them as surely as if the argument had only just been voiced.

"What are you doing here?" Dagobert demanded tightly.

"I might ask the same of you," Thierry retorted, his tone colder than he might have intended it to be. His father's nostrils flared slightly, the only outward sign of his anger, and he glanced up at the brooding fortress with almost a casual air.

"This is my home," he asserted stonily. "I would ask again, what brings *you* here?" The challenge in his eyes was unmistakable. This was not Thierry's home.

"I had thought I might find something of home here myself," Thierry maintained proudly. His father lifted one fair brow.

"No legacy have you here," he said flatly.

The memory of what Eustache had said filled Thierry's mind. The realization that his sire had deliberately chosen to deny him his heritage cut like a well-honed knife.

"So I have been told. No idea had I that you were so ashamed to have me as your son," Thierry commented bitterly. His mother gasped, but both men paid her no heed.

"Not half as ashamed as evidently you are of having me as your sire," Dagobert snorted.

"No shame have I in my lineage, even if my own sire would deny me," Thierry argued.

"Ha!" Dagobert charged. He urged his horse forward as the color rose in his neck. "'Twas not as I recall your last words to me," he spat venomously. "Or mayhap you find no shame in having a 'coward' as your father?"

Thierry felt his own color rise at the reminder. "I was young and spoke in haste," he said defensively.

"Oho! In haste indeed did you speak, not to mention that in haste did you leave," his father countered. "And nary a word in the years between. Have you not a shred of compassion for your mother's worries, at least?"

"Well I understood that you were relieved to see the back of me," Thierry snapped, his anger finally beyond constraint.

"Me? And what had my concerns to do with any of this? Headstrong you were from the first and determined that you alone knew what was for the best!"

"Headstrong?" Thierry repeated angrily. "'Twas not I who deliberately denied my only son his rightful legacy! Tell me, Father, am I a bastard born? Is that what lies at the root of this?"

"Thierry!" Alienor breathed in shock. Dagobert's eyes blazed and he spurred his mount yet closer to his son.

"Were you not my own spawn, I would take a lash to you for speaking thus of your mother," he spat.

"So you claim me, then?" Thierry demanded proudly.

Dagobert's head jerked up and his silver eyes blazed. "Always have I claimed you as my own," he retorted.

"Indeed?" 'Twas Thierry's turn to arch an inquiring brow. "'Twas not what old Eustache told me."

Dagobert's features paled despite his tan and when he spoke, his voice was strained. "Eustache could not have told you that I denied you, for he knows better."

"To deny me my legacy is not to deny me?" Thierry snorted in disgust. "Indeed, it seems you play a game of words with me, milord."

Dagobert's eyes flashed. "I denied you *naught!*" he fairly shouted. "Claimed you as my son and heir I did all those years past." He jabbed one finger through the air to the fortress high above. "There in that bailey under the spring moon did I claim you as my own son!"

"Then what of this legacy that all speak of in whispers?"

"'Tis naught for you to concern yourself," Dagobert insisted stonily. He turned slightly away. Rage rippled through Thierry as he realized that his father still had no intention of confiding in him the tale.

"Has it to do with this?" he demanded, tearing his *kalat* open to bare his mark with a vicious gesture.

Dagobert looked up with evident reluctance. The tension crackled between the two men until Dagobert glanced away from Thierry's mark and swallowed carefully. "What do you know about that?" he asked quietly.

"Well enough do I know that you sport one much the same."

Dagobert shrugged with feigned nonchalance. "'Tis a birthmark, no more, no less," he maintained calmly. Even with the years between them, Thierry knew his sire lied.

"'Tis a birthmark that nearly saw me slaughtered!" he cried. His father's eyes widened in shock. Thierry felt a surge of satisfaction that his point had been made.

"Where?" Dagobert demanded tightly.

"At the court of the king in Paris," Thierry supplied proudly, savoring his father's astonishment.

"You bared your mark there?" his sire asked incredulously. Older he looked, though his new appearance of vulnerability did naught to cool Thierry's anger. "Well does it seem that *you* cannot be called a coward," Dagobert charged. "Although mayhap a *fool* would be closer to the mark! Know you what you have done in this? Know you what you risked?"

"How could I? 'Tis a *birthmark,* no more, no less," he taunted. His father's jaw tightened.

"Fool!" he spat. "Know you what you have risked by such foolishness?"

"Evidently not!" Thierry shouted in exasperation. "How could I know when all refuse to confide in me the tale?"

Dagobert glared at him and his lips thinned. "Always did I mean to tell you the tale. When you were older."

"I *am* older," Thierry retorted. "And your reticence has nearly seen me dead."

"'Twas you who called me a coward," his sire accused. Thierry glared back at him, having naught with which to explain away those angry words. "Well did I understand that I was simply some coward with the good fortune to have fallen upon your mother at an opportune moment," Dagobert continued when Thierry did not speak. "And now you would ask of me a tale of your heritage."

"Dagobert," Alienor chided under her breath, but Dagobert's expression did not soften.

"'Twas precisely that the boy charged, as I well recall." His eyes narrowed as he looked to Thierry once more. Thierry winced at the familiarity of the words, wondering how he could ever have been so cruel.

"I erred," he said simply. Dagobert's eyes flashed angrily.

"Quickly indeed does that confession come for all the years spent awaiting it," he said tersely. "Should I not know better, I might conclude that you were solely concerned about your status as heir. Have you seen Montsalvat and decided you fancy it better than roaming ceaselessly over the hills?"

Thierry impaled his sire with a glance. "I seek no more than to know the truth of something that might see me dead," he maintained tightly. "Indeed, it seems little enough to ask of a father."

"I would tell you the fullness of the tale, were you not clearly leaving Montsalvat," Dagobert answered stiffly. Thierry met his father's gaze slowly.

"I ride only to seek you out," he said quietly and saw the surprise register on his father's features.

"Why?" Dagobert demanded.

"Eustache did I ask for the import of my mark. He declined to tell me the tale out of deference to you." Something eased in his father's expression, encouraging Thierry to plunge on and ask the question to which he most feared to hear the answer. "He bade me seek you out," he confided hoarsely. "I would ask you myself whether you had disclaimed me by not granting me the fullness of this legacy."

"Never."

Dagobert's flat denial hung in the silence between the two men so long that Thierry wondered if he had imagined the sound.

So long had it been. And for what? Heartless words exchanged in anger. Surely his sire knew that Thierry did not truly believe him a coward.

Was it possible his father had not swept Thierry from his heart?

"And well it seemed that I owed my sire an apology," Thierry added quietly.

Then Dagobert shook his head and dismounted hastily, closing the space between them with hasty steps. Thierry knew not his intent, but echoed the older man's move lest his father think even less of him. Their gazes met again when they were but a pace apart and Thierry did not dare to hope when his father laid one hand heavily upon his shoulder.

"Never would I deny you, no matter what charge was made in anger," Dagobert asserted with quiet resolve. "My son are you, blood of my blood and fruit of the vine. One night long past, I claimed you as my son and heir in the bailey at Montsalvat. I but left the decision to you whether you would assume the burden of the family legacy."

"What *is* my legacy, Father?" Thierry demanded softly. His sire frowned into space for a long moment, then met his son's gaze once more.

"Well do you know that we share a mark in common," he said quietly. Thierry nodded. "A mark 'tis of our lineage and the heritage of our bloodline." His voice dropped and Thierry had to strain to hear the words, even though they stood but an arm's length apart. "Well might you have heard tell of the lost kings of Rhedae, the forgotten kings whose line was divinely chosen to rule."

"Aye."

Dagobert's gaze grew serious and Thierry fancied he saw sadness in those gray eyes. "A line of kings wrongfully displaced by usurpers and overthrown from our rightful role. Long centuries have passed, each with their attempts, some noble, some covert, to regain that which we have lost, to regain that which is our rightful legacy. Each attempt has been a failure. I watched my sire die in battle and took the pledge at his hand that very day."

Dagobert sighed heavily. "I, too, failed at the task and nearly lost all I held dear in the transaction. 'Twould have been too much to pay for something mayhap no longer within our grasp, for well it seems to me that the days of regaining lost legacies are passing. Such doings are of the matter of myths and fireside tales and not a way for a man to earn his way. Centuries has it been and oft have I wondered if the blood royal ran too thin in my veins to see the matter successfully resolved."

He cleared his throat carefully and looked into Thierry's eyes once more. "When we had retreated to Montsalvat and were besieged, well we knew that the fortress would fall to the invaders. Alienor and I decided to stay but long enough to grant you your name. 'Twas when you should have been granted the burden of your legacy according to family tradition, but I—" Thierry watched in amazement as his sire shook his head wonderingly and smiled sadly "—I could not so readily commit you to a path I feared to be folly.

"That night, beneath the stars at Montsalvat, I claimed you as my son, granted you my name and bestowed upon you the choice of whether to take up the family quest or not. Never had another in our line done this for his heir, but times change and opportunities fade, and I would not see you pay a high toll for what might well be whimsy."

The lost kings of Rhedae culminated in him. Silence reigned between them for a long moment as Thierry fought to make sense of his father's words.

'Twas impossible to believe, yet the tale struck a chord of truth within him that told him his sire spoke aright. Of a line of kings was Thierry. Of a rightful line of kings destined to rule by divine choice. Here was the meaning of his mark. Here also was the grand destiny he had envisioned for himself, should he but regain the crown.

Quickly Thierry reviewed what he had observed in Paris and the vigor with which those summoned by Eustache had taken up his cause. A lost line of kings. Never would Thierry have imagined this to be his fate, but even now, his pulse quickened at the prospect.

"Make no mistake, Thierry," Dagobert said with utmost seriousness. "Never did I imagine 'twould be so many years before I told you the fullness of the tale."

"No fault was it of yours that I would behave so foolishly. 'Twas that quest that drove you from home, not cowardice as I charged," Thierry guessed intuitively and his father almost smiled at his low words.

"'Twas that, indeed," he admitted. "Already had I lifted my hand to the battle and failed. A hunted man was I in these parts and well had my desire grown to see many more days in Alienor's company." He spared a crooked smile over his shoulder and Thierry followed his gaze to find his mother's eyes glazed with tears. Dagobert's voice dropped to a confidential whisper.

"'Twas Alienor's desire once she had saved me from certain death that I live long enough to see my son become a man." The two men looked into each other's eyes once more and Dagobert lifted his other hand to rest companionably on Thierry's shoulder. He tightened his grip and summoned a smile that warmed the silver of his eyes.

"And so I have," he said softly. "So I have."

The two men looked away for a moment, Thierry struggling to clear the tears from his vision. His father cleared his throat gruffly.

"Not easy is it for a man to admit when he is wrong," Dagobert added quietly. "And I would not be churlish enough to hold words spoken in haste against you." No mistaking his pride was there and emotion rose in Thierry's throat fit to choke him. Dagobert's grip tightened on

Thierry's shoulder. "Glad I am indeed that we chose this time to come home."

Home. Thierry followed his father's gaze back to the heavy stone walls and knew exactly what the older man had meant. Naught did he recall of this place, but still Montsalvat invoked a powerful magic in his heart.

'Twas here he wanted to raise his family with Kira, he realized suddenly. 'Twas here he wanted to make his home. Well did Thierry know that he had not imagined Kira's comfort with the old keep. Here would they set down their roots.

A sudden thought disturbed Thierry's thoughts and he glanced to his sire in alarm.

"Why do you ride home now?" he asked urgently. "Is something amiss? Are you ill?"

Dagobert shook his head slowly, his calm expression soothing Thierry's fears as naught else could. "Nay," he said finally, squinting as he looked up to the high walls. "'Twas a dream that set us on our way west."

"A dream?" Thierry prompted. His father nodded once, then turned to face his son.

"Aye," he confirmed solemnly and his grip tightened slightly on Thierry's shoulder. "A dream that the time to regain what we had lost was upon us again."

Thierry's heart soared at the import of the words. 'Twas *his* time! 'Twas from Montsalvat that he would launch his attempt to regain his rightful legacy.

A thrill tripped through Thierry at the thought that his destiny was once again within his grasp, and he stifled a grin of anticipation. From here would he hold court over his domains that he had no doubt he would regain.

Were the knights not already loyal to the cause? Had not Eustache and the others already risked their hides and their reputations to save him from certain slaughter in Paris? He would lead them to the victory they desired, the victory they had hoped for all these centuries. He would grasp his legacy with both hands and make the old tales ring true.

The blood of two divinely appointed lines of kings mingled in his veins. Was this not everything of which he had ever dreamed? Not a doubt was there that he would succeed, for destiny was on his side.

Under Thierry's hand, the lost kings of Rhedae would soon be found again.

Chapter Fifteen

"Did you travel alone?" Alienor interjected hastily. Thierry returned reluctantly to the present at her question.

"Nay, I did not ride west alone," Thierry admitted warily. He indicated his silent friend, still sitting astride his mount in the shadows. "My *anda*, Nogai." His parents nodded, and greetings were exchanged in Mongol.

He knew he should tell his parents of Kira. Suddenly Thierry was nervous beyond recollection and he unexpectedly feared that they would not approve of the woman he had taken to his side.

"Just the two of you were there?" his mother inquired politely.

"Nay," Thierry conceded awkwardly. "My woman was there, as well."

He did not miss the look his parents exchanged. "Your woman or your wife?" Dagobert asked in a precise tone of which Thierry well knew the import. He straightened and deliberately looked his father in the eye.

"Indeed, there is naught of difference betwixt the two," he maintained stonily. His father arched one brow high and made to speak, but Alienor intervened.

"What is her name?" she asked in an obvious bid to avert an argument.

"Kira," Thierry supplied, feeling suddenly in poorer temper than he had expected. "Persian she is," he added for no explicable reason.

"And lovely, I am sure," his mother said quickly. Thierry fancied she spoke thus to keep his father from interjecting but he flatly refused to meet the older man's gaze. "Mayhap we could meet her," Alienor suggested. Thierry's gaze flew to his mother's in dismay.

Kira meeting his parents? The idea was more disturbing than it should have been.

What if they did not approve?

"She is not here," he said. His parents looked confused and his rationalization for leaving Kira behind suddenly seemed inane beyond compare. "Small she is and delicate. Well I thought that I would have to go to Khanbaliq to find you, so Kira I left in Eustache's care—"

"You left her alone at Montsalvat?" his sire demanded tightly. Thierry did not miss the agitation in his father's tone.

"Aye, for safer she will be there," he began, but got no further.

"Safer? But with you she was in Paris?" his father demanded skeptically.

"Aye," Thierry agreed warily. "My woman is she, as all know."

Dagobert leaned closer and his eyes gleamed. "Tell me how you left Paris," he ordered.

Thierry shrugged uncomprehendingly. "We fled, for as soon as I bared my mark, we were attacked."

"Fled with Eustache?" Dagobert insisted tersely.

"Aye," Thierry responded irritably, still not seeing the way of things.

"Fool!"

To his complete astonishment his sire wagged one indignant finger directly beneath his nose. "Addlepated fool!" Dagobert spat and whistled impatiently for his attendants. "Surely I raised you to have more sense than this!"

The charge was so reminiscent of precisely what Eustache had said in Paris that Thierry was momentarily taken aback.

"Eustache said they would be prepared," he protested.

"It matters naught," his father snapped before he turned away.

"Töde! Make the horses ready immediately! We ride on to the fortress with all haste!" Dagobert muttered an expletive under his breath. He spared his son one eloquent glance of disgust before he spun and hauled himself back into his saddle.

"Surely they can defend the fortress—" Thierry said to his mother. Alienor leaned over to grip Thierry's hands for a long moment.

"He but fears for your Kira," she confessed quickly before releasing his hands and hastily turning her mount. Already had Dagobert given spurs to his horse and Thierry was left staring after them.

Had Eustache not spoken aright? Had he left Kira in danger?

"For Kira?" Thierry was in his own saddle in an instant. "Why? What risk has she at Montsalvat? Safe she should be there." Thierry's heart went cold but evidently no answer was he to have. The rest of his father's retinue followed in the older man's wake, naught but a cloud of dust left before Thierry.

"What does this mean?" Thierry shouted in frustration. He spurred his beast and raced to catch up to his sire. "What is the threat to Kira?"

"Haste must we make," Dagobert called impatiently over his shoulder. "You have but to think upon the matter to see the truth. Poorly indeed does it serve the king's interest to leave any of us breathing. 'Twas that alone that had me flee my homeland. 'Twas that alone that bade me grant you a choice in taking this legacy."

"What is the price to Kira?" Thierry demanded again as he stood in his stirrups, already half certain he knew the answer.

"Your Kira may be forced to bear the price of being the woman of the fruit of the vine," his sire said enigmatically.

Kira could not be in danger because of his mark alone. 'Twas preposterous.

"Nay!" Thierry retorted sharply. "Safe she is at Mont-salvat! 'Twas why I left her there. Naught has this to do with her. Naught." His father shook his head slowly as Thierry drew up alongside, sympathy dawning in the older man's eyes as he regarded his son.

"We can only hope that 'twill not be too late," he advised.

The very words set a chill through Thierry's heart, but no more could he ask, for his sire was already digging his heels into his mount.

Had he abandoned Kira to some cruel fate? It could not be thus, but Thierry feared that he had done precisely that. Surely naught could have happened in the short span of a day. Surely Eustache would protect Kira, he thought wildly, urging his horse on with renewed vigor.

Surely this legacy of his that promised so much could not steal away the one person he held most dear.

Kira was over the wall and a dozen steps down the slope before she realized that she was being watched.

She stopped abruptly and clutched her bag to her chest, not at all liking the look of the two dozen men who confronted her. Half-hidden they were, lurking in the shadows of boulders and leaning against the trunks of trees, but their eyes gleamed.

And every eye was fixed upon her.

Kira's pulse took off at a gallop. She stepped cautiously backward, knowing full well that she could not scale the cursedly smooth wall. Jumping down had been one matter, but now she was truly stranded on the outside.

Mayhap leaving Montsalvat had not been a well-conceived plan.

One man stepped forward, the ripple of his cloak revealing a sliver of azure and gold that fairly stopped Kira's heart.

Knights from the court in Paris. One look into the steely gaze of the one who approached her with relentless steps told Kira that this was no social call. She panicked and turned to run just in time to see old Eustache leap from the wall in her wake.

He bellowed and drew his blade before he hit the ground. Kira was certain she had never been so glad to see another mortal in her life. The knight stalking her shouted a response. Kira spun to see his blade clear its scabbard as well and knew instinctively that this would be a battle to the death.

With her as the spoils.

Eustache shot her a glance and Kira instantly understood. She scurried out of the way and leaned against the chill of the heavy wall, wincing when the blades clashed for the first time. She opened her eyes and was relieved to find Eustache was yet unscathed. The men backed away from each other and circled. Kira licked her lip, her gaze drawn unwillingly to the figures lurking in the trees. Something cold took hold of Kira's stomach when she realized the import of their presence.

Should Eustache best this cold knight, he had yet twenty-three more to conquer before he earned her freedom.

How could she have been so foolish?

"Eustache de Sidon, are you not?" the cursedly agile mercenary inquired conversationally.

"Aye, 'tis my name," Eustache responded with a vicious swipe of his blade that belied his age to Kira's eyes. "Heard tell of me, have you?"

The mercenary cocked a skeptical brow. "Aye, plenty have I heard of you and your liege lord over the years."

"Many years has it been since my liege lord passed away." The lie fell so easily from Eustache's lips that Kira knew he had told it before. Was that why Montsalvat had been left in peace?

"Passed away?" the foreign knight inquired mildly. "Mayhap passed away over the hills." He backed Eustache determinedly across the deadened grass with a renewed attack. Kira felt her hands rise to her mouth. The two men danced across the dawn-tinged ground, more evenly matched than she might have guessed.

Suddenly the mercenary tripped over a stone and lost his balance. Eustache took advantage of the opportunity to lunge forward. The knight swore and twisted, managing somehow to raise his blade with lightning speed. Kira gasped when the sword slid between Eustache's ribs and surprise lit the older man's features. Eustache swore vehemently and backed away, the other knight watching with eerie steadiness.

To Kira's astonishment Eustache took a deep breath and lifted his blade once more.

"*En garde,*" he said with icy precision.

Even Kira's inexperienced eyes saw that the stakes had been raised. Eustache fought now for his life and his vigor was astonishing. Their blades clashing with deafening force, they crossed the clearing back and again.

Eustache's blade caught the other knight across the cheek and those impassive features contorted in pain. The foreign knight swore as a trickle of red meandered over his skin. Anger tightened his lips but Eustache had already jabbed again. The knight twisted and the tip of the blade but traced an ineffectual line across his throat. He roared in fury and lunged, slamming Eustache's blade so hard that the sword clattered across the few stones embedded in the grass.

Too far away to be readily retrieved. Kira dared to take a step in pursuit but two of the other foreign knights drew their blades and stepped over the sword.

Eustache drew his dagger in a flash as the knight swung for the final blow. Eustache kicked out and caught the other knight's ankle. The mercenary swore again as he lost his balance, but his blade still found its mark.

Kira's heart stopped as Eustache fell, the length of the knight's sword buried in his belly. She waited but he moved naught.

'Twas over. The foreign knight ignored Eustache, calmly inspecting his own wound.

This could not be. Eustache could not be gone so quickly. Kira's gaze flicked over the party of foreign knights in trepidation.

She swallowed in anticipation of her own fate. And her foolishness had cost Eustache dearly as well!

To her astonishment Eustache suddenly leaped to life. His dagger caught the morning light as it arched toward the other knight's chest. The mercenary shouted in outrage and jerked away. Eustache buried the blade in his shoulder with a grimace of pain and wrenched the blade downward.

His grip loosened and he slowly slid bonelessly back against the dirt, his features lifeless in truth now.

Well it seemed that the pounding of Kira's heart might deafen her when she met the cold gaze of the foreign knight. The cursed man smiled a most predatory smile and she knew naught good was in store for her.

The sun was well past its zenith when they passed beneath the barbican again. All seemed normal, but Thierry liked it not. Dagobert shouted for Eustache as they gained the bailey, but Thierry had no interest in finding the older man. All of his fears focused on Kira. Never should he have left her alone. He leaped from his saddle and dashed up the stairs to the solar.

'Twas empty. Thierry tore open the bed curtains to find that space similarly voided.

She was gone.

It could not be. Thierry turned over stools and prowled the room angrily until he saw that his other saddlebag was gone. Kira had left him.

Impossible it seemed, but the chilling truth could not be denied. He dashed back down the stairs to find a frown on his sire's brow.

"None have seen Eustache all day," Dagobert said with dissatisfaction.

"Kira is gone," Thierry said flatly.

"Something is amiss," Dagobert concluded. He snapped his fingers and raised his voice. "Search the grounds! Summon all to the task! The lady's life may be in danger!"

There was a scurry of activity as the men within the hall left to do Dagobert's bidding. Thierry fought against the tangle of emotions within him as he struggled to make sense of it all. Why would Kira have left him deliberately?

And what would he do if she was lost to him? Already there was an aching hollow within him and he yet knew not her fate.

To his surprise he found his mother's hand resting on his arm. Thierry looked up and found sympathy in her eyes.

"Well I think that you hold your Kira in regard," she said softly.

"Aye," Thierry agreed roughly. The press of his mother's fingers increased slightly.

"And yet she is not your wife."

"'Tis the *same*," Thierry insisted, knowing all the while that his mother was not convinced.

"Mayhap 'tis the same to you," Alienor said smoothly. "But is it the same to your Kira?"

Was that why Kira had left? Did she think he did not care for her? The very thought made everything turn cold within Thierry. Well should he have given her the *aljofar*. Well should he have told her the truth.

He could only hope that he still might have the chance.

"Here!"

The cry brought Dagobert and Thierry simultaneously to the guard post on the curtain wall. Dagobert muttered a curse and stepped immediately back from the scene below.

'Twas Eustache lying below, bloodied and dead. Thierry studied the older man's corpse until he located the telling wound. Swordplay. Several men were gathered around Eustache and looked to be making preparations to lift him back within the fortress walls. Thierry's gaze lifted over them to scan the ground and the periphery as he sought some sign of Kira's passing.

Had she come this way?

Thierry met Nogai's gaze. The Mongol nodded thoughtfully, visibly tracing the bloody trail marking the path where Eustache's body had been hauled.

"Dragged behind the rocks and trees was he, milord," the man who had accompanied them supplied tersely.

"'Twas why the sentries did not spot him sooner. 'Twas Beauregard who saw him.''

Thierry looked at the men below and spotted the young squire whose hair Eustache had ruffled in Paris. His jaw tightened at the signs of the strain the boy had borne, for his eyes were red rimmed and his countenance ashen. 'Twas evident the boy had worshiped Eustache, and 'twas a cruel blow that he should be the one to find his hero thus.

"And the lady?'' Dagobert asked. Thierry's gaze flew to the other man in time to see him shake his head slowly.

"Not a sign of her, milord,'' he confessed. Thierry saw sympathy dawning in the man's eyes and hastily looked away.

Not a sign. Mayhap not to him.

Thierry's gaze meandered over the jutting rocks and meager trees that covered the slope on this face of the mountain. Some small sign he sought that Kira yet lived, though when he spotted the broken branches, he thought at first his eyes deceived him.

Then he saw another snapped branch, a bevy of stones disturbed from the places they had long rested. The evidence was there and widely scattered enough that it could mean only one thing. A number of people had passed this way. Nogai lifted a finger and pointed to the same broken branches that Thierry had noted.

"Mayhap as many as twenty,'' he muttered. Thierry nodded, feeling his father's questioning gaze upon them both, but did not elaborate.

Only too clearly did Thierry recall the way they had departed Paris. Now that the fullness of his heritage was clear to him, he understood the king's response. Indeed, 'twas much like the thinking of Abaqa to eliminate all threats to one's hegemony.

But why this way? Why come to the wall, kill Eustache and leave without approaching the fortress itself? It made no sense to so quickly abandon an objective.

Unless . . . Thierry's heart chilled as the only answer became clear to him. Kira was the missing clue. Eustache had died defending her. Eustache had failed and they had taken

Kira. Mayhap someone recalled that she had been with
him, mayhap they sought to draw him out without sus-
taining the casualties necessary to storm an old fortress like
this one.

It mattered not what their intent was. The more Thierry
reflected upon it, the more certain he became. Kira had
been abducted and he could not leave the matter lie.

"Where are you going?" his father demanded. Thierry
glanced over his shoulder and saw the approval in his *anda*'s eyes.

"To fetch my pack," he said simply. "'Tis evident they
have taken Kira," he added grimly and turned away.

"Wait!" his father cried and Thierry halted unwillingly.
"We will summon a party to go with you. Already had
Eustache made preparations for battle." Dagobert paused
and swallowed carefully. "Should you choose to accept the
fullness of your legacy, well might this be the time to stake
your claim," he added quietly.

All eyes fell to Thierry and he felt the will of those surrounding him. All their lives had they hoped and worked
for the return of the rightful king. For years had this moment been their dream and for long Thierry had thought it
might be his.

The time was ripe. His own ambitions were within his
grasp.

But he could think of naught but Kira. Assembling a war
party would take time, time that might be critical to her
safety.

Thierry was surprised to realize that that fact mattered to
him more than any ambition he thought himself to have.
Should he be with Kira alone and be important to her, it
would be enough to satisfy his ambitions.

This task he would do alone.

"Nay," Thierry said flatly. "This is betwixt this king and
me."

He paused for a moment and acknowledged the concern
in his father's expression. Nogai stood silently and Thierry
knew his old friend understood his choice to go alone. "Let
the man see the manner of opponent he has engaged," he

added quietly. Something flashed in Dagobert's eyes, but Thierry turned hastily away, mentally composing a list of all he might need.

If they had harmed Kira in any way, he would see they sorely regretted the day, he resolved grimly.

'Twas dusk before Kira saw her chance.

The foreign knights had set a killing pace once mounted on the horses hidden at the mount below Montsalvat. That she was increasingly farther away from the fortress and any chance of aid did naught to reassure Kira, especially since the knight who had killed Eustache had yet to relinquish his grip upon her wrist.

They halted to let the horses drink from a passing stream and Kira dared to take a chance.

"I beg your pardon, sir, but I fear I must relieve myself," she said meekly. The knight granted her a skeptical glance and Kira was grateful to feel her color rise. More credence would that lend to her tale. She dropped her voice to a whisper. "I fear I may not be able to hold my water much longer," she confided.

"Troublesome bitch," the knight snarled. He dismounted all the same, hauling Kira in his wake. She struggled to give no sign of the thrill of victory coursing through her. The knight moved no farther and Kira's hope faded.

This would not do.

"Sir!" she declared in a scandalized tone. "Surely you do not expect that I...that I should, should...here amidst your men." Kira's cheeks heated yet further at her own audacity and several men around them chuckled.

"Oho, a lady fine have we," chortled one. Kira's chin shot up proudly and the knight who held her wrist granted her an assessing glance.

"For pity's sake," he snorted when she thought he might not give in. He turned and plunged into the woods, the chuckles of his men lending impatience to his step.

She would have to be quick about it, should she make the most of this chance. 'Twas dark in the shadows of the trees, yet still Kira played the demure maiden.

"Please, sir," she implored as she fingered the hem of her kirtle. The knight's lips set stubbornly and he turned his back upon her.

"Make haste, woman. Far have we to ride this night," he growled.

Had it been Thierry before her, Kira knew well he would have missed naught of what she did. She could only hope that this knight was less observant.

A man shouted and the knight's head turned. Kira's heart leaped. 'Twas her chance and likely the only one she would get.

Before she could question her impulse, Kira scooped up a broken tree branch. She crept up behind the mercenary, feeling it took a week to close the distance. She barely dared to breathe as she raised the heavy branch high. Kira swung it at the back of his skull with all her might. He turned, evidently hearing some hint of her presence, but had only time to open his mouth before the branch crashed into his brow.

He crumpled to his knees, his fingers grasped wildly for Kira's kirtle. Terror flooded through her. She danced out of range of his grip and raised the branch high. The knight curled his lip in a snarl. Kira panicked. He was going to summon the others! She swung the branch and squeezed her eyes closed so that she wouldn't have to see the damage she wrought.

The branch hit the ground with a thud. Kira had missed.

Something whistled past her ear. Her eyes flew open in time to see the knight lunge forward, then suddenly stop mid-gesture.

The shaft of the arrow buried in his throat quivered for a long moment, then he fell face-first onto the forest floor.

Kira gasped and spun on her heel. Everything within her dissolved at the sight of Thierry's grim countenance and she thought her knees might give way. She took a gulping breath of relief and he held up one finger for silence as he stepped to her side.

"Are you hurt?" he demanded with blazing eyes. Kira shook her head, not trusting herself to speak. Thierry slipped one hand into the hair at her nape, the warmth of his fingers there reassuring her as naught else could.

Thierry was here. She was safe, despite her foolishness. Kira willed her heart to slow its pace.

"Woho, Gunther! For whose relief do you take the wench?" The men laughed in the clearing beyond. Thierry stiffened, then crouched lower, his eyes narrowing as he peered through the forest growth.

"I will fetch him," another growled. "Is he not the one in such a rush to return to Paris?" The other men laughed amiably and the sound of the horses in the stream carried to Kira's ears.

"How many?" he whispered.

"Twenty-two," Kira supplied.

Thierry nodded, then a footfall in the brush brought his head up with a snap. He shoved Kira behind him and drew several arrows from his quiver. The silhouette of a knight appeared and Thierry moved so quickly that the arrow was planted in his chest before Kira saw Thierry draw his bow.

The knight grunted and fell, the thick carpet of leaves muffling the sound.

"Jean-Luc! Tell us not that the wench accommodates you both!"

A trio of men burst abruptly into the woods, but Thierry dispatched them with similar efficiency. Kira gaped at his skill, but he merely spared her a wink. He grasped her hand and tugged her hastily farther into the woods.

A cry rose behind them and Thierry ducked behind a tree, pressing Kira into the tree before him. He leaned against her protectively and silently threaded another arrow into his bow. Kira did not dare breathe lest she give their location away.

Thierry was completely motionless.

"What is this?" cried another man in dismay.

Another swore and Kira glanced up to see a third cross himself. They were close, too close for her comfort, but still Thierry waited.

"Who could have done this thing?"

"Where is the woman?"

"Naught did I hear."

A babble of outrage rose from the cluster of men. Kira felt their gazes rise to scan the forest and she closed her eyes, willing herself invisible. The scent of the cedars flooded through her and she hoped against hope that they would not be discovered.

Thierry had pursued her! Despite her fear, the thought sent a thrill through her. Was it possible indeed that he cared for her?

"Naught do I see," whispered another man. Awe there was in his voice. "How do we track a silent foe?" The group of men shuffled their feet in response to his question.

"Is the woman worth seeing our demise?" demanded another.

"But what will we tell the king?"

"Back to the fortress should we go!" cried one man. His suggestion was not greeted with enthusiasm.

"Nay! We should ride directly to Paris!" snapped another and Kira sensed this one would take the lead.

"Fool!" spat the first. "I would not darken that portal with this task unfulfilled."

"Mayhap you would not, but I fully intend to do so," the second man maintained frostily. "Any who would rather ride into battle uninformed are free to accompany you on your futile mission. Mayhap you will even manage to survive." A ripple of dissent rumbled through the company of knights.

"Uninformed?" argued the first man. "'Tis more than evident what we were bidden to do."

"Hardly that. Well you know that Gunther alone knew the fullness of the deed," the second knight snapped. "Without Gunther, we are best to return," he maintained haughtily.

"We need not a foreigner to conclude business here—" The first got no further before he was summarily interrupted.

"Have you not a whit of sense in your head?" the second knight said impatiently. "Can you not see that this is but a fairy tale we chase? The old king is becoming whimsical. Enough 'tis that we have ridden all the way to this cursed southern country, without wasting yet more time here."

"But this southern lord covets the crown."

"Plenty of others are there closer to Paris who covet the crown," sneered the second. Assent rippled through the ranks at that assertion.

"But he bears the mark of the old kings of Rhedae," the first knight objected, some of the vigor fading from his tone.

"Indeed," his companion said skeptically. "And you have laid eyes upon this mark?"

"Nay," the other admitted reluctantly.

"Nor have I," the second insisted, a telling confidence in his tone. "And that fortress does not inspire my fears. Poorly kept 'tis, for all its reputation, and any fool knows that a major battle of any kind, never mind a play for the crown itself, requires a fat purse. There is no threat in these southern hills."

"But the woman—?"

"Was not fetching enough to merit the trouble."

Kira might have gasped at his bold assertion, but Thierry's lips were suddenly warm against her ear. "He lies," he whispered, the fan of his breath making her warm all over.

"But what shall you tell the king?"

"Did you see this Mongol in Languedoc?" the second knight challenged his companions. Kira watched yet another knight bend over one of the fallen men and snap the shaft of Thierry's arrow. He turned it speculatively beneath the second knight's nose, though that man showed no sign of relinquishing the fight.

"'Tis said the bow is their weapon of choice," this new knight asserted calmly. "And this is fashioned unlike any arrows I know."

The second knight held his gaze for a long moment, then snatched the arrow from his hand. He snapped the shaft twice more, then cast the pieces on the ground. "I went to Montsalvat and found a deserted keep," he asserted boldly.

"Save Eustache de Sidon who lay dead from this arrow. Unfortunately, it seemed the old knight and his men were deceived by those he took in."

"And the Mongols?"

"Mercifully, we caught sight of them riding south on the road and gave pursuit," the knight responded smoothly. "Sadly, several of our companions were lost in the resulting exchange, but the Mongols—" he lifted one finger "—were chased along the road and into the sea just south of Montsalvat." His voice dropped and he eyed his companions speculatively.

"Which of you will call me a liar?"

The other knights avoided each other's gaze as Kira held her breath.

"The Mongols might return," one finally protested weakly.

The second knight laughed skeptically. "Only to hang your sorry hide," he retorted and leaned closer to the objector. "Think well, Didier, whether you would be more afraid of him or of me," he murmured before he straightened and cast an eye over his companions. "Be not fools. Subscribe to this tale and we shall all be paid in short order. Have you no desire to be paid and sleep well in your own beds?"

The question seemed to decide the matter for most of the knights. They nodded amiably to themselves, reassuring each other that their choice had been the right one.

One alone hung back from the others, his gaze rising to scan the trees. Kira's heart stopped when he seemed to look directly at them.

The knight who took the lead turned back, but he needed to say naught to his doubting companion. Kira heard the whistle of the bow and saw alarm cross that knight's features as he turned to find the man he had just argued with falling to his knees. Two more knights glanced back, their mouths opening in surprise. For a long moment, it seemed they could not move, then they turned and bolted as one from the woods.

When Kira gasped and doubled over, Thierry feared he had lost all he had gained. He glanced up to confirm that the knights were indeed gone, the jingle of their destriers' trap carrying to his ears.

"Kira? Are you hurt?" he asked and heard the thread of panic in his own tone. She shook her head, but the tears in her eyes when she straightened reassured him naught.

"You must tell me, Kira," he insisted. "Where are you hurt?" Kira inexplicably shook her head.

"'Tis the babe that kicks, 'tis all," she whispered. Shock enfolded Thierry. The babe? Kira carried a babe? Impossible 'twas, but when she drew back and met his gaze, he saw the truth reflected in her eyes.

"A babe?" he whispered. "But how?"

Kira smiled sadly. "In quite the usual way, I would imagine," she said, and her color rose becomingly. Thierry stared at her for a long moment before the questions erupted in his mind.

"But why did you not tell me?" he demanded finally. Kira tried to pull away, but Thierry tightened his grip around her.

"I feared you would not be pleased," she confessed quietly. Her lashes dropped demurely and Thierry cupped her chin gently, compelling her to look to him. Fear there was lingering in the depths of her dark gaze and intuitively he knew its source.

"Kira," he chided. "Never would I raise a hand against you." Tears filled Kira's eyes, though her doubt was still clear. "No man strikes a woman whom he loves."

The words had an unexpected result, for Kira abruptly pulled away and averted her face. "You know naught of what you speak," she maintained tightly. "My sire loved me well."

"Yet 'twas he who scarred your back?" Thierry guessed. Kira's only response was a nod and he felt his lips tighten. "No love is that, Kira," he said, but she did not respond. The silence hung thickly between them, then Thierry dared to touch her stomach. 'Twas rounding slightly, much to his amazement, and he marveled that he had noticed naught of the change.

"What of the babe?" he demanded urgently. "How far along is it?"

"But four moons along is it, as I figure, and I know not the import of its restlessness. No good can it bring, I am sure."

Four moons. Pride flooded Thierry and he stifled a smile. The child was his. Kira bore the spawn of his seed.

"Mayhap you have but strained yourself this day," he suggested. Kira's gaze flew to his and he lifted his brows encouragingly. "Come home and we shall ask my mother's advice."

"Your mother?" Kira asked breathlessly. Thierry nodded.

"Aye, a long way has she come to meet my bride." When he might have expected a smile, Kira turned abruptly away. "Kira?" he asked, but she resolutely ignored him.

And naught else did Kira say the entire way home to Montsalvat, though more than once Thierry caught her speculative gaze upon him.

Was it possible that Kira desired not to be his wife?

Chapter Sixteen

'Twas too much to be pampered within the great curtained bed, knowing all the while that Thierry's bride would soon arrive and cast Kira from this luxury. Could they not see how they made her ache inside with their consideration? Did Thierry's mother not guess how much it hurt to have her compassion, knowing all the while that it would soon be stolen away?

Kira rolled over and ran one hand over her eyes. 'Twas not that which troubled her most and well she knew it. More vexed was she by the thought that Thierry would soon be with another. Only too cruel was he to tease her at night and hold her close when they both knew their time together to be fleeting.

Had Thierry been right about love? Well it seemed that his affection bore its dark price, much as her father's had done. Kira concluded that the bite of the lash was easier to bear. She opened her eyes and stared about the solar, gasping in surprise.

Thierry stood against the wall some ten paces away from her.

Curse the man for his silent passing. Kira exhaled shakily and eyed him warily.

"I thought you asleep," he said quietly. Kira shook her head and felt her color rise.

She was unaccountably reminded of the first time she had laid eyes upon him. She felt the weight of his regard upon her and knew not what to do. When Thierry straightened slowly and deliberately stepped toward her, it seemed her heart would stop.

"Feeling more hale?" he asked as he sat on the edge of the bed. One finger rose to stroke her cheek and Kira shivered beneath the warmth of his touch.

Would that he would wed her. The scandalous idea shocked even Kira for daring to think it and she averted her gaze that Thierry might not guess the direction of her thoughts.

"Aye," Kira agreed. His fingertips wandered over her cheek, her throat and traced a path to the curve of her belly. Even through the bed linens, Kira swore she could feel the touch of his skin against hers and she closed her eyes against unexpected tears.

"A value for a gem do I need this day," Thierry said slowly. Kira looked to him in surprise. He lifted a fine chain and the *aljofar* dangled from his finger before her.

'Twas the gem from his saddlebag. Kira licked her lips carefully as she schooled her temper. How could he bring this gem to her for a valuation? More crass was his move than she believed him capable and she inhaled indignantly. Thierry's lips curved in a tentative smile when he noted her surprise and Kira could not believe his audacity.

"How dare you?" Kira demanded in a low voice that shook with outrage. "How dare you bring me this pearl to assess?"

How could he insult her thus by asking her to value his gift for another? Well it seemed he twisted the knife in the wound and Kira would hear no more of his prattle. She rolled over so that her back was to him and drew up her knees, not nearly satisfied by the way his smile had abruptly disappeared. Kira's hands clenched into fists and she wished there was some way she could hurt Thierry de Pereille in truth.

At least as savagely as he had hurt her.

"Kira!" he whispered.

Kira fancied she heard surprise in his tone and mayhap a tinge of injured pride but she refused to indulge her whimsy. No tender feelings had this man for her. That much had been clear for a long time had she simply had the sense to see what was before her.

She was a fool a hundred times over.

"Kira, what is wrong?" he asked, his breath warm against her ear.

Should he truly wish to know, Kira was angry enough to illuminate matters for him. She rolled over, enjoying the way he recoiled from the fury in her eyes. Kira propped herself up on her elbows and stared down the mighty warrior of whom she had once been afraid.

"What is wrong?" she echoed indignantly. "Here I lie with your child in my belly and yet you torment me with your bride's bauble. Have you not a scrap of compassion in your soul?" Thierry looked momentarily blank. Kira snatched the pearl from his grip and waggled it beneath his nose.

"This *aljofar*," Kira replied hotly, having no patience with his games. "Know you not what you hold? 'Tis a gift for a bride alone and none other. I would not watch you grant this to another woman and cast me aside for the crime of conceiving your child. Not alone did I manage that task, yet you would cast me out like a common whore."

"How do you know I would give this to my bride?" Thierry asked in confusion.

Kira acknowledged a niggle of doubt. Was it possible that he knew not the import of the gem?

"'Tis an *aljofar*," she explained patiently.

"Aye. Well do I know what the gem is called."

"Know you its import, then?"

"What import?" Thierry asked, and his scowl deepened. "'Tis a token for a woman, evidently."

"Nay." Kira shook her head firmly. "'Tis more than that alone. An *aljofar* is a traditional gift from man to wife on their wedding day a gift to celebrate their vows and bless the match with good fortune."

To Kira's consternation Thierry smiled crookedly. "Then 'tis an apt gift indeed," he said smoothly. He lifted the chain toward her once more and the pearl rocked invitingly. "Would you not value the gem for me?"

"I would *not* value the pearl you would grant your bride," Kira snapped. She would have rolled over again, but Thierry grasped her arm.

"You would wear it, then, without knowing its worth?" he asked. Kira glanced up to find a puzzled frown marring Thierry's brow. When he spoke again, his voice was so low that he fairly undid her resolve to turn him away. "In truth, Kira, I do not understand your objection."

It could not be. He could not have said that he intended for her to wear the *aljofar*. Mayhap she had misunderstood him.

But she had to know for certain. Kira swallowed nervously.

"To whom would you give this gem?" she asked, feeling her voice was far too unsteady under the circumstances. Thierry shook his head indulgently and pulled her closer.

"Kira," he chided in a warm undertone. "Know you not that this *aljofar* is for you?"

"Tease me not," Kira protested, but the warmth of Thierry's fingers spread to span her arm more determinedly and his gaze bored into hers.

"No jest is this," he said solemnly. "Always has it been for you but I found not the right moment to give it to you."

"What of your bride?" Kira demanded.

"My bride has yet to accept my offer." Pain flickered through Thierry's eyes and he leaned so close to Kira that she could smell the heat from his skin. "Well it seems that she will keep me begging in her bed."

Kira's heart skipped a beat.

Thierry intended to wed her? It could not be. But a glimpse of the sincerity in his eyes told her 'twas so, though Kira still fought against the conclusion. She would not believe what she most wanted to hear for fear she saw something where 'twas not.

"I thought you were to wed another," she protested weakly, but Thierry shook his head with maddening slowness.

"I would wed you," he said firmly. Kira's pulse rose in her ears

"But—" she protested. Thierry dropped one hard finger to rest gently against her lips and silence her words. Her gaze flew to his and he shook his head slowly.

"But *naught*, Kira. Will you accept my *aljofar* and be my wife?"

Kira's gaze slanted to the gleaming pearl and she forced herself to breathe evenly. "Stole the gem, you did," she accused in a last effort to prove her earlier conclusion right. Too much 'twas to believe that Thierry would be hers alone. So long had she wished for exactly this that Kira could not believe 'twas her heart's own desire Thierry offered her. "'Tis the bounty of an attack or some pilfered tribute you offer me, in truth," she charged wildly.

"Nay, Kira," Thierry replied with a resolve that told her he spoke the truth, though his next words challenged her conclusion. "Bought with hard coin 'twas."

She spared him a disparaging look. "Never would a Mongol buy a gem with hard coin," she charged flatly. Thierry arched a single brow high.

"And never had I until I saw this pearl in Constantinople," he confessed with utmost seriousness. "This I knew I had to see grace the lady who holds my heart."

Kira's heart pounded at this revelation. But a glance to Thierry's expression told her he spoke the truth. Thierry loved her. She eyed the pearl and let her heart flood with hope that happiness might truly be hers.

"But a token 'tis, Kira, and naught compared to what you give to me, should you consent to take my hand." An appeal there was in his deep voice, an uncertainty that Kira had never expected to hear from him and of which she could not bear the sound.

Thierry still knew naught of her feelings. Kira looked at the gem and lifted the chain from his hand with trembling fingers. She rolled the gem between her fingers consideringly and felt Thierry's breath against her ear.

"Marry me, Kira, and I will cherish you with all my heart and soul."

But one doubt remained in Kira's mind and she could not avoid giving it voice. "My father cherished me," she said quietly. Thierry's features immediately grew stern and he braced himself over her. His hands framed her face and he stared down into her eyes.

"Your sire knew naught of love," he said urgently. "Never will you know abuse at my hand and never will I stand by to let another harm you. I love you, Kira, and that you may take as my pledge to see you safe and well."

'Twas an opportunity she could not refuse. Kira looked up into Thierry's eyes and smiled as she reached up to smooth the frown of concern from his brow.

"Well it seems to me that this pearl is beyond price should it carry such a pledge from you," she whispered unsteadily. Hope flickered in Thierry's eyes.

"Nay, Kira," he murmured. "Should you accept the token, 'twill be but the setting for the richest treasure of all."

Should she accept the token. Still he knew not what she desired. Kira reached up and framed his strong jaw in her hands, wanting no more than to erase his doubts.

"No greater honor can I imagine than to be your bride," Kira said softly. "In truth, I have loved you long and wanted naught other than this."

Relief flared in Thierry's eyes and he scooped the gem jubilantly from her fingers. He slipped the chain over Kira's neck and smiled down at her as he traced the line of the gold chain against her skin.

"My Kira," he murmured wonderingly.

Kira smiled outright at his pleasure. "My Thierry," she corrected impudently and threw her arms happily around his neck. He was here and he was hers. Truly she could ask no more of the fates.

"Kiss," she demanded mischievously, readily recalling one of the first words she had learned in Frankish.

"Aye, a kiss would be in order." Thierry's eyes sparkled as he agreed.

"Mayhap more than one," Kira teased. Thierry tipped his head back and laughed outright for the first time that she had ever heard him do so. No time had she to wonder at his happiness, though, for he was quick to comply with her request. Indeed, the force of his arms closing around her was fit to take her breath away, but Kira cared naught when she tasted his lips upon hers.

For her was the *aljofar,* Kira thought triumphantly. She arched against Thierry with pleasure as she tasted the kiss she had feared she would live without for the rest of her days.

For her was Thierry alone.

* * * * *

Harlequin® Historical

What do A.E. Maxwell, Miranda Jarrett, Merline Lovelace and Cassandra Austin have in common?

They are all part of Harlequin Historical's efforts to bring you longer books by some of your favorite authors. Pick up one of these upcoming titles today and see what a difference an historical from Harlequin can make!

REDWOOD EMPIRE—A.E. Maxwell Don't miss the reissue of this exciting saga from award-winning authors Ann and Evan Maxwell, coming in May 1995.

SPARHAWK'S LADY—Miranda Jarrett From this popular author comes another sweeping Sparhawk adventure full of passion and emotion in June 1995.

HIS LADY'S RANSOM—Merline Lovelace A gripping Medieval tale from the talented author of the Destiny's Women series that is sure to delight, coming in July 1995.

TRUSTING SARAH—Cassandra Austin And in August 1995, the long-awaited new Western by the author whose *Wait for the Sunrise* touched readers' hearts.

Watch for them this spring and summer wherever Harlequin Historicals are sold.

HARLEQUIN®

PRESENTS
RELUCTANT BRIDEGROOMS

Two beautiful brides, two unforgettable romances...
two men running for their lives....

My Lady Love, by Paula Marshall, introduces
Charles, Viscount Halstead, who lost his memory
and found himself employed as a stableboy by the
untouchable Nell Tallboys, Countess Malplaquet.
But Nell didn't consider Charles untouchable—
not at all!

Darling Amazon, by Sylvia Andrew, is the story of
a spurious engagement between Julia Marchant
and Hugo, marquess of Rostherne—an engagement
that gets out of hand and just may lead Hugo to
the altar after all!

Enjoy two madcap Regency weddings this May,
wherever Harlequin books are sold.

REG5

Harlequin® Historical

Ruth Langan is at it again!

Don't miss this award-winning author's
return to Scotland
with her new prequel titles to

THE HIGHLAND SERIES

Look for #269 HIGHLAND HEAVEN, the sequel to THE HIGHLANDER,
coming from Harlequin Historicals in May 1995.

If you missed THE HIGHLANDER, you can still order it
from the address below.

WOMEN OF THE WEST

Exciting stories of the old West and the women whose dreams
and passions shaped a new land!

Join Harlequin Historicals every month as we bring you
these unforgettable tales.

Don't miss any of our **Women of the West!**

Harlequin invites you to the most romantic
wedding of the season...with

MARRY ME, COWBOY!

And you could WIN A DREAM VACATION of a lifetime!

from HARLEQUIN BOOKS and SANDALS—
THE CARIBBEAN'S #1 **ULTRA INCLUSIVE**℠ LUXURY RESORTS
FOR COUPLES ONLY.

Harlequin Books and Sandals Resorts are offering you a
vacation of a lifetime—a vacation of your choice at any of
the Sandals Caribbean resorts—FREE!

LOOK FOR FURTHER DETAILS in the Harlequin Books
title MARRY ME, COWBOY!, an exciting collection
of four brand-new short stories by popular romance
authors, including *New York Times* bestselling author
JANET DAILEY!

**AVAILABLE IN APRIL WHEREVER
HARLEQUIN BOOKS ARE SOLD.**

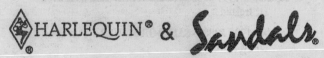
HARLEQUIN® & *Sandals*®

MMC-SANDT